A DANGEROUS KISS . . .

"As far as going yourself?" He laughed and shrugged the idea away. "You have absolutely no idea where it is, Miss Cooper . . . You'd get lost and I'd have to rescue you again. I forbid it."

Bailey rose from the swing to grip the porch railing. Frustrated anger filled her . . . "You have no right to forbid me to do anything."

He rose just as quickly as she. Instantly, without warning, his arms swooped down and wrapped around her, turning her until she faced him head-on. He crushed his lips to hers with a hard kiss.

Bailey was so surprised by his action—by the heat, by the intensity, by the passion behind those lips—that she couldn't respond. A man didn't just sweep you into his arms to silence you. That only happened in old black-and-white movies, and then only when the hero couldn't win an argument any other way. She struggled to be free of him, pushing against his chest, but he refused to lessen his hold.

As swiftly as it had started, the force of his kiss changed from punishing to promising, from hard to inviting, from deadly to dangerous . . .

YESTERDAY AND FOREVER

Vickie Presley

JOVE BOOKS, NEW YORK

TIME PASSAGES is a registered trademark of Berkley Publishing Corporation.

YESTERDAY AND FOREVER

A Jove Book / published by arrangement with
the author

PRINTING HISTORY
Jove edition / March 1999

The Penguin Putnam Inc. World Wide Web site address is
http://www.penguinputnam.com

ISBN: 0-515-12478-8

A JOVE BOOK®
Jove Books are published by The Berkley Publishing Group,
a member of Penguin Putnam Inc.,
375 Hudson Street, New York, New York 10014.
JOVE and the "J" design
are trademarks belonging to Jove Publications, Inc.

PRINTED IN THE UNITED STATES OF AMERICA

10 9 8 7 6 5 4 3 2 1

To Dottie Mazzola,
my mother by marriage

Chapter 1

"PEOPLE DISAPPEAR UP here."

Bailey Cooper stared at the ancient Indian man standing at her side. His face was leathery and worn, and his eyes bespoke years of wisdom.

"Surely not," she replied. "Wouldn't the park service close the area if it were dangerous?" The wizened man shrugged. He stared steadily at Bailey with intense dark eyes, then turned his gaze toward the withered expanse of the mountain ridge.

"They've tried over the years, but the Wheel is a holy place to our people. It is not possible to keep us away."

They stood high atop the crest of Wyoming's Medicine Mountain, overlooking the mysterious remnants of an Indian worship site. According to the National Park Service brochure she held in her hand, it was probably centuries old, although no one actually knew who built the structure or when. The "Medicine Wheel" was made up of several hundred limestone rocks and stones that had been painstakingly formed into the shape of an enormous wagon wheel. Bailey counted twenty-eight spokes where the rocks had been placed from the outside circle of the wheel inward toward a huge doughnut-shaped center. From one side to the other, the remains of the timeworn landmark measured probably more than eighty feet across.

The land immediately around the monument was a stark contrast to the scenic mountainous terrain she had hiked through the past few days. This place was rocky and barren, as if the plants or shrubs could not muster the courage to take root and grow. The few trees looked bent and beaten, still not fully recovered from the harsh snows of last winter even though it was now August. She had read that the Medicine Wheel was a holy place for Native Americans, but she didn't expect it to feel . . . well, so eerie.

The few tourists standing nearby also seemed to sense the foreboding aura as they whispered to each other in hushed tones. They quietly surveyed the white rocks and boulders, taking obvious care not to step too close to the wire fence that surrounded the Wheel and kept intruders away. The stillness was broken by the gleeful shrieks of two curly-headed girls who played chase around their parents. Bailey watched the mother bend and lovingly wrap her arms about the youngest of the two, while the father lifted the other onto his shoulders.

A perfect family.

Bailey turned away and fought the familiar tug of jealously, then matter-of-factly reined in her envy. She was on vacation to get away from kids. The last thing she wanted was to mope around because she didn't have a family of her own. She focused her attention back on the Indian man who stood at her side. He watched her with compassion, as though he somehow sensed her deepest yearning.

"You love children, I see. It is a natural thing for a

woman, yet your aura is sorrowful, your face full of pain. Do you have a son or daughter of your own?"

"No, it's just me," Bailey replied more brightly than she felt. The Indian man's unwavering interest in her was unnerving. Bailey had noticed him immediately when she first arrived. He was on his knees, apparently in prayer, and like the other people nearby, she had kept her distance, not wanting to intrude on the stranger's apparent meditation. She had been more than surprised when he looked up, met her gaze directly, then lifted his hand toward Bailey as if he'd been expecting her.

"However, I do work with many kids in my job. Generally, they're either lots of fun . . . or lots of heartbreak."

The man chuckled and nodded. "I, too, find the same in youthful spirits. Rewarding and annoying at the same time."

Bailey turned back toward the monument. "Why is the Medicine Wheel surrounded by a fence?"

"To protect the Spirits who reside here," the shaky voice answered. "Only Native Americans are allowed inside the fence, and then only to worship in some way."

The venerable man closed his eyes and hummed a soft rhythmic tune. He appeared to be in deep concentration, a trance almost. Bailey considered him as carefully as she would one of her clients back home in Memphis. He appeared to be harmless. He was dressed in ragged clothes, a frayed jacket, and worn suede moccasins, but his distinct features, dark weathered skin, and the single feather in his long gray hair left no doubt of his proud heritage. Bailey's training as a lawyer had made her wary when he had slowly shuffled toward her earlier. Experience had taught her that an innocent appearance was often the most deceiving. All he had done was start a conversation and tell her more about the monument. Bailey relaxed when she realized he wanted to talk to someone who would listen. The Indian's low voice was tired and slow . . . and lonely.

That she understood. And that was why she hadn't excused herself and walked away.

The Indian people had apparently chosen this site for worship because it was so isolated. The Medicine Wheel was on the crest of the mountain with only a steep, gravel road as an entrance. The park brochure said it had been only a footpath up until they built the road a decade prior. Anyone who ventured up on foot would have faced a challenging trek almost straight up the mountain. Challenge appealed to Bailey. She had parked her car at the base of the drive and hiked up the treacherous road just to prove to herself that she could.

Across the ridge to the east, there were endless craggy sierras. To the northwest, the flat, windswept land of the mountaintop was practically void of life. In its own way, the landscape was just as haunting as the primeval structure. Maybe that's why the place was so fascinating. It had endured despite the forces of nature that worked against it.

She heard the Indian man as he shifted, then once again opened his eyes and met her gaze. He lifted a weary hand and pointed toward the bent and rusty wire fence surrounding the Wheel. "Our people come here to commune with the Great Spirits who make this their eternal home. Those are their offerings."

Bailey studied the bizarre objects tied to the old fence. There were hundreds of them. Feathers, strings of beads, wisps of dried flowers, roots knotted together in bunches, bones and skulls of dead animals, even little cloth talismans filled with who knew what. A sudden shiver raced up her spine, and the skin on the back of her neck instantly tingled. Her first instincts must have been right. This was very eerie and more than a little spooky.

"The Wheel may seem frightening to some, but it should not," the man assured her. "For centuries, our people have traveled to this point to seek harmony with the powerful

Spirits who dwell here. It is a place of communion, a place to obtain spiritual guidance. Our people come to give thanks for an answered prayer, or to leave a gift or sacrifice in hopes a prayer will be granted. My own son experienced his vision quest at this very spot many years ago."

The old man inhaled a deep breath as if it gave him strength. A strong breeze carried the faint aroma of pine from the trees in the basin below. The fragrant mountain air was invigorating, a stark contrast to the desolate land surrounding the Medicine Wheel. Bailey shivered. The temperature had started to drop and, despite the afternoon sun, a chill began to envelop them. She pulled a light khaki jacket from her backpack and shrugged into it. It didn't matter that it was a late summer afternoon, the air was getting downright cool.

"We believe that the circle is the essence of life," the man went on as he buttoned his own coat with shaky hands. "Everything begins and ends and begins again following the same path. A boy is born, becomes a man, marries, begins a new circle with his own children. He grows weary, then passes on to better places only to see the circle repeat itself time and again. The Spirits here can interrupt that circle if they so choose."

The low moan of wind on a mountaintop filled their ears. The Indian man looked toward the sky then nodded silently. Bailey took an involuntary step back. Lonely or not, this old fellow was getting way too creepy. She turned to leave as he spoke again.

"There is a Spirit here you might find interesting. Her name is Dark Fawn."

Bailey nodded and inched farther away. Many of the other tourists had already started back down the mountain, some hiking like her, others driving. It wasn't wise to be left alone with this stranger, practically out in the wilderness, even if he did just want to talk. The Indian didn't seem to notice her apprehension as he continued his story. "It is told that Dark Fawn's father was the son of a tribal chief and her mother the daughter of a shaman. Her father was a fearless warrior who was tragically killed in battle while she was yet a child. Dark Fawn's mother was so distraught by the death of her husband, she grieved herself to death. Died of a tearful heart.

"The child was left alone in this world by the ones she loved more than life itself. Dark Fawn grew into a maiden of great beauty, but she refused the attentions of even the bravest and strongest men of the tribe. She claimed that she would never again endure the loss of love, especially not as her mother had."

Despite herself, Bailey was mesmerized by Dark Fawn's story. It was so . . . sad. Almost like her own. She had also lost everything just like Dark Fawn. She, too, had been alone as a child, without her parents, and without the love of a family. Bailey shook her head and turned back toward the Medicine Wheel. The man's words were just a freak coincidence. There was no way he'd know that her own story was so similar.

"Legend speaks that Dark Fawn's tribe journeyed here to worship. She vanished without a trace, and her people never saw her again. They knew that she had been chosen. The Spirits had been so inspired by her serene face and pure, undying love that they chose her to dwell with them. They allow her to share her grace with the young maidens who come here seeking their dreams."

"What an interesting tale," Bailey replied carefully. "Dark Fawn must be a kind and loving spirit."

He nodded, a slight smile tilted his chin. "That's why so many people disappear up here. The Spirits answer their prayers. Sometimes in ways no one can imagine." He studied her under half-closed lids. "Only special people, though. People who are ready."

"Hmmm." She nodded and glanced around. It appeared

that the other few hikers had long departed back down the road. She pulled her jacket closer to ward off another sharp bite of the wind. "Thank you again for telling me the history of the Medicine Wheel and Dark Fawn. I am honored to understand why it is so special to your people."

The man reached out and touched her arm before Bailey could move. "Do you have a prayer for Dark Fawn?"

Bailey started to jerk away, but hesitated. He really did seem to be harmless. Spooky, but harmless. Ultimately, her compassion won out. It couldn't hurt to humor a lonely old man. After today, she'd never see him again anyway. Cautiously, she turned back toward him. "I'm not a Native American. Wouldn't it be disrespectful?"

He nodded his approval at her reverence. "The Spirits hear every word," he answered. "But not all requests they choose to answer. You pray now. Dark Fawn is nearby."

Bailey copied his actions and bent her head to speak with the tragic Indian maiden. She really didn't know what to say, but it seemed to please the stranger beside her. "Dark Fawn," she began, "please hear my prayer. You and I are much alike in the loss of our parents. The gentleman beside me has said that you grant the desires of special people. While I am not special, Dark Fawn, the children I work with are. I face a challenge after this vacation. I've been appointed as a juvenile court judge. When I return home, I will be deciding what is best for many neglected children who have suffered like you. And . . . well, and like me.

"I pray for faith, Dark Fawn, so that I should never discount a parent's pure love for their child. I ask for hope so I may convince those who don't believe. And, above all, I wish for charity so that I may see problems through the eyes of the person or the child before me."

When Bailey opened her eyes a pleasant inner warmth of contentment and peace cloaked around her. Somehow, she wasn't surprised that the Indian man had quietly disappeared during her prayer, and she was left standing alone, comforted in a way she didn't know she had needed. Bailey smiled. Perhaps Dark Fawn had heard her prayer after all.

The family with the two little girls was getting into their car, almost the last of the afternoon sightseers. Kind spirit or not, she certainly didn't want to be up here all alone. Bailey lifted her nylon backpack over one shoulder then headed toward the road that led back down the mountain. When the park rangers had told her that hikers often parked at the cutoff road and walked up to the mountaintop, she had thought it an exciting idea to do the same. This was a vacation, after all, and what better way to see the real beauty of the area than a good long hike? Now she wasn't so sure it had been a great idea. True, the hike back to her car was downhill, but the sudden cold wind and late afternoon sun certainly wasn't conducive to a lonely hike down the mountainside. She hadn't meant to stay up here so long, and now she'd better hurry.

She reached the gravel-covered road and started down, careful to stay in the center on the good footing. The whipping wind grew almost brutal. When she reached the tree line, there would be more trees to break the force of the wind, although right now it was intemperate. It was almost as if the Medicine Wheel didn't want her to leave. Bailey quickly shook off that weird thought. The rangers had told her that the weather was known to be unpredictable at close to ten thousand feet above sea level, even in August. That was all it was. She had taken her chances deciding to hike instead of drive. Now she had to make the best of it. Bailey reached into her backpack for a pair of leather gloves and pulled them on. They weren't really made for cool weather, but they would do until she got back to the car.

She continued downhill, being careful not to slip on the loose layer of gravel that covered the road. She hadn't remembered the road being so treacherous on the hike up. Bai-

ley stepped over to one side of the road, hoping for more secure footing. The sky started to lose its blue and turn grayish. The air continued to grow dense and heavy. Despite the
sun, a heavy mist began to seep across the mountainside and
dampened the gray gravel at her feet. Bailey moved even
closer toward the edge of the drive as a descending car
slowly edged by, its windshield wipers rhythmically slash-
ing through the mist. She thought about flagging a ride but
hesitated a second too long. The car continued slowly down
the road and disappeared out of sight.

The fog grew more blinding with each step Bailey took
until it completely enveloped everything around her. She
slowed her pace and finally stopped when she could no
longer see the road directly at her feet. These mountains
were as unpredictable as the rangers had said. Less than two
minutes ago, the sun had been shining and birds chirped
from the trees. Now it was foggy, deathly quiet, and still.

Bailey readjusted her backpack with a firm tug. She had
taken this vacation by herself as a refresher in confidence
and self-reliance. The fog merely presented an unexpected
obstacle, yet another challenge for her to overcome. Challenging, but not impossible. She took one cautious step, then
another. As long as she kept on the road, she should be all
right. The problem was that the fog was now so thick that
she wasn't exactly sure where she was on the road. Was she
in the center or on the side? And, if she was on the side, was
it to the left or the right? Only the downhill grade kept her
headed in the right direction, even if it was inch by inch.

Bailey shifted her backpack from one shoulder to the
other and heard her car keys jingle inside. She had planned
to hike for only a few hours so she hadn't packed much extra
in her backpack, only her wallet, a bottle of water, and a
sandwich. Like any good hiker, though, she had her cellular
phone, a pack of matches, and a topographic map of the
area. If she did have the misfortune of getting lost, she'd at

least have a good chance of finding her way back. There was no excuse not to be prepared, especially when one traveled alone as much as she did.

With another careful step, Bailey quelled her rising fear. She told herself she was probably more than just a little spooked from talking with the Indian man, and it wouldn't be long before she reached her car.

Trying to keep her mind off her nervousness, Bailey thought of the other treasure tucked inside her backpack, something she had found at an old gift shop at the base of the mountain. It was a 1900 edition of the *Old Farmer's Almanac*, still bound in the original worn leather. Bailey had bought it instantly. Antique books had long been her passion, and she'd spent many a lonely night with her nose buried deep inside the pages.

Another step.

Her confidence returned as she carefully edged along the road. It shouldn't be much farther now. Her car had been no more than a mile off. Bailey wondered if the other hikers had made if safely down before the fog rolled in. "Hello? Anyone out there?" She raised her voice in hopes another hiker might be nearby. Silence answered her. Deathly still silence. Bailey walked on.

In her anxiousness to get back to the car, Bailey picked up the pace and that was when it happened. Her foot slipped in the gravel and she stumbled, desperate to regain her footing. Bailey knew instantly that she hadn't missed a step. She was pushed. Hard. Deliberately. Forcefully.

Bailey turned and tried to strike out at whoever had pushed her. But she wasn't fast enough. The gravel beneath her gave way, and her hiking boot slipped off the path and broke through the fog into emptiness. She hadn't realized she'd been so close to the edge of the road.

Bailey screamed, scratching wildly for anything to stop

her fall, but there was nothing. The fog refused to show her the danger, to show her how to protect herself.

Suddenly, as quickly as it had started, it stopped. Bailey landed on soft, wet ground, her body was covered in mud, while her head and arms hung over the brink of what seemed to be a ledge of some sort. At least she was alive and no worse for the wear. No telling how far she had fallen. *This blasted fog!* Without stopping to breathe, Bailey edged herself away from the emptiness beyond the ledge.

Kneeling to catch her breath, Bailey heard a horrible cracking and suddenly the ground gave way beneath her. She frantically clawed at dirt, weeds, anything to stop her slide down the mountain. In desperation, Bailey managed to hook one arm around what was probably a tree root. The force of her action caused her body to slam into the mountainside and her backpack to slip off her shoulder. She heard a solid *thunk* as it hit the ground seconds later. She wasn't about to let go and find out how much farther it had fallen.

The fog was still heavy and blinding. Sheer willpower helped Bailey pull herself up onto a narrow ledge created by the tree root. The ledge was small and circular, almost cradling her against the wall of the cliff. It smelled of rotting wood and mud, which terrified her as much as her helplessness. Who could have pushed her, and why? She was certain she'd been alone. Certain. And how could she have not noticed such a deep ravine on her trip up the mountain? She'd have been extra cautious if she had.

Just as quickly as it began, the thick mist began to dissipate. The temperature started to rise and the sun returned to its place in the sky. Bailey leaned into the cliff to catch her breath and tried to calm her rapid heartbeat. She was lucky to be alive, that was all there was to it. She had fallen about twenty feet or so. Above her was the edge of a cliff where the land had broken away to reveal black dirt, rocks, and jutting roots. Below her was a deep ravine, maybe sixty feet deep or more. If she had fallen farther . . . Bailey shuddered. She certainly wouldn't have lived.

She looked beyond the ravine, out into the distance, surprised to see it no longer appeared so barren and desolate. The scraggly trees and rocky outcrops that had dotted Medicine Mountain were gone. In fact, the mountains themselves seemed to be gone. All she could see were acres and acres of rolling hills and lush green grass. Her gut instinct clamored a warning. Something was wrong. Very wrong. A wave of dizziness washed over her, and Bailey fought to keep calm. She leaned back against the dirt ledge and closed her eyes. A warm trickle seeped down the side of her face. She knew instinctively it was blood, and tenderly fingered a gash above her temple just at the hairline. Her face also burned where the skin had been scraped by the harsh dirt and rocks. She groaned and tried to spit out a mouthful of grit. Her right hand was hurt, but it didn't seem to be broken. Overall, she was in pretty good shape for her predicament. If only her head didn't hurt so badly.

Bailey weakly called for help, although she knew there wasn't much chance anyone would hear her. She had been the last one on the mountain. It was unlikely anyone would hear her cries. Her phone was in her backpack twenty feet below her. Using one arm as a lever, she sat up and carefully looked below. Separating her from her backpack was not only another sharp fall, but more rocks, mud, and roots.

There was no way she could reach it. No way at all.

Nausea gripped her as the dizziness she battled grew too strong. Bailey leaned back against the dirt and closed her eyes. Black oblivion consumed her.

Chapter 2

A DEEP RUMBLE of thunder reverberated across the prairie sky. The gray clouds hung low, hiding the sun and casting a yellowish hue in every direction. Zach Gooden glanced upward, then lifted his hand to readjust his hat. The sky looked ominous. Another thunderstorm was brewing. Certainly no time for dawdling, especially not on J.T. Thompson's land, and especially not leading this particular stray bull.

A surging wind suddenly whipped around, knocking Zach's black hat from his head. His horse tossed his head and snorted, sidestepping right into the startled bull. "Easy there, fella. Just a little tempest dancin' across the plains. Settle down." The horse continued to stamp nervously and pull at the bit. Something had sure spooked him, although Zach couldn't tell what. Reliant was generally steady, calm, and true to his name. Then, very faintly, over the howl of the wind, he heard it. A scream. A woman's scream.

Hell. That could only mean . . .

Quick as he could Zach loosened the lasso from around the young bull's horns and tugged it free, coiling the rope back on his saddle as he did so. He spurred Reliant toward the copse of trees a half a mile in the distance. He knew Thompson's ranch almost as well as he did his own. There was an unusually deep ravine just beyond the smattering of trees in the distance, probably cut out of the ground by the river before it changed its path. The ground was always soft and muddy around that area. Zach could remember more than one ranch hand and a few good horses who had lost their lives from a wayward step over the years. If someone had gotten too close to the edge it was likely the ground had given way and they'd fallen. The scream had been faint, but it was definitely female, which meant that one of his sisters had gone and done something foolish.

Again.

Which one this time? Probably the same culprit who had let his prized bull escape from the corral. She probably thought she'd make amends by helping to look for it. Zach leaned farther over Reliant's neck and urged the horse faster. He quickly covered the distance to the trees.

Another scream.

Without waiting for the horse to come to a complete halt, Zach jumped from the saddle and rushed as close to the edge of the ravine as he dared. "Faith? Hope? Is that you?"

No answer. Zach inched up to the edge of the cliff. Damp earth broke away and fell, leaving a gaping hole where he had started to place his foot. Cautiously, he peered over the edge. There she was, lying on a narrow ledge about twenty-five feet down, curled tight against the side to keep from falling farther. He released a quick breath when he realized this wasn't one of his sisters. This one had copper hair instead of the telltale Gooden blond, and she was wearing mannish clothes, something the Gooden sisters would never be allowed to do. In fact, if it hadn't been for her hair, he wouldn't have been certain she was a woman.

"Ma'am? Are you able to move?" Still no answer. He could see blood on her ashen face, and her eyes were closed. She'd probably passed out cold. Either that or she was already dead. Zach hated to think along those lines. He inwardly groaned as he stared down at her still form. The cliff was slick, muddy, and dangerous. If he was to climb down to her, his added weight would crumble the precarious ledge she was on and they'd both fall to their deaths. He whistled low and shook his head. His relief that it wasn't one of his sisters in danger was short-lived. This woman had to be rescued, and that left only him and his horse to do the rescuing.

His other dilemma was J.T. Thompson. Zach Gooden was no more welcome on Thompson's land than Thompson was on Zach's, and being caught with a stray bull would only make Zach's situation worse. If any of Thompson's men happened by, he'd have some explaining to do, and most likely at the wrong end of a gun. Despite the real danger posed by Thompson and his men, Zach rose and strode to his horse with quick, purposeful strides. He undid the coil of rope tied to his saddle, then knotted one end around the saddle horn and led his horse farther away from the edge of the cliff.

"Steady here, bud. The ground is soft." He cued the horse, who planted both feet firmly into the dirt. He lifted a second rope from his saddle to tie around the injured woman. Zach knotted the end of the first rope under his arms and around his chest, then walked back toward the ridge, and glanced back at his horse. The bay gelding stared at him with dark eyes, then snorted and tossed his head.

"You don't have to tell me," Zach sighed in agreement. "Females mean nothing but trouble. You hold me steady and I'll do the rescuin'." The horse tossed his head as if he understood completely. He leaned back on his haunches to hold Zach's weight with the taut rope.

Carefully, Zach lifted himself over the edge. More dirt and mud caved in and slid down the side of the ravine. He could hear the plop as it landed on the ground below. He whistled twice, two short shrill sounds, and his horse slowly moved forward. The rope jerked his ribs as his weight settled into the motion. Zach dropped farther and farther down the side of the cliff until he reached the woman. Reliant walked forward a few more steps, then halted to give Zach enough slack to work. Zach steadied himself, then bent to check the woman. Blood seeped down the side of her face, but the constant rise and fall of her chest indicated that she was alive.

Zach straightened and quickly considered the sky. The afternoon rain clouds had gathered earlier than usual, probably due to the intense wind that had whipped around. A roll of thunder reminded him that he'd better not dally. Another storm would soon let loose. Crossing the swollen river to get back to the Double Bar G was going to be dangerous enough with an unconscious woman in his arms; it would be even worse in a downpour.

He shifted the woman and started to tie the second rope he carried around her chest, just under her shoulders. She was soft and bosomy although not terribly heavy. Exactly what he liked in a woman. He smiled to himself and then the slick mud beneath his boot gave way. Zach fell forward, then toppled facedown in the muck right beside her. He grunted as the safety rope around his chest caught him hard. He didn't have time for thoughts like that. He had to get himself and the woman to safe ground.

Suddenly the woman slipped from his grasp and started to fall; he hadn't finished tying the knot so it instantly came loose. He quickly grabbed her arms before the force of the rope around her chest could yank her back. He didn't know if she had any broken ribs from the fall, but she certainly would from the rescue if he weren't more careful.

She still lay unconscious on the ledge while he hung precariously from the rope. He couldn't risk putting his weight on the narrow ridge again. The best he could do was to hold the woman in his arms and hope she didn't slip from his grasp while Reliant pulled them to safety. He used one leg to carefully brace himself against the side of the ledge, then reached for the woman. In one quick motion, he lifted her over his shoulder, then signaled again, this time three short whistles. Slowly, his horse began to back up, pulling them from the ridge treacherous inch by treacherous inch.

Zach shook his head in admiration as he steadied their slow ascent. A trained cow horse was worth his weight in feed any day of the year. He'd see to it that good old Reliant got an extra helping tonight.

Once over the top and back on solid ground, Zach laid the unconscious woman gently on the grass. Quickly, his hands skimmed her limbs as he felt for broken bones. Her right wrist looked swollen. He reached for his handkerchief to dab at the nasty gash on her forehead. He would have to spare a man to ride for the doctor in Box Bend.

He studied her face carefully. She had to be a stranger to these parts, since he'd not seen this woman in town before. Ladies were scarce and he'd have certainly remembered this one with her tangled red hair. He'd never seen hair quite so remarkable. It was silky despite the mud, and it glistened even with the sun behind the clouds.

Her painted nails were odd, something usually only worn by saloon girls. Her clothing, though, was like a man's with a jacket, button-up shirt, thick leather boots, and denims. Was she a guest of J.T.'s out riding on his ranch? Zach stood and stamped the mud from his boots. No, J.T. would never allow a woman to ride alone, especially not with the type of ranch hands the man notoriously hired. Zach glanced around, half expecting to see his neighbor watching from nearby. No sense in pressing his luck. He carefully picked up the unconscious woman and mounted his horse. There was probably a simple explanation as to who she was and why she was out on the range by herself. He'd feel much better searching for answers back on his own Double Bar G.

In his hurry to rescue the woman, Zach had left his hat on the ground, and the bull grazing loose. He needed to get this woman to safety then round up the bull again. He hoped the fella hadn't wandered too far off. That young bull had cost Zach a small mint, and Thompson had made it clear he wanted the animal dead. Zach sighed; between his lost hat, the wayward bull, and an injured woman it was going to be a long ride home.

A streak of lightning lit the room as a deep roll of thunder shook Bailey's bed. She woke with a start. Three beautiful angels dressed in frilly white guarded over her. Her head pounded violently, and she could barely focus on their faces. The one closest to her carried a brass candleholder, and the glow of the candle's flame cast an aura of warm welcome. The room was completely dark otherwise.

Bailey closed her eyes. Except for the steady pounding of rain, this could all be a dream. When she looked again, the angels came into better focus. All three smiled sweetly, although worry marred their expressions. They were not quite cherubs, yet not grown angels either. Was there a proper term for teenage angels?

"We're so glad you're here," the one with the candle said as another bolt of lightning illuminated the room. "Zach was so angry at me for leaving the gate open and letting that silly bull escape, but if I hadn't, he wouldn't have been there to rescue you. Besides, you're the answer to our prayers."

"Shhh," whispered another. "Not so loud, Hope. She doesn't want to hear all that right now."

Bailey didn't understand. Why should she be the answer to *their* prayers? She opened her lips to ask but no words came. Bits of sand and grit still lined her mouth, and her throat was parched.

"We thought you might like some water," the first angel added in the most serene and peaceful voice Bailey had ever heard. "Zachariah is working on the record books. He's so involved that he'll probably be there for a while and forget that you might need a drink." She gently lifted Bailey's head and held a cup to her lips. The water was sweet, cool, and refreshing, better than any she had ever tasted.

"I'm Faith," the second angel said softly. "These are my sisters, Hope and Charity. You rest now, we'll be back later to check on you."

Bailey laid her head back down on the pillow and closed her eyes. Surely, she was in heaven. Where else would such sweet, innocent angels take care of her?

Zach Gooden bent and grabbed the rolled bandage he had dropped on the floor. He'd wanted Hope to change the dressing on this mysterious woman's head but, as usual, his sister was nowhere to be found. The morning sun was already high in the sky, which meant she was probably out near the small creek reading yet another novel before the afternoon rains set in. There was no telling where Faith and Charity were either.

He turned back to the sleeping woman and began to remove the soiled dressing covering the gash on her head. Doc McConnell had come last night to check her injuries. The gash was deep, which meant she might have a concussion, but nothing was broken. Her ribs were bruised and her wrist was sprained, but she ought to be all right in a few days or so. Doc had wanted to keep her still as much as possible just to be on the safe side. That hadn't been hard. She'd been out like a light ever since he rescued her yesterday. Zach was to

watch her carefully over the next few days and send for the
doc if she didn't come around.

Zach's fingers brushed the soft skin of her check as he
pulled back her hair to keep it out of the way. Actually, this
wasn't such an unpleasant task. She had the most remarkable face he had ever seen. Her complexion was fair, as if
she rarely went out in the sun. Odd for a woman living in
Wyoming. Light tiny freckles swept across the bridge of her
nose and dusted each cheek. He gingerly began to remove
the old bandage, taking care not to disturb his guest. Her
eyes were still closed, but he imagined them a vivid emerald
green in stark contrast to her coppery tresses. Her vibrant
red hair was thick and long, and shone from the early morning sun that seeped through the window. One of his sisters,
probably one of the twins, had already been here and
brushed away the mud and tangles.

Zach shook his head and mentally reprimanded himself.
He was gawking at her as if he'd never seen a woman before.
Of course, sometimes it seemed as if he hadn't. The thought
of having to deal with his sisters had pretty much dissuaded
all of the local women from showing any interest in him
whatsoever. Their botched attempts at finding him a wife
had become fodder for gossip three counties over. Besides,
he didn't have time to waste on yet another female. The
three he had were more than enough for any man.

Once the old bandage was removed, Zach reached for a
warm cloth to clean the wound. It was deep, but just in the
hairline. Luckily, no scar would mar her lovely skin. He
placed a new bandage on the injury and carefully lifted her
head to wrap the roll of cotton around her forehead to hold
it in place. Zach straightened and gazed down at the woman
resting in his stepmother's feather bed. His sisters had neatly
stitched the light quilt that was draped over her just before
their mother had died four years ago. Even though the girls
behaved like firebrands most of the time, he was certain they

at least remembered some of the manners their mother had taught them. He knew they could act like ladies and do needlepoint and such if they really wanted to.

They just didn't want to. Period.

And if they didn't want to, they didn't. Period.

He couldn't remember when he had lost control of his sisters. It seemed like he just looked up one morning and noticed that they were no longer cute little girls. The twins, Faith and Hope, had become beautiful hellions, and Charity was their younger apprentice. They caused trouble wherever they went. Not bad trouble, mind you, just annoying trouble. And he had no idea what to do about it.

The woman stirred briefly under the patchwork quilt, her lips lifted slightly. Zach ran his hand over his scratchy chin and pondered on her situation. It was logical to assume she must have something to do with J.T. since she was found on the man's ranch. If that was the case it didn't bode well for him. He hadn't sent word to his neighbor that he had found the injured beauty because he wasn't certain she wanted to be found. If she had been trying to escape J.T.'s grasp for some unknown reason, then they had something in common.

He knew absolutely nothing about her, not even her name. He'd never seen her around the nearby town of Box Bend. Perhaps she had been traveling through the area and somehow become separated from her companions. If that was the case, it probably meant she also had a husband or another man to watch after her. Zach frowned and bent to tuck the edges of the quilt under the mattress. When he had rescued her, she'd been in the ravine alone. As near as he could tell, there was no evidence that she had a horse or that another person had been out there with her.

He walked across the room to check the ranch activity outside the window. His two prized Aberdeen Angus bulls grazed in separate wooden corrals near the barn, the half-grown bull calf in a third. Their coats were a shiny black, the color of newly spit-polished boots. He stared at them proudly. Those bulls were his future—and his gamble.

Zach stared at the young bull he'd tracked down. The animal seemed no worse for his adventure on the plains. A sly grin crossed Zach's face as he wondered if the bull had gotten to any of J.T. Thompson's fertile cows while he was loose. Thompson already hated Zach's Angus. Zach could only imagine what the man would do if he found any crossbred calves nursing his Herefords come spring.

The woman moaned softly. Zach turned toward her and covered the distance between them in two strides. She moved again, then reached up to touch her injured head. He caught her hand and stopped it in midair. "Don't worry with the bandage, ma'am. I've just now put on a fresh one. Do you remember your name?"

"Bailey Cooper," she answered weakly, slowly opening her eyes. He was right. They were deep green, although not quite the color of emeralds. Jade, perhaps. "Am I in heaven?"

He gently brushed a strand of hair away from her face. "Some folks say this is as close to heaven as you can get, but I don't think it's the kind of heaven you mean. I'm Zach Gooden. You're at the Double Bar G." He leaned his head close to her lips to listen as she tried to say more.

"Last night," she whispered, "three angels visited me. They were all dressed in white. One carried a candle."

So, the trio had disobeyed his orders to let her rest. He sighed. Why couldn't they mind? Just once. "Trust me," he said grimly. "Those three are anything but angels. They're my sisters, Faith, Hope, and Charity."

Her features visibly lightened. Zach felt a strange surge in his chest to see her effort to smile. "I'm waiting for Hope now," he added. "She's to take care of you today, find you some clean clothes and get you breakfast. Doc McConnell wants you to rest. You've had quite a blow to the head.

Should I send word to anyone? Do you have any family?" The woman weakly shook her head and closed her eyes once more.

Zach walked back to the window. Just where was his sister? The sun had been up for more than two hours. He had a ranch to run, no time to play nursemaid to a stranger, no matter how beautiful she might be.

"Morning, Zachariah." The door behind him quickly opened and Faith stepped inside.

"Finally," he snapped. "Where's Hope? I told her to be here to help change the bandage."

"Oh, she's here and there, I suppose." Faith smiled nonchalantly as if she had no worries in the world. "You've managed quite well, so everything has turned out fine, don't you think?"

Zach glared at his sister but, as usual, he had to bite his tongue to hold back a sharp retort. Not only did each sister cover for the other two, all three had logical explanations for their actions. There was never any intended disobedience, instead it was a misunderstanding, and always on his part. Unfortunately, his sisters all knew that no matter what he said, he was all talk where they were concerned. Zach swore under his breath. They were his three baby sisters, and they had him firmly wrapped around their little fingers. He would put an end to their behavior if he could just figure out a way.

"She *is* beautiful, don't you think?" Faith walked over to the woman and sat down on the bed beside her. "I'm glad Hope got her out of the muddy clothes. She probably rested better. I'm going to help her into one of my dressing gowns. A pink one would look lovely, don't you think?"

Without acknowledging her words, Zach grunted and headed for the door. He knew exactly what the sixteen-year-old was up to. She was trying to put thoughts in his head about how beautiful this woman was. Only Faith didn't know that his manly desires had already led him to that conclusion. Faith's goal was to find him a wife . . . any wife and as soon as possible. "You will be around the *rest* of the day, won't you?" he asked. "Or do I need to check on you as well?"

"Now, Zachariah. When have I ever been irresponsible?"

He stopped in the hallway just outside the door. "Well, let's see," he replied sarcastically. He held up his hand to count with his fingers. "How about last month at the Ogdens' barn raising? There was that shipment of loose apples at the mercantile in town. Don't forget the incident at the church with the cow, and we all swore to never again mention the name of the schoolmarm who got a sudden case of unexplained vapors. The widow Garrett is too embarrassed to meet my eye, and wasn't it just last week that you . . ."

Faith at least had the decency to flush and look embarrassed. "Perhaps you're right, I do get carried away sometimes. However, today you have my sincere word that I will remain by her side."

"And no big ideas," he reminded her firmly as he headed toward the stairs. "I don't need a wife."

Bailey slowly opened her eyes as the door snapped shut. She was still quite groggy, but as much as her head hurt and her body ached, she wanted to laugh out loud. It was obvious who was in control of this house, and it wasn't the handsome man wearing the genuine cowboy duds. She glanced over at the girl named Faith, who stared back at her with unblinking blue eyes.

Bailey had represented plenty of girls just like her over the years. Surprisingly innocent for all their grown-up ways. They were usually high school dropouts in trouble with the law, or drug addicts who had lost all hope by the time the court had appointed her as their attorney. Still, it was apparent this angel-girl named Faith had a kind heart beneath her troublemaking nature. Bailey could easily see how she got away with her pranks. Even a brother would have difficulty saying no to such a beguiling smile.

A sharp pain stabbed across her temple and reminded her of the terror of the ravine. She wrinkled her face and lifted her hand to the bridge of her nose. She couldn't recall anything of being rescued.

"Here." Faith had carried in a cup of steaming liquid and now placed it on the table by Bailey's bed. "Doc McConnell wanted us to get some broth in you the minute you woke up." Faith helped Bailey pull herself up into a sitting position, then watched as she lifted the white porcelain cup to her lips.

The warm liquid was soothing as Bailey swallowed. "Bailey Cooper." Her throat cracked slightly with the introduction.

"Pleased to meet you, Miss Cooper. My sisters and I are so glad you are here, and not hurt very badly."

Bailey noticed the odd prairie-type dress that Faith wore. Each time the girl moved, the blue calico skirt swirled around her black, lace-up boots. Bailey took another sip of the liquid and tried not to stare. If she had learned one thing about working with teenagers, it was that kids take pride in wearing the weirdest things. This teenager was no exception, although Bailey had some clue as to where she had come up with her look.

The room was as old-fashioned as the girl. It was furnished with an antique assortment of dark and massive furniture. There was a dresser with a white stoneware basin and pitcher sitting on top. The oak highboy had a wooden jewelry box on a lace doily, and a pink crystal oil lamp sat on a table beside her bed. Someone had placed a vase of wildflowers next to it, too, a warm touch to an otherwise sparse room. The bed was an unusual three-quarter type, not small enough to be a twin and not quite wide or long enough to be considered a double.

There was a polished dresser against the wall across from the bed, and hanging on the stark beige wall above it was an old mirror framed in the same dark oak as the furniture. Bailey focused on her reflection in despair. She looked as if she had been beaten up and left for dead. She felt like she looked, too. The bandage on her forehead was bad enough, but the various assortment of scratches, cuts, and bruises silently spoke of her fall. She was going to be one big ache for at least a week. Why hadn't she remembered such a perilous edge from the hike up? She would have certainly made every effort to avoid it on her return, especially once the fog had settled in so heavy. There was a nagging thought, too. That she had been forcefully pushed off the road. Nothing was making sense.

A giggle beside the bed brought Bailey's attention back to Faith. The girl's lack of makeup did nothing to dim her beauty. Her golden-colored hair was accented by eyes the color of the bluebonnets that grew wild on the mountainside.

Faith returned Bailey's stare with no attempt to hide her curious excitement. "I'm so glad you're here," she rushed. "You don't know how boring it is on the ranch. Nothing but smelly cows, dirty cowhands, and a bossy brother."

Bailey grinned. Faith might have the sweet voice of an angel, but the girl could probably fast-talk the devil if she had to.

"Zachariah said you fell down the ravine. Didn't you know the rains made it dangerous?"

"We're on a ranch?" Bailey shook her head. "No, I guess I didn't realize where I was. I was walking back down the mountain and slipped."

"The mountain?"

Bailey barely heard Faith's softly spoken words. She watched as the angelic face clouded with confusion. Why would she be confused about a mountain? Surely it was just off in the distance. The girl acted like it was light-years away. Bailey struggled for something to say to fill the gaping silence. "May I please use your bathroom?"

"Our what?" Faith immediately resumed her buoyant self, impatiently pushing her blond hair away from her eyes.

"Your rest room. I have to . . ."

Faith's confusion returned as she met Bailey's gaze, then she blushed as realization dawned. "Oh, you must mean the chamber pot. I'll get it for you." She hurriedly bent to look under the bed, then lifted a heavy ceramic chamber pot and carried it to a discreet corner. Bailey stared at it in horror. "Don't you have indoor plumbing?"

"No. I've read about it though," she said excitedly, oblivious to Bailey's discomfort. "I understand that it's only in the best homes in the largest cities. Certainly nowhere in Wyoming. Does your house have it?"

"Certainly." Bailey politely tried to keep the horror from her voice. "Where do you go?"

"The outhouse, of course. It's just behind the kitchen, although we have chamber pots, too." Bailey battled disbelief as she stared at the clean white container.

"I'll give you some privacy." Faith quietly turned and headed for the door, seemingly embarrassed. "I'll be back in a little bit with something to wear and to help you dress. Doc McConnell doesn't want you up and about until you feel a little better. Maybe tomorrow we'll go downstairs if you feel up to it. Besides—" She stopped suddenly and looked back at Bailey. "You're not married, are you?"

The sudden shift in conversation caused Bailey to stare blankly at the cheerful girl. "Of course not . . . why do you ask?"

"Just curious," Faith replied in a singsong voice. A wicked grin spread across her features like a slick Siamese cat who just discovered a bowl of cream. "My sisters wanted me to ask." With that, Faith almost skipped out the door.

Bailey cocked an eyebrow. She didn't need her courtroom

training to deduce that Faith was scheming and plotting. Unfortunately, she also had a sinking feeling that Faith had already cast her as one of the main characters.

True to her word, five minutes later Faith returned to the room with a dressing gown for Bailey. "This is one of my favorites," she said with a grin. "It will look wonderful on you, and Zachariah will be especially glad he rescued you."

Faith held up the lovely light pink dressing gown for Bailey's inspection, then glowed when Bailey smiled her approval. Faith had obviously brought the best in her wardrobe. It didn't matter a single bit that the rosy shade of pink would clash with Bailey's red hair.

Bailey tossed back the quilt and managed to stand. Then, exhausted, she dropped back on the bed as a wave of dizziness washed over her. When the nausea had passed, she slowly and carefully sat straight up.

"Zachariah is so thankful he happened to be nearby and heard your screams." Faith carefully lifted Bailey's injured hand and guided it through the billowy sleeve. "My sisters and I want to make sure . . ." The incessant flow of words stopped suddenly. Bailey looked up to find Faith biting her lip, hesitation on her face. "You'll have to forgive me." She smiled brightly. "Zachariah says I chatter constantly. I'm quite a bother, actually, and he's always getting on to me about it. Half the time I don't know what I'm saying. I just talk to hear myself talk. He's right, you know. I . . ."

Bailey laughed as Faith continued on nonstop. Her brother was a wise man. Talking came naturally to teenage girls, this one more than most. "Thank you for getting me out of my torn clothes." Bailey changed the subject when Faith paused for a breath. "I couldn't bear the thought of sleeping in them." She managed to stand on shaky legs.

"You're welcome. Hope and I took your wet clothes to be washed." Faith started to say something further, but went abruptly silent, as if something unusual had occurred to her. She sat down on the edge of the bed beside Bailey, then giggled softly in what must have been embarrassment. "That reminds me. Your . . . well . . . um, your underthings. We've never seen anything like them before, not even in the Sears and Roebuck Catalog. They were so . . . soft and light. Are they French?"

Bailey grinned. The kid had guts, that was certain. She liked that. Too often many of the kids she represented in court were either too frightened to speak, or too angry to listen.

"You've discovered my secret passion." Bailey lowered her voice and darted her glance around the room, pretending to look for eavesdroppers. "Irresistible lingerie. Although it's not French, it's just from Victoria's Secret."

Yesterday morning, she had chosen to wear a particularly daring white bra and matching French cut panties that were almost nothing but lace. The set was not the sexiest she had ever purchased but rated pretty high on the scale. She was glad it was Faith and her sister, not their brother, who had changed her into the white cotton nightgown. He would have gotten quite an eyeful. An unexpectedly warm shiver tickled up her spine. He was a handsome man, after all.

"That would explain why they're not in the mail-order catalog," Faith replied earnestly. "Of course, I see why you would want to keep underthings a secret, but who is Victoria? Do you suppose she might tell Hope and me about such finery, too?"

Bailey's amusement dimmed. She stared at Faith, who sat on the edge of the bed and waited hopefully for an answer, the skirt of her plain calico dress tucked carefully around her legs. From Faith's excited expression, it didn't appear she knew about the chain of lingerie stores.

"I don't see why not." Bailey nodded at Faith and once

more suppressed the growing worry that had nagged at her since she woke.

"Wonderful!" Faith jumped up from the bed and bent to plump Bailey's pillows. "You really must rest now. I'll be back later with dinner and my sisters. They are dying to meet you."

Bailey nodded quietly. She'd met many unusual people as a court-appointed juvenile attorney. She was the first to speak that all people had the right to live as they pleased, but there was something unusual about this family. She sighed. It must just be the blow to the head. Why else would everything seem so odd?

It was just after dusk, not quite dark enough for the moon and stars. Those wouldn't have mattered anyway. Another rain shower had started in the early afternoon, sometimes heavy and sometimes light, but it had not let up all afternoon. That was just as well for Bailey, she still didn't feel much like getting up and exploring. When she brought lunch, Faith had chattered for an hour or so before Bailey had given in to the urge to close her eyes. As they must have promised their brother, the three sisters had checked on her several times throughout the rainy day, but the fall seemed to have sapped most of her strength. They'd peek in, see that she was resting, and tiptoe back out, giggling softly. Frankly, talking with the oldest one this morning had not been easy. She was pleasant enough, but her conversation was quite odd even for a teenager. Still the family was very kind to take her in like this, no matter their eccentricities.

She had wanted to call the ranger station, just to let them know she was safe, but there was no phone near her bed, or apparently in the room. Faith had only looked puzzled when Bailey asked for a cordless. The effort to make the girl understand was too taxing for Bailey's aching head, so she had given up for the time being. She figured the park rangers would have found her car at the cutoff road, and hoped they hadn't launched a massive hunt to find her. She obviously wasn't lost in the elements up on Medicine Mountain.

Bailey hadn't seen the attractive cowboy since his visit this morning. Faith's sisters, Hope, an identical twin, and Charity, just a few years younger, had brought her supper a little while ago, but Bailey didn't have much of an appetite. The tray with a thick beef stew and bread sat untouched on a nearby dresser. She was thirsty, though. The pitcher Faith had placed within arm's reach was long empty. It shouldn't be too difficult to refill it herself. Bailey tossed back the blanket and sat up in bed. She touched her toes to the floor and carefully stretched. Everything ached from the top of her head to the bottoms of her feet. What didn't ache had a scratch or a cut instead of a bruise.

She lifted the heavy ironstone pitcher with her uninjured hand and opened the bedroom door. The empty hallway was dimly lit in a yellowish hue by a small oil lamp sitting on a tall narrow table by the wall. Bailey hadn't seen one with a burning wick in years. She felt a cool damp breeze on her face. A window at the far end of the hall had been left open, the curtains ruffled from the rainy wind. Bailey paused to listen for the sound of a television or radio in the house, but it was quiet. Perhaps the family had gone to town for dinner or a movie. She softly knocked on the first door to the left but there was no answer. She recalled Faith's statement about no indoor plumbing, but perhaps she'd find another pitcher still full of water. She opened the door to see a large bedroom that clearly belonged to the three sisters. Like the hallway, it was also softly illuminated with an oil lamp. There were three beds with fluffy thick mattresses and pillows, an assortment of hair ribbons, books, and dolls. She noticed one doll in particular. It was a beautiful Indian maiden dressed finely in a deerskin dress with intricate beading. For some reason, it reminded her of Dark Fawn, the

Spirit she had prayed to. Bailey stepped softly toward a pitcher, identical to the one in her hand, that sat on a nearby nightstand. Empty.

Disappointed, Bailey ran her tongue across dry lips, then turned back to the hallway. Perhaps if she could manage the stairs, she could find the kitchen. It was truly odd not to have running water or plumbing upstairs, especially with three teenage girls, but surely there would be water in the kitchen. She looked around at several closed doors, then softly tapped on one across the hall. No answer. The door creaked as she pushed it open. Despite the dim light, she knew instantly it was a man's room. It smelled woodsy, musky, masculine. She didn't know if any other man occupied the house except the girls' brother. They hadn't mentioned anyone, and she hadn't asked. Suddenly, Bailey felt guilty for snooping. Granted, she needed something to drink, but this was someone's private space. The last thing she needed to do was to offend the man who had saved her.

Bailey backed out of the room and carefully closed the door with a click. She turned, intent on finding the stairs. In the fading light she didn't see the figure standing close behind her until it was too late. She crashed chest to chin with her rescuer. The ironstone pitcher slipped from her grasp and landed on Zach Gooden's toe before crashing to the floor and shattering into chunky pieces.

Zach's hands quickly encircled Bailey before she could do likewise and fall to the floor. Thousands of tiny heat prickles soared where his skin touched Bailey's through the soft fabric of her gown. Bailey managed to regain her balance and stepped away from the shocking sensation.

"You startled me!"

"What are you doing up?"

"I . . . I needed something to drink. I was hoping to find it myself and not disturb you further." Bailey swallowed hard and fought to control the rising fluttering of her heart.

Nerves. That's what it had to be. Why else would her heart be beating so fast and loud?

He had obviously just come in from outside. His clothes were dusty, his body hot and damp. Even in the vague light of the hallway, Bailey could see Zach's eyes leave her face and travel slowly down the length of her body, then back up again. The dressing gown Faith had loaned her suddenly seemed extremely sheer and revealing, even though it had a high neck and tight belt. Just as quickly as it began, it was over. The look she had seen on his face, the desire, the want, the need, was instantly gone. He carefully stepped back and bent to pick up the shards from the pitcher.

"I'm sorry you had to get up to look, ma'am. I'll have one of the girls bring up a fresh pitcher for you. Are you feeling better?"

Bailey nodded. "I apologize for being such a burden, Mr. Gooden. Your sisters told me how you rescued me from the ravine. I don't know what I would have done if you hadn't come along."

Zach nodded. "That is a dangerous area, but we can talk about that tomorrow. You best be back to bed. I'll send Faith up with another pitcher." He walked her back to the open door of her room, then tipped his head and disappeared into his own.

Chapter 3

"SIT HERE, BAILEY, and I'll get us something to drink. Charity makes wonderful lemonade. Just like our ma used to do." Faith guided Bailey to an enormous chair in the middle of the great room downstairs, being careful not to jar her injured hand.

"Where is your mother?" Bailey lowered herself into the chair. She grimaced to feel a sharp twinge at one of her ribs.

"She died," Faith answered solemnly.

"Oh, you poor dear!" Bailey reached to pat the girl's hand. "I'm so sorry."

Faith nodded, her eyes downcast and sad. "She's in a better place now. At least that's what the good reverend says. Zach had a different ma. She died, too, but years and years before I was born." Bailey nodded. How terrible for these precious girls to be without a mother. It wasn't fair to any child, much less three.

"If you're settled now I'll go get us the lemonade." At

Bailey's nod, Faith smiled sweetly and headed past the dining table and through a door to the left.

Bailey curiously glanced around the ranch-style house. It was obvious there was no womanly presence in the house. There were several glass oil lamps sitting on the tops of ruffled lace doilies. Those were about the only frills in the room. It was decorated rustically with more antiques similar to those in her room. The wood was polished to a beautiful sheen, but dark and masculine throughout. The sunlight from several windows across the front, sides, and back of the house allowed more than enough light to make the room comfortable. All of the windows were open, and a cool late morning breeze rustled functional yellow gingham curtains. Bailey inhaled deeply. The air from the outside carried a faint scent of wildflowers, and the house smelled rich and inviting.

Her chair was covered with deep brown leather, overstuffed and quite comfortable. At the far end of the room was an enormous fireplace with a stone mantle. Black ashes and soot were evidence of a recent fire. She slowly rose and moved to look out one of the front windows, then self-consciously tightened the fabric belt at her waist. Another borrowed dressing gown was draped over her body and rustled against her bare thighs. The soft, lightweight wool made her feel just as feminine as her fancy lingerie.

Beyond the broad front porch, Bailey saw only open prairie. Blooming flowers added vivid dots of color to the solid sea of silver-green grass. Other than the few shady cottonwood trees planted near the house, there was not another tree to be seen across the vast expanse of land.

Over to the left stood a huge barn, the wood weathered to a light gray. The doors were open, but it appeared to be empty. She assumed that this was a working ranch, and all the employees were out riding fences or branding calves, or whatever it was they did on ranches. An old buckboard wagon sat unused near the barn. Farther to the left were several corrals. Two wooden corrals held black bulls, one of which was the largest Bailey had ever seen. He lifted his head from the grass and seemed to stare toward her, his bottom lip steadily moving as he chewed a mouthful of grass. Another corral separated the two bulls. It held three horses, each a different color.

The mountains loomed a majestic purple off in the distance. Mr. Gooden must have carried her quite a ways after he found her in the ravine. She started to turn back toward the room then stopped. Something outside wasn't quite right, there was something missing. Bailey looked out the window again. It all appeared normal. She lifted her hand to her chin as she did when she had to think through a scenario for a court case. Granted, she didn't know much about ranch life, but wouldn't there be a work truck or family car around somewhere? Or a plain old tractor? Surely there had to be some type of vehicle. How else could the cowboy have brought her here? Bailey touched the bandage on her forehead again. Perhaps the blow to her head was worse than diagnosed and she did have a concussion. Why else could she not remember things clearly?

She turned back to consider the inside of the house again. While it was attractive in a rustic sort of way, her hosts certainly chose to live sparingly. Oil lamps instead of electric lamps, open windows instead of air-conditioning, and an outhouse instead of plumbing. First thing this morning, Faith had brought her fresh water in a wooden bucket. Without so much as a how-do-you-do, the chattering girl had walked over to the dresser and poured some of the water into the ceramic pitcher and the remainder into the matching basin. It was clear that Faith thought nothing was odd. To her, it appeared to be everyday life. Were they just so very far from civilization that modern conveniences were unavailable? If that were the case, surely such places could be self-contained? This didn't seem quite reasonable, yet everything seemed to work fine as far as the family was concerned.

Bailey returned to the chair and settled back down. She was still tired. Her injured hand continued to ache, and her head really did hurt. She rested against the soft leather and looked around. The house was almost like the set of an old television Western. She closed her eyes and imagined she was sitting in Ben Cartwright's living room on the Ponderosa. Little Joe and Hoss would come barreling through the front door any second now to tell their pa that the bank in Virginia City had been robbed. Oh, but it was the eldest son, Adam, who would sweep her off her feet.

A deafening crash came from the kitchen and interrupted Bailey's brief daydream. Loud yelling began in an Asian language she didn't understand. The distressed cries of what sounded like a goose came bellowing next. What must have been the kitchen door opened and a white blur sailed into the dining room, wings flapping, feathers flying, followed by Faith, who was dancing around and carrying on, obviously tying to shoo the poor bird away.

Behind Faith came a small Oriental man wielding a huge butcher's knife. The goose landed atop a bookcase against the far wall and stared down at the scene below, honking indignantly. Faith waved her arms, trying to keep the goose safe while the man began another diatribe in his native tongue. He proceeded to flail the frightening knife as he tried to maneuver around Faith to get to the goose.

Bailey jumped to her feet to help the girl, certain the knife would slash across the teenager's face at any second. A surge of nausea flashed through her, and the room began to spin. The man saw Bailey move to jump to Faith's defense. He rushed toward her, words still flowing, butcher's knife raised dangerously high.

The room continued its spinning, and Bailey did the worst

thing she thought imaginable in a deadly situation like this. She passed out cold.

"Look what you've gone and done, Jin Lee! Zachariah is going to be angry!"

"Not my fault, Missy. If Mr. Zach is mad it'll be because he's not having goose for supper tonight."

"That goose is Charity's pet. I can't believe you were going to make her eat it!"

Bailey slowly came awake to hear the indignation in Faith's voice. She opened her eyes to see two blurry figures kneeling beside her. The Oriental man leaned closer, fanning her with a white cloth. His butcher's knife was nowhere to be seen.

"I think she's coming around," he said to Faith. "You better hope Mr. Zach doesn't find out about this. He's going to be even more angry with you and your sisters. The bull Miss Hope let loose was one thing, but his dinner is another."

Bailey blinked and shook her head. She remembered having the wildest thoughts that she was in an old episode of *Bonanza*. And now leaning over her had to be none other that Hop Sing himself.

She stared at the man's concerned face then lowered her lids as reality sunk in. This man wasn't Hop Sing, this wasn't Ben Cartwright's house, and she wasn't at the Ponderosa. Another wave of dizziness floated over her as she tried to lift her head.

The man put his hands around her back and helped Bailey to the chair. "My name is Jin Lee," he said with a reassuring smile. "Mr. Zach told me you hurt your head. He also told me to make sure you didn't get overworked today. He's going to be angry at Miss Faith for causing all this trouble." He smoothed a hand over his white knee-length apron.

"I didn't cause any trouble!" Faith declared defiantly. "I was trying to keep you from killing Charity's goose."

"Mr. Zach told her not to get attached to that bird. He's for eating, not for petting," he snapped right back as he rapidly fanned Bailey's face with his white cloth.

Obviously forgotten, Bailey glanced from one to the other. She reached up to stop Jin Lee's moving hand. "May I please have something to drink?"

Jin Lee and Faith ceased their fussing long enough to blankly consider Bailey. Despite her scare with the butcher's knife and the wooziness left over from her brush with death, Bailey worked to suppress a grin. Clearly, these two had gone head-to-head before. Jin Lee muttered something in his native tongue, probably about manners, Bailey figured. He glared at Faith, bowed slightly to Bailey, then headed toward the kitchen, pausing to glance back her way and bow again before he disappeared through the door.

Within minutes he had returned with a single glass of lemonade, pointedly excluding Faith. After another glare at the teenager, he exited once more. Bailey lifted the glass to her lips. Faith was right, the lemonade was excellent. Even without ice cubes it tasted cool, tart, and refreshing.

"I apologize about the goose calamity," Faith started. "Charity would have been devastated if he had roasted Clarence."

Bailey smiled. "You must love your sister very much to fight off a man wielding a huge knife."

"I do, and she'd do it for me, too," Faith admitted. "Both of them would. In fact, I need to go find Hope and Charity and let them know you're up and about. Will you be fine alone for a few minutes?"

"No more wild-goose chases and angry cooks?"

Faith grinned, her eyes sparkling with laughter. "I promise."

"Then I think I'll be all right." Faith headed out the front door, leaving Bailey alone in the great room. Bailey couldn't help but be a little envious of her hostess. It must be nice to have not one, but two, special sisters. As she waited for Faith to return, Bailey noticed two family portraits near the fireplace. She carefully rose from the chair and stepped closer to study them, pulling snug the tie of Faith's pink dressing gown as she moved.

The first one had only three people in it. Even from a distance, Bailey stared straight into the eyes of a solemn young Zach Gooden. He stood behind a gray-haired man and a beautiful brunette woman. Bailey leaned closer to study the woman's serious expression. She had to be his mother; the family resemblance was clear. In the second portrait, a much older Zach again stood behind the same serious-faced gray-haired man. A different woman, this one blond and fair, sat on a small sofa next to Zach's father. She was obviously the mother of the two nearly identical young girls on the floor and the toddler in her lap. What a pretty woman, too, and to die so young. Such a shame.

In the black-and-white images of both photographs all the people were somber and dressed in beautiful vintage clothing. The photographers must have gone to great detail to create such a timeworn look to the pictures. Considering the ages of the girls now, it had probably only been five or six years since they posed for it. She stepped closer to examine the oval frames. They were made out of some type of material that looked like tortoiseshell. The photographs were certain to become heirlooms one day.

Through an open door to the right, Bailey caught a glimpse of a mahogany desk stacked high with books. "That's Zachariah's office," said Faith, coming into the room. "Usually off-limits to all of us." She shrugged with a wicked grin. "Or so he thinks. He's so provincial, don't you think?"

Bailey grinned at Faith's attempt to sound sophisticated. "Did you find your sisters?" she asked, settling back down in the chair.

"No. They were supposed to be at our 'secret spot,' but they're not there," Faith replied with a devilish twinkle. She headed toward the leather sofa across from Bailey's chair, sat, and pulled her feet up under herself. "We've planned something special. It's a surprise." The sparkle in Faith's eye made Bailey suspect that she was somehow involved in their plan whether she wanted to be or not.

Bailey reached for a large leather-bound book resting on the table by her chair. *Wyoming Territory: A Judicial System for the Common Man.* Using her good hand, she flipped open the green cover to the copyright page. *Published 1876, Laramie, Wyoming, James J. White, Publisher.*

"This is a lovely book," she exclaimed as she thumbed through the pages. "It's in remarkable condition. Just like new."

"That old thing?" Faith giggled. "Zachariah's had it for a couple of years."

Bailey shook her head as she looked from Faith to the book in her lap. Suddenly, an idea dawned on her, a concept so ludicrous she thought herself flighty. She studied Faith's appearance for a long moment. It was almost like she was back in another time, another century. She leaned her head against the leather chair and lowered her lids to stop the endless spinning of her mind. That thought made no sense at all.

"Are you all right, Bailey? Shall I take you back upstairs?"

Bailey heard Faith rise and felt her hand pressed against her forehead. She smiled to ease the young woman's worry. "I'm just a little dizzy. It will pass, I'm sure." Bailey opened her eyes and reached for her glass of lemonade. Obviously relieved, Faith returned to her seat. "Why do you call your brother Zachariah?" Bailey questioned. "He introduced himself to me as Zach."

"Because it annoys him," Faith answered with a light-hearted grin. "Our pa insisted that all our names come from the Bible. Zachariah rebuilt the temple for the Jews. It was one of his mother's favorite stories. My sisters and I were christened Faith, Hope, and Charity. Zach said that everyone hoped our names would reflect our personalities."

"Do they?"

"Hell, no."

Faith and Bailey both jumped at the deep baritone voice. Zach Gooden leaned against the doorway, his dusty hat pushed back from his face. Bailey couldn't help the nervous swell that rose from her toes straight up her back and into her heart. She hadn't remembered him looking so . . . well, so exciting.

"Those are three of the most misnamed girls in Wyoming." His drawl was amused. "They're more like Havoc, Chaos, and Plague."

"Or Curly, Larry, and Moe?" Bailey teased. She quickly sobered when her handsome rescuer didn't pick up on her weak attempt at humor.

"Are they in the Bible, too?" Faith asked with solemn chagrin. "I haven't been keeping up with my verses."

"No, you won't find them there. Maybe on Sunday morning in old black-and-white movies," Bailey clarified, embarrassed her joke had fallen flat. Faith and her brother both looked confused this time. These people really didn't get out much.

Her glance stole back to the man as he walked into the room, a newspaper in his hand. He was taller than she remembered, and much more attractive, especially in his tight jeans and boots. An inexplicable anxiousness seeped through her veins. He was dark and lean like a big cat with powerful muscles. And, although he appeared relaxed, Bailey sensed it was a deliberate pose. Her years of training in jury selection indicated that he was probably always guarded, confidently looking for just the right time to spring on his prey. He would probably be a fair juror, she deduced, but she would still ask to excuse him since his face and demeanor were so restrained. She was paid to know how people would react given a specific set of circumstances, and it seemed certain that this man gave none of his emotions away. Not to mention the fact that she wouldn't have been able to concentrate if he was on a jury anyway, not with those dark eyes and sexy grin.

As he moved into the room, Bailey noticed how the light from a nearby window accented the slight red in his dark brown hair. He wore it brushed back away from his face. It wasn't overly long, but perhaps a bit ragged around the ends. He dropped his black cowboy hat on the table between them, lowered himself into the other leather chair, then met her gaze. His chiseled jaw was clean shaven, and the brown eyes that considered her were unyielding. She wondered if his deep tan covered his entire body or if it was limited to his forearms and leathery face.

She blushed at the thought and quickly glanced down to study the binding of the book that still rested in her lap. This man was her rescuer, nothing more. As soon as she could get in touch with civilization, she'd be on her way and away from his charmingly odd family.

When Bailey finally looked up again, Faith had quietly disappeared out the door so that she was alone with the rugged rancher. He looked as if he belonged to another era, a time when real cowboys ran the West. His legs were covered with dusty leather chaps, which molded his thighs better than Levi's ever would. His boots were dirty and worn, like they'd seen a lot of hard work. His tarnished spurs jangled as he moved, reminding Bailey of a feline with a bell. Only he was more like a dark panther than a house cat.

The only cowboys she had ever met were "wanna-bes" who dressed that way for barbecues and fund-raisers. They certainly didn't evoke the instant raw physical attraction this man did. She forcefully quelled her nervousness and, as if he were the opposing attorney for an important case, met his gaze squarely. "You have a lovely home, Mr. Gooden. Thank you for your hospitality."

He nodded, his lips lifting into a careful smile. Her heart did another sudden sway to see dimples. Not one on the chin like the stereotypical cowboy, *real* dimples, one in each cheek.

"My pleasure," he replied. "I'm relieved that your injuries were not more serious. Do you remember how you got in your predicament? Should I send a man over to Thompson's place and let him know you are here and safe?"

Bailey sensed that his opinion of her was somehow hanging on the answer. "I don't know any Thompsons," she replied truthfully. He visibly relaxed at her admission. "All I remember is that I was hiking back down the mountain road toward my car. It was late in the afternoon, but still a couple of hours before sunset. I was at the top of the mountain. On the way back down to the cutoff, I must have walked through a thick, low-lying cloud because it suddenly became intensely foggy, so dense and thick I couldn't see. I tried to keep going, knowing I just had to walk through it. I guess I slipped and fell, either that or I was . . ." Bailey stopped. Had she fallen or had she been pushed? The memory was suddenly vague.

"You were . . . ?" Zach prompted.

"Nothing." Bailey shook her head. "I must not be remembering things clearly."

"Obviously. There's not a mountain near the ravine, only foothills and a river."

"No, we must be discussing different places. I was at the very top of Medicine Mountain visiting the Medicine Wheel National Landmark."

"Impossible. Medicine Mountain is more than fifty miles from here in a very dangerous area."

Bailey stared at him. Now she was truly confused. "Nonsense. It can't be that far."

Zach Gooden shrugged, shifting in his chair without a response. Absently he tossed a newspaper he was holding onto the table between them. Bailey waited. She had no idea what to say, and he hadn't made it any easier. Minutes ticked by in silence.

Nervously, Bailey reached for the paper. "Am I reported missing in here? Surely the rangers should have found my car by now." She unfolded the paper, noting it was an unusual size compared to the Memphis paper back home. It wasn't nearly as thick and the few pages were printed in an old-timey flowery type.

Box Bend Herald, August 12, 1878.

She gasped. A sinking feeling sapped her body and drained all rational thought. Suddenly everything seemed to make sense. Or rather nothing at all made sense. The clothes, the plumbing, the chamber pot, the portrait, the furniture, the wagon outside. Everything and nothing.

"I must have hit my head harder than the doctor thought, Mr. Gooden, I can't seem to recall the date." She whispered the words, almost afraid to hear his answer.

"August fourteenth. I found you three days ago, late in the afternoon."

"No, no . . . I mean, thank you . . . but I meant the year." She looked at him fearfully, hating the desperation she knew was in her eyes. "I don't seem to remember things clearly."

Concern crossed his face. He rose and moved toward her, then kneeled down and cradled both her hands in his, being careful not to squeeze the injured one. "I should have been more cautious. You've had a blow to the head and a terrible gash to prove it. I'll send for Doc McConnell again just to be sure." He smiled empathetically. "It's August fourteenth, 1878."

She inhaled sharply and grasped his hands tightly as if she

could draw his sheer physical strength into her being. It was 1878? How could it be possible? That would mean that she had fallen down the ravine and somehow fallen back into the past at the same time. Surely not, that was simply too far-fetched . . . but . . . could that explain why everything was so . . . weird?

She mentally retraced her actions on Medicine Mountain. She had breakfast at the lodge, milled around the gift shop and bought the old almanac, and then set out on a pleasant drive through the mountains. She parked the rental car at the foot of the road leading to the Medicine Wheel National Landmark about three and hiked up to see the circle. She had only stayed about an hour or so, looking around and talking to the Indian man. He stopped her before she could leave and asked if she'd like to pray to the spirit of Dark Fawn for . . .

Bailey gasped. Horror filled her soul as she looked up at Zach. "I prayed for faith, hope, and charity!"

"Thank you for your thoughtfulness," he replied stiffly. "I suppose their reputations are truly notorious if a perfect stranger feels the need to pray for them."

"No, no. I didn't mean your sisters. I meant after I took the bench. After I became a judge!"

Bailey felt faint and light-headed at the sheer insanity of it all. It was all too crazy, too weird, too unbelievable. She was a normal, everyday kind of person, way too stoic to be unusual. Nothing strange ever happened to her.

Nothing.

This simply couldn't be true.

"Miss Cooper." Zach stood and gently pushed her back so that her head rested against the chair. "Can you remember any of your family, a husband perhaps? I'm certain he would be concerned for your safety."

"No . . . no. I have no one," she whispered. "No one at all." She lowered her gaze to the floor, unwilling to let anyone, especially not this skeptical man, see the tears that wanted to form. She hadn't cried since the sad day she realized her parents were truly dead. That they weren't in some tropical country, as she had always liked to pretend, due to return anytime. She hadn't cried since the day she learned she was in this world all alone; that no one cared about Bailey but Bailey.

Well, she wouldn't cry now either. She pushed away the tears and his hands, then rose to her feet and began to pace the floor as she did when presenting a case in court. The rhythmic stride of pacing back and forth comforted her, especially in a crisis. As usual, the movement began to push aside some of the fear and filled her with a calm resolve. This was simply not acceptable. She had worked too hard and come too far to accept this anomaly without a fight. She stopped and faced her rescuer.

"Mr. Gooden, this will sound unbelievable to you, and I can appreciate the absurdity of what I'm about to say. However, I swear to you that it is the unquestionable truth. I am not from this time, and it is imperative that I return to my own home immediately. You must take me to the Medicine Wheel National Landmark. I'm not certain, but I believe it is somehow connected with the future."

Zach Gooden straightened and watched her levelly. When he spoke his voice was calm and soothing as if he was talking to an hysterical woman. Which, of course, he obviously thought he was. "Even though the area is supposed to be safe, Medicine Mountain is deep in Indian country, and the Wheel is a sacred religious ceremonial site. Plenty of adventurers have traveled up there and only a few lived to tell about it. Hell, I even looked for it once myself. I actually made it up the mountain and saw the strangest thing . . ."

His voice dropped off as if he were remembering something odd. The room was quiet for a second, then he stood and reached for his hat, obviously to cover his lapse. "Anyway, I couldn't find the path. There's no way I could take you there even if your story was true."

Bailey watched the rugged man approach her. "What did you see up there?"

"It doesn't matter now. It was just the wild imagination of a boy who was somewhere he shouldn't have been."

"Was it an old Indian man?"

He glared at Bailey, but shook his head.

"Then it was an Indian woman . . . an extremely beautiful one," Bailey persisted. At his surprised face, she pushed harder. "I'll bet her name was Dark Fawn, the same one I prayed to."

"You're distraught, Miss Cooper," he said gently, ignoring the implication of her words. He touched her shoulder to offer some type of comfort. "Get some rest while I send for Doc again. This will all make sense later. I'm sure of it."

Bailey brushed aside his hand as if it stung. "I'm not confused," she calmly insisted. "I have never been more certain of anything in my life. There has to be a connection somewhere, and if you've seen her, too, I'd suspect Dark Fawn and Medicine Mountain appear to be it. Does anyone else know how to get up there?"

"I suppose old Tag does, but I haven't seen him in a couple of weeks. He's probably out mining gold or whatever it is he does when he wanders off. He'll be back sooner or later."

Bailey hardly heard his words as she resumed pacing across the wood-plank floor. There had to be another way. She couldn't afford to sit around here and wait for someone who might not be back. Plans were made for her to be sworn in as a juvenile court judge in less than a month. She had to take action with or without the help of Zach Gooden. But how? He didn't believe her, and she didn't blame him. It was hard to believe it herself. If only she could find some evidence, something to prove she was who she claimed.

She snapped her fingers. *Of course!* Her backpack. She had plenty of identification with dates and everything. Perhaps that was the answer. Surely he could take her there. "Where's my backpack?" At his blank stare she stepped closer to him with each word. "A backpack, knapsack, carryall, traveling bag, whatever it is you want to call it."

He shook his head and narrowed his eyes at what he presumed was a distraught woman. "If there was one there, I didn't see it. All I saw was you."

"Then you must take me back to the ravine so I can get it. I can prove to you who I am. Just let me find my clothes and jacket and we'll go." She headed toward the stairs, loosening the tie belt of the robe out of habit and hurry.

"Miss Cooper. Bailey . . . stop."

Annoyed by the delay, Bailey paused on the fourth step and faced him.

"I'm not sure what is in your bag that is so vital to you, but we can't go back to the ravine." He headed toward the stairs, stopped at the bottom, and looked up at her face. "At least not right now. We would have to cross the river again and it's dangerously high. The thunderstorms have only made things worse. I was lucky to get us both across when I did."

"This is the only way I can prove to you who I am, and if you believe me, you can't help but find me a way to get back to Medicine Mountain." Bailey lifted her chin and set her resolve. She couldn't give up, there had to be a way to cross the river. Zach Gooden just had to be willing to find it. He studied her silently, then slowly lowered his eyes to scan the length of her body, then brought them up to rest just below her shoulders.

She felt the heat of his stare and glanced down herself, shocked to see she had forgotten to readjust and tighten the belt. The lapels of the floor-length robe hung apart, giving Zach Gooden an eyeful of her skimpy lingerie through the thin cotton of the gown. Worse than that, her nipples stood erect through the silky sheer of her bra. She whisked the robe closed while her face took on a darker shade of pink.

The cowboy slowly raised his eyes and met her embarrassed gaze. He rubbed a hand across his stubbly jaw then turned away. "I wish I could oblige, ma'am, but the answer is no. A wrangler drowned crossing that river earlier this summer, and I'm not going to chance it. You can borrow what you need from my sisters for now. We'll get your bag when it's safe." He strode into his office and shut the door behind him with a bang.

Bailey stared after the man, uncertain what to do. Even though he didn't believe her, he *had* to help her. She had too much at stake in the future to risk losing it. If there was any way possible, she had to get back to her own time, and soon. Her rational mind understood Zach Gooden's position, but he didn't comprehend that her desperation was genuine.

She headed toward his door and reached for the worn brass knob. This conversation certainly wasn't over, not by any means. She hesitated. Her entire profession was based on presenting a logical case. Emotion was involved, of course, but it was fact that usually turned a reluctant juror to her way of thinking. The only way she could realistically prove her identity was with her identification in her backpack. And the only way to get the backpack was to convince this man to take her to the ravine. Or was it? She was an experienced hiker after all. All she needed was directions, then she would take care of herself, just as she'd always done.

Bailey let go of the doorknob and glanced out the window toward the vastness of the open prairie. She'd always loved wide-open spaces since they were so unlike the cosmopolitan landscape of Memphis, Tennessee, where she lived and practiced. No matter what window she looked through, the view was identical in every direction: a cloudy blue sky and green grass dotted by wildflowers dancing with the wind. A herd of brown and white cows grazed in the distance, a few black ones intermingled. It was all so alike. Could she really find her own way?

She moved away from the door. Unless she could convince Zach Gooden to help her, she'd probably need the assistance of someone else to find the ravine. Lucky for her, there just so happened to be one young adventurer and her two sisters somewhere around this place. If they were as rambunctious as she'd been led to believe, they would probably be more than willing to show her the way.

Chapter 4

ZACH LOWERED HIMSELF into the dark leather chair behind his desk. He had a crazy woman on his hands, that was all there was to it. Beautiful, yes, but delusional. He'd send Hoop to fetch the doctor shortly; she had to be hurt worse than Doc realized. She couldn't have been up at the Medicine Wheel. It was impossible.

Absolutely impossible.

The area was considered safe since the army had destroyed all the Indian tribes and relocated the few that remained. Yet Zach had known several men—and heard of others—who had tried to find the Wheel. Few had ever returned. Most were presumed killed by renegade Indians, who refused to leave their religious site unguarded. "Considered safe" didn't mean much to a dead man. Even if, by some strange chance, the redheaded Miss Cooper *had* been up there, it was downright foolish to take her back.

And that story of the Indian woman. How had she known

what he had seen that day? Hell, it had been such a long time ago, well before his pa had been killed, he wasn't even sure what he'd seen himself. A young Indian woman, true, but almost like a vision or a dream. Certainly not real, and certainly not anything he'd care to repeat.

Zach ran a tired hand along his jaw, then picked up a worn pencil and thumped it on the desk in a rhythmic beat. If she was telling at least part of the truth—and he wasn't admitting she was—but if she really had been up on the mountain, that still didn't explain how she ended up alone at the ravine. It was at least a four-day ride from the Wheel.

Zach sighed. He probably shouldn't have been so harsh with her. Demanding answers and barking orders might command respect from hired ranch hands but had absolutely no effect on women. Not on Faith, Hope, or Charity. And certainly not on the odd woman with the unusual name.

He tossed the pencil back on the heavy leather blotter, then leaned back in the chair and lifted his boots to rest them on the top of the desk, his spurs jangling off the edge. Where had she come up with the wild story of being from the future?

More important, why?

And who would believe she was a judge or about to become one? That was the most ridiculous of all. He thought of himself as a progressive man, and certainly supported the rationale for allowing Wyoming women to vote, but wasn't that pushing it a bit too far? Besides, Theodore Horner had been the circuit judge for years. Why did she so convincingly maintain that she was something she was not? It just didn't make sense. She didn't make sense.

The wisest thing to do would be to send her to town and let Rand worry after her and her tall tales. Wasn't that what a good sheriff was supposed to do? He fidgeted with the desk blotter. He'd grown up with Sheriff Weeks, knew him almost like a brother. Rand would waste no time in "rescuing" the lovely stranger then using his good looks to charm and beguile her. Zach wasn't about to turn over his beautiful stray kitten to that smooth talker, no matter how odd she seemed to be. This woman needed real help. She had no money and nothing in her pockets that told who she was or where she was from or how to find her kin.

Zach gazed out the window toward the mountains. The very top of the sierras were still capped with last year's snow, creating a lavender haze across the distant skyline. He knew the soft, white clouds overhead would eventually turn into yet another thunderstorm. The heavy summer rains had been a boon for the prairie grass but hard on the already swollen river.

He lowered his lids and let his mind wander to the night he found her. She had been light as a butterfly when he carried her up the stairs and gently lowered her onto his step-mother's old feather bed. She wore denims—another strange thing, and odd boots. Her skin felt soft and warm to his calloused hands as he washed the dirt and mud away from her face and neck. Surprisingly, Faith and Hope had brought a clean nightgown and, without being asked, they began to remove the woman's soiled clothing. It took a glare from each of his sisters before he remembered to leave the room to give them some privacy. He just couldn't draw his eyes away from her for some reason. Zach shook his head and frowned, feeling a tightening in his groin. He'd been too long without a woman, way too long.

This couldn't have happened at a worse time. There was so much at stake right now. The financial success of the ranch depended on his new hybrid cattle. The mortgage would be due after the fall round-up. Even then, it'd be next fall before his efforts really paid off. J.T. made no pretense of hiding his hope for Zach's failure. J.T.'s friendship with the banker didn't help matters either.

Hell, Zach's Angus bulls had proven themselves a big

enough problem on their own. He'd risked practically every-thing to find them in Scotland, go through an agent to buy them, and import them to the United States. Once that was done, they had to be shipped cross-country to the Double Bar G. It was really amazing that the two bulls and dozen cows had even survived the arduous journey.

Zach sighed, rose from the chair, and walked toward the bookcase to get his ledgers. The success of the ranch still wouldn't eliminate the whispers about his sisters, though. The injured Miss Cooper had thought them angels. Little did she know his sisters had pulled one too many devilish pranks over the past few years. Now the entire population of Box Bend openly dreaded the days they came to town.

He knew it was all his fault.

Slowly, he returned to his chair and tossed the financial books onto the desk. He'd already spent too much of the day dawdling. He had a ranch to run, books to figure, cattle to feed, fences to check, hay and grain to put up for the winter. He didn't have time to waste worrying over things that would more than likely resolve themselves in the end.

Zach opened the desk drawer to drop the pencil inside. Quick as a bullet, a small furry animal scampered up his sleeve. He jumped and shook his arm. His leather chair flipped over backwards as the fuzzy creature dug its claws through the thin fabric of his shirt and clung to his skin. His head hit the hard wooden floor with a solid thud.

Zach opened his eyes to see a small gray kitten scurry up his sleeve and onto his chest, hissing, spitting, and swatting. A tiny claw stung as the kitten scratched deep enough to draw blood. He grabbed the mongrel by the scruff of the neck and held it out from his body. He tried to rise from the floor but the animal took another swipe, twisting its body until the back claws grabbed on to his wrist. Zach fell again, this time banging his head on the arm of the chair. He cursed silently, then twisted awkwardly and managed to stand still holding the angry kitten. A flash of blond curls ducked away form the window followed by the sound of three gleeful female giggles.

He suspected as much.

Zach stormed to the window, ignoring the sweet smell of the early afternoon breeze. He held the kitten, still wrapped around his wrist, as far away from his body as he could. Faith and Hope sat side by side on a white wooden porch swing, Charity in a nearby rocking chair. Their faces tried to proclaim no knowledge of Zach's troubles, yet the twinkles in their eyes and the quivering laughter on their lips gave them away.

Zach stared at each one, slowly counting to ten before he spoke. "Charity Grace, you will remove this animal from my arm immediately or else . . ."

"Don't hurt it!" she cried. "It's just a helpless kitten." Faith and Hope rolled their eyes, obviously knowing their sister's plea gave everything away.

"Who said anything about a kitten?" he asked smoothly, pleased he'd caught them practically red-handed. Charity rose and reached for the kitten, who immediately settled into her arms with a tiny purr. She smiled, he glared.

"Don't do it again." Even as he made the threat, he knew nothing would prevent their shenanigans. Lord, he'd let this go on too long, now he didn't know how to stop it. "Faith, tell Miss Cooper that Sheriff Weeks, Hoop, and Mr. and Mrs. Mack will be coming to dinner tomorrow evening. Make sure she has a proper dress so she can join us." With that, he pulled his head back into the office and moved to straighten the overturned chair.

This was the last straw. He had lost control of his sisters. Today proved it. Even a guest in the house didn't deter them. He'd been so busy saving the ranch, and creating a new breed of cattle, that he hadn't given them the attention they needed. Their ma was Zach's father's second wife. She had died when Faith and Hope were only twelve and Charity only eight. His father hadn't been much of one to him or to them. He'd been too busy running the ranch and feuding with neighboring ranchers. That left Zach to raise them.

He'd tried to be everything to them, but a womanly influence he just couldn't provide. They needed a real woman for that. But the ranch had been so close to ruin for many years. Finding a wife had been the last thing on his mind.

Now Zach was paying for it. Faith, Hope, and Charity, while as beautiful as their mother, had the happy-go-lucky spirit of his father. They were incorrigible minxes who took delight in torturing souls with their erratic sense of adventure and their love of havoc. He had allowed them to grow up like ranch hands. It was time someone taught them how to act like ladies. Time someone taught them proper manners before they were completely out of control.

Deep inside, he couldn't help but wonder if the woman upstairs might be an answered prayer. Despite the head injury, Bailey Cooper was obviously poised and well-educated. She aggressively demanded he take her to Medicine Mountain, and then the ravine, like she was used to giving orders and being obeyed. Like she was queen of the prairie and all it contained. She might just be the person he needed to rein in those sisters of his.

Zach leaned forward and picked up a small miniature of his sisters. He smiled and ran a finger over the golden gilt of the frame. Like it or not, they were his family, all he had left other than this struggling ranch. He needed to do what was best for them even if they didn't like it.

While he solved the mystery behind Miss Bailey Cooper, she could return the favor by way of his sisters. If it was true that she was all alone, no husband or family, then she needed him as much as he needed her.

Something told him she wasn't going to be happy about it.

*   *   *

Bailey sat cross-legged in the middle of the small feather bed, the belt of the dressing gown wrapped firmly around her waist. She cradled her injured right hand on her lap and rested her aching head on the other. For one of the first times in her adult life, Bailey Cooper could prepare no course of action. She had no idea how she had arrived, no idea what to do now that she was here, no idea of how to survive in this time, and no idea, much less a concrete plan, of how to get home. There were too many questions, and all were unanswered. Her logical mind was in overload.

The sun glistened through the open window, inviting the warm afternoon inside. For a moment, she allowed the essence to absorb her. The air was clean and invigorating, although darkening clouds dotted the sky. Refreshing, despite the vague scent of horses, cattle, and hay. Bailey shifted position so that her good hand could outline the various patterns on the patchwork quilt covering the bed. The mindless repetitive movement was comforting.

Hundreds of thoughts raced through her head before she could find answers for a single one. If this was the past, did the future still exist? Had it stopped? Did it run concurrently? Had it yet occurred? Had she been reported missing? How long did a search party look for a lost person? How long before they gave up?

The only people who would immediately suspect she was missing would be the park rangers who supervised the Medicine Wheel National Landmark. And then only because her car would be abandoned at the base of the cutoff road that led up to the monument. Surely the Indian man would remember her, if they found him. He had spent a good hour telling her about the Wheel and the Spirits who reside there, including Dark Fawn.

Dark Fawn.

She had prayed for the three things she thought she would

need to be a good and fair judge: faith, hope, and charity. What she got instead were three misnamed girls who lived more than a hundred years in the past. If there actually was a spirit of Dark Fawn, why would she think Bailey needed them?

She mentally counted who else might become concerned over her absence. She had just paid her rent, so her landlady wouldn't expect to see her for several more weeks. Her girlfriend, Faye, was spending the summer in Europe. She'd met a barrister with a sexy British accent and a house in the country. Knowing Faye, she might not surface until Christmas. Her coworkers at the social services offices knew she was on an extended vacation hiking in the Big Horn Mountains. Once she returned, they expected her to prepare for her new position. They might wonder what she was up to, but they certainly wouldn't worry about why she hadn't called or stopped by. Her appointment hadn't occurred, so Bailey had yet to meet any of her new colleagues. No one was expecting to hear from her until closer to her swearing-in ceremony. No one would be overly concerned when she didn't call.

No one at all.

She lived alone in a condo without so much as a cat for companionship. She had many office buddies, but that's all they were. Outside working hours she was still a loner. It was one of the side effects of being raised in foster care. When it came right down to it, she'd always be alone. Bailey frowned and released a deep sigh. She was used to being by herself, she just never realized how solitary she really was. Until now.

While she was still very young, she had determined to rise above the disheartening odds that faced foster kids. She worked hard in school, put herself through college with grants and scholarships, and finally made it into law school. Other than Faye, who simply forced Bailey to open up, she hadn't stopped long enough to make any friends. Bailey approached her career with the same diligence and single-mindedness. That left room for colleagues, acquaintances, and peers, but no lifelong connections and friendships. She never trusted them to be there forever anyway.

Another terrible thought filled her with despair. How soon before her judicial appointment would be given to someone else? A very real possibility existed that she would lose it all in the blink of an eye. She'd had nothing to begin with, and what little she did have might be taken away from her. Bailey leaned back against a pillow and sighed.

"Miss Cooper?" A soft rap came from the door. Bailey ignored the voice, hoping it would go away. When she heard a second knock and a click of the lock, she sat up on the bed and wiped away her troubled thoughts.

Faith gently opened the whitewashed paneled door and stepped inside, followed by her two unmistakable sisters. The other twin was almost identical to Faith, just a smidgen shorter and eyes a bit more blue. The third was a bit younger and remarkably similar to her older sisters. They all looked just as angelic, all with flaxen hair and eyes that twinkled even as they stared at her. The picture downstairs didn't do the beautiful girls justice.

"These are my sisters, Hope and Charity."

The youngest smiled sweetly and walked toward the bedside; her long golden hair was pulled back into a single braid down her back. She carried an Indian doll tucked under one arm, obviously a favored toy. She reached for Bailey's hand and patted it softly.

"Don't be sad," she encouraged. "My brother will take care of everything. He always does."

"She's right, Miss Cooper," Faith added. "Zachariah may seem like a grumpy bear, but you can depend on him." These three didn't know her at all, and yet they were genuinely concerned. Bailey nodded and blotted the corner of her eyes with the fabric belt of the dressing gown. She was deeply touched.

"Hope and I went through our wardrobe and bought a few things that might fit." Faith held out several cotton shirts in white. The second girl held three long skirts in various calico colors and an array of what had to be underwear.

"That's very thoughtful of you," Bailey replied, smoothing a hand over her borrowed robe. She hadn't thought about what she'd wear while she was stuck here. "Where are my own clothes?"

"They were muddy, but not ruined. Jin Lee will wash them for you." Faith smiled and crossed over to sit on the bed beside Bailey. She was immediately followed by Charity and Hope. Bailey was forced to readjust her position so everyone would fit. After realizing that no one back home would miss her, it was kind of nice that these three sisters were obviously glad she was here.

"May we try on your denims later?" Hope asked mischievously. "Zach won't let us wear them, but we all desperately want a pair. He says that proper ladies don't wear pants. He says—"

"He says," Faith interrupted loudly as she glared at Hope, "we shouldn't overwhelm Miss Cooper with questions." She turned back to Bailey. "Zachariah wanted us to invite you to a special dinner tomorrow evening. Sheriff Weeks and Mr. and Mrs. Mack are coming. He thought you might like to join us."

As Faith was speaking, Hope stood up and placed all the skirts carefully over the edge of the bed. Then she held up a gorgeous satin gown for Bailey's inspection. "He wanted you to wear this," Hope added. "Isn't it lovely?"

Bailey cocked a brow at the unusual request. It was a very pretty gown, but compared to the other skirts and blouses, it seemed out of place. Hope carefully draped the deep emerald satin across Bailey's lap. Bailey fingered the ivory lace decorating the round neckline.

"It's my best party dress," Faith said proudly. "We thought it would look wonderful with your hair."

"I brought you these," the youngest girl piped in. She held out two ivory satin ribbons. "You can pull back your hair, then Zach won't be able to resist you—oomph." Charity winced as Hope pinched her arm. All three girls glanced back at Bailey with feigned innocence. These angels were up to something non-angelic.

Bailey rose from the bed and walked around in front of them, her bandaged hand resting on her hip, her face impassive. She stopped suddenly, directly in front of Faith, and stared her straight in the eye for several long seconds. Finally, the teenager lowered her gaze. She moved to Hope, who didn't bother to lift her head and meet Bailey's stern face. She sat back down on the bed, and studied her hands. Charity, however, stared at her with twinkling eyes, although wary of Bailey's practiced intimidation. Bailey bent at the waist until Charity's nose was inches from her own.

"You're not trying to fix me up with your brother, are you?" Charity shook her head no at first, but as Bailey continued to stare, she slowly changed to an affirmative.

"Us?" Faith stood up next to Bailey. "Why, we hardly know you."

Bailey couldn't help the laughter that built inside her. These three were sweet. Transparent, but sweet. "Thank you for thinking of me, ladies, but I'm not interested in your brother. Besides, even if I were—"

"You don't think he's handsome?" interrupted Charity. Her earnest expression indicated she would be appalled at someone who didn't.

"Well, yes. I suppose he is handsome. It's just that—"

"He's rich, too," piped in Hope. "At least as soon as he sells the new cows."

"Rich is always helpful," Bailey replied, suppressing a grin. "But I have to get back. People are expecting me."

"It's his temper, isn't it?" Faith asked solemnly. "He's just a toad sometimes. We just don't know what to do with him." She opened her hands as if at her wit's end by her uncooperative brother. "We try to make him laugh, but he just gets mad at us."

"He didn't seem so bad to me," Bailey tried to assure her. "It's just—"

"You do like him!" the trio exclaimed in unison. Exasperated, Bailey rolled her eyes heavenward. No wonder Zach couldn't win. He'd been lassoed without a rope.

Bailey ignored the last statement, and picked up the green dress. The rich fabric was soft and inviting and—well—romantic. Just like something Victoria Barkley would have worn in *The Big Valley*. "The dress is lovely, but isn't it a bit much for dinner?"

"Oh, no." Hope smiled. "I'm going to wear my blue satin." Faith and Charity nodded in agreement.

Bailey wavered. If all the Goodens were dressing up, it might not be so bad. The green *was* a very flattering color, and it might be fun to wear a dress like this at least once in her lifetime. Plus, it would only be this once, since she had come up with a getaway plan. The plan involved these three imitation angels, so it couldn't hurt to humor them.

"OK, girls. I'll wear the dress on one condition."

"Wonderful!" all three chimed in, delight written all over their faces.

"It's a big adventure," Bailey whispered, glancing toward the window as if to ensure no one else was nearby. "Really, really big. You must promise not to tell your brother anything."

The three girls exchanged silent looks.

"That's our favorite thing in the world, Miss Bailey. Adventure that Zach doesn't know about." Charity glanced at her sisters to see if she had said something wrong. Obviously not, since the other two leaned forward and excitedly looked at Bailey for more.

Too easy, Bailey though smugly. Way too easy.

Chapter 5

"IN HERE!" CHARITY excitedly pulled Bailey by the hand into the dusty-smelling barn the next morning. The young teenager opened the door to an empty stall and rushed over to the corner. There, nestled amongst dried straw, was a large multicolored dog and eight hungry puppies fighting for a dinner spot on their momma's belly. Charity picked up the smallest, the runt of the litter, and hugged it to her chest.

"Zach has warned me not to grow too fond of them. They're all going to be work dogs," Charity confided. "I don't care what he says. Precious is mine." The puppy licked Charity's finger, then cuddled against the soft yellow fabric of her cotton dress. Sheer happiness shone on both faces.

"You named your puppy Precious?" Bailey watched Charity and the tiny pup with a mixture of envy and regret twinging inside. She'd never had her own pet.

"Precious will be an extraordinary dog so he needed a special name. I'm going to train him myself." Charity confi-

dently lifted her gaze. Without having to ask, Bailey already
knew that look meant Charity's brother must have already
said no. The less Bailey knew, the better.

Just then, a large white goose meandered into the barn. It
walked right up to Charity and pushed at the girl with its
head. "Not now, Clarence. I'm playing with Precious."
Charity brushed the bird away as the momma dog began a
low growl. The goose honked indignantly right back at the
dog before heading back out of the barn. Bailey wasn't sure
if a goose could be irritated, but it looked like that one was.

Bailey glanced back at Precious' brothers and sisters and
saw the momma dog now glaring suspiciously in her direction. Bailey couldn't help but stare right back. The puppies
were adorably cute, like fat little spotted fur balls, but the
momma was the ugliest dog Bailey had ever seen in her life.
Not only was her short dense coat an unusual mottled combination of white, gray, black, and brown, she had several
solid black, brown, and gray patches dotting her chest and
front legs. Even some of her patches had spots. The dog's
oversized pointed ears were too large for her narrow head
and chunky body. One ear was black, and the other was gray
with little black spots that extended along the side of her
face, down her throat and chest, all the way to the end of her
front paw.

After a few minutes of perusal, the momma dog decided
Bailey wasn't a threat and returned to licking her puppies.
"I've never had a dog of my own. What kind are these?" Bai-
ley asked from the doorway.

"Cattle dogs," a deep voice answered. She glanced up as
Zach approached from the far end of the barn. Far behind
him, the enormous barn doors were open. As Zach drew
near, the morning sun flooded through, blinding all but his
silhouette. Bailey couldn't see the expression on his face,
but the powerful image of his lean form caused a catch in her
throat. She watched, mesmerized by his slow, steady gait, by

the way his muscular legs fit perfectly with his hips and chest. When he was only inches from her, she slowly exhaled.

His black hat was cocked at a jaunty angle, his eyebrow tilted as if he could read her thoughts. Bailey turned back to the puppies to hide her embarrassment, unsure why she was suddenly so warm and nervous. She fidgeted with the high collar of the borrowed white blouse then smoothed a shaky hand down her borrowed skirt. Why on earth did these women wear such long hot skirts in August?

"I've never seen such a thing before," she stammered, then grimaced at how he would probably misconstrue her statement. From the corner of her eye she could see him grin as if he fully understood the underlying meaning of her comment. Thankfully, he pointed to the puppy.

"That's because there aren't many around these parts. I'm fortunate to have two. The other is out with the men, working the cattle." He walked into the stall and reached for another puppy. This one had a lighter, reddish brown tint to his fur. Zach smiled at his littlest sister before bringing the pup over to Bailey. "I bought them from a Texan who was traveling through last spring. He said they were originally from Australia, supposedly an accidental cross between their shepherds and wild dingoes. Now every rancher for miles around is yammering for one of the pups. This is her first litter."

"Why? They're so . . . so unusual." She really wanted to say ugly but thought better of insulting her hosts. Bailey cuddled the puppy in her hands as Zach stroked it, his fingers brushing against the sensitive skin all the way from her wrist to her thumb. Bailey tried to block the sensation that shot through every nerve ending in her body. Why did this man put her instantly on edge?

"They're smart. They can round up a cow faster than a man on a horse in most cases." Bailey suddenly realized that he suspected the effect his touch had on her. She narrowed her eyes but said nothing as he continued the repetitive motion. "They have a natural instinct for herding. They keep the cattle moving along or keep them from wandering away by nipping them on the heel until the cows go where they're supposed to."

"You mean the dog annoys a cow until it obeys?"

"That's one way to sum it up." Zach laughed. "Sort of like Faith, Hope, and Charity. As for how the dogs look, and how annoying my sisters are for that matter, they have to grow on you."

She was surprised to find a deliberate spark in the deep amber depths of his eyes, and surprised that she was responding to him like an innocent schoolgirl. She'd certainly been attracted to handsome men before, but this particular man was having such an odd effect on her. It must be the cowboy thing again, she thought.

Bailey dropped her gaze back to the mother and the other puppies. Naturally, she wasn't surprised to see that Charity, like her sister earlier, had disappeared without a sound, taking Precious with her. "I see why Charity was so insistent that I come see the puppies right this very minute. I think there was a conspiracy to get us alone, Mr. Gooden."

Zach shrugged noncommittally and reached for the puppy she held. She instantly missed the warmth of the animal nestled against her. He gently set it back with its mother, then swiftly brushed by her and out into the aisleway of the barn.

"I'm afraid you're the latest victim."

"Victim?"

"The girls are notorious for trying to find me a wife, Miss Cooper. Not out of great concern for my well-being, mind you. Faith is convinced that if I had a wife, I wouldn't be so hard on her, Hope, and Charity."

"Are you hard on them?"

"They think so," he said. "They're almost grown. They

can't keep acting like farm boys." As he spoke, he led a horse from another stall into the middle of the barn and tied him to an iron ring on the wall. He picked up a hammer and a few nails from a wooden box, then turned his back toward her and bent over to pick up the horse's hoof, unaware the position gave Bailey a most interesting view of his backside. The strap of his chaps buckled around his waist. Dark leather tightly wrapped around each leg, leaving his denim-clad rear end exposed. The result was an image that left nothing to the imagination.

The man certainly knew how to show off his best features.

Sensing the mutual truce they had just established, Bailey ventured a bit more conversation. "I understand you're having guests tonight. Thank you for including me."

"You have to eat," he said, without looking up.

She walked over to the horse's nose to pet the soft black muzzle. She didn't know much about horses, but she wasn't really afraid of them. "What's his name?"

"Reliant. He's the one who really saved your life. Without him, we'd have both been goners," Zach answered, reaching up to pat the brown shoulder. The horse lifted his ears forward and nudged the back of Zach's hat with his nose. "He was the first horse I ever raised on my own. Birthed him, broke him, trained him. He's a damn good cow horse."

Bailey smiled at the pride in his voice. "There's something about the outside of a horse is good for the inside of a man," she quoted. Zach straightened, released the horse's foot, and turned to face her.

"Interesting thing to say. I've always judged a man by how he keeps his horse. Dead giveaway as to character, if you ask me."

Bailey nodded. "Wish I could take the credit, but those aren't my words. President Reagan said that, but even then I think he was quoting Churchill."

"Smart man. What's he president of?" Zach asked. He

tossed the hammer back into the wooden box and turned to face her, casually resting his hand on Reliant's rump.

Bailey moved away from the horse, away from the overpowering nearness of Zach Gooden. "Reagan? He was President of the United States."

"Last time I checked, Mr. Rutherford Hayes was still the man in charge. I've never heard of this Reagan fella."

"He was . . . *will be* . . . president from '80 to '88. *That's 1980 to 1988*," she stressed the last part.

Zach shook his head, as if trying to muster up enough patience to reckon with her. "What about this Mr. Churchill?" he persisted. "How do you know about him?"

"From the history books. He was a great military leader in World War Two."

"World War Two?" Zach asked with disbelief. "Don't you mean The War Between the States? It ended nearly thirteen years ago."

"No, World War Two." She knew before she answered that he wouldn't believe her. World War Two was her history, but it was his future. "The U.S. didn't get involved until the Japanese bombed Pearl Harbor in 1941."

He gently took her arm and guided her over to a bench near the barn door, then sat down beside her, the leather of his chaps brushing up against the soft thin cotton of her skirt. "Miss Cooper, you've had a bad experience and a head injury. One or both may be so bad you must be refusing to remember what actually happened. There is no President Reagan. There has not been a world war, and I've never heard of this Mr. Churchill. The Wyoming Territory may not hear news as fast as other places, but I can promise you I would know about major events like those."

"But I am from the future," she argued. "I can prove it to you once I get my backpack. I have plenty of identification, all with names, dates, and numbers. I'll prove what I say."

He smiled at her tenderly then touched her forehead just

below the bandage. His face was only inches from hers, his breath warm on her cheek. "Once this has healed I'm sure you will remember things more clearly. Until then, please don't rush yourself by making up such ridiculous stories. It doesn't do any of us any good." He reached down and lifted her hand into his. Bailey could feel the heat of his calloused skin. The rough texture silently conveyed the strength and vigor of a man who knew hard work.

She pulled her hand away, irritated he thought he could soothe her with just a touch. "Don't look at me like I'm crazy, Zach Gooden, and drop the head injury bit, too. I'm telling the truth, whether you want to believe it or not."

Zach rose and turned to face her; his lips were drawn in a thin line. "Tonight is very important to me—to the Double Bar G, to all of us. Charlie Mack, the owner of the bank in Box Bend, is coming to supper. I put up part of the ranch and my herd of Herefords as collateral, and he loaned me the money to buy and import the Aberdeen Angus cattle you see outside. Now he's suddenly wanting to call in the loan with practically no explanation. If I can't convince him to extend my loan, I'll lose my Herefords and the Angus. I'll still have the ranch, but there won't be much left. I'd probably have to hire out just to make it through the winter. I have a feeling that J.T. Thompson is behind the foreclosure. Undoubtedly, he's got a ready promise to pay off the note and take my cattle."

"Does he want your Aberdeen cattle?"

"No." Zach shook his head in irritation. "He wants the Double Bar G. He's certain that if I lose the cattle, the ranch won't be far behind. That can't happen, Miss Cooper."

Bailey leaned her head back against the wooden wall and silently considered the man in front of her. Tonight *was* extremely important to Zach Gooden, and she understood that the last thing he needed was to have a seemingly crazy woman at the dinner table discussing the history of the future. If he had dropped into her world, she wouldn't have hesitated to send him directly to the mental hospital. And she certainly wouldn't have taken him into her house like he had done for her, especially if she had such an important agenda.

"All right then, I'll make a deal with you."

"A deal?"

"Yes." She nodded, ignoring the smirk on his face. "I've told you that I have proof of all I say. You've said you'll help me find it but you can't do so immediately. That being the case, do not assume that I'm lying or that I'm deranged, and certainly don't pat me on the head and tell me I am until I have my backpack in my hands."

He levelly returned her glare. "And in return?"

"In return, I'll keep my mouth shut about being from the future with everyone but you."

After a long silence, he slowly moved toward her. He lifted a leg and rested his booted foot on the bench beside her and leaned forward to rest his bent arm on his knee. "Fair enough on your end, but I need a little more on mine. My sisters."

"What do you mean?"

"You've seen them but haven't yet experienced them," he replied, shaking his head. "Even I know they're hellions. They're not little girls anymore, and I can't go on raising them like they are. I can barely control them, much less teach them how to look, act, and dress like ladies. They need someone strong, someone who can stand up to their antics, yet someone who is also soft, lush, and beautiful. Someone like you."

He looked down at her hands, picked one up, softly rubbed the tender area of her palm with his middle finger. Unlike his own hands, she had no calluses or cuts marring the skin. "You're obviously used to the fine things. You're educated and charming, and speak with a confidence I admire. You'd be perfect to teach them some of the better side of life."

"I do see troubled kids at my job, but I have no children of my own and no experience when it comes to raising them," she objected. "Not a clue as to how to turn three tomboys into homecoming queens."

Zach stood and stared down at her, his brows drawn together. "I don't need royalty. I just need acceptable ladies. Something you could help me with while I find out who you are and how to get you home."

Bailey withdrew her hand and rose to stand beside him. This man seemed convinced a head injury or some other horrible event had made her crazy, yet he still thought she'd be a perfect baby-sitter. "How do I know I can trust you to do what you say? You might just want to keep me around as a nursemaid with no intention of helping me."

Zach's eyes blazed in anger before he averted his gaze to consider the darkening rain clouds in the distance. Bailey heard the faint rumble of thunder and wondered if the potential storm was as ominous as his fury. "I can only give you my word," he replied stiffly.

It was clear that was all she would get from Zachariah Gooden.

He made it clear that he was skeptical, and he didn't much care whether or not she had proof. To him it made no difference whether he took her today, tomorrow, or next week. He probably *would* do what he said, but he would do it in his own good time. She still had little choice but to accept his offer and let him think she would abide by his decision. Then she could set about finding the ravine on her own. There had to be another way, and it was up to her to find it.

If he wanted three impressive ladies, that's just what she'd give him. She'd show them everything she knew about being a successful modern woman; about being progressive thinking women of the future. Chances were, he'd probably rue the day he recruited her help. Zach Gooden had no idea what he was asking her to do, and he wasn't going to like it when he figured it out.

Not one iota.

"All right. Agreed." She expected him to smirk in satisfaction, but there was only concern and relief on his face. "I've dealt with more juvenile delinquents than you can possibly imagine. How much trouble could those three really be?"

Zach started to say something but must have thought better of it and stopped. He finally shrugged. "You're right, how hard could it be?"

"Famous last words," Bailey muttered out loud. It hadn't been six hours since she and Zach struck their bargain, and she was already wondering who got the best deal. It wasn't that the girls were mean-spirited or rebellious. They were fearless and . . . well, just so *in* to everything. Charity wanted to romp around the ranch playing with the animals. All the animals. The dogs, the goose, the chickens, the horses, even the bulls Zach warned her to stay away from. Bailey had spent the better part of the afternoon following Charity around doing just that. Faith and Hope, meanwhile, had made it clear that they were far too old for a chaperone, and Bailey had absolutely no authority over them, no matter how much they wanted her to marry their brother. They immediately took off for a ride on their horses without so much as a backward glance.

Now she and Charity sat on the porch swing waiting for the twins to come riding back. A tiny white kitten was nestled in Bailey's lap, contentedly purring as it dozed.

"There they are," Charity said, pointing to two approaching riders. "I told you they wouldn't be gone that long. They like you."

"They sure have a funny way of letting me know."

Bailey watched from the porch as Charity rushed to meet her sisters. Once the two older girls had dismounted, the three huddled together in whispers; every now and then one glanced over at Bailey. Charity shook her head, horrified, but the older girls appeared to be swearing her to silence. Bailey supposed the three didn't think she was paying attention. Either that, or they figured she wasn't bright enough to figure out they had something planned.

Bailey watched silently, stroking the soft kitten as Faith reached up and untied a saddlebag and handed it to her twin. Hope took the bag, glanced toward Bailey, then gathered up the reins for the two horses and headed toward the barn. Faith and Charity, meanwhile, headed in Bailey's direction. Charity spoke nonstop, telling her older sister about what she had missed while she was gone. Faith wrapped an arm around her little sibling and smiled. Bailey felt a tug at her heart. No matter if they were truants, it was obvious the sisters loved each other very much. Bailey saw the genuine affection on their faces as they stepped onto the porch and headed her way.

"Did you have a nice ride, Faith?" Bailey kept her voice friendly but reserved. Behind her, she heard a rustle of bushes. Charity's glance over Bailey's head confirmed something was amiss. There was no doubt now that the twins were up to something. What?

Before she could speculate, Bailey felt something brush her foot. She looked down in time to see a little green snake slither on the porch between her feet. Her first instinct was to scream, jump, and run, but she used all her might to quell it. She forced herself to continue to pet the sleeping kitten with steady even strokes.

"Oh, my, how did that fella get here?" Bailey stared down at the snake, hoping she wouldn't have to prove a point and touch the thing.

Speechless, the girls stared at her. "You didn't scream,"

Faith said accusingly. Hope emerged from the bushes behind her.

"Of course not, it's just a little snake. Did you expect me to?"

Hope nodded, not realizing she'd walked right into Bailey's trap.

"So, you let the snake go on purpose, hoping to frighten me? That's pretty weak, girls." Bailey handed the kitten to Charity, then stood and stretched. "It'll take a lot more than that to scare me. And I know how to get even. I mean . . . *really* even." Using every bit of courage she could muster, Bailey calmly bent and picked the snake up with two hands. She then walked over to Hope and draped the wiggly creature around her collar. "I tell you what, let's call a truce. I'm here for a few days until your brother can help me get home. He'd like me to spend some time with you, you know, girl talk and all that stuff. But I'm not about to wonder if you're up to something or out to hurt me all the time. I'll be your friend, but only if you'll be mine. Otherwise, I can play rough with the best of them. What do you say?"

The twins could only nod speechlessly while Charity grinned from ear to ear.

Chapter 6

Bailey GLIDED DOWN the deeply polished stairs feeling regal in the green satin gown and matching slippers. She was surprised that Faith's dress had fit her almost perfectly. The bodice area was the only problem. The outfit had obviously been made for a younger woman rather than a mature one, and the seamstress hadn't allowed much room for growth. The tightness of the fabric caused the dress to push her cleavage up toward the scooped neckline. Bailey knew she wasn't overly endowed, but the dress let it be known that she was all woman. Unmistakably so.

"Here she comes!" Charity called excitedly. Bailey felt all eyes turn toward her as she reached the bottom stair and turned back toward the living room. Instead of smiles and greetings, it was awkward stares and a pounding silence that filled the room.

Instantly, she knew she'd been had by the sisters. Overdressed to the ultimate embarrassment.

Hope was not wearing the gown she'd promised. She was wearing a simple dress of solid blue brushed cotton, not luxurious satin. Bailey clenched her fist and fought to control the fury that started from her toes and rose straight to the top of her head. She glared pointedly at the middle girl until Hope flushed and dropped her gaze to the floor. She did the same with Faith, who was sitting in one of the dark leather chairs, and Charity, who stood by the fireplace next to her brother. Charity's face was lit with delight, obviously unaware of any problem. She puzzled over Bailey's stern look then glanced at her sisters in confusion. The youngest sister clearly thought Bailey was beautiful. She didn't understand the rueful faces. To Bailey, that meant she wasn't the instigator.

Bailey finally met Zach's gaze squarely. He wore an immaculate white shirt that was pressed without a wrinkle, a narrow black tie at his neck. His pants were dark, just like his expression. Dark and unreadable. He was dressed nicely but certainly not as fancy as she. He watched her steadily, not saying a word to ease her discomfort or admonish his sisters for their prank. He'd tried to warn her, she supposed. A suppressed cough came from across the room, and Bailey looked up to see several strangers, three men and a woman, gaping at her as well.

Did she look that bad?

"Excuse me, I've dressed inappropriately." She stiffened her spine and shoulders. "If you'll give me another minute, I'll change into something more suitable." She lifted a slippered foot back toward the first step.

"Oh, but you look beautiful, Bailey!" Faith exclaimed. All three girls rushed forward at once, delight written all over their faces, their previous chagrin long gone. They each looked back and forth between Bailey and their brother. "Don't you think so, Zachariah?"

So that was the plan. Bailey should have figured. The

dress was for the benefit of their brother. They weren't trying to be mean, they were playing Cupid. They wanted their brother to notice her. Despite her annoyance, Bailey couldn't help being slightly amused at their ridiculous plan. It felt good to be wanted so badly. She glanced at Zach, his face a mixture of impatience, irritation, and hostility. She'd still better go change. She gathered the long skirt and reached for the staircase banister.

"Miss Cooper . . . Bailey." Zach fumbled for words as he reached for her arm. His hand lingered on her sleeve. "You look lovely. It's been a long time since anyone dressed so appropriately for supper around this house." He guided her down the stairs and brought her close against his side until her arm brushed against his chest.

It felt . . . possessive. And inviting.

"Zach is right, Miss Cooper. You light up this room like a rare flower. I understand now why Zach is reluctant to talk about you. He doesn't want anyone else knowing how beautiful you are." An older man walked toward her, taking both her hands into his. His smile was warm. "I'm Charlie Mack. This is my wife, Abigail." Mr. Mack led Bailey away from Zach toward a thin woman who was seated on the edge of the sofa. She appeared wary and uncomfortable as her eyes darted back toward the three sisters. The older woman finally rose and extended a hand toward Bailey.

"It is a lovely gown, Miss Cooper," she offered nervously, fidgeting with her own plain dark brown dress. It didn't take a supersleuth to realize poor Mrs. Mack had apparently been the brunt of at least one of the girl's escapades. From the worry on her face, Bailey sensed the woman was truly fearful. One could only imagine what might have happened between Mrs. Mack and the Gooden girls.

"So nice to meet you, too."

"You haven't yet met Hoop, Bailey." Zach rescued her from the timid woman and led her over to a tall man leaning against the mantle of the fireplace. "He's the foreman of the Double Bar G. Been with us for a good fifteen years now. Just like family."

"Hoop." Bailey offered her hand to a man equally as tall as Zach although much thinner. His light brown hair was starting to gray, and he wore it slicked back, away from the sun-weathered skin of his narrow face. The foreman was dressed in dark pants with a white shirt and looked decidedly uncomfortable as he tugged at the collar.

The man studied her carefully, as if sizing her up, then glanced toward Zach and his sisters. After a quiet pause he straightened and took her hand. It was obvious he wasn't accustomed to shaking the hand of a woman, but he did it just the same. "Ma'am." The man gave a polite nod but said nothing more. Clearly, Hoop had just made up his mind about her. Whether or not he approved, she wasn't sure. Another uneasy silence settled over the room.

"And then there's me," a wonderfully clear baritone voice drawled from just behind Bailey. She turned to see a tall man with sun-kissed blond hair and a sort of Robert Redford twinkling grin. "Sheriff Randall Weeks at your service, Miss Cooper. Zach's told me a little of your unfortunate plight, and rest assured, I stand ready to assist you in any way possible."

She smiled at his humor as she instantly recognized the opportunity the charming sheriff had just presented. He might be exactly the person she needed to help her get to her backpack. Bailey glanced at Zach, then averted her eyes before her host could decipher her thoughts and object. "Why, thank you, Sheriff. I might just take you up on that offer."

Immediately Zach stepped forward, placing himself directly between Bailey and the sheriff, virtually cutting off their conversation. "I believe our meal is about to be served. Miss Cooper, you are seated to my right. Rand," he looked pointedly at the grinning lawman, "you are at the *other* end of the table."

"Whatever you say, partner. Shall we, Miss Cooper?" Rand deliberately stepped around Zach and held out his elbow to Bailey. She looked from one to the other then decidedly accepted the sheriff's arm. If Rand Weeks would be willing to help her find her backpack and figure out how to get her home, she'd be the first in line to take him up on it. What she didn't understand was why Zach Gooden seemed irritated that someone else might offer assistance. *He* didn't believe her, why would he begrudge someone else for possibly helping her? She'd honor her promise not to discuss her dilemma in front of Mr. Mack. But, if she could get the lawman alone for a few moments, she might be on her way home by morning.

Bailey cast her sight over the table as they approached. She'd been so concerned with getting into the green satin gown, she hadn't thought much about supper. The dining table could not have been more elegant. A soft, ivory-colored linen cloth covered the oak table; a small vase full of fresh tiny pink roses graced the center.

Each place setting was of beautiful white china with delicate flowers in various shades of red painted on the rim. Polished silver knives, forks, and spoons lay beside each plate. Four crystal candlesticks each held a white candle, and the flames cast an inviting atmosphere. Zach Gooden was serious about impressing the banker and his wife.

"Please call me Rand," her escort said softly as he settled her into the chair. He gave a reluctant smile as he stepped down to his own place beside Charity. Immediately, she felt the presence of Zach Gooden standing behind her. He bent forward, his fingers lightly resting on the ticklish skin at the base of her neck. She stoically quelled the warm tingle that slowly blossomed then raced over her entire body. Rand Weeks might be the ticket back to her own time, but Zach

Gooden and his magic fingers would make the ride a lot more fun.

He leaned close, his breath warming her ear as he pointed to the china. "This was all my mother's. Jin Lee brings it out for special visitors."

"Mmmm. Beautiful," she murmured nervously. The fire from his touch immediately cooled as he removed his hands and moved to stand at the head of the table, opposite Mr. Mack. Jin Lee approached with a large platter of sliced beef and steaming potatoes. Bailey couldn't help a grin when the cook glared coldly at Faith as he set the food on the table. Clarence had lived to see another day.

Suddenly, three shots rang out in rapid succession. Bailey jumped as the hollow sounds reverberated loudly from just outside the house.

"Everybody down!" Zach ordered. He moved toward the front door, grabbing his rifle off the wall. Hoop and Rand followed, both men heading for their guns and holsters, which were hanging on pegs near the entrance.

"Gooden!" a deep angry voice called. "We've got business to attend to, boy."

"Thompson," Zach snapped angrily. Hoop said nothing but moved to the side of a front window to peer out through the curtains. Sheriff Weeks shook his head in frustration.

"When will you two cease your aggravating ways, Zach? Enough is enough."

"You're preaching to the choir, Rand. You see who's causing the problems. Thompson's determined to destroy me no matter what it costs him." Zach looked toward Hoop, who dropped the curtain and nodded. Zach threw open the heavy wooden door and stalked outside. The sheriff, still holding his gun, was next, Hoop right behind him. Mr. Mack rose from the table and headed outside, intent on finding out what was going on. Faith, Hope, and Charity did likewise.

"Oh, no," Bailey said as she stood to block their path. "I

don't know what the problem is, but it's no place for young ladies."

"You're absolutely right, Miss Cooper," Mrs. Mack nervously piped up. "Someone needs to keep a tight rein on those three. They've caused enough trouble already."

Bailey stared at the woman, who suddenly didn't seem as timid as she'd first thought, then back at Faith and her sisters. "Would the conversation outside have anything to do with something one of you instigated?"

"Depends," Hope admitted reluctantly, wringing her napkin with fretful fingers.

"On what?"

"If he's mad about the bull. I'm the one who sort of . . . accidentally, you understand . . . left the gate open, and . . ."

"Let the bull get out?" Bailey rolled her eyes at Hope's nod. "I see. You three stay with Mrs. Mack. I'll watch from the window and let you know what's going on."

Surely there wasn't going to be a shoot-out over a bull. Outside, the faint red glow of the setting sun cast an eerie aura over the ranch. Six men, all of them on horseback, watched as Zach and Sheriff Weeks approached. Although the air was thick with tension, she noticed that not all of them held guns or seemed ready to shoot. Hoop had taken a seemingly relaxed position near the front door, his gaze never leaving the group of men as he pulled a pouch from his pocket and casually began to roll a cigarette.

Bailey watched as the man obviously in charge of the group dismounted from his horse and walked slowly toward Zach, his stare never wavering. Even with the waning sunlight, she could see his silver hair. He was not as tall as Zach, but solid and powerful with an overwhelming air of meanness. Even the crickets had stopped their evening songs as if they waited for his permission to resume.

She studied the other men still on horseback. Most of the half dozen or so men appeared to be ranch hands or the like.

Two bore striking resemblances to the leader. Probably sons, Bailey surmised. The youngest was about twenty. He was a good-looking kid with sandy blond hair that would, no doubt, mature gray identical to his father.

"That's Joe Junior," Hope said as she joined Bailey at the window. At Bailey's glare, the girl laid a hand on her arm. "Please don't make me sit back with Mrs. Mack. I did cause the problem you know."

Bailey considered the girl through narrowed eyes. Hope's worried face seemed genuine. After a second's hesitation, Bailey nodded, put her arm around Hope, and turned back toward the activity outside. "Who's the man to his right?"

"That's Sloan, Mr. Thompson's oldest son. According to Joe Junior, he just showed up a couple of months ago. Nobody knows much about him. Joe Junior doesn't like him."

"How do you know that?"

Hope shrugged. "He told me."

Bailey saw the oldest brother adjust his reins to settle his horse. He looked as if he was a good bit older than Joe Junior, although still much younger than Zach. Unlike Sloan's father and brother, his hair was almost black. There was something else about him that seemed different. Even though his horse stood close to the others, he was apart from the group. He looked as if he didn't really belong, as if he didn't really fit in, and as if he didn't care to, either.

"Who are the other men?"

"They all work on Mr. Thompson's ranch. They're the main reason Zach won't let us go riding alone. Hoop says they're all mean enough to have seats reserved in hell."

"Hope!"

"Well," the teenager reasoned. "That's what he says."

Bailey refocused her attention on the stranger outside. "Gooden, I warned you about letting those black bulls get out and roam the range. I told you a year ago that they're too big to cross with these scrappy longhorns. The sheer size of the bastard calf will kill its mamma before it's born. If I lose a single cow next spring because one of your monsters got loose, I'm gonna butcher every single one of them."

Zach nodded toward the corrals over by his barn. "Looks to me like they're all accounted for, J.T." Bailey heard the controlled anger in Zach's voice. This wasn't going to look good to the banker. She wondered if this unfortunate confrontation would have an effect on Zach's loan. In fact, if Zach hadn't exaggerated his concerns, this whole situation could have been staged specifically for the banker's benefit.

Thompson didn't turn to confirm Zach's claim. "Only because you found the damn thing before I did. Next time you ain't going to be so lucky. You or the bull."

"You threatening me, Thompson?"

"No, I'm promising. If a single one of my good Hereford cows has an ugly crossbred calf at her side next spring, you won't have a single fancy black *A-beer-deen* Angus to your name."

Even in the dimming light Bailey could see by Zach's body language that he was hot. Hoop straightened from his place by the rail. The foreman slowly took off his hat and removed a match from the band. He moved to strike it on the bottom of his boot. Every eye in the area studied the sudden flame as if it might cause the situation to ignite.

Zach seemed to regain his composure during the distraction. He deliberately closed the distance between him and Thompson, coming nose to nose with him before he spoke. His voice was calm, deep and threatening.

"We both know what you want, Thompson. The Double Bar G. You think you'll get it by destroying my herds, but that won't happen. I'll kill you first."

Bailey gasped. Zach had just threatened the man in front of a sheriff, *and* the banker he was trying to impress. The other man returned Zach's threatening stare with equal hatred. It didn't appear that either of them was going to back down in the growing dusk. A slow movement of one of the horses suddenly caught her attention. Sloan Thompson cued his horse closer until the two men were forced to step apart. Bailey released a breath she didn't realize she'd been holding as the horse effectively broke the tension.

"Charlie, you might as well go ahead and foreclose. Gooden's a fool to think hybrids can save this lousy spread. Save what money you can by calling in the loan and selling his herd to me. I'll give you top dollar."

Thompson waited for a response, but Charlie Mack said nothing. Thompson turned on his heel, mounted his horse, and spurred angrily. Joe Junior and the other men did likewise.

Sloan watched the others ride out, then turned back toward Zach. Silently, almost apologetically, he tipped his hat and turned his horse to follow at a much slower pace.

Chapter 7

DINNER WAS A disaster.

After Thompson had ridden away in such a fury, neither Zach nor Mr. Mack knew what to say to reassure the other. Less than ten minutes later, Mrs. Mack declared a blinding headache and asked her husband to take her home. A stone-faced Sheriff Weeks opted to accompany the couple back to town.

Hoop quickly said his good nights and headed for the bunkhouse.

The twins and Charity obviously knew when to leave Zach alone. One by one each girl fled up the stairs. Hope paused long enough to cast a worried frown at Bailey.

Zach disappeared into his dark office without a word.

Bailey escaped the confines of the house for the weathered swing on the edge of the porch. It squeaked as she settled into it and began to slowly rock back and forth. She ran a finger over the rough wooden slats then quietly considered the past few days. In the flicker of an eye, she was thrust into a situation she'd never dreamed, never imagined, never thought possible. Not just with Zach Gooden and his hot-tempered mess but also with her own dilemma.

Was this what happened to the countless number of people who simply vanished without a trace? Were they really hurtled back in time instead? If so, that also meant that those who were never found must never return. Otherwise, modern science would give at least some credence to the viability of time travel. She might have heard it was possible, at least in some checkout lane tabloid.

The brewing storm had finally drawn closer and rain began to fall. An occasional claw of lightning batted across the sky followed by the distant sound of thunder. The air was thick and heavy with a sharp chill. Bailey wished she had a shawl or cape to cover her bare shoulders.

The hinges on the front door groaned. A sliver of light appeared, grew wider, then quickly disappeared after Zach walked onto the porch and shut the door behind him. He leaned against the railing, seemingly unaware of her presence. He was clearly still enraged at tonight's events. She spoke cautiously. "That was pretty much a disaster I suppose?"

Zach shot her a dark look, although he did not appear surprised to see her. He nodded sharply and lifted his hand and wearily ran it through his hair. "The last thing I need is more trouble with J.T. Thompson, especially in front of the banker."

"What is it about those cows that makes him hate them so much?"

Zach shrugged as he considered the sky. He cupped his fingers to catch falling rain, then splashed the water on his face. "He wants the Double Bar G. Always has. This is just his latest way of manipulating to get it. He knows that I mortgaged a large portion of the ranch. I guess he thinks he can convince Charlie Mack of his way of thinking."

"Maybe not," Bailey replied. "Mr. Mack seems like a reasonable man." Bailey continued to rock back and forth on the swing.

"Charlie was opposed to the mortgage from the beginning. He only agreed because he owed my pa a favor from years back." Zach turned to face her, resting his hands on the porch rail behind him. "I needed the money in order to import the three bulls and a dozen cows from Scotland. My plan is to breed the Angus with my Herefords and produce a hardier animal, one that could better withstand our harsh winters. Hopefully, they will also regain weight faster than the pure Herefords. If I'm right, Double Bar G beef will be ready to sell when prices are at a premium, long before any of Thompson's head are ready for market. Not only that, every rancher around would want their own Aberdeen Angus hybrids. It's all a gamble. I'm either going to win big or lose big."

"That's business, Zach. You have to be innovative and take risks. I admire you for that." He smiled slightly, obviously pleased she understood. Then he sighed heavily.

"Unfortunatly, that's not all of it. About five years ago, the feud between my pa and J.T. came to a head. J.T. almost won the Double Bar G in a poker game. Pa had a straight flush, Thompson had a royal flush. Pa accused Thompson of cheating as did several other players. The other men in the game and in the saloon that night refused to let Thompson take the ranch. He and Pa got into a terrible fistfight right there in the saloon."

"Where is your father now?"

"Dead."

"I'm so sorry."

He nodded. "A few weeks later, we found him with a knife in the back. He still held the winning hand of cards in his pocket. No doubt he planned to badger Thompson about the cheating. He and J.T. had hated each other for years. The card game was just the latest battle in their personal war."

Bailey sensed that Zach told her probably more than he intended. It could not have been easy for him then or now. "Did they ever prosecute the man who killed him?"

"No. J.T. had an alibi. He was up at a line cabin on the far side of his ranch the night of the murder. His son, Joe Junior, and several ranch hands were there with him. They'd been checking for lost cattle and stopped there for the night. Anyone else who would have done it was long gone by then. Ever since the murder, Thompson has claimed that he rightfully won the ranch. He's determined to have it one way or another."

"What happens if he ever gets it?"

"My sisters and I become penniless for one thing. For another, he'll have complete and total control of the river. He could build a dam at the bend and literally force everyone to rely on him for water. That will make his the most powerful ranch—and him the most powerful man—in these parts, a dangerous combination for someone so arrogant."

"So there's more to it than just ruining you."

"Exactly. Last year was a hard winter, and I lost almost every head I had. I can't afford to do that again. That's why I took the gamble to buy the Angus."

An oil lamp from inside cast a golden glow through the window. In the light Bailey noticed how a large freckle on the side of Zach's neck moved as he spoke. She fought an unbidden thought of what it would be like to run her tongue over it, then continued on to trace the edged profile of his chin and straight up to his lips.

Zach looked her way suddenly as if he could read her thoughts. His gaze lowered to her mouth and throat, then dropped further to the lace of the low-cut dress. Suddenly warm, Bailey flushed and pretended interest in her fingernails. There was no way around it. Zach Gooden excited her, and he knew it.

"Why didn't you reprimand your sisters for embarrassing me with this dress? I thought you wanted to curtail their devilishness." It was a weak question, but she had to say something to break the tension between them.

"Frankly, because I couldn't take my eyes off of you."

Zach shifted against the rail, then headed toward her. She watched like a nervous doe about to be pounced on by a mountain lion. The wooden slats creaked as his weight settled onto the narrow swing. His lean thigh brushed against the soft fabric of the dress; he draped his arm across the top slat as if it was the most natural thing in the world. Bailey once again wished the bosom of her dress were not so low or so tight. She nervously lifted her hand and casually rested it on her exposed skin. It didn't cover much, but the action gave her a little bit of comfort.

The rain had started just after the Macks' departure. The wind moaned softly. "Looks like your guests got caught in the rain," Bailey said, trying to keep her voice steady.

Zach groaned. "Just another thing to go wrong. I'll bet Charlie calls in the loan first thing in the morning."

She grinned, absently stroking the skin below her throat. "I doubt it. He seemed pretty impressed with your determination to succeed."

He grinned ruefully. "You mean my unfortunate and poor choice of words to kill J.T.? My temper has always been my downfall."

"Did Hope leave the gate open on purpose?"

He shook his head. "Hope's probably the smartest one in the family, she just doesn't think sometimes." He pushed the swing into motion and they slowly rocked back and forth.

"Why do you suppose his son stepped between you two?"

"How did you know Sloan was his son?"

"Hope was commentating for me."

"No idea. I don't know what to make of Sloan Thompson. He's an odd one. Apparently, he's Thompson's illegitimate son. He grew up with his mother's family in north Texas and only recently took up with his father. He doesn't say much, so no one knows anything about him."

"You don't know anything about me, either." Bailey glanced over toward him, then back at the rain.

"Right as rain. I don't." He turned toward her. "Tell me about yourself, Bailey. Where do you really come from? What do you really want?"

She stared at him, knowing her truthful answers would annoy him. So much had already happened, she didn't want to spoil what was left of the evening. Redirecting the conversation would be better. "When do you suppose the rain will let up?"

"It could stop tomorrow, or it could rain for the next two weeks. Just don't know. The river was already swollen from the melting snow off the mountains. This constant rain has only made it worse. That's why we can't go back to the ravine for your traveling bag right now. We barely made it across the first time."

She looked at him carefully. There was no moonlight to study his features. What little light that was available came from the oil lamps just inside the living room windows. The stubborn set of his jaw told her he hadn't changed his mind about taking her to find her backpack. Carefully she tried to piece together a scenario that would make him want to go. There had to be something in it for him.

Of course! *The Old Farmer's Almanac.* Not only was it copyrighted in 1900, it held a history of the weather patterns for fifty years back. There just might be something in it for him after all. The knowledge she could give him would surely be beneficial to his ranch. In fact, it might mean the success or failure of it. A sudden thought stopped her cold. Would it be inappropriate for her to literally show him the future? What he could learn from that book would surely affect the decisions he would face in the coming years from weather patterns to crops and cattle.

No, she determined. It was evidence, and evidence was what she needed to get out of this mess. She couldn't imagine being sent back into this time without a way to defend herself.

"I also have something you would find interesting," she added.

He cocked a brow at her. "I doubt you'd have anything I need in a traveling bag, Miss Cooper," he replied stubbornly.

"I have an almanac."

"I already have my own."

"Perhaps, but do you have one from the year 1900? One that would tell you about the major floods, droughts, and other natural disasters of this year and next? One that will tell you where the major railroad spurs are built ten years from now? Well, I do—"

"And it just so happens to be in your traveling bag," he interrupted sarcastically.

"Yes, and if you want it, you must take me to get it. Tomorrow. My backpack is water-resistant but not waterproof. This constant rain could ruin the book and my other belongings. Besides, I plan to find it with or without your help. Sheriff Weeks seemed more than willing to assist me."

"Rand Weeks is a good lawman and an even better ladies' man," Zach replied with amusement. "He's good about saying whatever a woman wants to hear. He knows how bad the river is, and he'd probably insist you wait even longer than I would. As far as going yourself?" He laughed and shrugged the idea away. "You have absolutely no idea where it is, Miss Cooper. You were unconscious when I carried you here. And, since you'd wandered so far away from the mountain you claim you were on, I'd say you have no sense of direction either. You'd get lost and I'd have to rescue you again. I forbid it."

Bailey rose from the swing to grip the porch railing. Frustrated anger filled her as it did every time the system let a criminal go free. "You have no right to forbid me to do anything."

"If I weren't afraid you'd do something that might cost you your life, I wouldn't have to forbid it." He rose just as quickly as she. Instantly, without warning, his arms swooped down and wrapped around her, turning her until she faced him head-on. He crushed his lips to hers with a hard kiss.

Bailey was so surprised by his action—by the heat, by the intensity, by the passion behind those lips—that she couldn't respond. A man didn't just sweep you into his arms to silence you. That only happened in old black-and-white movies, and then only when the hero couldn't win an argument any other way. She struggled to be free of him, pushing against his chest, but he refused to lessen his hold.

As swiftly as it had started, the force of his kiss changed from punishing to promising, from hard to inviting, from deadly to dangerous. He didn't release his hold, but he shifted to tickle the inside of her upper lip with his tongue, then drew her deeper into his arms, into his embrace.

The anger at his audacity slowly faded. It had been a long time since she had been so thoroughly kissed. In fact, she didn't think she'd ever been kissed quite like that. Her hands ceased to struggle. The feel of his hard muscles scorched through the fabric of his shirt. His arms loosened yet continued to hold her close. His calloused hand rose to lift her hair from her neck and brush the delicate skin underneath. The cool night air tickled the tiny wisps of hair as his lips left hers and trailed down to caress her neck and bare shoulders. He lifted his head again, this time to dance around the outline of her mouth.

"You are the most beautiful, the most interesting, the most willful, the most infuriating woman I've ever met," he said, pressing against her lips.

Bailey stopped cold. *Infuriating?* She was in a battle to save her life as she knew it, and he thought she was infuriating? She pulled away, staring up into his dark eyes. She wasn't sure if they were unreadable from passion or from mocking laughter.

"And you are intensely obnoxious. Kissing a woman into submission may be proper procedure here, but it went out long before my time. Don't do it again." Bailey jerked out of his grasp and stiffened her back with dignity. She lifted her chin and walked back inside the house. She tried her best to ignore the deep chuckle that filtered in through the open window, and the three familiar giggles that came from a hiding place underneath the stairs.

Two days later Bailey stood by the corral and stared at the three elderly, overweight horses. A quick check in the barn had confirmed there were no others. She doubted the large black one would make it half a mile, much less gallantly carry her across the river to the ravine.

She had risen and dressed before dawn, watching from her window as the ranch became an active hub. Hoop was the first, coming out of the barn even before she was fully awake. He forked hay into each of the corrals for the bulls and horses.

Cowboys, a few at a time, had filtered out of what must have been their bunkhouse, saddles slung across their backs. They readied their horses, then climbed up on the top rail of the corral to have a smoke before the day started. A few minutes later, she saw Zach stride toward them. His ebony hat had created a vivid contract against the rose-colored sun that brought the day. She had hoped the red-streaked sky would give way to a cloudless blue, but it didn't look like that was to be. Bailey stared at the overcast sky and inwardly groaned. Did it ever stop raining in Wyoming? Zach barked out orders, and group by group, sometimes one by one, all the cowboys rode off to start the tasks of the day. He and Hoop were the last to leave. Neither spared so much as a glance toward Bailey.

She bent to brush away a new splotch of mud from her jeans. Jin Lee had left them, her jacket, her chambray blouse, and her boot socks on the bed sometime after dinner last night, washed, dried, and folded. Each night, she had washed out her underthings. There were garments Jin Lee just didn't need to see. Although her clothes were stiff from drying by the kitchen fire, they were clean and fresh. She couldn't imagine how anyone could live without a regular washing machine and dryer, much less other modern conveniences. These people worked hard for everything they had, no matter how minute.

Out of habit, she looked at where her watch should have been, irritated and a bit distracted to find it missing. She'd apparently lost it and her gloves in the fall. Faith had agreed to meet her around seven, well after Zach, Hoop, and the other ranch hands would be out with the cattle, but still early enough to find the river before anyone knew they were gone. When Bailey had told the girls of her plan yesterday afternoon, they had grown quiet. She knew they wanted her to stay, especially since in their minds she was practically walking down the aisle to the altar with their brother.

Fortunately, each had a spirit of adventure that couldn't be quelled. They had agreed, in the end, to take her as far as the river. From there, she would cross and find the ravine on her own. Zach had made it abundantly clear that the river was dangerous. If this did turn out to be a harebrained idea, she certainly didn't want to put them in danger.

Contrary to what Zach Gooden believed, she had an excellent sense of survival. Her love of solitary hikes had confidently polished that skill. She knew she had a decent chance of finding the ravine on her own. All she needed was a point in the right direction and a horse to get her there. Heck, for that matter, she could probably make it to Medicine Mountain by herself as well.

"I told you so," a girlish voice whined.

Bailey turned as Faith and Hope approached. They each wore white cotton blouses and cotton skirts that stopped mid-calf, Faith in a midnight blue, Hope in bland tan. Charity followed a little ways behind wearing sort of an olive drab that matched the dress on the Indian doll she carried. All three girls wore dark leather lace-up boots. Bailey couldn't help but notice how dull the clothes were. The girls had a kind of drop-dead beauty that needed bright, bold colors to accentuate their hair and flawless complexions. She made a mental note to gently mention it to them along the way.

"You told them so about what?"

"I told them Zach would leave Plug, Bear, and Sparky for us to ride." Hope frowned, frustration marring her face. "He never lets us ride anything with spirit. He's afraid we'll do something foolish."

"You mean like take me to the river?"

All three girls burst out laughing. "Exactly!" Charity grinned.

Hope was the obvious horsewoman of the bunch. She led Faith and Charity inside the corral, caught the horses, and brought the tired animals close to the barn. "Can you cinch up a saddle?" Hope asked.

"I can learn." Bailey followed her into the dim barn and reached to lift the heavy saddle Hope indicated. On her first try, she couldn't even lift it, much less raise it high enough to get it on the back of a horse.

"Here, let me help. I'm used to doing it by myself," Hope confided. "I sneak out sometimes and ride Reliant."

Bailey laughed. "Zach's horse? Aren't you afraid he'll clobber you?"

Hope smiled, but said nothing. Unsettled alarm swept over her. Bailey's instincts told her Hope wasn't telling all of her story, but she brushed it aside. She'd deal with that later, too.

"We can get you to the river and then point out the direction to the ravine. Are you sure you don't want to stay with us?" Faith interjected hopefully.

"If things were different, I'd seriously consider it. Besides, I'm planning to come back."

Charity stepped forward and hugged Bailey solemnly, her blue eyes clouded with gathering tears. "Be careful."

Bailey was touched. In a little more than a few days, these girls had made her feel welcome despite their prank with the dress. Charity pulled away and dramatically sniffed to hold back her tears. Bailey would certainly miss them when she left, but there was no need to get too attached. It wouldn't last anyway.

"Zach is usually predictable," Hope told her. "In a couple of hours, he'll come back to the house just to make sure we're not hurt or into any trouble." She looked over Bailey's shoulder to the three saddled horses, then rolled her eyes. "As if Plug, Sparky, and Bear could get up the energy to hurt anyone."

"Charity will tell him that you, Hope, and I went riding, that we promised to stay within sight of the ranch, and that we'll be back shortly," Faith added. She turned to Charity with a stern look. "*Do not* let him know that we headed toward the river. Our plan won't work at all, then."

Faith stressed her words to Charity with such conviction that Bailey wondered for a brief instant if "the plan" was more than originally decided. She quelled her anxiousness. Either Faith and Hope would help her, or they wouldn't. If she didn't find the river today, she'd find it somehow.

Faith hiked up her skirt in a most unladylike manner and swung herself up into the saddle of the tall black horse named Sparky. She settled her skirt back around her without a care in the world. At first Bailey was shocked by the girl's actions. How else did one ride a horse in a skirt, though?

Bailey swallowed nervously. Her own time of reckoning was here. When she formulated her plan, she didn't mention that she had ridden only a few times in her life on hired trail horses that followed one another on the same path around the same park a dozen times each day. Other than her ride with Zach, which she didn't remember anyway, she was a true novice.

"Is this one gentle?" Bailey worried aloud as Hope helped her mount the flea-bitten gray they called Plug. She watched as Hope turned back to her dark brown horse. Hope copied her sister's actions with the skirt, and casually mounted her horse.

"As gentle as any, I suppose."

Bailey looked down at the horse Hope had saddled for her, and patted his neck. Faith and Hope made it look so easy. Besides, how hard could it be to ride a horse named Plug?

Chapter 8

For the tenth time, Bailey glanced up at the late morning sun and wondered how much farther to the river. They had been riding for almost three hours, and she didn't know how much more she could stand. Faith and Hope rode ahead on their horses, Sparky and Bear, and had quickly settled into easy canters. Plug, on the other hand, continued along at a fast bone-jarring trot. Although he was keeping up with his stablemates fairly well, he stoically refused to put any more effort into the ride than he had to. Bailey's body, nerves, and patience were ready to snap.

The girls had told her to kick Plug in the sides and he would break into a comfortable canter like the other horses. It didn't work. No matter how much she kicked, the dirty gray horse still ignored her and continued the same rough gait. If and when she ever got off, Bailey doubted she'd ever ride again.

Even though she was a beginner, she could see that someone needed to speak with Zach about getting the girls better mounts. Plug seemed to be a gentle soul despite his determination not to move any faster. He had to be after all the kicking she'd done. Plug, Bear, and Sparky were obviously horses for beginners like herself, not experienced horsewomen like Faith and Hope. If they had more of a challenge in other regards, maybe they wouldn't need to create so much mischief for entertainment.

Bailey realized she was already forming an argument on behalf of the girls. She didn't want to stay an hour longer than necessary, yet here she was ready to talk to the three sisters about wearing more flattering colors and convince their brother to get them suitable horses. It was uncanny how easily she seemed to fit right into their lives.

Bailey held the flopping reins together, gripped the saddle horn with both hands, and once more kicked good ol' Plug in the sides. The horse grunted and tossed his head but never wavered. He continued along at the same jolting pace, rattling Bailey's teeth and causing aches and pains in places she didn't want to think about. Faith and Hope were quite a ways ahead of her now. She prayed they wouldn't forget she was back here.

As if they heard her thoughts, they slowed their horses to give Bailey and Plug a chance to catch up. Bailey bounced painfully toward them, promising herself a long hot soak in the tub when she finally got home. Off to the right, she could see a dull gray metal windmill slowly spinning in the breeze. A herd of about a hundred or so cows, some brown and white, several solid black, grazed nearby. A few stood at the base of the windmill drinking water from a wooden trough. The scene was vaguely familiar. In fact, she could swear they had passed this way once before.

"Are you certain you know how to get to the river?" Bailey called to Faith and Hope as she drew alongside them. "It seems to be taking more time than I recall."

"We're almost there," Hope replied quickly as she reined her big brown horse to a halt. "Zach said you were out cold when he brought you back, do you think you remember the way?"

"No, I don't," Bailey answered truthfully. She stood in the saddle to stretch her weary legs. Plug had stopped on his own and was now sniffing at the grass on the ground. She considered both girls carefully. "It seems to me that we've passed that windmill already. Are we going in circles?"

"Oh, that." Faith shrugged nonchalantly. "There are several on the ranch. The river is just up ahead." A covert look between Faith and Hope instantly confirmed Bailey's suspicions. They were up to something all right. It didn't take a rocket scientist to figure out that one.

Suddenly, Faith's horse reared and flayed its front legs. Faith played with the reins to try to settle him but it was no use. The horse snorted and reared again. Startled, Plug swung his head up from the tall grass he'd been sniffing and shied away from the commotion. Bailey lost her balance and fell backward onto the hard ground, landing with a loud thud, the impact knocking the wind out of her.

Faith's horse gave an angry snort, then reared a third time. When he came down, he swirled around in tight circles and took off at a dead run across the grassland, Faith hanging on for dear life. "Help me, Hope! Help me!"

"I've got to catch her!" Hope called to Bailey. "Stay here, we'll be right back." She spurred her horse and took off after Faith at breakneck speed.

Bailey had not yet regained her wind after falling to the ground. She lay still and listened to the fading sounds of the horses. Plug wandered up and sniffed at her face as if he was checking to be sure she was all right. Then he sneezed all over her shirt and turned his attention to a juicy spot of vegetation up by her ear.

Bailey closed her eyes. She'd been had. The rearing and

spinning had been too perfect, too controlled. Faith and Hope knew she couldn't ride and took advantage of it. Heck, she couldn't even get on the horse by herself. When she finally figured out they were going in circles, they changed their plan and left her out here in the wilderness with nothing but a tired gray horse, a bunch of cows, and two buzzards circling overhead.

It was easy to figure who they planned to have rescue her, and after their heated exchange last night, Zach Gooden wasn't going to be happy about it. Well, if he was going to be the one who rescued her, she might as well go for broke.

Bailey struggled to her feet and reached for Plug's reins. He darted away and pulled them from her grasp. "Easy, boy," she soothed. "I'm just going to try and get on and we'll go find the river ourselves. I just need to cross it and hopefully find my backpack. I promise we'll walk. I don't think I could stand anything faster anyway. We'll take it nice and slow. No stress, no worries." She bent and grabbed a handful of grass and held it out to him. Plug flicked his ears toward her in interest and stretched out his neck so his nose almost reached her hand.

Just before she could grab the reins, the sly horse skittered away again, stamping his feet impatiently and blowing with indignation. He wanted her to hand-feed him, but he didn't want to be caught. She tried a third time, actually touching the soft hairs on his nose, before Plug jerked away. The fourth time, Plug didn't even bother to look at the grass offered in her hand. He just turned and walked away when she got too close.

Bailey sighed and looked around. Other than the windmill, the cattle, and the foothills in the distance, the scenery was identical in every direction. Not even a row of trees to indicate a possible river. It would be a guess. Even if she could catch the horse.

"Plug, old boy," she called to the grazing horse. "I'm

walking over to the windmill. If I have to be rescued, I might as well make myself easy to find. You're welcome to tag along." The horse lifted his head, silently stared at her, and continued to chew a mouthful of grass. He started toward her, stopped just out of reach, and tossed his head, clearly wanting her to get moving.

Bailey sighed. The people and the animals seemed to like her so much that they didn't want her to leave. She turned and watched the tarnished metal wheel turn in the breeze, then made her way toward it.

Plug stared after her for a minute then slowly began to follow.

"I told you I wouldn't rescue you again." Zach gripped the reins as he stared, aggravated, at the redhead sitting cross-legged on the grass, a short distance from the windmill. Her glorious hair was pulled back in a single braid, a worn straw hat, probably one of Hope's, covered her head and shaded her eyes. Even as she stood and met his gaze defiantly, he couldn't help but notice how the tight blue denims outlined her shapely long legs. He remembered how the open dressing gown had inadvertently exposed the rosy skin underneath all those clothes.

"I had to get my backpack."

"Did you have to include my sisters in your plan? You're just as sneaky as they are." He knew the sun behind him restricted her view of him. She raised a hand to block the sun and squinted to see him clearly.

"I would not have allowed them to cross the river. They were only going to show me where it was and point me in the direction of the ravine. It wasn't their fault I couldn't catch that irritating horse."

"Perhaps, but it's their fault you're out here alone." Zach pushed his hat toward the back of his head, then leaned forward in the saddle to rest his forearm on the saddle horn. He wanted to be angry with her but he couldn't. It was hard to be furious with anyone who had been so neatly outsmarted by his sisters. The same thing had happened to so many folks on a few too many occasions. Like the time at last year's roundup festival. A she-cat brawl ensued when two of the local ladies accused a third of switching all the jars in the jellies and jams contest and hiding the real first-place winner. He remembered how Faith, Hope, and Charity stood innocently by while the husbands had to pull apart the fighting women. The third woman had accused the girls of pulling the prank, but they had each vehemently denied any part in the mess. Zach had stood by them, too.

It wasn't until the ride home that Hoop found the missing jar hidden in the corner of the buckboard underneath a sack of corn. It was then Zach realized he had true hellions on his hands.

He glanced around. "Where is your horse?"

"He wandered off that way more than an hour ago," she said, motioning toward the south. "Cows, no matter how pedigreed, are not the sweetest smelling things, you know."

Zach stifled a grin, then tossed his leg over Reliant's back and dismounted. The bay stared at both of them with interest, then dropped his head to look for a clump of grass. Bailey looked nervous as Zach walked closer, so he maintained a tough face. "I ought to turn you over my knee."

He saw disbelief flicker across her features as she shook her head. "Just you try, Gooden. I can hold my own." She immediately took a stance as if she were ready to pounce. Her legs were bent at the knees and her arms held in front of her body, crooked at the elbow and almost crossed as if to protect her body.

He stopped abruptly, stared at her, then started to laugh. Before he could catch his breath, Bailey lunged forward, grabbed his right wrist, hooked her leg behind his knee, and pushed backward. Zach landed on his back with a thud, still

in the grass but barely missing the thick mud that surrounded the water trough.

He glared up at her as she stood over him with her odd-
looking boot resting on his chest. "You tripped me!"

"No, I dropped you on your butt. I told you, I can protect
myself." She said it so matter-of-factly that Zach had to
laugh again. He sat up and considered this Bailey Cooper in
a new light. He'd never met a woman so . . . so amazing. She
was smart, resourceful, independent, and dangerous, a combination that couldn't help but excite him. Despite her foolish tale of being from the future, he was beginning to think
that she and he might—

He stopped cold. What was he thinking? Surely he wasn't
trying to convince himself she was telling the truth. Her
story of being from the future was too far-fetched. Granted,
he'd never seen those fancy fighting moves, especially from
a woman, but that didn't mean she came from the future.
She could have learned them anywhere.

"Now, do you want to talk about this situation like adults,
or do you still want to turn me over your knee?" Bailey
stood a few feet away, again in her unusual stance, ready to
strike at any moment. Zach knew she'd be too quick for him
while he was still on the ground. There were other ways to
conquer and control. He rose to his feet and wiped the dirt
from his backside. When he straightened, he deliberately
lowered his eyes to her toes and began a slow upward perusal, taking in every curve, every part of her body. His gaze
lingered on the open collar of her blouse, at the base of her
throat, just above her breasts. He noted the rapid rise and fall
of her chest, the only thing that indicated her nervousness.
When he continued farther upward to consider her face, she
stared back at him just as boldly.

"Taking you on is something I definitely have in mind,
woman, but not out here in the mud. There are better places

for that." He watched smugly as her face reddened to match her hair.

Slowly, then, Bailey mimicked his actions, her gaze studying every inch of his body, resting momentarily just below his belt. Zach shifted uncomfortably as his body responded with obvious desire. "Perhaps I'll let you take me on," she replied, giving back as good as she got. "And, if it happens out here in the grass and mud, well . . ." She let her voice trail off with the possibilities.

Zach grew warm all over. He didn't know whether to be offended or aroused at the idea of taking her right here and now. His body knew, though, and it was giving him away. She wasn't afraid of saying what she thought; she wasn't afraid of defending herself; and she wasn't afraid of him. He suddenly began to doubt Bailey Cooper could have been attacked or left for dead. She simply wouldn't have allowed it to happen.

Zach coughed before he lost all sanity and carefully moved closer a step at a time. The last thing he wanted was another back flip to the ground. "I suppose you know Faith, Hope, and Charity planned all this. They had no intention of helping you leave."

"I figured as much the second time I saw the windmill. They have brilliant minds to concoct such a way to get us alone. If only you could bottle that brilliance and sell it. You'd be a rich man."

He grinned, then looked up at the windmill. "We have two other windmills on the ranch. How did you know this was the same one?"

"The bandanna tied to the stand." Bailey pointed to a place about halfway up the stand where a red kerchief was knotted. The kerchief had obviously been there awhile since it was soaked with last night's rain.

"I've never noticed that before." He quickly climbed the stand and removed the knotted cloth with his knife. Once back on the ground, he tied the kerchief on his saddle then looked back toward Bailey. "I wasn't putting you off about the river. It is very dangerous right now."

"And I'm very desperate. That gives me more motivation to find an alternative way to cross it."

"Just to prove your story?"

"Not only that, but also the almanac. It could be helpful to you, and being out in the elements may destroy it." Bailey sighed and shook her head. "There might also be a chance that the area holds the key to why I'm here. I don't know, but I have to review all the evidence. It's just my nature."

Zach lifted a finger to tip his hat. "If there were another way, don't you think I'd know about it? But I'm a reasonable man. If seeing is the only thing that'll convince you, I'll take you to the river myself." He walked over to Reliant and mounted, then rode forward and halted the horse beside Bailey. Zach reached down to grab her extended hand and lifted Bailey into the saddle behind him.

She tried to hold on to each side of his waist, to touch him only where necessary. But, when he spurred the horse into a gallop, she quickly changed her mind and wrapped her arms tightly around him. He smiled in satisfaction. She thought she was more than he could handle. It would be a hell of a lot of fun proving her wrong.

He felt the firmness of her breasts pressed against his back as her arms encircled his body. He thought about her brazen suggestion of wrestling in the mud. She might think the decision to take him on belonged to her, but it didn't. Not completely, at least. Not after the hot stare they gave each other. He straightened in the saddle. They were playing a game of want and desire, and if he played it right, he just might come out the winner.

*   *   *

Bailey heard the rushing river water before she saw it. After an hour of riding, they drew near an outcropping of trees. He guided the horse toward a wide opening in the trees where the area was wet and muddy. It was easy to see how an animal could get bogged down if it got too close to the water.

Zach kept Reliant close to the edge of the trees, avoiding the dangerous area. When she finally saw the engorged, white-crested river, Bailey was speechless. What had she been thinking? That Zach's dangerous river was merely a flooded stream? A babbling brook gone haywire? This was raging water, torrential water, vicious churning water that hurtled past them, carrying tree branches, logs, even dead animals. The rancher had not exaggerated in the least.

Reliant halted at Zach's signal. Zach turned in his saddle to help Bailey dismount then got off the horse himself. She walked as close to the river edge as she dared, avoiding the muddy area where the cattle came to drink or cross to the other side.

"Isn't there anywhere else to cross?"

"A few other places, but most just as bad."

Bailey felt all her hope wash away with the river. She was trapped somewhere she didn't want to be. True, the place was interesting and pleasant, but it wasn't home. It wasn't where *she* chose to be. Bailey closed her eyes to try to regain control before she despaired. Good lawyers learned early to seal away their emotions and rely on the facts, especially when it came to some of the atrocities facing innocent children. It was a skill she'd proudly perfected as an attorney. Now she knew it wasn't such a good one for a woman who had lost everything she'd ever known not once, but now twice in her life.

Zach was used to female tears. You couldn't live with three sisters and not be. He'd learned to pretend they didn't affect him. But watching this woman who was so visibly shaken, so desperately trying to hold back tears, was more than he could bear. He'd never doubted she had a traveling bag. What he doubted was the urgency to retrieve it and what she claimed was in it. He watched her anguish now, and wished he had at least tried.

He studied the river as he had many times over the years. It was higher than he'd seen in a long time. The current was swift, especially right in the center. But, if they went upriver a half a mile or so, maybe they could cross. The river was not as wide, although the water was much deeper. Reliant would have to swim a good twenty feet right in the center. If his horse could tolerate the swim and fight the current with both of them on his back, they could probably make it to the other side. He'd have to deal with crossing back later. Then there was the issue of being on Thompson land.

Hell, he couldn't believe he was about to do this. If they made it across safely, and he found her traveling bag, she'd be closer to leaving, something that nagged uncomfortably. However, it wasn't fair to her to think along those lines, and there was no sense in refusing. He was certain that she'd try again on her own, and next time he might not be around to prevent her from getting hurt.

He walked up behind her and gently wrapped both arms around her waist. She stiffened, but when he pulled her back to rest against his chest, she relaxed and accepted his comfort.

"You were right, Zach," she admitted softly. "I doubted your word when I had no reason. The river is everything you said. I wish I could somehow prove to you who I am. I wish I could give you the almanac to help you know the future. I . . . was even hoping that once I was back at the ravine there might have been a slim chance I could somehow get home. Without it . . ." She let her words trail off.

"Is that what you really want, to go home?"

"Wouldn't you?"

He sighed. He had to do it. "All right, then. You have to listen to every word I say and don't get any bright ideas."

Bailey turned in his arms and met his gaze, her hands resting lightly on his chest. "How? The river is even worse than you described."

Zach shrugged. "If it's gotta be done, it's gotta be done, and I guess I'm the man to do it." He pulled away from the warmth of her body and headed toward his horse. Bailey followed and stood quietly as he removed a long length of rope from the saddle. He tied one end around her, coiled the middle section around the saddle horn, then knotted the other end around his waist just as he had when he brought her across the river several nights ago. He put her up on the saddle, this time sitting in front, and mounted behind her.

"Hold on to the saddle horn, not his mane. Let Reliant do the work. And for goodness sake, whatever you do, don't let go. The current will knock you off his back in a second."

Zach headed Reliant a short way up riverbank to where the grass and trees grew closer to the water. "The first step will be rough, just hang on."

Bailey let go of the saddle horn long enough to reach back and touch Zach's cheek. "Thank you for doing this, Zach."

He was so close, he thought, so close to losing himself in those deep green eyes. Yet here he was helping her leave. He nodded gruffly. "Ready?"

Bailey's hand dropped back to the saddle horn. Zach guided Reliant to the river's edge and let him step into the rushing water to feel the bottom. Then he guided the horse back to the bank and turned him around.

"Yah! Yah! Yah!" He spurred the bay and Reliant burst toward the bank and plunged into the river.

Water splashed into Bailey's mouth and eyes and down her throat. She sputtered to breathe. The river was frigid, the current as strong as she'd been warned; she could hear the gush of the water as it swished by. She'd never been more terrified in her life, not even when she fell down the muddy ravine.

Once under way, Zach continued to urge the bay forward, pushing him to give it his all. Quickly, his hooves lost touch with the bottom and he began to tread water. Bailey held on with all her might. How could Zach have carried her across the river while she was unconscious? She tried to be alert, to somehow help, but all she could do was hold on for dear life. When the horse began to swim, his head came up and his back settled into the water. Bailey and Zach were waist high in rushing water. Zach seemed calm, his steady encouragement to his horse was the only sound he made.

After what seemed like an eternity, the heavily breathing horse reached solid footing. Reliant took another step, then another, only twenty feet more and they'd be out of the water. Relieved, Bailey dared to glance around and see what they had just endured. What she saw instead sent a flash of terror through her soul. A solid log, thick and heavy, hurtled toward them with the current; a large branch still holding leaves protruded out from its side.

Bailey lifted a foot to push the log around them, but she wasn't fast enough. The force of the blow knocked Zach out of the saddle and into the water. The slack in the rope wrapped around the jutting branch and dragged Zach under.

Bailey did the only thing she could think of to save him.

She jumped in, too.

Chapter 9

BAILEY SURFACED QUICKLY. She needed to work fast to keep Zach from being pushed underwater and possibly trapped by the tree. Zach had been swept off the horse's back to their left. Bailey had jumped into the river on the opposite side, so Reliant was between her and the rancher. She braced herself against the horse's neck, hoping to put a solid object between Zach and herself. If she didn't act quickly, she'd also be swept away since they were tied together.

She still couldn't see Zach as she bounced in the current, but she heard his call as the force of the river continued to press down on both of them. Bailey knew she didn't have the strength to pull him from the water herself, but his horse did. She urged Reliant forward and the tired animal continued to move toward the shore.

As soon as she felt the river bottom against her feet, Bailey tugged on the bay's reins to slow him, then struggled to maneuver underneath and around his neck. The rope began to pull as the river carried Zach farther away. She reached for the saddle horn and wrapped the remaining slack in the rope around it.

Reliant resumed his steady movement toward the shore. Bailey searched the frantic river for Zach. He was less than ten feet away, but she couldn't let go of the horse's neck. She couldn't reach him through the rushing water without being swept away, too.

A few more steps and Reliant was close to dry ground. Bailey urged him forward until Zach was out of the water. Finally, the horse stopped, lowered his head, and looked back toward his master. She quickly untied her end of the rope and ran to Zach. Bailey knelt, checked his pulse, and breathed a sigh of relief that he was alive and conscious. Zach struggled to sit up, sputtered, and leaned away to cough the water from his lungs.

"You saved my life." His breath came in ragged gasps.

Bailey was breathing just as hard as she returned his stare. She shook her head. "No, Reliant saved your life. I just helped out."

Zach considered his weary horse, then Bailey. "I guess we're even. Reliant and I saved your life, now you and he saved mine."

She wiped water from her eyes with a soggy sleeve. "Yep. I guess we're even."

A short while later Bailey held her fingers out and warmed them in front of a small fire. She could still hear the loud cry of the rushing water through the small copse of trees. She shuddered, and pushed away the nagging thoughts of how close they had come to drowning. Why had she been stubborn beyond reason? They never should have attempted to cross that river. Never. It was illogical, and she had always prided herself on being painstakingly rational.

Zach had almost drowned, but now he was the one caring for her. Once he had regained his breath, Zach settled her in this small clearing and set about collecting an armload of firewood. Most of it was damp from the past rain, but there was enough for a tiny flame. Thanks to the contents of a tightly sealed match tin in Zach's saddlebag, he managed to get some of the damp grass and leaves to catch, followed by scrub, then the rest of the fire.

The smell of wet horse, human, fabric, and leather mingled with the dank fragrance of the trees, leaves, and ground. Everything had been soaked, their clothes, the saddle, the horse, even a blanket Zach kept tightly rolled and attached under the cantle of his saddle. He had unrolled it and hung it over a low tree limb to dry. It was still cloudy but the afternoon sun shone through the trees above, and its rays reached down and added to the fire's warmth.

Reliant grazed in the sun just a short distance away. Zach had unsaddled the horse and rubbed him dry with handfuls of grass. The horse seemed appreciative of the attention, but he acted as if he'd crossed rivers like that on a daily basis. Every so often, he would wander a bit too far off, and Zach would softly whistle a short tune without looking up. The horse would immediately turn and begin grazing back toward them. Too bad Plug hadn't been so well trained, Bailey thought wryly.

Zach had positioned Reliant's saddle in the sun so the wet parts of it could dry. He now stood by it, unloading his rifle. The Winchester carbine, he had assured her, would hold up under the worst of circumstances, including a little river water. Once he finished, he rested the rifle against his saddle. With a quick nod in her direction, he headed through the trees back toward the river.

Bailey considered the sound of the rushing water and couldn't help but worry about the return trip. This whole mess was her fault, after all. She'd wanted her belongings and was willing to risk her life for them, but she hadn't planned to include anyone else in the danger. Not Faith, Hope, nor Charity, and not their brother.

When Zach had shown her how vicious the river was, she'd been ready to force herself to accept the necessary delay. Then this handsome rancher, a virtual stranger, had taken pity on her plight and agreed to the dangerous journey across the river. Bailey pulled her knees to her chest, wrapped her arms around them, and lowered her head. Zach and his aptly named horse had almost been killed because of her stubbornness, because of her rash, emotional behavior. She was so frightened of being stranded in this world, this century, that she had lost her cool. She'd lost her normal calm thought process and reacted impetuously. Look where it had gotten them. Wet and almost drowned.

"Found it."

Bailey glanced up to see Zach approaching with a black hat in his hand. It was wet, dirty, and practically flat. "Is it salvageable?"

"Hell, this hat's been through worse things than a swim down a river." Zach's pleasantness grated on Bailey's nerves.

How could he be so . . . so calm, when he'd almost drowned? She watched as Zach studied his hat, trying to work it back into shape. His shirt was hanging on a branch close to the fire so it could dry. He was bare-skinned, his muscled chest smooth and dark. This was no farmer's tan as Bailey had wondered that first day. From what she could see, the bronzed tan colored his torso then dipped down below the waistband of his jeans and rested just below his navel. The jeans were still damp, and clung to the lower half of his body, outlining his powerful thighs. Bailey couldn't help but notice a narrow scattering of dark hair that seductively drew her attention toward his narrow hips.

After she'd almost tossed him in the mud earlier, he'd been so bold, practically assuring her that he had every intention of seducing her sometime in the future. As she watched him now, she couldn't deny that the thought held some pretty obvious attractions.

She mentally shook herself to regain a bit of self-control and drew her attention back to his face. He returned her steady gaze, unblinking. She realized that he had been considering her as she considered him. Bailey felt the heat rise in embarrassment. Zach hung his soggy hat on a tree limb close to the fire and boldly approached her.

"Take off your shirt," he commanded, "then your pants and boots."

"I beg your pardon?"

"You heard me. Take off your shirt."

Bailey stared up at him, shocked by his words, unsure of what he intended. She'd be damned if she'd let him think she was frightened. She mustered every bit of bravado that she had. "One step closer and you'll be back in the river, mister."

He looked at her blankly, then grinned like a sly polecat. "Calm down, *Miss Cooper*. It's not what you think." He reached for his shirt. "This is almost dry. I want you to put it on and give your clothes a turn in the sun. If not, you'll turn to ice when it gets dark."

"What about your pants? They haven't dried yet."

Zach held the shirt in front of him and reached for his belt buckle. His hand hesitated. "You really want me to take them off?"

Bailey flushed again. She glanced down at the heavy wet fabric of his jeans and thought about the lean muscles it covered. "That won't be necessary. I'll wear your shirt. Now turn your back."

He handed her the sun-warmed fabric then did as she was told. Quickly, Bailey slipped out of her dripping chambray blouse and sticky jeans. She wasn't about to take off her bra and panties. There was no sense in asking for trouble.

Zach's shoulders were so broad that the shirt practically

swallowed her; it buttoned well past her hips and hung almost to her knees. She was decent at least. Bailey carefully walked around him and placed her clothes over the same tree branch. Her bare legs accidentally brushed against him as she pushed by. When she finally turned around, he no longer stood waiting.

Zach strode up the riverbank, away from her, as fast as his feet could move. He didn't think he could take much more. First, she'd caught him off guard as she openly admired his body when he walked up with his hat. He'd meant to make her blush with his equally bold perusal, but once again, she twisted the conversation until she was the one in control.

To top that, he realized as he sat down on a fallen tree trunk a goodly distance from the woman, he had asked—no, demanded—that she remove her clothing and wear his shirt until her own could dry. He never actually expected the aggravating woman to obey him, much less discard her wet jeans, too. How did he know she'd look so irresistibly inviting? The very instant she walked around him and he got a glimpse of her glorious bare legs, he thought he would melt. Actually, that wasn't the right word. He thought he'd burst if he got any harder. He'd had to hightail it out of there before she turned around and caught him staring like a teetotaler in a saloon. Otherwise, he might have had to rip his shirt off of her and tumble her to the ground.

His mood wasn't much better an hour or so later as he returned to the clearing. He'd had about all the teasing a sane man could tolerate in one afternoon, yet he knew he had to go back for more. He cast a lingering doubt at the sun overhead. There was enough daylight left to ride Reliant down to the ravine and check for her traveling bag, but there was no way they could make it back across the river before sundown. And, after the last fiasco, he wasn't about to cross it in the dark. They'd have to camp here for tonight and head back to the ranch first thing in the morning. He didn't like being on Thompson's land at all, though, especially after the sun went down. No telling what Thompson or his men might do if they found them.

He whistled to his horse, who immediately answered the command. Zach put Reliant's bridle back on, looped a coil of rope around the horse's neck, then led him toward Bailey. They would ride bareback the relatively short distance to the ravine, look for her traveling bag, then be back to the river by dark. If they found it, she'd be satisfied and their mission would be over. If they didn't, she'd have some explaining to do and he wasn't leaving until he had answers.

He had jumped up on Reliant's back and silently offered a hand to Bailey. Zach felt the heat of her skin as she took hold and he pulled her up behind him. Zach inwardly groaned to feel Bailey riding so close against his bare shoulders. She didn't have on enough cloth to dust a fiddle, and he could actually feel the peak of each of her breasts through the thin fabric of his borrowed shirt. Her arms were once again wrapped around his waist, her bare legs nestled full-length against his. It was heavenly torture, and he'd inflicted it on himself. If he died right at this moment, he'd be one frustrated man.

Half an hour later, Zach guided his horse up to the muddy area overlooking the craggy divide. They weren't in the mountains, but the wind had carved a treacherous gully on this hill. The pouring rain over the past three weeks had made it muddy and dangerous. During the daylight, it looked less threatening than it had the evening he rescued her. Zach reined Reliant to a halt and quickly dismounted, leaving Bailey to her own devices. There was no way he could watch, much less assist, as she slipped off the horse and slid those creamy legs down to touch the ground. When she finally joined him at the side of the ravine, Zach avoided her eyes and glanced back at Reliant, who evenly returned his stare. If ever a horse could smile, his faithful mount was doing it.

"Look!" Bailey cried suddenly. She pointed toward the side of the clearing almost behind them, well away from the edge of the ravine. "It's the almanac." She rushed to a dark book lying open in the dirt, picked it up, and held it toward him. She started to laugh. "You would think as much as I paid for this old book, I'd be furious that someone tossed it aside. But," she looked up at him and smiled, "I've never been more glad to see something in my life. You have to believe me now, Zach. I may have had a head injury, but I'm not crazy. I've been telling the truth. I am from the future. This proves it."

She brought the book closer and handed it to Zach. "*Old Farmer's Almanac*," he read aloud. "*1900 Edition*." He looked from the book to Bailey and back to the book, searching for the answer to his unasked question. How could anyone possess a book that hadn't yet been printed?

Unless it was a misprint.

Unless it was a fraud.

Unless . . .

Unless she is telling the truth. Unless this person is from the future. But that's impossible, isn't it?

"Here," Bailey said, interrupting his shock. "Let's find the weather reports from 1878. It'll tell you what to expect this winter, maybe even when the rains will let up."

"No," Zach snapped before she could open it. "I don't know what's going on here, but I don't like it at all. There is no way you can be from the future. I don't care what you say or what you show me. I don't believe it." Zach threw the book back at her as if it burned.

Confused, Bailey caught it, then retreated to the other objects strewn nearby. Zach had seen the surprise and hurt on her face at his rejection. The sweet closeness they had felt after their near brush with death suddenly evaporated into bitter distance. He watched her kneel to the ground.

"Someone must have already found the bag," she said softly. Her voice was soft and timid. It was as if she didn't trust him enough to share too much. He hated that, but couldn't she understand the impossibility of what she expected him to believe? "I hope whoever took my backpack enjoyed my lunch. I had a sandwich in this."

Zach reached for the small clear bag she offered. It was made of an odd, slick material that was as thin as paper, but wasn't quite paper. It wasn't fabric either. He stared at it curiously.

Bailey reached for a leather glove lying in the mud, and its mate a short distance away. The farthest looked as if it had been tried on, then tossed away. She quickly moved a few more feet to retrieve something else. It was obviously something she didn't want him to see because she tried, covertly, to hide it inside the pocket of his shirt. He held out his hand for her to show him. She shook her head. "It's nothing, Zach. I promise." He advanced forward, palm extended. "It's a woman thing. You really don't want to know."

"Yes, I do. Either hand it here, or I come get it."

"You wouldn't dare."

"At this point, Bailey, I'd just about dare anything." He continued to walk toward her. "Now give it to me."

"Don't say I didn't warn you." She reached into the pocket and slowly pulled out another bag of the same clear material. In it were two white cylindrical objects wrapped in soft paper. There was light blue printing on the side, but it meant nothing to him.

"Cigars?"

"No, not quite," she stammered. "Please, Zach, you really don't want me to explain. They're personal." He found it odd that these two little things could create such tension in this normally fearless redhead.

Was it fear, though? She was acting like his sisters did when they were . . . well, *embarrassed*. Instinct told him to drop the issue. He handed the unusual objects back to her. He'd figure out the secret later.

Clearly relieved, Bailey returned them to the bag, then put it in the pocket of his shirt. She walked over to the edge of the ravine and bent slightly forward to peer over the edge. "This was right where my backpack landed after the fog dissipated," she called to him. "It was right down there on that piece of exposed granite. There's nothing there now." Her voice was tremendously sad.

The late afternoon sun made his shirt almost transparent, illustrating every sensuous curve of her body. She looked so inviting yet so despondent. The protector in him wanted to comfort her as he had before they crossed the river. He knew if he reached for her, he wouldn't stop at just comforting. He'd take her right here by the ravine, then he'd push for the truth about who she really was. He'd use their growing attraction to get what he wanted—and in more ways than one. That wouldn't be fair to either of them.

"Get away from the edge. You'll fall again." He had spoken more sharply than he'd intended, but the sight of the book still in her hand bothered him more than he cared to admit. She had told him that he'd find an almanac from the future in her bag, and she'd willingly given it to him just as she said she would. Why?

He was being forced to make a decision on the reality of something he'd never even thought about. *Could* a person drop back into another time? If it was a genuine almanac, it would contain weather and crop reports and other information. If it was an almanac from the future it would have documented the heavy rains and harsh snows over the next twenty years. Knowing details like that would make a man extremely successful, and rich and powerful. That alone was certainly intriguing, but there had to be a catch.

"Bailey." He squatted down and propped his elbows on his knees. "If that almanac tells what's going to happen in the future, why are you willing to give it to me? Whether it's actually true or not, you could probably sell it for more money than I could pay you. Why me?"

"Why not?" she answered simply. "In my time, it's nothing but an old book. Its value comes from surviving over time. For you, it could be the success or failure of the Double Bar G. If giving you the almanac helps me get home, then we've both profited, haven't we? Besides, you're the only genuine Wyoming rancher I know, and you and your sisters have been kind to me. Well, at least you have. Your sisters . . ." She tried to lighten the mood between them.

Zach nodded. It was a difficult admission, especially after he'd snapped at her only minutes before. He glanced toward the ravine. "Whoever took your traveling bag must have taken everything they wanted. What else did you have in it?" He still didn't know what to think, but it was obvious that there was a bag somewhere.

"Let's see, my phone, my wallet with my driver's license, money and credit cards, my map . . ."

"Map?"

"Yes, a topographical map of Medicine Mountain. I bought it at a sporting goods store before I decided to hike up to the monument. They map out the landscape rather than the roads. It helps when you're hiking off the beaten trail."

"Bailey, all maps are of the land."

"I guess in this time, you're right. Where I'm from, though, the maps now consist of cities, interstates, streets, and roads. People rarely travel by foot anymore, and even less by horseback. They drive cars. Kind of like a horseless carriage. I think they may have already been invented or are just about to be, although I have no idea where."

Zach looked puzzled but said nothing as he moved toward Reliant and gathered the horse's reins. He jumped up on his back in one simple motion. Bailey put the empty bag and her keys in the shirt pocket. She handed Zach the almanac, then stepped near the horse and allowed him to help her up.

There was an air of sad acceptance about her, Zach noted. She might have believed this was her one shot to prove she was from the future and to find her way home. She had shown him that there was at least something to her story, and he wasn't acting very gentlemanly about it either.

He wished he could offer some type of comfort, but he didn't know how. To do so would mean he believed her story of being from the future.

He wasn't ready to go that far.

At least not yet.

Chapter 10

ZACH HAD BEEN sullen since they left the ravine. Bailey sat quietly behind him on the horse, trying her best not to touch him as they headed back to the makeshift camp. It was dusk. The chirping crickets kept time with Reliant's slow steady gait. When Zach finally signaled the horse to stop, Bailey slid off unassisted and headed for her clothes that still hung on the low branches. Although the fire was low, her blouse was pretty well dry. The fabric was stiff and scratchy. Her jeans were still damp, but they'd just have to do. There was no way she was wearing Zach's shirt a second longer than necessary.

"How long will it take us to get back to the ranch?" she asked, watching Zach dismount and remove the horse's bridle.

"We'll head out at first light. We pushed our luck crossing the river in daylight, there's no sense taking another foolish chance by crossing at night."

Bailey felt his gaze as she disappeared into the cover of the trees to change back into her clothes. "You mean we're going to sleep out here in the open? Together?"

He didn't answer until she'd returned to the clearing. He politely took his proffered shirt from Bailey, his eyes skimming over her rumpled clothes as he did. "Looks that way, ma'am. I set a trap earlier. I'm going to see whether we're eating roasted rabbit or beef jerky for supper."

Bailey watched his retreating back without a word. As far as she was concerned, beef jerky would be fine. She had managed to make it her entire thirty-five years without eating rabbit. She didn't plan to start now, thank you very much.

She had to admit to herself that when the shock finally wore off, when she really accepted the fact that she was in 1878 Wyoming, she had thought there was an exciting feel to this time. After all, she was in the rugged West with a real rancher, a man's man, a genuine cowboy. She'd thought there was something sweetly romantic about the green satin dress and passing an evening on the porch swing with a handsome stranger. She'd thought it exciting and heroic the way Zach had come to her rescue and how he had braved the river, even though it was dangerous, just for her.

Today had changed all that. Yesterday she'd had a chance of going home, she could afford to think along those pleasant lines. Now that had dwindled and with it went any romantic notions about this time. Life was hard here, and she wasn't made for it.

Bailey spread Reliant's saddle pad on the ground close to the warmth of the fire and sat down on it. Earlier this afternoon she might have been intrigued by the idea of spending a night in the wilderness with Zach Gooden. Now she wasn't so sure.

Whatever was brewing between them, be it plain lust or something more, had definitely been dashed at the ravine.

Just as much as she needed him to believe what she said was true, he needed for it not to be so. She reached up to touch the healing gash on her head. Another few days and it would probably be gone. Bailey leaned back on her hands, dropped her head, and closed her eyes. She'd never been one for co-incidence; being a believer in facts prevented her from such. But, if it was the prayer to Dark Fawn that had brought her here, was it also possible that the same prayer was holding her here? She had prayed for faith, hope, and charity. Was it mere coincidence that there were suddenly three similarly named girls in her life? Was she here to help them, as Zach had asked? He had already made it clear that taking her to Medicine Mountain was out of the question. Crossing a swollen river was one thing, he had said, but possible scalp-ing was another. She would find her own way, no doubt of that, but even if she did, would Dark Fawn actually let her go home? It did seem to come down to letting her go home, since she had not a clue about how to manage it herself, even when she got to Medicine Mountain.

It looked as if becoming a female role model for Faith, Hope, and Charity was about her only option. She had no money, no identification, and no chance of surviving on her own without this family. She could probably do some re-search and find out how to become a proper 1878 attorney, but even that would take time. She had to support herself in the meantime. Even though Wyoming was said to be a pro-gressive state, it was still a man's world.

She heard a rustle just before Zach walked through the cottonwoods holding the carcass of a rabbit. Although he had already cleaned and gutted it, Bailey still had to turn away when he drew near the fire. If Zach noticed her queasi-ness, he said nothing as he placed the rabbit on a spit di-rectly over the fire.

Yes, she'd certainly been wrong. There was nothing romantic about this time, not when it came to catching, cleaning, and cooking Thumper straight from the forest.

It was completely dark now. Bailey looked up at the sky; several stars twinkled in the light. "I can't believe it's not raining," she murmured. "Perhaps it's going to let up." Zach followed her gaze upward.

"Isn't it amazing about the moon and the stars?" she asked.

"What's that?"

"They're probably the only constant things in this universe. No matter what time you're in, they're still the same. Sometimes, back home in Memphis, I'd drive my car way outside of town, far away from the noise and the lights, just to see how bright the moon and stars could get. I always marveled at the clarity. Even so, they were never this bright."

Zach continued to stare at the stars without speaking. Bailey wished he would say something. Anything. She reached for the almanac and flipped through the pages. Zach had yet to pick it up and look at it.

"I understand why you're reluctant to look at this," she said. "If you do, you have to make a choice whether or not to believe what it says. If you choose to believe it and make preparations based on what is recorded in the book, then you also have to admit I am who I claim."

"Sometimes, Bailey, it's not good to tell a man what he's thinking." He reached into his pocket, removed the clear plastic bag with the two tampons, and tossed the bag to her. She had obviously forgotten to take them from his shirt pocket when she'd given it back to him. "I have no idea what these are for, but I guess they belong to you," he said. Bailey was glad she sat just outside the light of the fire. Explaining the purpose of tampons to a virtual stranger would not be an easy task. She could do it if she had to, of course, but she didn't relish the thought.

There was no telling how long those tampons had been in

her backpack. She was always prepared in case of any emergency, and they rated right up there with her flashlight and compass.

The silence between them continued to grow awkward. Zach was stoic, merely nodding noncommittally each time she tried to draw him into a conversation. He slowly turned his dinner to let it cook over the fire. Each time she watched it turn, the more agitated she became.

Finally, she could stand it no more. She jumped to her feet and stomped over to Zach, who was sitting on a rock on the far side of the fire. She bent until her face was only a few inches from his. The surprise in his eyes was evident.

"First of all, I am *not* eating wild rabbit for dinner. I have never done so in my entire life. I refuse to start now. Beef jerky for me is just fine.

"Second, what the hell is your problem? I'm the one who is trapped where I don't belong. You're the one moping around like your life is over." She walked away, then spun around and paced back and forth like she did in the courtroom.

"Frankly, I don't care what you believe, because the problem is mine, not yours, and I *will* solve it. However, allow me to recount the facts for you. Five days ago, I was on vacation looking at an old Indian monument called the Medicine Wheel. I was in my time, 1999, minding my own business.

"At the urging of a nice old Indian man, I prayed to Dark Fawn, some Indian Spirit who grants the prayers of lonely women." Bailey stopped her pacing and pointed a finger at Zach. "And yes, I am a lonely woman. I *didn't want* to pray to her, I thought it might be irreverent since I'm not an Indian. The man assured me it was acceptable. So, innocent me asked Dark Fawn for faith, hope, and charity, three things I thought I'd need as a judge."

Bailey resumed her pacing. "Next, I found myself on the

side of some dangerous gully calling for help. You rescued me. Since I was unconscious, I did not know where you were taking me, or who you were for that matter. I learned I was at your ranch only when I regained consciousness the following morning. I thought I'd been visited by three beautiful angels during the night, but they turned out to be three troublesome teenagers conveniently named Faith, Hope, and Charity, who, it just so happens, need a governess, or whatever it is you want, in the worst way.

"I asked you for help. You refused. I tried to find some way to get home on my own, but I couldn't do it without assistance. You finally agreed to help me locate my belongings to prove to you who I am, only it was too late. Someone else had already taken them. Now, right this minute, somewhere out in that vast darkness is a person who doesn't have to be convinced my story is true because he or she has the evidence in front of them."

She stopped and again bent down inches away from his face. "Can you imagine his or her shock to see the color picture on my driver's license? What about my date of birth? Think he knows what a flashlight is? Or a cellular phone?"

Bailey turned back to her path. "It's a fact that I told you about the almanac two nights ago, long before you actually saw it. You didn't believe me, yet here it is. Now, for some strange reason, you're afraid to open it. Why? Because that means you'll have to admit my story is true, and that's too far-fetched for you to believe.

"Well listen, buddy, it's too far-fetched for me to believe, too. The only problem is that I'm the one living it." She stopped again, dead center in front of the rancher. "Now get over yourself and help me figure out what to do next."

Bailey knew her eyes flashed with passionate anger. The same thing happened every time she offered a closing argument. She couldn't help it, not then, not now, and especially not when the evidence was so damning.

Zach stared up at her. His expression divulged that he thought she was certifiable. She was used to that, too, especially from tired old judges who no longer cared about the lives of the children in their courtrooms.

"Look," Bailey sighed, "what you believe is up to you, but I need help. You mentioned a man, Tag, I think. Will he take me to the mountain? I have no money, gold, or whatever you guys use for currency, but the almanac has to be worth something. Since you don't believe it's of any value, you might as well give it back to me so I have something to barter with."

Seconds painfully dragged by as Bailey stood before him. She knew he was a smart man. He was struggling with the facts, and faced probably one of the biggest decisions in his life. When he finally spoke, his voice was so soft Bailey strained to hear.

"You're right, Bailey. There seems to be every indication that your story is true. The problem is I have no idea what I'm supposed to do. I'm anxious to study that almanac, but do I *really* want to know the future? Why was I the one who rescued you? You weren't on my land, and I shouldn't have even been nearby. Yet I'm the one who found you." He studied her face carefully, then Bailey saw a slight glimmer of amusement. "I'd certainly never deny that you are a lawyer. You'd make anyone stand up and pay attention."

Their gazes locked over the fire. In spite of all the bravado, Bailey had never been more frightened in her life. So, did he believe her or not? He still hadn't actually said, and the sheer unbelievability of the entire situation continued to loom over her. Then, ever so slowly, the corners of Zach's lips began to rise and Bailey heard a deep chuckle. The sound built until it burst forth into full-fledged laughter. She stared at him blankly, unsure of what he found so amusing. This was her life, after all. She didn't know whether to

be angry or join right in with the laughter. After a moment's
hesitation, the laughter won.

She sat down beside him and placed her injured hand on
his thigh. "This really is crazy, isn't it?" Zach reached across
with his far hand and covered her fingers with his own. He
nodded as their amusement died down. She returned her
gaze to the stars above, and sighed.

"Who'd have thought plain ordinary me would be swept
into such an adventure?"

"There is nothing plain or ordinary about you, Bailey.
Nothing at all." Zach released her hand and leisurely circled
his fingers up her arm. He didn't meet her gaze. Instead, he
stared at his deliberate action. Bailey's eyes were drawn
away from the stars to his face. Her skin tingled in the wake
of the warm connection. This man exuded the scent of all-
male. It combined with the faint smell of the rushing water,
the crackling fire, and the few evergreens nearby, enveloping
her with a sensation of the natural order of life. Man,
woman, darkness, starlight, warm fire, chilly breeze . . .

The sounds of the night grew quiet as she focused on how
his simple action felt. Only the chirp of the crickets remained. Their steady calls seemed to intensify as Bailey
closed her eyes to shut out everything except what his touch
did to her senses.

Zach lifted his hand and studiously drew it up to her neck
where it nestled just below her ear. Her skin instantly grew
cold when he removed his hand to release her hair from its
thick braid.

"You have the most beautiful hair," he whispered. "You
should never wear it up."

Bailey lifted her lids to meet his amber eyes. She could
see the image of the fire reflecting back in them. "I have to.
It's the only way people take me seriously."

"You're wrong. I've never met a woman I've taken more
seriously." His fingers ran through her mussed hair and en-

circled her shoulders. Unhurried, he pulled her body toward him, into his lap. He cradled her in his arms like a butterfly who could escape at any second.

Tenderly he leaned forward, his mouth only a hair's width from her lips. She felt the heat from his body, from his breath, as a tremor of anticipation ran through her. He'd kissed her two nights ago, but that was about control. This was different. This was about longing. The unsaid promise of his touch was almost more than she could bear.

She sighed, closing her eyes and waiting for their lips to meld.

Zach didn't move.

A vague aching feeling settled over her. Surely a man like Zach wouldn't play games, especially not after what they'd been through. He wanted her, he'd made that clear. She'd been equally direct about wanting him. Just when she could stand the anticipation no more, just before she could open her eyes in question, his lips brushed just below her ear. Her body tensed from the slow intensity then melted from the elation caused by his touch. He traced his lips up an down her neck, making her dizzy with his thoroughness.

Finally, when she felt she could stand it no more, Zach deliberately moved to kiss the sensitive skin around her anxious mouth. After what seemed forever, his lips joined hers. Bailey was so impatient from his methodical stalking, there was no way she could have resisted what he offered. No way she would have wanted to.

His tongue seductively played against the opening of her mouth until she answered his silent inquisition for more. The kiss became deeper, stronger, almost ravishing as Bailey's own desire fueled the burn. One of Zach's arms was wrapped around her back, drawing her closer to his chest. The other hand rested against her neck, holding her face close to his.

Bailey felt his hand drop from her collar. His fingers once

again began a slow exploration. This time, he encircled the buttons on her shirt just above her breasts. She longed for the heat from Zach's fingers to slip inside and rub the sensitive area just under the lace of her still-damp bra.

She grabbed his inquiring hand with her own and pressed it against the fabric of her blouse. Zach understood the silent message, undid the offending button, and reached inside. Bailey had never so fully realized the power of anticipation.

Suddenly, Zach stopped. His lips, although pressed against hers, stilled. His hand ceased its intimate exploration, his body tensed. Bailey jerked away and opened her eyes to see a steely resolve in his. Something was wrong.

Zach casually bent his head next to her ear; his voice tickled as he spoke. "Kiss me, Bailey, just as you did a minute ago. We're being watched."

Chapter 11

ZACH HELD FAST to the woman in his arms, giving her no time to voice fear as he tightened his hold. He kept his voice low, calm, and assuring. "I'm going to pick you up and carry you over to the saddle as if I'm going to lay you down and love you. I'll turn with my back toward where I think he is, and when I kneel, act like you're reaching for my bedroll. Instead, grab my carbine, hand it to me, and hit the ground. That's the most important part, Bailey. Get flat on the ground. He may start shooting."

Bailey silently nodded and slowly smiled. He saw she was careful not to give any indication of alarm. Zach squeezed her softly to offer courage. He didn't know who was out there, probably one of Thompson's men. Many of the neighboring ranchers were even restless about the situation. It should be obvious that Zach's experiment with hybrid cattle should have no effect on their own, but they had listened to

Thompson spew his anger about the Aberdeen for so long, they didn't know who to trust or what to believe.

It could even be Thompson himself out there. Once again, he was here on Thompson's land, doing things in the darkness that he probably shouldn't be doing. Thompson would have every right to object. Bailey wrapped her arms around Zach's neck as he lifted her in his arms and stood. He positioned himself so any potential gunfire would strike him before his beautiful redhead. Zach continued to stroke Bailey's ear with his lips while he covertly studied the area where he had seen the strike of a match and the lighting of a cigarette. He moved toward the saddle and his belongings as if he were intensely anxious to culminate what they had started.

"Grab the bedroll, woman," he commanded in a gruff voice, just loud enough to be heard across the small clearing. Zach knelt and Bailey released her hands from his neck. Right on cue, she kissed him in return. Her hands shook, and Zach knew she was frightened. This was all his fault. Against his better judgment, he'd allowed himself to soften at her distress. Had he been more unsympathetic, they would not have crossed the river to search for her bag. They would both be safely at the ranch watching the stars from the porch swing. Perhaps he'd have taken her in his arms and carried her up the stairs to his bedroom instead of moving over to get his rifle. Perhaps they wouldn't have been interrupted. Perhaps Bailey would have trembled because of what he'd have done to her magnificent body, not due to a stranger hiding in the darkness.

Bailey found the roll and held it up to shake it open. At the same time, she leaned forward and located the wooden butt of the rifle. She pulled it straight back, felt it connect with Zach's waiting hand, then dropped from his arms and did a forward roll, flat on the ground beside the saddle.

Zach immediately turned, dropped to the ground, cocked the trigger and aimed the carbine toward the far side of the clearing. "Stupid thing to light a cigarette in the dark, especially when you're trying to sneak up on someone. Come out now or I start shooting."

He could see the tiny glow of the cigarette. It grew brighter as the person slowly took a pull. The seconds dragged by like minutes before it was tossed down and snubbed out. Zach heard the shuffle of leaves, and a man moved out from hiding, leading a large black horse.

"Wasn't stalking you, Gooden, just trying to be a gentleman and warn you of my presence before things got hot and heavy between you and . . ." Sloan Thompson nodded toward Bailey, still on the ground, "your woman."

She lifted her head and steadily returned his appraisal. She didn't blush or look away, but stared back at him, unblinking. Zach was proud. His woman didn't cower from fear, she faced it head-on. He liked that.

"What do you want, Thompson?" Zach asked. His finger still rested on the rifle's trigger.

"I'm unarmed."

Zach considered the man before him. Why would Sloan Thompson be unarmed in the presence of a man who'd threatened to kill his father? They both knew that Zach had the upper hand, but was he willing to set it aside so readily? "I suppose if your business was to shoot, you'd have done it before I had my gun handy."

Zach uncocked the rifle and pointed it toward the ground, although he didn't release his hold on the trigger. Sloan Thompson was still a stranger in these parts. No one knew his past, and until recently Thompson didn't talk about his eldest son at all.

Sloan slowly approached the campfire and sat on the log Zach had used to dry his gear that afternoon. "I didn't want to interrupt what was going on. You two seemed to be getting to know each other right well. But, if you had heard me, it might have been shoot first, ask questions later. I'm not anxious to get a bullet in the back."

"I don't shoot men in the back, Thompson. You've got me confused with your pa."

Sloan returned Zach's distasteful glare. "Don't say." He shook his head as if correcting a mental error, then quietly studied the burning fire. Zach sensed there was controlled anger underneath the surface. Somehow, though, he doubted that he and Bailey were the reason.

"I struck the match hoping to tactfully get your attention off your lovely lady. I'd about decided to leave and let you two get on with business."

Bailey rose from her spot by the saddle and walked toward Zach. She was cautious but also clearly interested in why Sloan had gone to such trouble to be polite.

"Since I'm supposed to be on watch," Sloan continued, "I guess I need to ask the obvious. What are you doing out this late and why are you on J.T.'s land?"

"We were looking for my backpack. I lost it when I slipped down the ravine," Bailey answered before Zach could speak.

Zach released the rifle and leaned it against the saddle. Sloan Thompson didn't appear to be out to kill. Not tonight, at least. "She's right. We ran into trouble crossing the river about mid-afternoon. I decided not to cross it again in the dark. We'll head back at first light."

Sloan glanced through the darkness toward the river. He didn't comment. Instead, he reached inside a pocket for his packet of tobacco. His attention then focused on rolling another cigarette.

Zach pulled Bailey's hand and they both sat down on the same rock they'd just vacated. Zach stared at Sloan across the crackling fire. He was curious. Even though he was J.T.'s eldest, the man had made an honest effort to get their attention. He seemed to have something to say, and there was no harm in listening.

"Find your pack?" Sloan asked Bailey as he completed the cigarette and lifted it to his mouth. He pulled a match from the same pocket and struck it on the sole of his boot.

"No, someone had already beaten us to it."

"I doubt it was any of the hands; I would have heard. There was an old drifter with a white donkey passing across the ranch early this morning. The boys called him Tag. Said he was on his way to Box Bend."

Zach glanced at Bailey, knowing she recognized the name. A sudden emptiness enveloped him as he saw the pleased look on her face. He'd selfishly hoped Tag wouldn't show up for several weeks yet. She claimed that "time was of the essence," yet he wasn't so sure. If she had no family, why was it so all-fire important that she get home immediately? For a job? She had a job, taking care of his sisters. If anyone could help them, it would be this woman. At first, he'd wanted her around if only for that reason. Then, he had kissed her, and she had kissed him back with equal abandon. The reasons were multiplying.

He pushed aside such worrisome thoughts. Of course she wanted to go home, and he couldn't prevent her from doing so. "Tag's harmless enough," Zach said. "Although I'm not sure about his ornery donkey. Mildred's kicked me one too many times. Those two are so used to climbing up and down mountains mining for gold, Tag would've had no trouble getting to your bag."

Bailey nodded and steadily met his gaze. Was that relief he saw in her eyes, or reluctance?

Sloan coughed slightly to remind them of his presence. "Gooden, I'd planned to meet up with you next time I saw you in town, but since you're here, now's as good a time as any."

Zach focused his attention on Sloan, who took a long drag

on his cigarette. He watched as the man stared into the fire, obviously trying to weigh his next words with care. Zach rose, stoked the flames, and added several more branches. "I'm listening."

"J.T. has to be stopped."

"I know that, I'm surprised to hear you agree."

He shrugged. "I have reason enough. I heard he killed your pa."

Zach glanced toward Bailey at her quick intake of breath. He nodded imperceptibly. "That's what they say. No one can prove it, though. He claims he won the Double Bar G in a poker game. My pa claimed J.T. cheated. Two weeks later, my pa was found dead, knifed in the back with cards in his pocket. The cards were supposedly the same ones J.T. held in the game."

"Were there any witnesses?" Bailey interjected. Zach could almost see the wheels begin to turn as she processed all the information.

"No. They found him down near the windmill where I found you this afternoon. There were some neighboring ranchers in the saloon that night who overheard everything, but the other two men in the game were just passing through. They were long gone by the time of the murder. That's why it was my father's word against J.T.'s word."

Zach turned back toward Sloan. "That doesn't explain why you think J.T. is up to no good. You're a stranger to these parts, and you're his son."

"A man can't help who sired him," he replied with a shrug. "Thanks to him, I've been a stranger everywhere." Sloan tightened his mouth as if he'd said too much already. He rose and headed to his horse.

"I haven't quite figured out what he's up to, but no good will come from it. He's irrational when it comes to your bulls. He searched three states to find me and spent six months to convince me to come. Never said he wanted to make amends for the past, just that I was the best and he'd pay me well. Joe Junior's about as cross as a snapping turtle. Thinks I'm here to take over the ranch. Hell, I don't know the first thing about being a rancher. It's the last thing I want to do."

"Why should I trust you?" Zach asked.

"No reason that I see," replied Sloan. "I didn't come out here asking you to, either. Just wanted you to know not everyone is your enemy. The way I figure, J.T. is either going to try and convince me to solve his problem, or he's going to take care of it himself and let me hang for it. That won't happen."

"Why would you hang for it, Mr. Thompson? Are you talking about murder?" Bailey studied the mysterious stranger.

Sloan was silent for a long moment. Zach had begun to doubt he was going to give Bailey an answer, an answer he'd also like to hear. Finally, Sloan considered Bailey steadily, then spoke carefully. "I go by Sloan, ma'am. I'm not real proud of the rest of it as I'm sure you've figured. Tempers are too short between J.T. and another fella right now. It doesn't all have to do with you, the Goodens, or the Double Bar G and the hybrids. I mean to stop J.T. I just haven't decided how."

Zach stood as Sloan Thompson mounted the black animal then touched the tip of his hat and reined the horse back into the darkness.

"He didn't answer my question," Bailey said as she turned toward Zach.

Zach shook his head. "I don't trust him. There has to be something in it for him. Why else would a stranger care about what happens to my family?"

"I'm a stranger, and I care," Bailey offered. She stood beside him and touched his arm. "I've watched people lie on the stand for years. No one could be more naturally skeptical than me. There's something about him, though, maybe his loner persona, that makes me think he's telling the truth."

"Could be. More than likely, though, J.T. pressed his eldest into extending the proverbial olive branch so I would lower my guard. J.T. has a way of manipulating things to suit him." Zach studied the darkness where the man and the horse had disappeared. He'd always been a good judge of character, and he agreed with Bailey's assessment. Even so, he had no intention of accepting Sloan's statements at face value. There was potentially too much to be won or lost.

"Why do you think J.T. went to the trouble of tracking down his son?"

"That I don't know. He's got something planned, though."

"Why wouldn't he consider having Joe Junior marry one of your sisters? Another few years and you might have been family. He could have gotten at least some of the ranch that way. Been a heck of a lot easier."

"Hadn't thought about that, but you're right. I still think of my sisters as little girls, but they're not really. Besides, Pa left the Double Bar G to me. I plan to give the girls their share when it's time, but it's not something anyone can force me to do." Zach rose and walked to the edge of the clearing where Sloan had disappeared. He breathed deeply, then exhaled. "You know, nowadays it's not always easy to tell who are your friends and who are your enemies."

"It's still the same in my time, too. Especially when you work with so many malfeasants who prey on innocent children. It's hard not to be discouraged."

"What about you, Bailey? Can I trust you? Can I believe you are who you say you are? Can I believe that you are from the future?"

"I've answered those questions already, Zach. You have to decide whether or not to accept me as I am. I can't help you with that." Her voice was soft yet her tone was firm, and there was an air of resignation about her.

Zach walked over to the fire and the now burnt rabbit. He reached into his saddlebag, then offered Bailey a piece of cold jerky. She stared at the dried beef for a long moment, then shook her head. He wasn't hungry either.

He picked up the bedroll and straightened it out on the ground without looking at the woman standing near. He knew if he did he would want to forget the questions he'd asked. He would want to sweep her into his arms, to resume where they had left off earlier, and that wasn't fair to either of them. She'd been so certain that she would find her traveling bag, but they hadn't. She'd been so certain he would believe her story once he saw the almanac, but he hadn't. Now she couldn't help but be distraught. The heat of the moment had cooled, and he still wasn't certain what he believed, no matter what he'd said earlier.

Whether Thompson's eldest son was straight as an arrow or crooked as a knotted pine, he really had done them both a favor when he interrupted. This beautiful stranger had pushed him to the brink with desire, and she was intent on getting home. It didn't appear that she would rest until she did. That being the case, he would take her to Medicine Mountain himself. He was too involved. He cared too much. There was no way he could let her go alone with only Tag for protection. Tag was a good guide, but Zach had come to think of Bailey as his. If she thought she had to go back to her time, he would make sure she got what she wanted.

"You go ahead and get some rest," he said more curtly than he intended. He reached for the almanac and moved closer to the fire. He felt Bailey staring at him as he opened it to the first page. She studied him for a moment, then dragged the bedroll to the opposite side. Without looking his way, she lay down and presented her back to him. Her thick hair spread out behind her, reminding him how he wanted to unbraid it and wrap it around both of them.

A lonely owl hooted in the distance.

It was going to be a long night.

Chapter 12

A SHARP NOISE woke Bailey from deep sleep.

She sat up and stared, confused by her surroundings. It was intensely dark despite a bright moon and twinkling stars. For a few long seconds she couldn't recall where she was or what she was doing sleeping outside. Then she remembered. The ravine, the fall, her rescue, the year. She remembered it all.

"Zach?" She didn't know where the rancher had intended sleeping, but he was no longer by the fire. It had burned down until it was just glowing embers. She could barely see Reliant, who stood at the edge of the clearing saddled and ready to ride. Bailey was certain the horse had been tethered before she had gone to sleep, and unsaddled. At least she thought he was.

She swung around at the sound of rustling leaves and breaking branches just beyond the glow of the fire. Before she could react, Zach entered the clearing carrying a small armload of wood. He didn't notice that she was awake but went straight to the flame and added several pieces. After a minute, the wood ignited and began to burn.

"That's wonderful," she murmured as the fire began to build. "I'm freezing."

Zach met her sleepy gaze. "It'll be light in a couple of hours and we'll head home. Get some rest."

"I can't. It's too cold." She wrapped the thin blanket tight about her shoulders. "Come keep me warm. We can share body heat."

He hesitated, then slowly closed the gap between them. "You know as well as I do that me keeping you warm isn't a good idea, Bailey," he said as he settled down beside her.

"I know, but I'm freezing. Just keep your hands to yourself." They both lay back on the ground and Bailey nestled her back against Zach's chest. She closed her eyes and enjoyed the feel of his body resting full length against hers. Even their legs entwined in a perfect match.

"Where were you? I woke, and you were gone," Bailey asked softly as their warmth began to envelop them.

"Went to gather firewood. Did you miss me?" He gently leaned forward and kissed her earlobe, then moved down to nuzzle her neck. Bailey felt the prickly sensation of desire consume her entire body as Zach stroked her hair away from her ear, then outlined it with his lips.

She tried to relax and enjoy the sensation but something didn't seem right. Why would he have saddled Reliant just to get firewood? Had he ridden somewhere else? It was difficult to concentrate with him awakening such intense feelings deep in her body, but the investigator in her knew there was more to it than just that. All the memories of last night tumbled into her already jumbled thoughts. Had he decided to follow Sloan? Wherever he had been, he didn't seem anxious to share it with her.

"Stop, Zach."

She heard a deep sigh as he pulled apart but not completely away. "Why? You wanted me to get you warm."

"Yes, I did. But now I agree it wasn't such a good idea. We're out under the stars in the wee hours of the morning. It would be really easy for both of us to forget who we are and even why we're out here. There's too much that separates us. Once the sun comes up, we'll go back to being who we really are. I truly understand why you can't believe who I am, and at the same time I can't let myself begin to care for someone who lives a century before me."

He gathered her close in his arms and pulled her back against him. "Does the past really matter, Bailey? Can't you just make your future here with us? With me?"

Indecision gathered in her heart. Dark Fawn was not a kind spirit at all. She was mean and bitter to taunt Bailey with something she could never have. Not in her own lifetime, and not in this one either. "You don't know how much I wish that could be, Zach. All my life I've wanted what you have. I've wanted a family, roots, somewhere to belong. But just wanting doesn't make it so. I don't belong in your life, you know that as well as I do. There's no sense in getting involved when I won't be here to see it through. We would both get hurt before it's over."

Zach said nothing as he held her tight. They lay together, neither moving, neither sleeping, just sharing the warmth between them. After a while, Bailey heard his deep, even breathing and knew he had managed to drift off to sleep. In a way, she envied him. He would wake up to the same world he knew. Not so for her.

When Bailey finally stirred again, the sun was rising with glorious hues of yellow and orange. The place at her back was cold.

"Get up, you lazy woman," Zach said cheerfully. "I want to cross the river and head back to the ranch as soon as you're moving. I know for a fact that there's a pan of hot biscuits and a pot of Jin Lee's coffee already made. They're beckoning to me."

Bailey stood, a joint or two popping as she stretched. She was stiff and sore from sleeping on the ground. Her clothes were dirty and rumpled, even her hair had been pulled out of its braid and hung loosely about her back. "Do you always wake up in such a good mood?" she asked grumpily.

"Only after I've spent the night with an angel."

"Smooth talker." She stood by the fire and watched as he rolled up the bedroll and tied it to Reliant's saddle.

"I went down and checked the river this morning. The water has receded some, but the current is still dangerous. We need to be just as cautious as we were yesterday." He had rinsed out the bandanna he'd found yesterday and now handed it to her so she could wash her face. Zach moved to put out the fire, spreading the logs and throwing dirt over the remaining embers. A quick whistle brought Reliant closer, and Zach mounted, holding out a hand to pull Bailey up behind him. "Since it didn't rain last night, the mud on the bottom has cleared a bit. I think I've found another place to cross. It's rocky, but I don't think it's as deep."

They walked upriver for about half a mile then came to a break in the rocky bank. "The water still has a bite to it," he warned. Bailey nodded as she wrapped both arms around his waist and held on tightly. Zach cued Reliant and the horse plowed into the frigid water. Inch by inch Zach carefully guided his horse around and over several rocky places. Once the horse slipped and skittered as he fought to maintain his balance. Bailey released the deep breath she'd been holding once they reached the other side.

"Wish we had known about that spot yesterday," she offered.

Zach shook his head. "The river bottom was too muddy, we would have never been able to walk across the rocks. Do we need to stop and dry your denims, or will you be all right? We can be home in a couple hours."

"It's only wet up to my knees. I should be OK. Besides, if Jin Lee can add a hot bath to that steaming coffee and biscuits, I say we haven't a minute to lose."

Zach grinned and spurred Reliant into a fast gallop.

"You three are dead."

It was mid-afternoon, and Bailey wasted no time in getting right to the point with Faith, Hope, and Charity. She had all of them sitting on the leather sofa in the main room of the house. They sat in a line, two heads level, one in between, their hands clasped, their heads bowed in supposed chagrin. Bailey didn't buy it for a minute. She paced back and forth in front of them, knowing the unsettling effect it had on them. "Faith and Hope, I know you two schemed and plotted to get me alone with your brother, and you dragged your little sister into it, too."

Faith feigned innocent surprise. Hope had the decency to look at least a little bit ashamed. Charity nervously fidgeted with her doll.

"Well, it worked." Bailey stopped pacing long enough to raise a hand to count out each indiscretion. "We almost drowned, then went without dinner, had to sleep *outside* with *one* blanket between us, and almost froze to death. But your plan worked. We were alone and together all night long."

"Did you share the blanket?" Charity's eyes were wide with curiosity.

Bailey considered the youngest sister. "Yes, we did. It was either that or freeze. But that's no reason—" She started to move again.

"Were you warm?" Charity asked again. "I hate being cold."

Bailey stopped and walked over to Charity. "Yes, ma'am. We were very warm. Now don't change the subject. I'm serious abut this. You three could have—"

"Then everything turned out fine, didn't it? I mean, you and Zach shared the blanket and all. Won't be long now before you are really our sister, right? Zach and you will have to get married now or people will talk." The logical look on Charity's face caused Bailey to smile despite her anger at the girls. The reddened face of her two sisters made it very obvious where Charity had deduced her information. Kids could be funny when it came to simple logic.

"From what I understand, people are already talking, but it's not about your brother and me. It's about these silly pranks you three insist on pulling. Stuff like this isn't funny, it's manipulation."

Faith and Hope looked as if they were about to argue. Bailey sat down in one of the leather wing back chairs and held up a hand to silence them. "I want a promise from all three of you that you will refrain from causing trouble for at least the next month. No manipulation, no plotting and scheming, and especially no more bright ideas to make your brother marry me." In unison, all three girls tilted their noses upward, crossed their arms over their chests, and refused to acknowledge Bailey's words. Bailey expected that. She hadn't worked with unruly teenagers for nothing. She ignored their actions and pressed on. "In return for your promise, I will make a promise of my own."

One by one, the three girls darted their eyes at Bailey. They were interested, although they didn't want her to know how much. "My promise is to stay with you for a while, not as a chaperone, but as a friend. As friends, we'll do anything and everything you want, from styling our hair to talking about boys to riding the range on horses. I'll even talk to Zach about getting you new ones. In fact, once I see an improvement in your behavior, I'll talk with him about not being so strict on you."

Faith threw herself against the back of the sofa. Hope, however, had an interested gleam. "You will?" she asked reluctantly.

Bailey nodded. She waited while the girls conferred together in whispers. It appeared that Faith was the holdout on cooperation. Unfortunately, Bailey realized, Zach was right about his sisters. They were beautiful girls, but they had no sense of being ladies. Oh, sure, they used their feminine guiles when it suited them, but she had never seen three more capable—or conniving—young women.

Bailey considered the three heavenly faces bent close in serious discussion and wasn't fooled. They were not angels behind halo-colored hair and light blue eyes. They were more like poltergeists. One hundred percent mischievous terrorists.

The three separated again. Faith glared, Charity smiled, and Hope nodded. "All right," Hope agreed. "You've got a deal. At least for a little while."

"Good, now let's go up to my room. I want to get started."

A short while later, she considered the ever-drab clothes and plain ponytails of Faith, Hope, and Charity with a critical eye. She couldn't help but point an accusing finger toward Zach. It was his fault the girls were the way they were. Had he given more thought to them instead of his hybrid black cows, he wouldn't have near the anxiety, complications, and lack of cooperation when it came to their future. She had seen it plenty of times before with fathers who sacrificed their families under the guise of providing for them.

Bailey sat on a bench near the dresser and studied their

reflections in the mirror as she fashioned her own newly washed hair into a French braid. She worked hard at being nonchalant about the whole arrangement. She knew that she had to win the trust of all three sisters before they'd truly accept her. Along with that trust, she hoped, would come respect and caring. That was another thing that bothered her. She still had every intention of finding her way home just as quickly as possible. What would it do to these lovely ladies when she left?

All three sisters watched intently as Hope handed her hairpins. "Have you ever worn your hair this way?" Bailey asked Charity. At the youngest's negative nod, Bailey slid over and patted the seat beside her. She placed one last hairpin to hold the style, then took the borrowed hairbrush and began to unfasten Charity's ponytail.

"You should," Bailey replied with a light hug around the girl. "It will flatter your high cheekbones. One of my foster moms taught me, now I'll pass it on to you." Bailey began brushing Charity's long tresses. "How did your mother die? Was she not able to teach you any of this?"

"Consumption. She was so sick all the time," Hope answered for the three. "Faith and I took care of her the best we could, but she died anyway." Bailey rested the hairbrush on the bed and moved to bring both twins in her arms.

"That sounds like you think you could have prevented her death. That's not so. My own mother died when I was younger than you. For a long time, I thought it was my fault. If I had been a better girl, or prettier, or smarter, or anything, she wouldn't have died. But that wasn't true. Just like it's not true for you."

"That's what Zach says," Hope admitted, "but it's hard sometimes to remember that when you don't have a ma."

Bailey's heart tugged as she turned back to brush Charity's hair. "I know, and you two had a little sister to raise, too."

Faith and Hope sat down on the edge of the bed so they could get a good view. Each girl had lovely hair, healthy and shiny, but they needed a new style to make them feel grown-up and sophisticated. Too bad the town mercantile did not stock mousse and hair spray. She didn't believe either had been invented yet. Bailey grinned. If she were to stay in this time, she'd make a fortune with all her new inventions and products. It would be a woman credited in the history books with all the innovations. She giggled at the thought. First, she would start with hair products, move on to makeup, mascara, and blush, and then not stop until every woman across the country had a pair of panty hose.

And a bottle of deodorant.

"Hope, while I show Charity and Faith how to do this braid, why don't you run down and ask Jin Lee to bring us up hot water for a bath. Also"—Bailey stopped her as Hope hurried out the door—"please ask Jin Lee to find Zach's razor and some shaving cream. I really need to shave my legs."

What Bailey really wanted to do was to start a little inspiration, then sit back and let them move forward on their own. Even though they had instigated her rendezvous with Zach, even though they acted as if they were happy with their lives, Bailey knew just a little dab of femininity right behind the ears would start the ball rolling. Then she'd have to keep up with their questions. That was the only way this whole scheme would work. Faith, Hope, and Charity had to discover femininity on their own. They had to think it was their idea to make these changes.

"Bailey," Faith said carefully, "what happened with Zachariah last night? Even though you said it was wrong for us to do it—and we promise not to do it again—we went to a lot of trouble to set that up. We were ecstatic when you didn't come home." There was a ring in her voice that didn't sit well with Bailey.

"Ecstatic? You should have been worried sick. You lied to me, then left me in the middle of a cow field all alone. When your brother came along, he was really angry. I did convince him to take me to the river, the place you were taking me, remember? Listen, girlfriend, the next time I ask for your help, do me a favor and say no."

"Everything turned out fine, didn't it?" Faith pressed. "You went to the ravine and you got to know Zachariah better. What else happened?" Faith had mastered the "innocent little me" expression right down to an art form. It irritated Bailey to no end, just like it did when it was used by the kids in her own time.

"Oh, no you don't. That won't work on me, young lady. You're not getting one iota of information from me. It's absolutely none of your business." Bailey refocused her attention on weaving Charity's hair into a French braid like her own. She figured from the apprehensive look on Charity's face, Faith wasn't finished.

"We're not learning anything until you tell us what happened with Zachariah." Faith crossed her arms and glared defiantly at Bailey. "Right, Charity?"

Charity didn't answer. Instead, she hugged her doll tightly. Big tears welled up in her eyes and her ears began to redden. The little sister was torn between loyalty to Faith and her sweet desire to be mothered by Bailey. It was unfair of Faith to put her sibling in the middle. "Explain your point, Faith," Bailey said.

"We are not children," Faith retorted, enunciating each word carefully as if Bailey was slow to understand. "You and Zachariah went to the river and stayed together all night. Did he kiss you?"

Bailey put the brush down on the dresser and rose to face Faith. She crossed her arms at the elbows. This might be a little harder than she thought. Faith was clearly used to sweetly manipulating, and if that didn't work, she quickly turned vicious and demanding to get what she wanted. Serious action was needed if Bailey was to earn her respect. Serious action. She reached down, calmly took Faith by the arm, and escorted her to the door. She opened it and ushered Faith across the threshold.

"That's between your brother and me. Ask him what you want to know."

Faith folded her arms across her chest and stuck out her tongue.

"I may be your guest, Faith Gooden, but I am also your elder. You will never, and I repeat, never, be disrespectful to me again. I will not tolerate it." Bailey knew her eyes flashed with anger just as Faith's did. Before the younger girl could react again, Hope, who had just come up the stairs, rushed over and punched her sister in the shoulder.

"Stop that, Faith! We *wanted* Bailey and Zach to spend time together."

Faith lightened her glare but continued to frown.

"Secondly," Bailey went on, "all three of you are guilty of conspiracy. That means possible jail time as far as I'm concerned. I *know* you planned for last night to happen, so don't pull the Miss High-and-Mighty act on me. I've worked with too many kids who would put your pranks and temper tantrums to shame. I even helped put some of them in prison, so don't *ever* get on my bad side."

Bailey reached for Hope's arm and pulled her into the room, leaving Faith to stand alone. "When you are ready to act like the lady I know you can be, you may join your sisters and me. Until then, Faith Gooden, don't set a foot across my path. I'll eat you alive and spit you out in little pieces."

Bailey stepped back and smartly snapped the door closed without even enjoying Faith's stunned expression.

It was clear no one had ever talked that way to her before.

It was high time someone did.

By the time Hope and Charity sported stylish new dos, there was a tentative knock on the door. The two sisters looked worried as Bailey hesitated before walking over and opening it. Instead of Faith, it was Zach who stared down at her. Bailey's heart gave a little leap as his eyes dropped to her mouth and then to what she was wearing: another skirt and blouse of Hope's that didn't quite fit as well as she would have liked.

"I found something out in the hayloft that belongs in here." He stepped to one side to allow Faith to enter the room. Her eyes were still red from crying, and she walked as if her rear end was sore. "My sister has something to say."

Bailey dragged her gaze away from the powerful man to Faith, who stood with her head bent, sniffing and embarrassed.

"Faith," Zach prodded.

"I'm sorry, Bailey. It is none of my business, and I was ugly about not getting my way." Bailey smiled cautiously. She looked from brother to sister before stepping forward to hug Faith like a sister.

"Apology accepted. Why don't you come back inside and let me fix your hair?"

Instantly, the recalcitrant teenager bubbled over with excitement and rushed to her sisters, now sitting by the bed. She oohed and ahhed over their new looks. They stopped when they realized Zach was still there. Zach's expression was one of stunned disbelief. He shrugged and backed from the room.

Bailey followed him into the hallway and pulled the door closed behind her. He stared awkwardly, then took her hand. "I don't know what you did, but thank you, Bailey. She was actually terrified that you'd never speak to her again."

"She just needed some boundaries, that's all."

He nodded, seemingly reluctant to move away. He started to reach for her face, then dropped his hand. "See you at dinner?"

Bailey nodded as he began to walk away. "Zach—"

He turned back quickly.

"There's going to be some changes over the next few days. Make a big deal over them, OK?"

He smiled then put his hat back on his head and snapped his fingers against the brim. "Will do, ma'am."

Faith was already in the tub when Bailey walked back into the room. If the girls noticed her smile, they didn't say anything. "All right, ladies, what shall it be? A manicure? A pedicure? Girl talk? Boy talk?"

Bailey laughed as their eyes grew wide with anticipation. She picked up a hairbrush and walked over to Faith. "We have a lot to do if you're going to catch up with your sisters. I've just about made them over into beauty queens." She dunked Faith's head under the water and reached for the soap as Faith came up sputtering.

"Oh, by the way." Bailey lathered the soap on a cloth. She met Faith's eyes in the mirror's reflection. "Your brother is a great kisser." She ignored the surprised and pleased smiles and Faith's covert thumbs-up signal to Hope and Charity.

"I really love this, Bailey." Faith stared in the mirror a short while later, turning her head from side to side as she considered her new appearance. Unlike Charity's French braid, Faith's long flowing hair was swirled up into an elegantly romantic twist. "How did you learn to fix it?"

"You can't have hair as long as mine and not be able to

pull it out of your face. When I'm at work, I prefer to wear it back. It makes me look older and more professional."

"Why would you want to look older?" Charity asked. "I thought men liked women who looked young."

Bailey laughed at her question. Some things were the same no matter what century you were in. "That can be true, but not all men think like that. Certainly not one you would want to marry. Anyway, I figure the more convincing and believable I look when I'm in the courtroom, the better chance I have at winning the case. You might say I stack the odds."

"You have a job? Zach said you had to go to college to have a job. Then he said they didn't let women in college, and we should just concentrate on being ladies."

Bailey made a mental note to speak to Zach about his primitive beliefs. "He's right about having to go to college to become an attorney, but wrong about not letting women attend. Even in this time—I mean, in this day and age women are enrolling in college by the hundreds. I suppose you'll have to find the right one, maybe even go east, but all three of you could go to college if you wanted to. I'll speak to Zach about it if you'd like. You would make a great attorney," she encouraged Faith, adding the final touches to her hair. "You have the brains and the determination not to let anything stand in your way. You remind me a lot of myself at your age."

"You know," Hope interjected almost sadly, "we've been through all this before."

"What's that? You've talked about going to college?"

"Having someone take us to raise into ladies."

"Your brother didn't tell me all that."

"Probably because he didn't want to scare you. He gets this wild idea every now and again, and hires some poor soul to teach us the ways of the world. They're usually chunky old ladies who want us to learn how to cook and sew and become proper wives. Not one of them ever considered that we had brains, that we wanted something more than life on a lonely ranch."

"We've become real good at running them off," Faith added cautiously. "Last time, it only took three days."

"Well, I approach things a little bit differently, and I'm here only for a short time anyway. I've got my own life to get back to. However, I promise we won't talk about cooking one single time unless that's what you want to talk about. In fact," she lowered her voice to almost a whisper, "I don't even know how to cook."

"No!" all three replied in disbelief.

"Then maybe we can teach you something, too," Hope replied.

"I can make lemonade and gingerbread cookies," Charity added. "Jin Lee taught me."

Bailey was touched. It was almost as if these three really were her sisters. She could close her eyes and easily convince herself that she belonged here. She mentally shook herself out of that reverie. Every time she'd gotten up her hopes about having her own family, they'd been dashed for some reason or another. She wasn't about to let that happen again. It hurt too badly.

Bailey thought she was being realistic about encouraging the sisters to consider college. Society at this time was limited for young women, but opportunities were available. Look at all the women throughout history who had accomplished more than folks expected of them. They were respected as pioneers by Bailey's contemporaries.

"Before I left home," Bailey added, "I was about to become a judge."

"Goodness, why did you leave?"

"Apparently, I said the wrong thing to the wrong . . . person," she explained. "I do miss my kids."

At their surprised look, Bailey added, "My foster kids.

They are very important to me. I represent them to the court system."

"The Foster kids? Where do they live?" Charity asked. The grown-up hairstyle Bailey had fashioned only added to her innocence.

It took Bailey a minute to figure out what Charity was talking about. Then she realized and chuckled. "No, no. Not the *Fosters'* kids. I work with kids who have no parents, or no brother or sister to watch after them."

"Oh, you mean orphans. They have special homes for them. Why were they in court? Did they get in trouble?" Charity asked, a horrified look crossing her face. "Do they put orphans in jail when they grow up?"

Bailey shook her head and decided not to go further. All they knew was that orphans lived in orphanages. That was probably best for now.

"Is that why Zachariah wanted you to work with us, because you know a lot about kids?" Faith asked.

"Actually, I think he was desperate." She tugged at Faith's hair and grinned. "If you were to go to college, what do you think you'd like to study?"

"I'd like to be a writer," Hope mentioned softly. "I've never told anyone, not even you, Faith, but I've already written my own novel."

"I'm not sure what I want to do," Faith answered truthfully. "I'd like to go to college, and study everything, and then make up my mind."

"That's very insightful. Sometimes we don't know what the world offers until we've learned more about it."

"I don't want to be the youngest anymore," Charity piped in.

"I don't think there is anything you can do about that, sweetheart." Bailey smiled and sat down beside her on the bed. She resisted the urge to pull the littlest angel in her lap and hug her. Charity wanted to be grown, not babied.

"However, I bet there is something that you can do better than either of your sisters. Other than the lemonade and gingerbread cookies, I mean." Bailey raised her brows and looked at Faith and Hope expectantly.

They thought a moment, a bit longer than Bailey would have liked, before Hope replied. "You are extremely good with the dogs, Charity. Zach says you have a way with animals that he's never seen before. I mean, just look at the way Clarence follows you around like you're his mama."

"That's wonderful, Charity!" Bailey replied with excitement. "Your brother told me those dogs will be valuable once they're trained."

Faith sighed, then rose from the tub and wrapped a towel around her blossoming figure. "This really isn't going to work, Bailey. We've begged Zachariah to let us do more than just sit around the house. He says girls don't need to bog down their pretty little minds with figures or hard work." She mimicked her brother and Bailey couldn't suppress the laughter. "That's why we have to sneak around to do anything. Otherwise we'd sit inside and sew all day."

"Is it that, or is it because of all your hijinks that he keeps you under wraps?"

"If he'd give us some responsibility, we wouldn't resort to so much mischief," Hope interrupted.

"It doesn't work that way, Hope," Bailey replied. "You earn respect and trust by your actions, not the other way around. Still, I think it's time to make some changes around here. Pretty big changes. How far is town?"

Their eyes immediately brightened. "You'll take us into town?"

"Zach promised to take me. I don't see why you three can't come along, too. I'm a firm believer that a new dress or two is the best cure for whatever is ailing me. I bet it'll work for you three as well."

*   *   *

Zach couldn't believe his eyes. His stepmother had been right to name them from the Bible. Faith, Hope, and Charity were three angels. Not only that, they were becoming young women. Beautiful young women.

He rose as the three came down the stairs for supper. Charity was first. She had fixed her hair in the unusual braid that Bailey wore. It started tightly against the top of her head and followed down to the back of the neck. The remaining hair had been tucked under and secured with a piece of ribbon that perfectly matched her calf-length pink cotton dress. She wore black button shoes and white stockings, just like she was ready to go to town.

He noticed that Hope's hair was swept up in a way that made her seem far more grown-up than he liked. Tendrils fell softly around her face, framing her vibrant eyes and porcelain skin. Faith's hair was a bit different, but she was equally as stunning as her twin. They both wore skirts of a deep green, the color of oak leaves, with white cotton shirts that buttoned up the front.

Bailey followed his sisters down the stairs. She had changed from the river-soaked pants she'd been wearing to another of the twin's dresses, a far cry from the mud-stained clothes he'd found her in. She was even more lovely than his sisters. At once, Zach realized how good it felt to have a woman around the house. Someone who made it a home. For a moment he put away his thought that she would be leaving them. Right now, he just wanted to enjoy the changes she had wrought in a single afternoon.

He walked past his sisters and took Bailey's hand as she descended to the last step, and escorted her to the table. Jin Lee had prepared a light meal of stew and corn bread.

As he listened to their banter, Zach had reservations

about taking them into town tomorrow afternoon. When word spread that the Gooden girls had grown up, he was certain every eligible cowpoke within a hundred miles was going to start calling. Besides, trouble could find those three walking down the street. He glanced around the table, ready to make up some excuse and delay the trip to town. Just then he met Bailey's pleased expression and a smile that promised more than he could imagine. He couldn't take his eyes away from her as his heart melted. There was no way he'd back out now.

Box Bend, Wyoming, he thought, the Goodens were coming to town.

Chapter 13

Zach PULLED BACK on the reins and hauled Plug and Sparky to a halt right in front of the ranch house the next afternoon. He stared up at Bailey, who was standing under the shade of the porch. Her hair was elegantly pulled back into a braid, but he'd decided he liked it much better loose and flowing. He wished he could take out the pins and work his fingers through the silken tresses.

The call of a mockingbird flying overhead startled him out of his reverie. It was as if the bird was laughing at him, reminding him that his destiny in life was not to have someone take care of him. He was to take care of others: his sisters, the ranch, even Bailey while she was under his roof. There was no sense in getting involved with this strange woman who believed she was from the future, especially since she'd made it clear that she'd take drastic measures to return.

"Oh, no, no, no. This just won't do. What will we do if it

rains?" He heard Bailey mutter softly. Zach glanced her way as he stepped down from the wagon and adjusted one of the brass hitch buckles. Sparky stood beside Plug; both horses looked extremely put-upon to be pulling the weathered gray buckboard to town.

"Beg your pardon?"

Bailey walked down the steps with her hands on her hips and surveyed the worn wagon. She shook her head, then turned to face him. "This won't do, Zach. Not an old buckboard. Don't you have something nicer? I know there's not a carriage in the barn, but don't you at least have something with a cover?"

He narrowed his eyes and glared. "Your three angels set the cover on fire last month. Besides, we always take the buckboard. We go to town for supplies, Bailey, not to impress people."

"Not today," she insisted. "Today we are most definitely going to town to impress people. We want them to see what beautiful ladies Faith, Hope, and Charity are becoming. Can't you borrow a surrey with a fringe on top or something like that? And a matching team of carriage horses?"

"A surrey?" He lifted a brow in irritated amusement. "Not quite sure what a surrey is, sweetheart, but here we use buckboards."

Bailey looked puzzled, then shrugged. "I thought . . . oh, well, maybe they were just in Oklahoma. It doesn't matter, though. We need a fancier carriage to drive us to town. If you want Faith, Hope, and Charity to be more ladylike, then they need all the details, or as you would probably say, they need the trappings that go with it."

Zach eyed Hoop, who leaned against the back of the wagon nonchalantly chewing on the end of a piece of grass. Hoop looked back and forth between the two, then rolled his eyes and grinned with an *I told you so* look in his eye. Zach glared at his foreman, then turned back toward Bailey. He had asked this fire sprite to calm his sisters, not make them too big for their britches.

"The wagon is fine." Zach motioned to Faith to load up.

"Maybe that's part of the problem, Zach. Maybe the people see the girls as common buckboards, not elegant surreys."

It seemed as if the whole prairie suddenly went quiet. The birds stopped chirping, Plug and Sparky turned their heads and pricked their ears, even Hoop sat up straighter. She'd pushed him too far, completely too far. Zach approached Bailey, who held her ground and lifted her chin. He stopped, her face inches from his own.

"My sisters are not common, *Miss* Cooper." Menace laced his words.

"Of course they're not," she replied, meeting his intimidating stare blink for blink. "I was trying to make a point, and you're not listening." She stepped away from him and started a slow pace back and forth right alongside the buckboard. In the brief time that he'd known this woman, he had learned that meant only one thing. She was about to reason him right around to her way of thinking.

"What you've done in the past hasn't worked. If you expect the town to change its view of Faith, Hope, and Charity, you'll have to change yours first. That means *you* start treating your sisters the way you expect others to behave toward them. And you." She halted right in front of Hoop. "*You* make sure the ranch hands do the same." Hoop spit the straw out of his mouth, started to refute her comment, then stopped and slowly shook his head. Hoop, the man who had quiet words of wisdom for every situation, was speechless.

"However, since there is obviously no way we can change the situation today, we'll take the buckboard into town for this trip. I ask that you take this matter under advisement, *Mister* Gooden."

Bailey spun on her heel and paced back toward Zach at

the front of the wagon, then stopped and waited for him to help her up onto the front seat. Zach stared at Hoop for support. Slowly, Hoop shrugged, his face a mixture of awe and intimidation. Even the cattle dog sitting at Hoop's feet tilted his head and stared in puzzlement.

"The pretty lady has a point, Zach," Hoop finally said as he tipped his hat at Zach's sisters, who now stood by the buckboard. He walked toward Faith, Hope, and Charity to help them into the wagon.

Bailey turned to Jin Lee, who stood nearby with a worried frown. "Jin Lee, would you please get several quilts to line the wagon bed? I don't want the girls to ruin their dresses." Jin Lee nodded and rushed back inside the house.

Perfect, Zach concluded wryly, she had Jin Lee rush to do her bidding, *and* she even had good old reliable Hoop snookered. *A surrey? A team of carriage horses?* Just what did this woman expect from him? She'd agreed to help his sisters, not turn them into princesses, and certainly not to take over his house. Yet it looked as if she was doing exactly that.

Why did she have to stand there so stubbornly when all he could think about was how the sunbeams made her fiery hair glisten? Why did she have to look at him like she needed to be tossed in the hay and kissed until she could no longer think straight? Zach came around and reached for Bailey, his two hands encircling her waist. He lifted her into the front seat of the wagon and allowed his thumbs to brush underneath her breasts as he slowly released his hands. Their eyes met and held for a second that seemed to go on for eternity. He could tell from the flush that crept across her shoulders that she'd been affected by his touch. He dropped his hands with a devilish smile. He'd found her weakness.

Jin Lee brought the quilts to pad the wagon, then Zach helped Faith, Hope, and Charity settle onto the floorboards. The three made a big show of ignoring him as they carefully sat down, trying not to muss their dresses. Zach rolled his eyes and stepped up to the driver's seat by Bailey, who silently stared straight ahead. He sighed as he clucked to the horses. This was going to be a long afternoon.

Try as he might, Zach still could not figure the fuss over the buckboard. A buggy was nice for riding and visiting and all, but the wagon was far more practical for life on a ranch. His sisters had never complained before, but now that Bailey said it was unladylike, he knew he'd never hear the end of it.

If he'd known it would be this much trouble to make them into ladies, he'd might have just preferred them as tomboys. Then, a single glance over his shoulder at Hope's smiling face, and Zach's heart swelled. He hadn't seen his sisters this happy and content since . . . well, since before their ma had died.

Bailey claimed that she knew nothing about being a sister or how to be part of a family, but she was wrong. She fit in better than he did in some regards. In a matter of a few days, she had given his sisters more than he had in the past five years. She'd given them respect. He'd been so busy trying to save the ranch from the mess his pa had caused, he hadn't given the same attention to Faith, Hope, and Charity. A wave of shame washed over him. He hadn't meant to neglect them, but for the longest time it was all he could do to keep the ranch going and food on the table.

Once the Double Bar G was out of the hard times, the girls were already troublesome mischief makers. It had been easier to let others deal with them instead of doing it himself. The problem was definitely of his own making. That being the case, did he actually need this persistent woman to resolve it? Another look at his sisters proved he did.

Bailey Cooper was exactly what they needed.

Exactly what he needed.

They drove in silence for a mile or two. Even though they

were irritated, he knew his sisters couldn't keep quiet for long. Not even if their lives depended on it. True to form, Charity was the first to speak, asking Bailey to teach them a song.

Bailey thought a minute, then turned back toward them, the tight confines of the narrow seat forced her knees to nestle against his, as she launched into a singsong story.

"It's a story about a man named Gooden,
Who was bringing up three very lovely girls,
All of them had hair of gold, unlike their brother.
The youngest one wore curls. . . ."

Despite his intention to remain stone-faced, Zach grinned at the silly song. No matter how much he complained, he sensed that this woman—this clear-thinking, fun-loving woman who gave him supposed proof she was from the future—was the answer to his prayers. In a single morning, she'd given the girls the very thing he couldn't: the sense of being worthy young women.

And she . . . handled them. She'd withstood Faith's demanding temper tantrum. She'd tolerated Hope's worrisome practical jokes about the green dress and losing her on the range as they supposedly escaped to the river. And Charity, his sweet, kind, and gentle baby sister. She'd been just shy of eight when their ma had died, only ten when pa was killed. She craved a mother's love even more than her sisters, and Bailey seemed to love her right back, honestly and openly.

Yes, the entire family needed Bailey Cooper. He slapped the reins to push Plug and Sparky up a notch. She needed them just as much. She claimed she had no family. The way Zach saw it, if she was really from the future, that meant there was nothing to hold her there except perhaps her desire to be a judge. That was a man's job anyway. She could be just as happy caring for his sisters, couldn't she? She could be just as happy loving him, couldn't she?

Whether she realized it or not, Bailey didn't need to go

home. She needed to stay, and it was up to him to do the convincing. If only she would listen to him, if only she weren't so stubborn, if only she didn't talk so much, if only . . .

Zach grinned to himself. If only he could keep a clear head when she was near. He'd never met a woman who could win an argument before he even realized they disagreed. In her own way, this Bailey Cooper was just as much trouble as his sisters. The thing was, it was a kind of trouble he liked.

Zach felt Bailey's eyes on him and turned to meet her gaze. "That five o'clock shadow is very sexy, Mr. Gooden." Her voice was soft and seductive, just like she'd been when they kissed.

Zach rubbed a hand around the stubble of his chin. "I meant to shave but couldn't find my razor. My three thieving sisters must have been up to no good again."

"Oh, no, they're innocent. Your razor and shaving bar are in my room. I really like your horsehair shaving brush. It tickles."

Zach sputtered to suppress a cough. He glanced down and met her beguiling stare, her eyes blended perfectly with the fields of grass behind her. "Do I really want to know why my razor is in your room?"

Bailey shrugged. "I needed to shave my legs. It took me a few tries to figure out how to use a straight edge and I ended up with a couple of nicks, but I finally managed. It actually works much better than my disposable razors at home."

He didn't want to, but he had to ask. "You use a razor?"

"Of course."

"Then you dispose of it?"

"Sure, otherwise it's too dull."

Granted, Zach didn't know much about female things, but it was hard to comprehend why a seemingly moral woman like Bailey Cooper needed a razor. He lowered his head close to her ear and spoke softly so only Bailey could hear. "I thought only saloon girls shaved their legs, and then only for special clients."

Bailey leaned toward him and lifted a hand to his jaw. Her touch was hot as she pulled his head to her lips so she could whisper in his ear. "Why, Mr. Gooden, would you happen to be one of those special clients?"

He couldn't help the flush that crossed his face at Bailey's teasing smile. The thought of Bailey's silky smooth thigh brushing against him, separated only by the fabric of her skirt and his pants, was almost too much to bear. The unbidden vision of those soft legs wrapped around his waist drove him nearly wild. His body reacted immediately, and Zach shifted uncomfortably on the hard seat of the wagon. He removed his hat and wiped his forehead with his sleeve. Hopefully, they'd reach the town within the hour, and he could get away from this tantalizing she-devil.

Get away, and go soak in the water trough.

Chapter 14

BAILEY SENSED IT the minute they drove into town.

The Gooden sisters struck fear in the hearts of the citizens of Box Bend.

It was first evident when a young mother glanced up and saw who sat in the buckboard. Her face turned white and her smile dropped as she hurriedly gathered her three toddlers and fled inside the mercantile. Immediately, Bailey saw a skinny balding man peer through the storefront window. The white apron wrapped around him indicated he must be the mercantile owner. She couldn't really tell, though, since she quickly pulled down the shade.

She looked back at Faith, Hope, and Charity. Their heads were bent together, and Bailey could hear their muffled whispers and sneaky giggles. She loudly cleared her throat to get their attention. One by one she gave each girl a no-nonsense look that meant any plotting and scheming would cease. Immediately, they separated and crossed their hands in their laps like the cherubs she had once thought them.

She glanced at Zach, who looked down at her with an air of satisfaction. He remained quiet, but Bailey knew what he was thinking. Coming to town may not have been the brightest idea. She might know the girls wanted to reform, but the town didn't. Well, they had to start somewhere.

On the steps of the white wooden church, she saw Sloan and Joe Junior talking to an older man with gray whiskers. She assumed he must be the minister from his dark suit and white neck band. All three men stopped their discussion and stared at Zach, who nodded as he drove the horses on. A charitable-looking woman, probably the minister's wife, glanced up from her sweeping, saw the sisters, looked toward the heavens, then immediately rushed back inside. What in the world could Faith, Hope, and Charity have done?

"The church, too?" Bailey asked in disbelief.

Zach nodded. "Early this summer on a Tuesday afternoon, they stole one of the Reverend Martin's milk cows, led her inside the church, and used a hair ribbon to tie old Bessie's tail to the bellpull."

Stunned, she looked back at Faith. "You didn't?"

"It was Hope's idea," Faith replied defensively.

"Only after you led her from the pasture," Hope argued. "I didn't have anything to do with snitching her."

"I don't care who did what," Zach interrupted. "You both sent the entire population running to the church thinking there was a terrible emergency. Sheriff Weeks insisted I keep you three out of town for at least a month while everyone cooled down. Next time, I'm going to let him lock you up."

"There won't be a next time, will there?" Bailey lifted her chin into the air and smiled confidently at the twins and Charity. All three nodded and copied Bailey's action. "Zach, you are privileged to be the first to see the new and improved

Gooden sisters. The people of Box Bend will come to love them as their own."

"That'll be the day," Zach muttered as he pulled the horses to a halt. "This dressmaker is new in town. She may not have heard about them yet and might be willing to make them a dress or two." He set the brake, then got down from the seat. Hoop, who had been following behind the wagon on his own horse, dismounted and helped Faith, Hope, and Charity from the back. Zach reached for Bailey's waist and literally picked her up off the seat with two hands. He brought her close to his chest and grinned as she slowly slid down against his body until her feet touched the ground. She'd felt every intimate part of him, including the fact that his body wanted her.

It was Bailey's turn to flush. She nervously glanced around. They had been playing a dangerous game since she'd first arrived, a game of want and desire and denial. The tension between them was taut and ready to explode with the possibilities, and the realization excited her and frightened her at the same time. Had she encountered Zachariah Gooden in her own time, or had she been born to his, Bailey doubted anything could have kept them apart. Time had a funny way of mocking people, especially when they were separated by a century.

"Stop it, Faith! I want to see, too." Charity pushed herself in front of her older sister as the Gooden ladies stared into the dressmaker's window. All three girls shuffled back and forth, hoping for a glimpse of the treasures inside. Anticipation illuminated their faces.

Bailey's gaze returned to Zach, who reluctantly released his hold and stepped aside as Hoop tied his horse to the back of the wagon and took Bailey's place in the front seat. Over the years she'd learned not to get too attached to her foster families, and then not to get personally involved with her clients. It hurt too much when it was time to say good-bye.

Now she faced the same dilemma. Faith, Hope, and Charity made her feel like she was family, like they were her very own sisters. Bailey knew she was going to leave soon, and she couldn't allow herself to fall in love with those devilish angels.

Bailey took a deep breath. Who was she kidding? She already loved the three, despite their reputation as bad apples. She was so well-suited for them, and they for her. All they needed was a mother figure. All she needed was a family.

It was heartbreaking to realize it could never be.

"Bailey, hurry!" Hope rushed back and pulled Bailey's hand toward the door of the dress shop. Faith and Charity immediately followed and pushed Bailey from behind. Bailey saw the dressmaker peer through the front window. She smiled at first, curious about the customers about to come inside. Suddenly, a look of horror crossed her face as she obviously recognized the Gooden sisters. She dropped a feathered hat and hurriedly moved forward to place a CLOSED sign on the window of the door.

Bailey rushed toward the glass-paned door, opened it, and managed to stick her foot inside. She narrowed her eyes and stared at the young woman through the slight opening. "I've come to purchase new dresses for my . . . sisters. They tell me that you're new to town, and a far better dressmaker than the other one. Naturally we came to you first.

"I know you'll want to help us. I plan to spent a great deal of money. And I do mean a *great deal* of money." Bailey removed her foot, straightened her dress, and smiled haughtily. "However, we can easily take our business elsewhere."

The woman didn't move for a moment, but stood considering Bailey's words. She glanced back at the girls, all standing perfectly ladylike and proper. Bailey watched the indecision on her face and realized Zach had not exaggerated about the terror associated with his sisters. Had they really been that bad? She made a mental note to ask Zach for details later. Right now, though, drastic action was needed.

Bailey deliberately jingled her purse, heavy with the gold coins Zach had given her. The woman cautiously stepped back and slowly opened the door, a tentative smile on her lips.

"Please," the woman warily brushed back a strand of hair, "do come in." Bailey saw the woman dart her eyes toward Hope, who rushed in before the seamstress could change her mind. "I have some lovely dresses already made that should certainly flatter the young ladies."

"Thank you so much," Bailey said. "I think you will be pleased." She turned back toward Zach and Hoop, who'd watched the entire scene from the wagon. A triumphant gloat crossed her face as she gave them a haughty nod. That would teach them to never underestimate the power of a woman.

A short while later, the dressmaker, who'd introduced herself as Mattie, had clearly decided the Gooden sisters were not as bad as she'd heard. She took their measurements and showed the girls a variety of fabrics and dress styles. Since Bailey knew little of 1878 fashion, she directed them to Mattie for guidance.

For herself, Bailey picked out only one dress, a traditional blue calico with tiny bouquets of flowers in the pattern. She hated to use Zach's money, but what choice did she have? She had to be practical. If she wasn't able to get home as quickly as she hoped, she'd need something more than her jeans and tight-fitting borrowed clothes. She also needed underthings.

She watched the joy shared by Faith, Hope, and Charity as they helped each other pick out clothes. She again stopped herself from thinking that the three were like her own sisters; she had given up that dream each time she was shuffled between foster homes. Besides, now she was virtually married to her career and things like that no longer mattered to her. She could argue and win the toughest of cases in the courtroom, but when it came to being a part of a real family, Bailey knew she was way out of her league.

She glanced out the picture window at the bustling town. The street was busy with wagons, horses, and mule teams as people hurried about their business. This was the day-in, day-out reality of their lives. What about her life in the future? Surely by now she would have been reported missing and, hopefully, a massive, well-publicized search was going on.

She would get home soon. She just didn't yet know how.

Bailey leaned her forehead against the cool glass. Even if people in her own time were searching, their efforts would be in vain if she couldn't reach them from this end. If Dark Fawn thought this place was the answer to her prayers, she was sadly mistaken.

A group of men had gathered on the boardwalk across the dirt street. They were a rough-looking crowd, and it didn't bode well that they seemed to be agitated. Since they were outside what was obviously a saloon, Bailey figured it was a card game gone wrong or something. She thought about Zach's pa and the unfortunate way he had died.

Across the street and down the main road a short ways, a small white donkey stood tied to a hitching post. On its back sat an enormous load that looked as if a sharp wind would topple the donkey over.

Mildred. That meant Tag was not far off.

"Girls, I'm stepping outside for a breath of fresh air. Do not, I repeat, do not step outside this store. I'll be back in a minute." The girls were so engrossed in soft leather slippers, they only nodded to Bailey as she opened the door. She stopped and turned back toward them. "Faith?"

Irritated at the interruption, Faith glanced up.

"You are in charge. I expect you to be here when I get back, and I expect the store to be as lovely as it is now."

"Of course, Bailey," Faith replied, clearly hurt Bailey doubted her. Bailey carefully closed the door behind her as worry nagged. The girls couldn't have converted that quickly. What if they had already plotted their latest scheme? She made a mental note to hurry.

As she crossed the street and approached Mildred from behind, a consuming stench grew stronger until it became almost unbearable. Bailey walked right up beside the animal and placed a hand on her rump. "Doesn't he ever give you a bath?" The donkey snorted as if she was offended by Bailey's question. Before Bailey could move, the dirty animal repositioned her rear end and swiftly kicked Bailey on the thigh with one of her back hooves. The donkey began braying as if she were laughing.

Rage and indignation surged through Bailey. How dare that flea-infested smelly *ass* kick her? She clenched and unclenched both fists in an effort to control her temper and resisted the urge to kick the animal back. If she wanted to get home, she needed this man and probably his donkey, too. Despite her less than warm introduction, there was no sense in making an enemy at the first meeting.

"Shouldn't have insulted her, lady. She's temperamental about such personal things." Still fuming, Bailey stared at the wiry man reclining underneath the shade of the saloon porch.

"You must be Tag," Bailey snapped through gritted teeth. "Your donkey just kicked me."

"Pleased to meet ya, too." He touched the brim of his dirty hat. "Mildred don't take kindly to strangers."

"You don't say." Bailey bit her tongue to stifle her true opinion of the smelly animal. If she was going to get home, he and this donkey would be the key. She wasted no time. "I understand you were on the Thompson ranch a few days ago."

Tag's bushy gray eyebrows drew together as his eyes narrowed. "Maybe I was, maybe I wasn't."

Bailey ignored his obtuseness and pressed on. This old man couldn't be any worse than some of the hostile witnesses she interrogated on the stand. "I also understand that you may have found a backpack or what you might call a traveling bag down a ravine."

Tag narrowed his eyes. Bailey could tell he was instantly on the defensive just from his body language. "Maybe I did, maybe I didn't."

"I understand you did," she persisted, ignoring his attempt to be cagey. "It belongs to me, and I'd like it back." The old man said nothing, just stared at her through droopy eyes. Bailey sensed he wasn't sleepy at all, just giving the impression he was. She also knew he was interested.

"I can pay for it," she pressed.

"Don't know what something like that'd be worth. I never had me a box that chirped like a bird."

"That box is my telephone. That means you have the rest of it, too."

"Maybe I do, maybe I don't." Tag scratched his scraggly gray beard. "Wouldn't matter if I had, I traded that chirpin' box for a new halter for Mildred. Looks mighty fine, don't ya think?"

Bailey turned to stare at the grumpy white donkey. Sure enough, the animal wore a new leather halter around her head. She started to ask who made the trade, but Tag shook his head before she could utter a word.

"And I ain't tellin' who, neither. I'd have ever'body and his mammy wantin' to trade for somethin'."

"OK, then," Bailey reasoned. "I'd like to hire you. I will *give* you the backpack and the rest of its contents, *and* I will make it worth your while if you and Mildred will guide me to Medicine Mountain. I have a book, a book that's extremely valuable."

The white-headed man studied her carefully. "Scary place, pretty lady. Why do you need to go up there?"

"That's where I—became separated from my people. I'm hoping they are still there."

"You don't look Indian to me."

Bailey counted to ten, then twenty, then thirty, to try to contain her temper. She'd have liked to throttle the old coot, who was being determinedly contrary, but she knew she couldn't. She had to convince him to take her to the mountain.

The old man stood and walked over to Mildred and untied her lead rope. "I'll ponder on it a bit. That can be a mighty dangerous trip, and I ain't got a notion to git killed quite yet." He tipped his hat again and led Mildred away from her.

Bailey started after them but stopped when Mildred readied her hind foot for another attack. Frustrated, she could only watch the pair as they headed down the dirt-packed street. She had learned a valuable lesson just now. Something she'd never known in all her years.

Nothing comes between a man and his donkey.

Nothing.

Chapter 15

ONCE BAILEY RETURNED to the dressmaker's store, Mattie had already completed her measurements and helped the girls pick several fabrics and designs for the dresses she would make. Mattie had sent the girls upstairs to her apartment to look through a dressmaker's book she had, and offered Bailey a cup of tea while they waited for Zach's return.

"I should have the dresses completed within the week, Mrs. Gooden."

"Oh, I'm not the girls' mother. I'm . . . a friend of the family. Please, call me Bailey."

"Bailey, then." Mattie glanced down at the last of the packages she was wrapping. "I am sorry I was so rude this morning. It's just that—"

"No apologies necessary. I understand your concern about the girls; they've been terrors in the past. I'm hoping to change that, and your beautiful dresses will look stunning on them."

Mattie still looked embarrassed. "Truth is, Bailey, I'm new in town. I've never sewn dresses for the Gooden girls before; I had just heard about the trouble they cause. I judged them before I saw for myself, and I apologize. They are really delightful young ladies." Bailey noted that Mattie was about her own age with a beautiful porcelain complexion, shiny mahogany curls, and eyes so deep brown they were almost like a fawn's.

"What a kind thing to say. I hope the rest of the town will give them a chance. What did you hear about them, if you don't mind me asking?"

"The owner of the mercantile told me to watch them carefully anytime they were in my store. He said they once stole a dozen apples and gave them to some mix-breed children who were camped outside of town with their family. Apparently, the family was looking for a place to settle and the good residents of Box Bend decided this wasn't the town."

Bailey was shocked. Was Zach that narrow-minded, too? Mattie went on before Bailey could ask. "Apparently, your man took pity on the family. According to the mercantile owner, Mr. Gooden offered the man a job. By that time, though, the man and his Indian wife were already being threatened. They decided to move on."

"So Faith, Hope, and Charity swiped apples to give to their children because the town was so mean to them?" At Mattie's nod, Bailey couldn't help but grin. "It's hard to be angry when their hearts were in the right place, isn't it? Still, I've got to put a stop to their misguided justice before they do something serious."

The bell above the door suddenly jingled as Zach walked inside. She watched as his eyes surveyed the shop with trepidation. What was it with men in dress shops, Bailey wondered. She rose from her chair by the counter, and he immediately headed toward her. His face was marred by an expression Bailey couldn't read, but she knew instantly something was wrong. He nodded to Mattie and took Bailey by the elbow.

"Get the girls in the wagon."

"What's the problem?"

"Just do as I say," he snapped.

"Certainly. They are your sisters. However, politeness, decency, and respect go a long way with women, Mr. Gooden." Bailey lifted her chin and started to turn away from Zach, who hesitated, then drew her aside and lowered his voice. He ran his hands through his dark hair and glanced out the window.

"J.T. Thompson was murdered. I want to get the girls back to the ranch where I can protect them."

"What do the girls have to do with this?"

He sighed. "Just do what I say and be quick about it. I wouldn't be here if it wasn't important."

Bailey struggled with her impulse to query further, then gave in. There was more going on than Zach wanted to admit, at least in front of Mattie. She'd work on him later. "They're upstairs. I'll get them and meet you outside." Zach nodded and turned back toward the door.

Several minutes later, Bailey walked out of the store and into the afternoon sun, Charity's hand held tightly in her own. Faith and Hope followed closely behind carrying the brown paper-wrapped packages. Mattie also followed and stopped at the door.

A crowd of a dozen or so dirty men had already gathered around Zach. Joe Junior and Sloan stood outside the crowd but nearby. Zach was near the back of the buckboard, ready to help his sisters inside. Hoop sat on his horse, his body relaxed as if he hadn't a care in the world. Bailey noticed that Hoop's hand rested on his thigh, ready for quick access to his pistol. One of the men pushed his way through the others and stopped directly in front of Zach, the brim of his dirty hat touching the edge of Zach's.

"Let's string him up now," the dusty cowboy said loudly. Murmurs of agreement rose from several similarly dressed men.

"Make the first move, cowboy. You'll be a dead man, too." Zach spat out the words through gritted teeth, clenching and unclenching his hands like the steady ticking of a time bomb. Someone had to stop these two before Zach's thin patience snapped. Bailey surged forward, then halted as the crowd separated for Sheriff Weeks, who confidently pushed his way through and stepped directly between Zach and the stranger. He hadn't been wearing the badge on his vest the other night, but it, coupled with the guns at his hips and the calm demeanor of his voice, reassured Bailey he was a man in control.

"Now, Fisher, you're not going to do that."

"Why not? Gooden has wanted our boss man dead ever since his pappy was killed." The cowboy's vengeful glare never left Zach, who coldly returned the stare.

"There won't be a hemp party in my town, boys. Now move along." The sheriff's voice spoke low and dangerous; the cocky grin and happy-go-lucky charm Bailey had enjoyed at dinner were gone.

"We've all heard you threaten J.T.," another added, holding up a coiled rope and shaking it. "You said you'd kill him dead. Looks like you're a man of your word."

The first one spoke up again. "Come on, enough of this yammering. Let's string him up."

The crowd moved closer to Zach and the sheriff. Hoop's horse danced around nervously, and Bailey saw Hoop place his hand on the butt of his pistol. At least they weren't in this alone. In all her years working in the justice system, she'd never experienced an angry mob, or misplaced mob justice. It frightened her. No, it terrified her.

She searched the eyes of Faith, Hope, and Charity standing beside her. Their faces were white with fear, and tiny tears ran down Charity's cheeks. Over their heads, Mattie met her glance and understood Bailey's unspoken plea. She ushered the girls back inside the shop, shut the door with a firm snap, and pulled down the window shades. Immediately Bailey saw one of the twins peek from around the edge.

The sheriff swung up into the back of the buckboard so he stood taller than all the other men. He rested one hand on the pistol at his hip, then used the other to motion to the bunch. "You boys know I'm not going to let you string anyone up." The sheriff looked directly at the Thompson brothers still standing off in the distance. He nodded his condolences. "Joe Junior, Sloan, I'm sorry as hell about your pa, but this isn't the way to handle things. There isn't going to be a lynching in my town. I will find out who murdered J.T., then we'll get the circuit judge to come for a trial. Now get along or I'm going to toss half of you in jail just because you're irritating me."

It took two more warnings from the sheriff before the catcalls subsided and the crowd began to disperse amidst loud grumbles and complaints. Bailey noted that Sloan Thompson and his brother held their ground. Joe Junior's expression was full of hate. Sloan's was unreadable as both brothers studied Zach. Neither said a word. Slowly, Sloan walked toward Joe Junior and put a hand on his shoulder. The younger man shook it away as if he'd been burned, then mounted his horse and, after a final glare toward all of them, dug in his spurs and rode out of town at a full gallop. Without emotion, Sloan watched Joe Junior ride out through the dust before turning toward Zach with an equally unreadable expression. He finally met Bailey's gaze, then tipped his hat, got on his own gelding, and headed out after his brother at a more leisurely pace.

Bailey stepped off the boardwalk and approached Zach, still standing in the road. "I have to take you in, Zach," she heard the sheriff say as he stepped down from the wagon.

"You know I didn't kill him, Rand," Zach replied stiffly.

The sheriff studied him for a long moment, then nodded. "Hot-tempered you are, Zach. Murderer you're not. The problem is that these boys are up to no good. They want revenge, and you're the likeliest suspect in town. Everyone knows the bad blood between you and Thompson."

Bailey placed her hand on Zach's forearm. The sheriff was after information, albeit in a roundabout way, and even though they were friends, Zach didn't need to say anything. Not until Bailey and he talked.

"You have no evidence, Rand, and protection is no reason for arrest," Bailey interjected before Zach could speak.

"I'm afraid I do—"

Zach interrupted before the sheriff could explain. "Bailey, go back inside with the girls. This isn't your concern."

Bailey's eyes flared. How dare he dismiss her as if she was one of his sisters. She stepped up to Zach until his face was just as close as the angry cowboy's had been. "At this point, Zachariah Gooden, I'm the closest thing you have to an attorney. Do you want to spend the night in jail?"

"Begging your pardon, Bailey," the sheriff interjected softly before Zach could respond. "That's what I was trying to tell you. I'm afraid he's going to have to do that anyway."

"Please explain," Bailey demanded.

"Zach's knife did the killing."

Bailey released Zach immediately. They both stood speechless at the sheriff's revelation. The sheriff spoke softly to Zach. "It was your pa's pearl-handled knife. The one that was used—"

Zach nodded before the man could finish.

"Was used for?" Bailey urged, irritated by their cryptic words.

Zach looked down, hesitated, then shrugged. "The one J.T. used to kill my pa."

"Zach, listen carefully to me." Weeks spoke softly. "No matter what you believe, J.T. had an alibi. You know that as well as I do. Now, do yourself a favor and don't remind folks of what you really think. It won't look good."

"When was Thompson murdered, Rand?" Bailey asked.

"As far as Doc McConnell can tell, a couple of nights ago."

"Then I know for a fact it wasn't Zach," she replied simply.

"Bailey, not now."

She ignored Zach's warning. "He was with me."

Zach grabbed her by the elbow and steered her away from the sheriff. "Give me a minute, will you? We need to straighten this out."

If the sheriff was surprised, he gave no indication. He merely nodded, then walked over toward Hoop, who still sat on his horse.

"Zach, I'm your alibi. You couldn't have killed Thompson. You were with me all night."

"Out by the river, all night, on Thompson's ranch, and seen by his son. Whose word do you think they'll believe, Bailey? Thompson's ranch hands were nasty toward me, but just wait until they get wind that you might have been involved, too. You must promise me that you won't say anything about this right now. Promise me." Zach ran his hands down both arms, then gripped her tightly.

"I can't do that, Zach. It can clear your name."

Anger flashed in his eyes. "I'm trying to be patient with your ways, Bailey. Even though you think you know everything, you don't know anything about this situation." Zach glanced around and lowered his head toward hers. "Telling folks we were together that night won't do anything but make you another suspect and drag you deeper into this. You are not to say anything."

"I can't abide by that, Zach."

"I want your promise, Bailey."

Bailey hesitated. Why was Zach so insistent on this? Unless . . . unless he had something to hide. She had awakened that night to find his horse saddled. "Did you kill him?"

The fire in Zach's eyes grew more fierce. "Is that what you think? That I'm a murderer? Fine." He released his grip on her arms and stepped back. "I talked with Tag earlier. He's willing to take you to the mountain or wherever the hell it is you want to go. Says he'll leave in the morning if you want. So go. Go back to where you came from. I didn't ask for your help to begin with."

Sheriff Weeks gave a polite cough to remind them of his presence. Zach glared at Bailey; the freckle on his neck ticked as he waited for her to leave. When she didn't respond, he pushed harder. "Go on, Bailey. Walk away."

"No." She crossed her arms and returned his glare. "That makes it way too easy for you, Zach. You want me to take care of Faith, Hope, and Charity, but taking care of you is not part of the bargain, is it? You don't trust me. You don't believe that I'm an attorney. You don't believe I can help. You want to brush me off like a timid mouse, have me scurry back with the women and let you be in control. No." Bailey firmly stood her ground. "Tag can wait. You need me."

He started to deny her accusation, but she interrupted him before he could speak. "I'm willing to compromise because you need me more than you know. I will go back inside the dress shop and make sure your sisters are safe. Then I intend to come over to the jail to assess the legal ramifications of your case. I know Rand is your friend, but I want your word that you will not answer any questions unless I'm present. Otherwise, I will find Tag and I will hit the road."

Zach stared down at Bailey's determined face. Now what was he supposed to do? She actually thought she could get him out of this mess.

"Bailey, I—" The words wouldn't come. He simply didn't know how to rely on someone else.

"Your word, or I'm gone," she insisted emphatically.

He stared into her resolute face, then nodded only once. It was more than he wanted to give, but he gave it anyway. Zach turned back to the sheriff. "All right, Rand, let's go."

Ten minutes later, Bailey headed across the street toward the jail at the far end of town. She knew it was difficult for Zach to accept her deal. For whatever reason, he didn't trust her. Apparently, giving him the almanac had convinced him of nothing.

Bailey mentally kicked herself. She had allowed herself to become a part of this family despite herself, and now she was postponing her chance to possibly get back home. Truthfully, a brief thought of staying here permanently had already flickered across her mind. Now she realized how silly that was. She needed Zach's trust and respect as much as she needed him and his family. And, even in dire circumstance, he wasn't willing to give it. She would help him because he needed it in spite of himself, because his sisters needed him. Once Zach was cleared, she was going home, and that would be that.

The few facts she knew were that J.T.'s body had been found stabbed to death with a distinctive knife owned by Zach's father. She knew that Zach couldn't have perpetrated the crime since he was with her all night by the fire.

But it couldn't be. Zach wouldn't risk losing everything by killing J.T. His sisters, his ranch, and his bulls meant too much for him to do something so rash. He had a quick temper, that was true, but surely he wasn't capable of murder. Where had he gone, for how long, and more important, why?

Bailey started walking again without lifting her gaze from the boardwalk. She was so deep in thought that she barely avoided a collision with an elderly lady in yellow. Who else would benefit from J.T.'s demise? Since the murder weapon belonged to Zach, it was apparent someone was trying to frame him. Who? His primary adversary was dead. The most valuable thing he possessed, next to his sisters, would be the ranch. There were plenty of people who would want that. Its location right by the river certainly made it quite desirable.

According to Zach, the girls would be equal owners of the Double Bar G once they came of age. If the worst happened, if Zach were hanged for murder, the property would probably be safe as far as the law was concerned. However, there were plenty more unscrupulous ways to take advantage of three children. Did Zach have any designated guardians for the girls? Who would run the ranch? Hoop? If so, then what was in it for him? In a worst-case scenario, she couldn't stand idly by and allow their only means of support to be taken from them. There were many questions that had to be asked and answered before she could rest.

Or go home.

As far as Bailey could figure, there was only one way to ensure that would never happen. It wasn't going to be easy to convince Zach, but it was for his protection as well as the girls.

The jailhouse door creaked as it opened. Zach and Rand sat on opposite sides of the desk. Each leaned back in his chair, their feet propped up on the scarred wooden desktop. It sounded as if they were talking about the weather, not a recent murder. Through a doorway behind the men, Bailey saw another room that housed three empty jail cells. At least Zach wasn't behind the black metal bars.

She had made arrangements for Faith, Hope, and Charity to spend a few more hours with Mattie. Hoop had headed over to the saloon to pick up the gossip about the murder.

"Rand." Bailey nodded toward the grinning man wearing the badge.

"Pleased to see you again, Bailey, although I'm sorry about the circumstances."

She returned the smile before getting down to business. "I don't know if Zach told you, but I am a practicing attorney and I will be representing him."

The sheriff glanced back and forth between Zach and her, and cocked an eyebrow with interest. Bailey still couldn't get over how handsome these Wyoming men were. Sure, some were sweaty and covered with dust, but if *Cosmo* could do a "rugged man" feature, this place would be overrun with women.

"Zach's told me a few things, but not that." He and Zach removed their feet from the desk, dropped them to the floor with heavy thuds, then rose. "I'll be glad for the help in finding the real killer, especially from such a pretty assistant."

Bailey rolled her eyes at his verbal pat on her head. He appeared to be a courageous and competent lawman and sincere in his desire to find the murderer. Zach clearly trusted Rand Weeks completely. She would have to reserve judgment until later.

The sheriff must have read her thoughts. "I've known Zach since we were boys, Bailey. I know that he didn't kill J.T. The unfortunate fact is that J.T. and Zach have both been loud and obnoxious about their mutual dislike. That crowd was mostly men from Thompson's ranch. They don't have much in the way of smarts, so it seems logical to them that Zach's the killer. When they find out about the knife that was used, all hell's going to break loose. They're really going to want to hang him then."

"Can you keep them from finding out?" Bailey couldn't prevent the horror that crossed her face.

"I'm trying," he replied. "Old Tag is the one who found the body and came and told me. He hid the knife in the donkey's pack. I didn't know he had it until I questioned him further. He let it slip that the knife was in his donkey's pack. He planned to sell it at the next town he visited." Rand turned toward Zach.

"Unfortunately, your pa made a big show when he won that pearl-handled knife from that cardplayer back east. Tag knows it belonged to your pa, and he knows it's worth a lot of money. That's why he didn't want to part with it. I asked him to keep all this quiet, but you know Tag, Zach. If there's a dollar to be made, he's going to make it."

Sheriff Weeks bent to unlock the bottom drawer of his heavy wooden desk. The lock creaked as it released, and the drawer groaned as he pulled it open. From the drawer he took out a small burlap bag, and from it a long object wrapped in dirty cotton fabric. Bailey stifled a shudder as the sheriff carefully removed the material from around a vicious-looking steel knife. The blade had been wiped clean, but dried blood still clung to the decorative crevices in the pearl handle and the hilt of the blade.

She wished it could be dusted for fingerprints, but she supposed that was impossible. She didn't really know when the police began to use fingerprints as evidence, but not in 1878. It was still a good hundred years before Miranda rights were given to arrested suspects as well. Zach needed to know that he didn't have to talk to anyone.

Bailey took a piece of paper and a pencil nub from the desk and sat down in the chair recently vacated by Zach.

Carefully, she began writing everything they knew so far. "You said he died two days ago?"

"That's what Doc McConnell thinks. Tag claims he found the body shortly after sunup this morning, and he came right into town and told me. I sent a couple of men to get the body." Rand replied with a slow drawl, clearly unwilling to relinquish control. His expression was unreadable as he sat back down in his wooden chair. The knife lay on the desk on top of the burlap sack. Rand directed his next question to Zach. "Who would have had access to the knife, Zach?"

Zach stared hard at the murder weapon, then shrugged. "I kept it hidden in a cabinet in my office."

"Could a person steal it?"

Zach shook his head. "I keep my office door shut, but not locked. The only guests we've had recently are Bailey, you, and Mr. and Mrs. Mack."

"Don't forget J.T. and his men. How do we know they were *all* out front that night?" Bailey asked.

The sheriff looked at her thoughtfully. Bailey knew what he was thinking and swallowed her indignation. She had to respect the sheriff for his speculation. Of course he'd consider her a suspect until he knew she and Zach both had alibis. "We can pretty much rule out J.T.," Rand finally said with a rueful grin.

"Don't forget Hoop and Jin Lee," Bailey added. "They both had complete access to the house."

"My sisters, Hoop, and Jin Lee have no place in this conversation," Zach snapped.

"We have to consider everyone before you can start eliminating anyone, Zach. We have to be thorough. Your life may depend on it." Bailey steadily met his glare.

"I agree," Rand added as he picked up the knife and wrapped the fabric around it. He placed it back in the burlap bag, then returned it to the drawer and locked it inside. "What do either of you know about Sloan Thompson?"

Zach walked across the office and lifted the window shade to consider the street outside. "Not much. You saw what happened at the ranch. I suspect he and J.T. didn't see eye to eye on things."

"How's that? I thought he was just trying to diffuse your tempers when he stepped between you two." The sheriff leaned back in his chair and studied Zach. Bailey had to give Rand credit. He was a persistent interrogator.

"Just an impression," Zach replied noncommittally. "Nothing specific." Bailey tensed. She intended to have Zach tell the sheriff the truth about Sloan and about their meeting that night by the river, but not until they had a chance to confer in private. It could mean the success of his entire defense. She breathed a sigh of relief when Rand moved on.

"What about Joe Junior?"

"Hell, Rand, he's just a boy." Zach motioned to his friend not to be ridiculous as he lowered the shade and moved to stand beside Bailey.

"Even though J.T. treated him like a kid, he is grown, Zach. Almost nineteen." The sheriff rose and stretched, then grinned at Bailey. "I'm planning to ride out to the ranch and talk to both brothers shortly."

Bailey returned his smile. Her fears that he might misconstrue Zach's words eased. He'd made it clear that he'd protect Zach as much as he could. What more could she ask for?

After the door clicked shut, Zach poured himself a cup of coffee, then sat down in Rand's vacated seat. An uncomfortable silence filled the room. Knowing that Zach didn't trust her, that he didn't believe she was from the future despite the proof of the almanac, made it even more difficult to share her plan. She had to proceed, though, if for no other reason than the welfare of his sisters. Bailey took a deep breath to muster her nerve. She rose from the chair, leaned across the desk, then looked him steady in the eye.

"You have to marry me, Zach. There's not a moment to spare."

Chapter 16

HOT COFFEE SEARED Zach's mouth as he heard Bailey's words. He sputtered, trying to keep the steaming liquid from scorching his throat. He fumbled to get the hot brew off his hands, but moved too fast, causing the tin to tumble over onto Rand's desk. Bailey jumped up and grabbed a cloth from a nearby table, then tried to help with the mess but only made it worse. He snatched the cloth from her hands and rushed to save the papers scattered over the desktop while trying to mop up the spilled coffee before it ended up in his lap.

It was a good five minutes before he could actually speak. "Now explain to me what in the hell you are talking about. Usually it's the man who does the asking." Zach sorted through the coffee-stained papers, separating them so they could dry.

"You have to marry me," Bailey repeated calmly. "I've

thought this through, and it's the only way to protect you and your sisters."

"How is that?"

"Two reasons. First, while I disagree, you've made it quite clear that you don't want anyone to know about us being on Thompson's ranch that night, and you don't want anyone to know that we talked with Sloan. Mark my words, it will come out. The sheriff suspects something already. When it does, I could be required to testify against you."

"About what? We were together all night."

She hesitated. "Perhaps. A good prosecutor would ask me if I could account for you *all* night long. The fact is that you *could* have ridden off once I finally went to sleep. In fact, I saw your horse saddled right before you got under the blanket with me. You *could* have murdered Thompson and returned without me knowing you were gone." She hated herself for such a low accusation. She wanted to believe in Zach despite how he felt about her.

"I saddled the horse to do a quick check of the area."

"Not a good statement from someone who threatened to kill his sworn enemy two days prior."

Zach stopped separating the damp papers and considered the woman before him. "So what does that have to do with marriage?" He heard Bailey sigh, clearly disappointed that he didn't seem to understand. He understood all right. He just wanted to hear it from her lips.

"Plain and simple. A wife cannot be forced to testify against her husband."

"You want to get married so you can protect me?" Zach shook his head. He'd been fighting his own wars for some time now. He'd be damned if he would fall for this trap or hide behind the skirts of a woman. "How convenient."

Bailey ignored his sarcasm and turned away from him to walk toward the jail cells in the far room. She placed a hand on the cool dark iron of a bar and leaned her forehead against it. She didn't face him when she answered. "That's only one reason. The other has to do with your sisters."

Zach considered her trim form. She seemed to be mustering her courage before she spoke again. When she finally looked at him, her expression was serious. "If the worst were to happen, what would become of Faith, Hope, and Charity?"

"Hoop would run the ranch for them until they married."

"Good plan." She nodded calmly. "How do you know Hoop's not somehow involved in the murder?"

Zach rose indignantly. "Hoop's as honest and loyal as any man I know."

"Perhaps he is. I don't know him like you do," she replied, pacing toward the desk. "At this point, though, he should be considered just as much of a suspect as you are. He had access to the knife. He knew the ramifications of killing Thompson with it. Does he stand to gain if you're out of the picture?" She halted, spun on her heel, and again headed toward the back room. "Most important, what if something were to happen to him? What about the girls then?"

"Make your point, Bailey. I'm short on patience right now," Zach replied stubbornly. He refused to consider that Hoop was somehow involved.

"Are you so boneheaded that you don't see this for yourself? Someone is trying to frame you, Zach. Whoever killed Thompson went to a great deal of trouble to make it look like you did it. Chances are they wanted Thompson dead and you to hang for it. Hoop might do a fine job taking care of your sisters, but he's not a legal relative. Once Faith or Hope were to marry, the new husband would most likely assume charge of the ranch whether Hoop objected or not. *Perhaps* that is the same person who has masterminded this entire situation. I know it's speculation at this point, but you must consider everything, no matter how far-fetched."

Zach's eyes narrowed. His voice was low and dangerous.

"I wondered when it would happen." At her surprised expression, he stepped closer, grabbing her arms and pulling her against his chest. "To think I was beginning to believe your poppycock story of the future. You're nothing but an opportunist. You moved right into our lives, ingratiating yourself and pretending to care about my sisters, probably knowing all along that this was going to happen. As my wife, the Double Bar G would become yours. Who's in this with you? Sloan?"

He saw all the emotions cross the delicate features of her face: hurt, anger, disappointment, outrage. "Are you really that blind, Zach? Do you think I staged the fall in the ravine just in time for you to wander by? Do you presume that I would cross that dangerous river to find my backpack to prove my identity to you if it were all for nothing? Do you believe whatever it is that exists between us is innocent flirtation? I've craved a family like yours to care for and to care for me all of my life. Knowing I had to leave was breaking my heart." She jerked herself free but refused to drop his gaze.

"Even though it's hard for you to accept, I am coming to love your sisters like they were my own. That's why I will delay my trip to help clear your name. And *that's* why I'm willing to marry you. It comes down to an issue of trust, Zach. You've spent the last five years of your life doing a really good job of proving that you didn't need anyone's help. This is a different matter entirely. You need me. Did you hear what I said, Zach? *You need me.*" Bailey slowly backed away from him and returned to stand by the iron bars.

The silence between them grew. Zach wanted to say something to ease her pain, but the words wouldn't come.

"Look." Her voice was soft but firm. "Either you trust me or you don't. If you do, then marry me. If you don't, I'm leaving with Tag tonight. I won't watch your stubbornness take away everything you have ever loved, starting with your ranch and ending with your sisters."

Zach saw the resolve in her eyes. For so long it had been just him. How could he let this unusual woman, whom he really knew nothing about, take control of his life? Her reasons seemed valid, but could he allow himself to rely on someone else? "Why are you suddenly willing to forgo your trip to Medicine Mountain?"

"I'm not forgoing it. Once this is settled, I'll be on my way. I've worked hard for that judicial appointment, and I want it."

"So you'll let the girls think you really are their sister. You'll let them get attached to you and then you'll leave them?"

"There is no other way, Zach," she replied sadly. "You can tell everyone that I couldn't take any more of the harsh Wyoming Territory. Tell them I went back east, or wherever. I don't care."

"What about you? You'll still be married even if you supposedly return to the future." He knew his voice was harsh, and he immediately regretted his tone when Bailey's eyes hardened.

"No, Zach, I won't be married. You don't exist in the future. It will be like this whole thing never happened." He returned her stare and for a moment neither of them spoke. Finally, Bailey sighed, regretfully shook her head, and started for the door. "I can still catch Tag if I hurry."

"Bailey, wait." Zach caught her hand gently in his. It was still wrapped to protect her injury. His pride and self-reliance were battered. It wasn't easy to accept that this woman was compassionate enough to help his family just because they needed it. He didn't have much choice, not withstanding everything else. She was right about his sisters, and she could be right that someone was out to get him. She was wrong about Hoop though. Very wrong. He reached out and took her other hand, too. "I recognize the truth in what you've just said. About the ranch, about the murder, about my sisters. They do need you."

"What about you, Zach? Do you need me, too?"

His heart cried out to tell her yes, but his mind refused to cooperate. He'd just given her more than he'd thought he could ever give anyone. Did he have anything left?

"Go get the minister," he said gruffly. She coolly extracted her hand as she turned away and headed out the door. He heard a firm snap of the lock as Bailey closed the door behind her. He didn't try to stop her, to make her understand. He couldn't, at least not right then. There was something building between them, and if he was honest with himself, he'd secretly hoped it would lead to more. Bailey, however, had made her feelings known. They had no future. Not now, not ever.

She had convinced him that he needed her. That his sisters needed her. But she had also made it clear the need was not mutual. As soon as she could, she was going back to her old life, wherever that life may be. What would happen to Faith, Hope, and Charity then? What would happen to him?

Quickly, he moved to the desk and sat down, reaching for a pencil and a clean sheet of paper. He thought a minute, then started to write. Bailey spoke as if she had all the answers. As much as he agreed with her logic on most things, he couldn't quite accept all of it. Hoop had signed on with the Double Bar G more than ten years ago. He'd hung on, too, helping Zach through the hard times, sometimes for nothing more than a hot meal and a place to lay his head. Bailey presumed too much if she thought Zach would give up on his best friend now.

An hour later, Bailey reached for the knob to open the door to the sheriff's office, the Reverend Horace Martin in tow. The small thin man was by no means inclined to perform such a sudden marriage, especially when the town's three terrors were bridesmaids. The promise of a sizable donation to the church's new building fund was more than he could resist. Mrs. Martin followed close behind, her prim nose tilted high in the air with not an ounce of compassion or forgiveness on her face.

Bailey had known better than to allow Faith, Hope, and Charity to accompany her to the church. According to Rand, the circuit judge wouldn't be in town until there was to be a trial; the reverend was the only person who could perform the nuptials. This marriage had to take place, and Bailey couldn't risk the preacher's refusal.

Mattie had graciously offered to escort the twins and Charity over to the jail, although all three girls smoothly assured Bailey they knew the way. Mattie had also agreed to stand as a witness to the ceremony. Bailey liked the dressmaker enormously. If she had planned to stay in this time, they would have certainly become close friends. *If she were staying.* Bailey mentally shook herself. This marriage was a temporary delay, nothing more, and it would be in her own best interests to remember that. She had no illusions that Zach was marrying her for any reason other than he had to. Once the real murderer was found, he would be the first to help her onto the back of any horse pointing toward Medicine Mountain.

"Ma'am?" Reverend Martin spoke from behind her. "I can't help but notice your hesitation. Are you certain this is what you want? You're not being forced into this union, are you?" He put a gentle hand on her shoulder with what seemed like genuine concern.

Bailey looked back at the quiet man and shook her head with a soft smile. Even though it wasn't the way she had imagined it, a family was what she'd wanted all her life. If it couldn't be forever, well, that was the price she'd pay. Yes, she wanted Zach and his sisters, despite how she was getting them. Bailey tightened her grip on the doorknob, then turned it and pushed her way inside.

Immediately, Faith, Hope, and Charity rushed toward her, delight on their sweet faces. "She's here," all three cried in unison as they danced around like Precious and the happy puppies back at the barn.

"Zach told us about your wedding." Charity laughed, clasping her hands together. "Now you'll really be our sister!" Bailey bent to encircle Charity in her arms as Hope and Faith joined the hug.

"I'm excited, too." She returned the teasing with a light-hearted grin that didn't quite reach her eyes. "Zach talked me into it even though you three were part of the bargain." The beautiful blond sisters giggled as Bailey scanned the room for their brother. Zach stood and watched, stoic and unsmiling. Again Bailey's heart sank. He could at least look a little pleased. She was trying to keep him from hanging, after all.

Hoop stood near Zach, hat in hand. Bailey thought she saw the trifle of a smile as he considered the joy and laughter of Zach's sisters. The sheriff, however, was another matter. He had said he'd been heading out to see the Thompson brothers when he learned of the immediate marriage. Now, he scowled at them both and demanded to know what they were up to. Neither Zach nor Bailey would explain, and he finally let the matter drop. Mattie and Sheriff Weeks stood side by side near his desk. She saw Rand dart a quick glance at Mattie, who blushed ever so slightly. Bailey sighed. If only things had turned out differently Zach might be flirting with her the same way.

Minister Martin took his wife by the elbow and moved toward Zach, who stood near the door leading into the room with the iron cells. "Zachariah." He nodded. "I understand you and Miss Cooper wish to be wed. Are you certain this cannot wait for a more appropriate time?"

The room grew silent as Zach considered the preacher. His gaze finally rose to Bailey. She lifted her chin defiantly. Even though he'd already made it clear that he didn't trust her, becoming his wife was the best strategy for his defense and for the future of his sisters. If he backed out now, he knew he would be on his own.

Slowly, Zach stepped forward and took Bailey's hand. "Yes, sir," he agreed tonelessly, "that's what we wish, and we would prefer not to wait."

"Well, then," the minister repled, opening his Bible and bowing his head. "Shall we begin with a word of prayer?"

It took less than five minutes, Bailey realized a short while later, to change the course of her entire life. Zach had kissed her to seal their vows, but it was nothing like the passion they had shared the night by the river. When the minister pronounced them married, Bailey tried to imagine the joy a true bride would feel standing by her new husband. All she felt was worry, confusion, and Zach's distrust.

Once the brief formalities were over, Faith, Hope, and Charity, as well as Mattie and Mrs. Martin, joined in to wish Bailey happiness. The men gathered around Zach, with plenty of backslapping and congratulations before they stepped over to kiss the bride. Hoop leaned forward and kissed her warmly on the cheek.

"If anyone can make this bunch happy, it will be you, Miss Bailey," he drawled. Bailey instantly snapped out of her melancholy to hear his kind words. Hoop was right. She could make Zach and his sisters happy, at least for a short while. In just a few short words Hoop had wisely reminded her of one of the benefits of this marriage.

"Thank you, Hoop." She smiled up at him. "That means a lot coming from you."

One by one, the crowd dissipated. The preacher and Mrs. Martin took their leave, still avoiding Faith, Hope, and Charity. Hoop excused himself to go check on the horses and wagon for the ride home. Sheriff Weeks offered to escort the girls to the buckboard, then take Mattie back to her apartment over the dress shop.

When they were alone, Zach considered Bailey carefully. "I hope you know what you're doing," he said finally.

"When it comes to the law, I know what I'm doing," she snapped. "If this mess isn't resolved quickly, and you are put on trial, I'll expect you to be much more gracious." She turned on her heel and headed toward the door. "I hope you find that jail cell comfortable for the first night of your honeymoon. It's a shame you're spending it *alone*."

Chapter 17

HOPE POPPED THE reins and cued Plug and Sparky into a fast trot. Bailey settled into the motion of the wagon as they headed back to the Double Bar G. Hoop accompanied them on his own horse. She glanced back at him and met his steady gaze. She wondered if Zach had told him of her doubts. It wasn't that she thought for certain that Hoop could be the murderer, but he was a suspect just like everyone else. She wondered if behind that relaxed air and lazy slouch in the saddle the foreman was hiding anything.

Surprisingly, Hope and her sisters hadn't yet bombarded her with questions. She knew they would, however, and that she didn't have any good answers. Zach, their only relative in the world, had just been arrested for murder then married a practical stranger all in one afternoon. All three knew that Zach had threatened J.T.; Hope had even stood at the window and watched. They didn't know yet about the knife, but it didn't take a legal expert to know that the circumstantial evidence did not look good. Often the truth was not strong enough to outweigh the circumstantial evidence either. She had seen it happen way too many times in the courtroom. She'd even used it herself when prosecuting kids with criminal records. Never once did she imagine she'd be so personally affected by the twists and turns of legal proceedings. Now she was about to be thrust into the middle of a fight for a man's life. A special man, she acknowledged. Her husband.

Zach's only alibi was that they were together the night of the murder, something he didn't want anyone to know about. Since they were now married, however, there was no reason to keep it quiet. She planned to speak to him about that first thing in the morning.

Zach was right about his sisters, too. The longer she stayed, the closer she would be drawn to his sisters and them to her. While getting home was still intensely important to her, the rush to do so immediately had dimmed slightly, judicial appointment or not.

Bailey scanned the horizon all around and saw nothing but the peaceful range. Not a single tree dotted the grassy hillsides, but the blue, purple, yellow, and white varieties of lupines provided splashes of color among the golden waves of tangled grass. The scent of flowers mixed with the breeze, creating the fragrance of fresh, clean air. Today, only a few clouds dotted the late afternoon sky.

Yes, she liked it here. Despite the lack of plumbing and despite a pretend husband who needed her but didn't want her. Bailey shifted on the buckboard seat and glanced at each girl in the wagon. "Who do you think killed Mr. Thompson?"

One by one, they all shook their head. "Almost everyone hated him, Bailey," Faith answered.

"Don't say things like that about the dead, Faith," Hope

snapped, turning from the seat to look back at her twin. "It's not proper."

"Well, it's true, Hope. Even Zach has said so," Charity added with childlike logic.

"She does have a point," Bailey said. "I met him only the one time and I instantly disliked him. But whether or not he was liked is still no reason for murder. We know that your brother didn't kill him, so let's figure out who did."

"Sloan," Hope interrupted firmly. "I didn't like him the minute he showed up. Neither did Joe Junior."

Bailey considered the teenager beside her carefully. Hope's normally pleasant expression was marred, and her lips had narrowed into a thin line. This situation with Zach was worrying her more than the teenager wanted to admit. Hope looked so pretty and grown-up wearing the skirt and blouse she'd chosen this morning with her hair up in the French twist. She drove the wagon and handled the horses with confidence, but her body was stiff and tense.

"You told me earlier that Joe Junior doesn't like his brother," Bailey reminded Hope. "Do you know why?"

"Hope thinks Joe Junior is handsome," Charity piped in. Bailey pretended not to notice Faith's hand that reached out to cover the smaller girl's mouth. Her gaze remained fixed on Hope. There was something here the three weren't telling.

"I need to tell you three something you don't know. It's extremely serious and you must *promise* me that you won't tell anyone else. Your brother's freedom may depend on it." She solemnly considered each girl. "Do you truly understand me?" All three faces were suddenly quiet and serious. One by one they nodded.

"Mr. Thompson was murdered with your father's pearl-handled knife."

Hope jerked her head away from Bailey and back toward the horses. She bit her bottom lip and nodded. "That must be it, then. Joe Junior told me that Sloan was going to ruin everything, but he didn't tell me how or why. Sloan had to have done it." Her voice was soft, but there was stubbornness in her eyes.

"All right," Bailey agreed thoughtfully. "Sloan could be a suspect. Anyone else?"

The girls began to name anyone they could think of that might have wanted J.T. Thompson dead. After about the twentieth name of neighboring ranchers or business owners in town, Bailey held up hand. "Okay, now of those men, who would have had access to Zach's office? This part is very important, think carefully."

"Probably not any," Faith replied earnestly. "The few who have been to our ranch usually come only once a year for a roundup party. Besides, the only people I've ever seen in his office are the three of us when we're not supposed to be, Jin Lee when he cleans, Hoop when he and Zachariah discuss the cattle, and Sheriff Weeks whenever he drops by for a visit." She looked deep in thought at Bailey's inquiry. Her mind was clearly hard at work on the mystery. Bailey grinned. Tenaciousness was a wonderful trait, especially for someone wanting to solve a crime.

A glance toward Hope reaffirmed Bailey's instincts. Her body had stiffened, and her face was pale. The girl's hands gripped the reins tightly, and the two horses tossed their heads in irritation. Hope wasn't telling all that she knew about Joe Junior and Sloan.

Bailey reconsidered the dead man's sons. Would either of them kill their own father? For someone who had never had a father or a mother, the thought was ludicrous. If Sloan had actually intended to murder J.T., he'd have never taken the time to seek Zach out and practically tell him so. On the other hand, Sloan had emphatically sworn that he was going to stop his father. Was Sloan's hate for J.T. strong enough to kill?

Why hadn't Sloan stepped forward and told Sheriff

Weeks that they were near the scene of the crime that night? That would have practically confirmed Zach's guilt to the angry cowboys. Sloan kept quiet. Why? Maybe because they could say the same thing about him. He was near the crime scene just like Zach was. And he had a motive, just like Zach.

They came over the crest of a small hill. Bailey noticed that Hope's gaze was intently focused on a windmill out in the distance that steadily turned with the slight breeze. Bailey squinted and looked more closely. Another kerchief was tied to the stand, almost in the same spot where Zach had untied the last one. Was it a signal of some sort?

Hope drew her attention back to the horses, deliberately ignoring Bailey's questioning look. Bailey made a mental note to talk to Hope privately.

Another half a mile and the buildings of the Double Bar G could be seen. As they rode nearer to the house, she saw a black horse with four white socks tied to the hitching post out in front. She recognized the distinctive animal immediately. Had the devil come a-calling?

Sloan Thompson sat on the porch swing, slowly rocking back and forth. He lifted a glass of lemonade to his lips as Hope pulled the wagon to a stop. He'd obviously been waiting awhile.

"Ladies, please go inside," Bailey said. "I want to talk with Mr. Thompson."

Hope reined the horses to a halt and set the brake on the wagon. She looked as if she was going to object, then thought better of it when Bailey shot her a warning glare. One by one, they all filed into the house, leaving Bailey alone with the tall man. Hoop took the team and wagon and headed toward the barn. His nod to Bailey indicated he'd be watching just in case.

"I'm sorry about J.T.," Bailey started. "I know it must be a difficult time for you."

"Not for me," he replied casually. "You and Gooden knew how I felt about him. Couldn't have happened to a nicer fellow."

"That's a little harsh, don't you think? The man is dead, after all."

Sloan shrugged but remained silent as he continued to rock back and forth in the swing. Bailey stared at his unwavering eyes and wondered if they were the eyes of a killer.

"Let's go for a walk, Sloan. I suspect there are listening ears behind those curtains." She pointed toward the window near the swing. Sloan finished his lemonade in one swallow, then rose. He joined her as they walked down the steps toward the corrals.

"Why didn't you speak up about the other night?" she asked when they were well out of earshot. "You were there. You know Zach didn't kill your father."

"Just as you know I didn't do it," he replied. They had come to stop at a paddock holding one of Zach's black bulls. "Sure is a fine animal," he added as he lifted a booted foot up on the bottom board, then leaned toward the fence and considered the two-thousand-pound bull.

Bailey ignored the diversion. "You could have killed him after you left us."

Sloan lifted both brows and considered Bailey skeptically. She knew he was silently pointing out the fact that the same was true for Zach, and for her. He turned back toward the bull. "I have a pretty good idea who the real killer is."

"Who?"

"I can't say right now."

Bailey impatiently shook her head. "Don't say you know who it is, then keep me in the dark about it. You started this conversation, now finish it."

"I came over here to tell you that I won't let an innocent man hang. You'll just have to accept it at that."

Bailey sighed. "I'm not sure I can do that, Sloan. Zach's life is on the line."

He shrugged. "Do what you need to do, Miss Cooper. But there appears to be more to the story than what's on the surface. I think J.T. had done this fellow wrong, just like he had me. But—"

"Are you saying there were mitigating circumstances?"

"That may be the name for it, I'm not certain. Just tell Gooden that there's more to this murder than fancy bulls. Then tell him everything else I've told you. But don't tell anyone else. Not the sheriff, not your foreman, and certainly not his sisters."

A red warning flag suddenly appeared in Bailey's thoughts. "His sisters? Does one of them have anything to do with this, Sloan?"

He looked at her steadily. "What makes you ask that?"

"Since I've been here, they seem to be somehow involved in everything else." She sighed and shook her head. Bailey was skeptical. Here was the son of a dead man telling her to bear with him and he'd find the real killer. "Why are you doing this, Sloan?"

"My *pa*," he said the word with disdain, "was not a good man. He used people, even those close to him, to get whatever he wanted. He sent for me because he needed my protection."

"Protection? He knew someone was going to kill him? Who?"

"Don't know, he never actually said. Just told me to keep an eye on everyone, even the most unlikely. I think my sudden appearance at the ranch is what got him killed."

"Why? You're his son."

"I'm also a hired gun," he replied. "A gunfighter."

Chapter 18

ZACH STARED AT the plate of chicken and dumplings Rand had brought him to eat. It had been hours since Bailey headed home with Hoop and his sisters. Not since his pa was killed had he felt so helpless. He'd always been the strong, self-reliant one of the family, even when his pa was alive. Once he was dead, it had been up to Zach to keep the ranch going and to raise his three sisters. He was the rescuer. Now it looked as if he was the one who needed to be rescued. With him behind bars, no matter how temporary, it was up to Bailey, Hoop, and Rand to prevent him from hanging.

Unless he could think of something to do from this blasted jail.

He pushed the plate across the table, then stretched in the uncomfortable ladder-backed chair. How had he ended up married on top of all this other mess? Bailey presented a logical argument, no question there. In truth, he wasn't so much worried about the possibility that she would be forced to testify against him. He was innocent, after all. He was more concerned that his sisters needed a legal guardian should anything ever happen to him.

That was part of the problem. Bailey had made it clear that this was a temporary marriage. Nothing permanent about it. Once he was out of jail, she was gone. He had just begun to realize that maybe he wanted her around permanently when J.T. was killed. He huffed. J.T. aggravated him even from the grave.

Truth was, he couldn't see clearly when it came to his fiery redhead. He wanted to sweep her into his arms and kiss her until her damn logic went haywire and her knees went weak. He wanted her more than he'd ever wanted about anything in his entire life. He had loused it up pretty bad, too, what with her badgering him to get married and all. What was in this for her? There had to be some angle. Other than Hoop, no one would willingly take on his sisters.

Zach rose from the chair and lowered the wick of the kerosene lamp. The room darkened and he walked toward the front window of the sheriff's office. He left the shade drawn, but stood at the side and lifted it slightly to look out at the town's single dirt road. It was late. The moon was high and the stars were bright. Together, they cast an eerie glow over the weathered buildings. Except for the noisy saloon, most of the town was dark and silent.

Rand had warned him, and Hoop had quietly confirmed, just how bad the gossip was in town. Both had told him to lay low in the jail at least for a few days. If not for his own safety, then for that of his sisters. The way Rand figured it, if J.T.'s boys knew he was behind bars, they'd be less likely to take their revenge on his sisters or at the Double Bar G. Zach wasn't sure he agreed with that logic, but Rand made it clear he'd officially lock Zach up if he didn't willingly cooperate.

Unfortunately, too many people knew about the animosity between Thompson and Zach's pa. Then Zach had taken up right where his pa had left off. It was hard not to when he knew in his heart that J.T. had killed Thomas Gooden because of a game of cards. He was sure most everyone in town suspected it, too, but Thompson had had a rock-solid alibi. He was with Joe Junior and several other ranch hands checking the herds. Rand never found anyone else, and Thomas Gooden had been buried, his murderer never brought to justice.

Perhaps until now.

Zach watched a solitary figure exit the saloon, mount his horse, then casually ride off into the darkness. He reminded himself that if he weren't so hotheaded, so free with his threats, he might not be sitting here, arrested for a murder he didn't commit. But hell, J.T. had cheated at cards, killed his father, relentlessly tried to destroy the Double Bar G, and then laughed about how it would all soon be his. Even a sane man had a right to be hotheaded when pushed that far. A hard lump formed in Zach's throat. He thought he'd feel satisfied that the scoundrel had finally gotten what was coming to him, but he wasn't. No one deserved to be murdered, especially so brutally, no matter what the reason.

Zach wanted to get even with J.T. all right, but it was through his hybrid cattle that he planned to retaliate. He intended to have his hybrids at the auction block early next summer, long before J.T.'s longhorns had recovered the weight lost during the winter. His hybrids would be bigger, the beef far tastier, and he'd sell his cattle while the prices were still high. If all went according to plan, he'd practically corner the market on Wyoming beef. The demand for Double Bar G crossbred beef would make Zach a rich man. All he needed was for Charlie Mack, the owner of the bank, to extend his loan. He wanted to keep this year's hybrid cows to breed next year. That should partially solve his problem with the calves being bigger than their mamas.

What, if by some strange twist of fate, this wasn't resolved, and he was hanged for Thompson's murder? As hard as it was to admit, Bailey was right. There would be a very real chance that his sisters would not be able to hold on to the Double Bar G. They'd be orphans, not legally old enough to oversee the ranch. He could easily imagine two or three particular townsfolk valiantly overcoming their dislike for his sisters to take over the ranch, using the flimsy excuse of doing what was best for them. He knew exactly what those same kindly townsfolk would do. They'd either take the ranch from them somehow or sell it outright.

Once that was done, Zach doubted anyone would continue a long-term family relationship with Faith, Hope, or Charity. Not with his sisters' reputations for trouble. Their ma had a younger cousin back east somewhere, but Zach wasn't even sure how to go about finding her. That would be the first thing he'd do once this was over. If there was one, he'd find this relative no matter how long it took. Faith, Hope, and Charity had already lost both parents, they didn't need to be completely alone in this world.

Zach sighed and turned from the window. They wouldn't be alone if Bailey was what she seemed. He headed back toward the jail cell. He knew without testing it that the cot would be uncomfortable. The thin lumpy mattress was a certain giveaway. He fluffed it up the best he could, then settled down onto it, placing his hands up under his head and staring up at the ceiling.

The image of his beautiful redhead once again haunted his thoughts. Bailey Cooper, this odd woman who claimed she was from the future, looked to be the answer to his prayers. For his sisters, for the ranch, and for himself. That's what bothered him. He had never really needed anyone, not even Hoop. Somehow everything changed the evening he brought her from the ravine. Now he suddenly needed everybody.

He had been talking to Tag when he heard the news about J.T. For the proper price, the old miner had said, he'd be willing to take Bailey all the way to Medicine Mountain. If he hadn't married her this afternoon, she'd probably have already been gone.

After Sloan disappeared back into the darkness that night by the river, he had sat by the fire reading the most unbelievable things in the almanac. If it was genuine, he now knew how harsh the winters would be for the next twenty years, and he had the potential to be a very rich man. Was it proper for him to have knowledge that no one else did? He supposed that depended on how he used the information. He couldn't tell many folks, of course; they'd think him as crazy as he initially thought Bailey was. However, if he were to advise his neighbors to prepare for harsh snows, dry summers, or even blinding rain, it might be acceptable to use it.

If it were true, and that was a big if.

Zach turned to one side and pillowed his head on his arm. Tomorrow, he would ask Bailey to bring the almanac to him so he could study it more. Looked like he was going to have a bit of time for reading over the next few days. He wished he'd read parts of it more closely, but the light from the fire had been too dim that night. And then an uneasy feeling had settled over him. He saddled Reliant and headed back to the ravine just to take another look around for her belongings. He hadn't found anything more, though. When he returned an hour later, he saw that Bailey hadn't stirred from her slumber. He hadn't killed Thompson, but he'd have a lot of explaining to do if she knew he had left her side that night.

He sighed. It was going to be a long night.

Would the night never end?

It had to be well past midnight as Bailey pushed aside the curtains and stared through the window of her bedroom. The rain had started about an hour ago, suddenly and without warning. The clouds had gathered as the sun was beginning to descend for the evening, and now they exploded with heavy rains, thunder, and lightning.

What had possessed her to marry Zach Gooden?

Although she hadn't wanted to admit it even to herself, Bailey knew that she had come to care for Zach despite the brief time she'd known him. It came to her not in a burst of lightning like tonight's vivid storm, but in a calm, gentle whisper like the morning dew.

As she saw it, not counting the murder, there were two problems that had to be overcome. Did she love Zach enough to want to stay with him forever? She knew that he physically wanted her just as she did him. And right now he needed her, but she held no illusion about his love for her. There was none. He'd made that perfectly clear this afternoon. He had something more that Bailey desired above all else. He had family. Was she willing to give up being a judge for the one thing she thought she'd never have? Was it good enough to have a family, but not the intense, need-defying love of Zach Gooden?

Bailey pulled the hand-stitched quilt from the narrow bed, then dragged a chair closer to the window. A burst of lightning spiked across the sky, its branches casting an eerie glow across the prairie. If it hadn't been so oddly beautiful, she might have been frightened by the storm. Bailey Cooper had survived far more terrible things than violent weather. Beginning with the death of her parents and now with a trip through time and a marriage to a man one hundred and twenty-one years her senior.

Perhaps that was unfair, Bailey thought. Being married to a man as handsome and interesting as Zach wasn't so bad. They definitely had some type of chemistry between them. It was the fact that Zach didn't want to be married to her that bothered her. Not that she blamed him. She would be suspicious, too, if a practical stranger had suddenly offered to solve all of his problems by saying "I do" in front of a preacher. But he had agreed, and now it was legal. The Double Bar G, and his sisters, would be her responsibility if anything went wrong.

Bailey tucked her feet up under her legs and leaned her head against the back of the chair. She wouldn't let things get out of hand; she'd made a promise to Zach. He wasn't a murderer, she knew that in her heart.

Then again, she didn't believe in time travel, and look where that got her.

"Well, what do you think?" Bailey asked as she carefully considered the expressions on the faces of Faith, Hope, and Charity. The early morning sun filtered in through the window. It was shortly after sunup. She hadn't been able to sleep, and neither had the girls. Together, they wandered around Zach's office looking for anything unusual. She wanted them to look through his office for anything that might indicate who had stolen the knife to try to frame him.

A surprising pang shot through Bailey as Zach's overpowering essence lingered in the room. The dark leather desk chair had comfortable indentations from his body. Entries in his leather-covered green ledger books were neatly written in black ink with flowing script. Bailey considered his entries thoughtfully. Zach was full of contradictions. He was a hothead with a quick temper, a man who reacted emotionally rather than logically, but Zach Gooden was painstakingly meticulous in his record-keeping.

Bailey walked over and tried the window behind the desk. It lifted quickly and easily, and there was no screen. She looked through the window frame to see that the front porch extended around the sides of the house all the way to the back. "Is the window always unlocked?" she asked.

Surprised, the girls stared at her. Faith spoke first as Charity joined Bailey by the window. "Of course. There's never been a reason to lock it."

Yet another difference between their time and mine, Bailey thought. Unfortunately, murder was murder no matter what century one was in. "If it was a warm night, Zach would leave the window open, right?" The three sisters nodded, and Bailey began her habitual pacing. She stopped suddenly. "Even if he wasn't working in here?"

Another round of nods.

"So literally anyone *could have* come inside."

"Anyone," Hope whispered urgently. "It could have been anyone."

Bailey deliberately took her time before meeting Hope's gaze. The teenager sounded worried, concerned, almost frightened.

"The problem would be how would they get inside without us knowing?" Faith asked as she walked to the window and stared outside. "There's nowhere to hide a horse except on the other side of the barn. And, if someone had done that, the dogs would have barked."

"Good thinking, Faith. You'd make a great investigator." The younger woman blushed at Bailey's praise. "Okay, let's create a list of suspects." She walked over to Zach's desk and took out a piece of paper and Zach's pen and ink. She'd never used such a pen before, but it didn't take long to get the hang of it. On the paper she listed the name of every person they talked about yesterday. To be completely thorough, she also listed the most obvious: *Zach, Hoop, Bailey, Joe Junior, Sloan.* She hesitated a minute, and then added another name to the list: *Tag.*

Sloan had said he had seen Tag and Mildred early the day of the murder. And it was Tag who supposedly found the body and told Sheriff Weeks. Since he'd been in the vicinity of the crime scene previous to the time of the murder, he was certainly a suspect.

Bailey read the names on the entire list to Faith, Hope, and Charity. Together, they determined where almost everyone should have been during the time of the murder as Bailey scribbled down notes beside each person. Now she had a place to start. She would confirm that the folks on this list were accounted for, then she'd see who was left over.

Faith walked over to the huge wooden secretary across from Zach's desk and started to open one of the lower drawers. Hope immediately rushed over and snapped it shut. Bailey saw the silent pleading in Hope's eyes as she met Faith's annoyed glare.

"Have you found something?" Bailey walked to the two and placed an arm around each one.

"N-nothing," Hope stammered. "Zach kept Pa's knife in there."

"I see," Bailey replied softly and turned the girls away from the cabinet and out of Zach's office. Their search had produced a very interesting bit of new evidence.

Zach had told Bailey that even the girls didn't know where he hid the knife.

"Don't think Zach would approve of that, ma'am." Hoop tossed a huge bale of hay down from the barn's hayloft. It was quickly followed by another, then a third and a fourth.

Bailey stared up at the tall foreman as he started to climb back down the barn's built-in ladder. It was mid-morning, and it once again looked like rain outside the cozy comfort of the barn. Charity was in the far stall playing with Precious and the other puppies. Faith and Hope had ascended upstairs after they had finished in Zach's office. They had said they were going to practice the new hairstyles, but Bailey was certain there was an avid discussion going on in their room. About what she wasn't certain. It was evident that Faith also knew her sister was hiding something. Perhaps she'd be able to pry it out of Hope.

"It doesn't look like Zach has much of a say in anything right now, Hoop. It's vital to the investigation. I need to go to Mr. Thompson's funeral this afternoon."

Hoop reached up to lift his hat and scratch his scalp. "It's not a good idea, Miss Bailey. Those boys are mean. It was J.T.'s first requirement before he hired them. They might decide to administer justice themselves, starting with Zach Gooden's pretty new wife."

"Then you go with me. Jin Lee can keep an eye on Faith, Hope, and Charity. The murderer is often someone who is close to the victim and usually attends the funeral. I want to watch the people; see who's there and who's not there. You can identify them for me."

Hoop walked over to the barn door and looked up at the cloudy sky. He was stalling. "I really got to check the southern fences, Miss Bailey. Zach's orders."

"Hoop, if we don't figure out who killed J.T., there may not be any southern fences left to check."

He rubbed his hand across his jaw for a long moment then reluctantly nodded. "You've got a point there. We'll have to take the buckboard, though, so don't be jumping all over me like you did to Zach."

"Fair enough," Bailey agreed.

"And don't tell Zach I was party to this," he cautioned. "I've got a feeling he'd really resort to murder if he found out I took you over to that nest of rattlers."

Chapter 19

LESS THAN AN hour later, Bailey stood outside the porch waiting for Hoop and the buckboard. The girls had wanted to go, Hope especially, but Bailey flatly refused. Hoop was right, it could be dangerous. Considering the anger that coursed throughout the crowd yesterday, she was a bit apprehensive herself. An appraisal of the mourners at the funeral was so very important, otherwise Bailey wouldn't go either. She couldn't leave Zach's future to chance. Not when she possessed at least some of the skills needed to clear his name.

Bailey looked down at the simple black dress she wore, once again borrowed from Faith. The bodice area was tight, but the neckline, edged with soft black lace, was high around her throat. The skirt came almost to the ground. Faith had offered her black satin slippers to wear with the dress, but after last night's rain, Bailey knew they wouldn't withstand the mud. Instead, she wore a pair of Hope's black lace-up boots. The youngest twin's foot happened to be just a bit larger than her sister's.

After talking to Hoop, she hadn't had much time to help the girls with their hair and then change clothes herself. She did manage to show Faith how to create the simple French twist she liked so much. Already, the three girls seemed much more demure and charming. Bailey knew it wasn't really due to her efforts. Zach's sisters had secretly craved this type of attention for such a long time. They just needed someone to get them started.

Either that or they were playing her big time, and all hell was going to break loose any minute.

Hoop drove the buckboard from the barn to the front of the house. Sparky and Plug were again hitched to the wagon; his own horse was saddled and tied behind as well. She had thought the two old horses were around for the sisters to ride. Apparently, the duo did much to earn their keep. As Bailey settled herself into the front seat of the buckboard, she noticed Hope standing by an upstairs window watching them. Bailey lifted her hand and waved as the horses began to move out. The minute she got back, Bailey determined, little Miss Hope was going to come clean about what she knew.

Bailey counted twenty-nine mourners at the funeral of J.T. Thompson. He was buried in the church cemetery right next to his late wife, Rosalie. It was mostly dusty wranglers who had gathered to pay their respects, along with the Reverend and Mrs. Martin, Mr. and Mrs. Mack, Sheriff Weeks, Joe Junior, and Sloan. Even old Tag and his flea-bitten donkey stood nearby.

Rand frowned when he saw Hoop help her step from the buckboard. He calmly walked toward them and escorted Bailey closer to the graveside. Hoop followed a short distance behind. They really were worried about her safety, she realized. The sheriff stopped near the fence surrounding the cemetery, a point where they could see the ceremony but could talk softly without being heard.

The preacher opened the Good Book in his hand and slowly began to read one of the passages. One by one, Rand quietly identified each person and explained how they were connected with the dead man in the coffin. Bailey mentally added or deleted them from her list of suspects as they talked. As usual, Hoop didn't say much unless asked. By the time the service was over, she reconfirmed her primary suspect list: Sloan, Joe Junior, Hoop, herself, Zach, and Tag.

When the crowd began to depart, the three walked back to the wagon. Rand offered his hand to help Bailey back onto the seat of the buckboard. "Hoop, you can head on back to the Double Bar G. I'll drive Miss Cooper over to the jail so she can talk to Zach. He's going crazy not knowing what's going on. I'll bring her back to the ranch later."

At Bailey's affirmative nod, Hoop untied his horse from the back of the wagon, then mounted. With a quick nod in their direction, he set out toward the ranch. She watched Hoop's retreating back and grinned. The stoic foreman had spoken at least a dozen complete sentences today, and they were all directed at her. Hoop was a genuine strong, silent type, so that had to be a record.

Sheriff Weeks had to slap the reins and cluck to Sparky and Plug all the way to the jail. Bailey felt ironically vindicated that she wasn't the only person who couldn't convince the horses to willingly obey.

"Who was absent?" Bailey asked quietly.

"As far as I can tell, everyone was there who would have meant anything to J.T."

Bailey nodded. "What about Tag? Why do you think he came?"

The sheriff laughed. "Curiosity probably. He's harmless."

"Maybe he is, maybe he ain't," Bailey mimicked the

grumpy old man's drawl. "I'm pretty certain he has some of my belongings. He found them before he found J.T."

"How do you know that? If he stole something from you, I'll bring him in and talk to him," the sheriff replied sharply.

"He didn't really steal it. I lost my traveling bag and I think he found it. But when I asked him about it yesterday, I foolishly commented on Mildred. I now have a terrible bruise on my thigh where she kicked me."

"You told Mildred she smells, right?"

Bailey grinned apologetically. "Guilty. Anyway, I wasn't as nice to him as I should have been. I feel sure he'll give me my bag. He's just trying to make a point."

"Yep, that's Tag. Contrary old coot. You have to convince him that you couldn't care less about what he has before he'll up and insist you take it. Whoa, now, fellas." Whoa was a command the horses knew well. They quickly stopped the minute Rand let up on the reins. Fortunately, it was in front of the jail.

"Tag was on Thompson's ranch the day of the murder. That's where he found my bag. He may not be the murderer, but it wouldn't hurt to talk to him. He may have seen something," Bailey spoke cautiously. The sheriff was just as determined as she to find the true killer. She didn't want to imply that he wasn't doing his job.

"I reckon you're right. That's why I talked to him last night." Rand didn't move from the wagon, neither did she.

"What did he say?" she asked.

"What you would expect. He was coming back from his latest, and usually useless, search for gold. He cut across Thompson's ranch, hoping to follow the river to a point where he could cross it easily. He literally stumbled over J.T.'s body. He claims he tried to bring it on in because of the wolves and the vultures and, of course, a reward from the grateful family. However, he couldn't lift it alone." Bailey shuddered at the mental picture.

"Was the doctor able to determine the exact time of death?"

"No, he said when a man stops breathing he's dead. End of story."

Bailey shook her head. She hadn't really thought the doctor would resist. Then again, it was still a century before good forensic medicine became recognized as a science.

"What's your opinion of Joe Junior?" Rand continued as he helped Bailey down from the wagon bench. She could see a growing respect in his eyes and it pleased her enormously.

"He's not all he seems, that's certain, but I haven't yet found anything connecting him with the crime. Did he and J.T. have problems?"

"I've heard gossip, but that's all it is at this point. Apparently, J.T. boasted to the ranch help that he planned to change his will so that Sloan inherited the largest portion of the ranch. That didn't sit well with Joe Junior."

"Motive." Bailey started to stop Rand as he moved to open the door but she hesitated. A gut instinct wanted to share her uneasiness about Hope. She knew she shouldn't, not until she knew herself what was going on. Hope had been involved in way too many shenanigans in her young life. If the townsfolk thought that she might somehow be involved, it might very well be the rambunctious teenager behind bars instead of Zach.

"What about Sloan?" she asked instead.

"He's the mystery," the sheriff replied as they walked inside. "I've sent out a few inquiries, but I haven't learned anything yet."

Again Bailey was torn. She also wanted to tell Rand that Sloan was waiting for her yesterday evening, but Sloan had exacted a promise from her. She was to tell no one but Zach about their conversation. Never in her life had she considered withholding information from the law, yet today she had done it twice. Go figure.

*   *   *

Zach was waiting inside as the door opened. He glared at both of them and immediately crossed over to Bailey. "You went to the funeral, didn't you? I told you to let me handle this—"

"Aren't you supposed to be *behind* the bars?" She looked from Zach to the sheriff.

"I trust him." Rand shrugged and nonchalantly walked over to his desk.

She rolled her eyes, took a deep breath as if to muster patience, then lifted her hand to count off on her fingers as she explained. "First, I had both Hoop and Rand with me so I was perfectly safe. Second, the funeral was in town with a couple dozen people all standing around. Third, the three of us combined our evidence-gathering abilities and discussed the possible suspects. And fourth, it's none of your business where I go or who I talk to. Now take a look at this list of names and see what you think." She held out a piece of paper to him.

Zach ignored the paper. He'd specifically told her not to do anything except keep an eye on his sisters. There was a man out there who was capable of murder. What if Bailey got too close with all this playacting and accidentally stumbled upon the real killer? Would she be the next one to die? He snatched the paper from her hand and sat down at Rand's desk. It was utter foolishness to allow her to get involved in the first place.

"You are now my wife, and that makes it my business."

"Why, you ungrateful—"

"If you will excuse me," the sheriff interrupted before Bailey could fully explode. "I see you two have some negotiating to do. I'm going to go find Tag and ask a few more questions. That is, if I can stand to be around that ugly jackass of his."

Zach heard the door softly click shut, and he and Bailey

were alone. He glanced up to see that she had stubbornly set her jaw and crossed her arms over her chest.

"Whether you admit it or not, you need my help, Zach Gooden. Rand is certainly trying to get to the bottom of this, and I can help speed it along. The sooner you are out of here, the sooner I can go home."

Zach threw the list aside and glared. *The sooner I can go home.* She had made that abundantly clear. Once this was over, she was out of here. He walked over to the desk. He had wanted to sweep her in his arms and maybe convince her that she wanted to stay, but her mind was already made up.

"Sloan was waiting for me when we got home last night."

"I'll just bet," he snapped.

"Oh, Gooden, cut it out," she said irritably. "If Sloan was the man I wanted, I wouldn't be standing here now. He believes he knows who killed his father."

"Who?"

"He wouldn't say."

Zach grunted, pushed his weight back in the chair, propped both booted feet on Rand's desk, then turned his attention to Bailey's list of suspects. She waited until he had read it before speaking again.

"Okay, if you won't talk about Sloan, let's get down to some of the other basic facts," she began. "It's time to tell Rand that we were together the night of the murder, and that we were on Thompson's land." Bailey sat down in the chair opposite the desk and mimicked his nonchalance by leaning back as well. "Also, since I am your wife, I cannot be forced to testify that I saw Reliant saddled during the night. Something that could only mean that you disappeared at least for a short while. Time enough to kill a man."

Zach's feet slammed to the floor. "Whoa there, woman. I didn't kill Thompson. You know that."

Bailey lifted an eyebrow. She rested her elbows on the

wooden arms of the chair and brought her fingertips together. "Do I?"

Neither spoke for a long minute. "No, you don't," he admitted harshly. "You only have my word. You have to trust me."

"Then don't accuse me of masterminding a brilliant conspiracy with Sloan Thompson to destroy your ranch. I do trust you, Zach. I don't believe you killed Thompson. I don't want to know where you went that night, or why because *I trust you.* The least you can do is give a little back, don't you think?"

Another overpowering silence enveloped the room as he considered Bailey. He realized right then that this was probably the smartest, most logical, and most cunning woman he had ever known. With the assuredness of a rattlesnake on a rabbit ranch, she had outwitted him at his own game, a game he really didn't want to be playing at all.

She was a damn good lawyer.

He lowered himself back into the chair and looked over the list once more. Sloan's name was neatly printed at the top. "What else did Sloan have to say?"

Bailey quickly relayed the rest of the conversation. "Why would he not want anyone else to know who he suspects? Do you think he's telling the truth?"

"Actually, I do," Zach replied slowly. "He was very obvious about his dislike of J.T. He wouldn't have been so free with his words if he intended to kill him. Plus, he would have left town immediately."

"We really don't know much about him. Perhaps we should tell Rand anyway."

Zach shook his head. "You think those men were nasty to me, imagine what they'd do to a practical stranger. I don't want the wrong man to hang."

"If we don't find the real killer, Zach, the wrong man *will* hang. That wrong man is you."

He could stand it no more. He rose from the chair, crossed the brief distance between them, and pulled her body close. He placed one hand behind her glorious, thick hair and studied the delicate skin of her face. Slowly, he lowered his head and kissed her with every ounce of fire he possessed.

With one arm wrapped around her waist, he lifted her slight weight and carried Bailey into the room with the jail cells until her back was pressed against the cold metal of the bars. He gently took one wrist, then another, and pushed them through the space between the bars. With one hand, he held her captive. She started to object, but he silenced her with his lips. There was nothing she could do but surrender.

Using his free hand, he released the pins in her hair and removed her borrowed tortoiseshell combs, allowing her radiant hair to fall free. He explored the gentle curve of her neck with his lips, then her ear, finally the delicate skin now hidden by her massive hair.

Zach pressed against her, letting her feel the full length of his masculinity, of his desire. Bailey's lids slowly lowered as she lifted her lips to meet his in the tenderest of kisses. The kiss deepened and became hungry and searching. He wanted her to melt in his arms, to stay forever entwined with him.

"When I'm near you," she breathed as his lips danced across her jaw, "I can't seem to think straight."

Zach smiled at her as his hand fingered the unfortunately high lace collar of her black dress. "And I want to pick you up, carry you off, and forget everything that troubles me." He leaned close again, this time his lips almost, but not quite, touching hers. "You said Sloan was not the man you wanted. Who is that man, Bailey? Who is the man you want?"

Bailey pulled back from Zach's hot touch as much as the cool bars would allow. Her gaze lowered to the top button of his shirt then back up to his face. "Oh, Zach. Don't you know? I want—"

"Oh, hell, you two," Rand stormed as he burst loudly through the door, Hoop following close behind. "Your sisters are at it again. This time they've run away."

Chapter 20

"RUN AWAY?" ZACH loosened his hold but didn't immediately release Bailey. He turned, pulling her away from the bars, then wrapped his arm protectively around her shoulders. "How can they have run away? Weren't they with Jin Lee while you were at the funeral?"

Hoop shrugged and looked toward Bailey. "I know you've been working with them and all, Miss Bailey, but I should've known better than to trust those young 'uns. When I got back to the ranch, there was a commotion coming from the kitchen. Jin Lee was screechin' like a plucked blue jay." Hoop shook his head and tried to fight the slow smile that crept across his face. "Those girls had trussed him up in a chair with the long ties from his apron. I don't recollect ever seeing a man sure enough mad as that little fella."

"Do you think it's another one of their pranks? Do we need to go look for them, then?" Rand moved to his desk.

Hoop's grin faded and silence filled the room as the three men considered the question.

"Excuse me, guys," Bailey interrupted. She couldn't believe the hesitation on their faces, especially from Zach. "Where I'm from, missing children is a very serious situation, no matter what those children may have done in the past. Of course we should go after them, and immediately. Let's not waste time speculating about it."

Rand looked embarrassed; even Hoop seemed to regret his indecision. Zach's face was dark and expressionless as he released her. Bailey couldn't tell what he was thinking, but she was ready to do battle with him about this, even if it meant she went after the girls by herself.

"You're right, Bailey," he said, ashamed. "Whoever murdered J.T. is still out there. We need to find them."

"Jin Lee said Faith and Charity tied him up," Hoop offered. "He said they were going after Hope. Your horse and the big brown were gone. I followed the tracks to the south windmill, but there were too many animal prints at the water trough to figure which ones were the most recent. I sent a few men on out to search, but I figured I'd come get you before I headed over to J.T.'s place for a look-see."

"Thanks, Hoop." Zach nodded as he moved toward the sheriff, who was pulling rifles off the wall. Bailey watched as the lawman checked to make sure each was loaded. "I have to go after them, Rand." Surprised, Rand looked up before tossing Zach a rifle.

"Do you think there's no smarts behind this good-looking grin? I got an inkling those three are going to lead us straight to the killer." The sheriff turned toward Hoop, still standing by the door. "Unhitch Zach's wagon and get one of those two nags saddled. I assume you'll ride behind Zach, Bailey?"

"No, she's staying here," Zach interrupted as Hoop disappeared outside, "and so are you." He calmly pointed the loaded rifle directly at his friend. Rand froze, but looked Zach squarely in the eye. For a long moment they just stared, neither moving, neither speaking.

Bailey could stand the tension no more. She rushed forward and positioned herself between the two stubborn men. "Zach! What do you think you're doing? He's your friend." He cast her a quick warning glare and held up a hand for silence.

"Yes, he is, and you're my woman." He stared directly into her eyes as he spoke. "That's why I'm not letting either of you get any deeper involved than necessary. I want this to look as if I broke out of jail and you two tried to stop me. I'll leave the keys were you can reach them so you can meet up with me later. But, Rand, as far as you're concerned, I jumped you, took the gun, and locked you up in the cell." Zach paused and enunciated his next words very clearly. "Now, if you two happen to escape from the cell and catch up with me outside of town, there'd be nothing I could do about it."

"Hell, Zach, that's embarrassing for a lawman." Rand placed the rifle he'd been holding on the desk and reached for the ring of keys hanging on a nearby peg.

"It's either that or I'll knock you cold. If any of the townsfolk realize that you let me out of jail just because my troublesome sisters were at it again, you'd have hell to pay. If I had been more responsible for my sisters months ago, maybe none of this would have happened. I'll wait for you both outside of town."

The door suddenly opened and Charlie Mack strode inside. He stopped instantly, his face a mixture of shock and rage as he surveyed the scene. "Never once did I really believe what J.T. said about you, son. And I certainly didn't think you would have killed him. Looks like I was wrong, or else you wouldn't be trying to escape."

Bailey recognized the sad resignation in Zach's eyes. If he

went through with this supposed "breakout," he was giving up virtually any chance that the banker would honor his loan. Zach stared at the man but didn't waver. Love for him coursed through her. His sisters were more important to him than what anyone thought.

"This isn't what you think, Charlie," he replied firmly. He pointed the rifle at the rotund man standing before him. "I'm going to have to ask you to step over by Rand and Bailey."

Charlie Mack stared at the barrel of the rifle, his normally flushed face draining of color. He slowly began to move to Bailey's side.

"I'm sorry to involve you in this, Charlie, but I have to find my sisters. I can't do that from a jail cell."

"I should have known your sisters would have something to do with this. Those girls are hooligans. They should be properly disciplined—"

Zach spun Charlie Mack and grabbed his shirt with one hand and brought his face inches from the banker's. Zach held the rifle at his side as he used the sheer force of his will to press the banker backwards to the jail cell, step by step. "Let's get something straight about my sisters. They may be a handful, and they may have done some foolish things in the past, but they are *my* sisters. I have a feeling they are trying on their own to find the person who really murdered J.T. Thompson. I call that bravery, banker. And if I ever hear you, or anyone else, talk bad about them, you'll answer to me."

Zach released the frightened man, then quickly walked back through the open cell door, slamming it shut behind him. He opened the door of the next cell and held it for Bailey and Rand. The sheriff stepped through first. As Bailey passed by, Zach grabbed her upper arm, then crushed his lips against hers. "Hurry," he whispered, "there's not a minute to spare."

*   *   *

Zach watched as Bailey and Rand rode over the small crest and closed the distance between them. He knelt on the ground about a mile outside of Box Bend. He'd been waiting impatiently for about fifteen minutes, and each one had dragged by as if it were an hour. His baby sisters were out there, possibly in danger, and at the very least they were somewhere they shouldn't be.

He'd suspected for a long time that Hope was smitten with Joe Junior, but he figured it was an innocent crush. When he saw the kerchief tied to the windmill stand the other day, he knew something more was going on. It was their signal to meet, he suspected. He had determined to confront Hope just as soon as he could, but it hadn't worked out. First they had all come to town, then he'd been locked up.

He prayed his little sister hadn't somehow gotten involved in something that would get her killed. The fact of the matter was that Joe Junior's pa was dead, and the boy probably thought Zach had killed him. Would he take his revenge with Hope?

Zach had wondered about Joe Junior and Sloan last night as he lay awake in the jail cell. The Thompson boys were very different. It appeared that Joe Junior wanted his father's approval at any cost, and Sloan didn't give a damn about J.T. or his ranch. Could either of them kill their own father? As Rand had pointed out, Joe Junior wasn't a boy any longer, and Sloan was the long-lost son who cast doubts on everything. If either brother had killed J.T., was he dangerous enough to kill other people?

Zach shifted his weight onto one knee and used a long hickory stick to draw a pattern in the dirt as he watched the horse and riders approach. Bailey rode behind Rand, holding tightly on to his waist, the long black skirt was bunched awkwardly over her legs. A stab of jealousy and a flash of irritation surfaced as he watched the two. He didn't like to see her so close to another man, even if that man was his friend. Rand was a charmer, and Bailey was a desirable woman. A man couldn't help but want her.

He saw that her hair was loose. She hadn't pinned it back after their kiss. It flowed behind her, making her look like a wild gypsy, the red glistening each time the sun peeked through the clouds.

He looked up at the sky and noted the lessening clouds. Hopefully, the heavy rains were over and the ground would begin to dry. He needed to get the ranch prepared for the winter, and the rains didn't help much. Not when he had so much to do.

He was assuming, of course, that they would find the murderer and he would be around for the winter. And, if he was back on his own, would Bailey still be with them? She'd wasted no words making it clear that she was going home after this was all over. That's what worried him. Truth was, he didn't want her to go. In just a few short days, she had made herself a real part of his family. Not just with their marriage, that was in name only, but with her eager and joyful love for his sisters. Perhaps there was some way he could convince her to stay, to become a true part of his life, or his family.

He stood as Rand reined his feisty buckskin to a halt. Zach reached up and lifted Bailey off the horse's back and brought her down toward him. He deliberately let her body slide against the full length of his. He felt the heat of her breasts pressed against his chest. His plan to tease her backfired. He was the tortured soul.

"We have got to hurry," Rand rushed. He surveyed the landscape behind him, effectively ignoring the entwined couple. "Charlie Mack is planning to round up a posse to come after you, Zach. I couldn't talk him out of it."

"You let him out?" Zach pulled his attention away from Bailey.

"No, not quite, but I couldn't leave him locked up. He already thought the whole thing looked a bit staged," Rand replied as Bailey nodded in agreement. "As it is, he'll be a hero since he was able to help us escape. He's rounding up a posse, though. We need to hurry."

"There goes my loan," Zach said ruefully.

"Not necessarily," Rand added. "Now that J.T. is gone, Mack doesn't have a willing buyer for your cattle. It wouldn't do him any good to call in your loan, especially when he stands to make much more next spring."

"Loan or not, Charlie Mack will never again speak ill of Faith, Hope, and Charity. I doubt Mrs. Mack will, either. I'm very proud of you, Zach." She stood on her toes and touched his lips with her own. Immediately, Zach's arms encircled her again.

He quickly released her, then lifted her up onto his saddle on Sparky. He briefly wished it was Reliant they were riding. That horse could practically read his mind, and probably knew right where to go to find the girls. He carefully mounted in front of Bailey and brought her arms tightly around his waist. He spurred the big black horse, who pranced around and tossed his head with an irritated snort, then broke into a fast gallop.

They had three bratty little angels to find.

Hoop waited on the far side of the river, resting comfortably on a smooth rock well away from the water. He stood when he saw them approach and mounted his horse, then guided it closer to the muddy bank. Bailey knew Zach and she had to cross the river again, and she was terrified. Seeing Hoop on the other side assuaged her fear a bit. He had obviously crossed safely on his own, and now he was prepared in case she, Zach, and Rand had trouble.

Zach wasted no time as he headed straight toward the rushing water. There was every indication that his sisters were somewhere on Thompson land, either by their choice or against their will. And if it was the latter . . .

Bailey determinedly pushed aside such worrisome thoughts. They had to find Faith, Hope, and Charity as soon as possible, no matter what the reason for their disappearance.

The big black horse stepped closer to the water, and Bailey tightened her hold around Zach's waist, clasping her hands together at his hard stomach. Zach must have sensed her trepidation as he briefly covered her hands with his own, then focused again on the deadly current. The river still rushed with an angry tempo, but it didn't seem nearly as threatening as before. The rain had lessened considerably over the past few days, and the waters had receded several feet. Still, the memory of Zach being swept away from her was vividly terrifying. She lowered her lids and sent a silent prayer for their safety.

Sparky entered the swift moving water and began to cross. The frigid water splashed up against Bailey's face. The shock of the cold water forced Bailey to open her eyes and pay attention. She needed to be watchful in case Zach had problems, not cower behind him in fear.

Sparky pushed into the river with each step. Zach continually urged the horse forward with his voice and legs. As they reached the center, the gelding stumbled slightly and another dose of cold water stung Bailey's arms and neck. She gasped, ready to jump into the water if she needed to, wondering how she could swim in the long, heavy skirt. Luckily, Sparky recovered his footing and plowed ahead. The water became deeper and deeper, rising up to Bailey's knees as she sat on the back of the horse. The flimsy black ankle boots she had borrowed from Hope were most likely ruined, and she fervently wished for her sturdy thick hiking boots. She'd managed to pull the long skirts up out of the way, exposing her bare skin to the frigid water.

Gradually, Bailey felt a change in Sparky's step as the horse began to leave the muddy river bottom for the firmer ground of the opposite shore. She released a long, thankful breath and gave the horse a quick pat on his rump. No matter his other eccentricities, Sparky had proven himself to be a good horse today.

Zach wasted no time on pleasantries and they joined Hoop on the riverbank. "What did you find out?" Hoop shook his head.

"The hands say they ain't seen either of the Thompson boys since the funeral. No one is up at the house 'cept the cook, who is sure they ain't together. Joe Junior threatened to kill Sloan last night after they read the will. Seems J.T. left the ranch to his eldest, and Joe Junior is mad as hell. Rightly so, if you ask me."

"What about the girls?" Zach asked. "Has anyone seen them?"

"Not saying so if they have."

Zach nodded. "Rand checked. They're not in town, and not at home. For the life of me I can't think of where else they'd be unless it's on the Thompson ranch. I'll bet they thought they could find the real murderer. Knowing those three fearless girls, I wouldn't be surprised if they did. But that also means whoever killed J.T. may kill them to save his hide." Zach worried with the reins as he brought Sparky around so he could watch Rand take a turn at crossing the river.

"The river's going down already," Zach said absently. Hoop nodded, then also turned his attention to Rand, who was just entering the water. Zach shifted in the saddle and glanced back at Bailey before concentrating on Rand.

Crossing the river was something they obviously didn't take lightly, Bailey realized. She regretted that she had so persistently demanded Zach cross the river to find her backpack. She hadn't really believed the threat until they crossed the first time. Now, seeing the serious attention they gave to crossing the river, she was even more ashamed.

Not just about the danger she'd placed them in, but also what she had done to this man who had been nothing but hospitable to her, a perfect stranger with an unbelievable story. If she hadn't forced him to take her to the ravine, they wouldn't have been out the night J.T. was murdered. They'd have been at the Double Bar G the entire time, and Zach wouldn't be the prime suspect. He wouldn't have had to marry her, and his sisters probably wouldn't be missing and possibly in danger.

This really was her fault, all because she didn't understand the ways of this era, and didn't bother to take the time to learn. She assumed that because she was from the future she was more intelligent and more advanced than the people of this day and age. That shamed her. She despised arrogance, and look where her own had gotten them. She had put her normally cautious and prudent behavior on hold and forced Zach to do her bidding. Her efforts at locating her backpack seemed insignificant compared to the problems they now had to solve.

She watched as Rand guided his horse through the water. Unconsciously, Bailey clenched her fists in fear. One wrong move, and Rand would be swept away just as she and Zach had been.

Zach and Hoop concentrated on their friend, watching carefully in case Rand should need them. It was remarkable how well the people of this time worked together. This era was so different from her own, exciting and challenging, even deadly at times.

After several long minutes, Rand finally made it safely across. Quickly, Zach relayed what Hoop had learned. Rand shook his head when he heard of the will. "What would possess a man to destroy his sons like that? He had to know the jealousy it would cause." Rand adjusted his position in the saddle. "Well, then, where should we look? They could be anywhere."

"We'd cover more ground if we split—"

A loud rustling noise from the trees and bushes nearby stopped Zach short. Bailey wasn't sure of what they'd heard; the rushing river water almost drowned out any other sounds. But there was something. They weren't alone. The moving leaves and branches proved that, although there was no indication of who would be trying to hide from them. Was it Faith or Hope?

All three men pulled rifles from their saddle scabbards but didn't take aim. From the sporadic rustling, Bailey could tell that whatever was back there probably wasn't human. Zach turned Sparky so he faced the unknown intruder, shielding Bailey with his body.

Another rustle.

Silence.

More moving branches.

Finally, the lower brush began to part, and the head and neck of a brown horse peeked through. The riderless animal stopped, lifted his head, and looked at them. He glanced at the river, as if weighing his options to cross, then seemed to sigh and went back to his search for grass.

Bear.

Faith's horse moved closer but generally ignored them. Hoop dismounted and walked over to the tired gelding, tossed a rope over his neck, and led him into the clearing. "He's not hot, so he's not running from anything. Looks as if he was headed home to dinner."

Zach frowned. "He's worn a saddle today, but since his bridle is off, too, I'd say someone deliberately unsaddled him. Do you suppose Faith released him, hoping he'd get back to us? He's a master at getting home before dinnertime, no matter what he's tied to or who's on his back."

Bailey stared at the friendly horse as Zach and Rand discussed the possibilities. If anything had happened to her beautiful angels, she'd see to it that whoever did it rotted in hell.

Hoop disappeared into the brush and reappeared a minute later. "Looks like the tracks lead west."

"That's a start. Let's go." Zach dismounted and settled Bailey into the saddle by herself. He took a long length of rope and fashioned it into a makeshift halter, then put it on the brown horse. The horse shied at the sudden action, but Zach was faster. He effortlessly jumped up on Bear's bare back and spurred the surprised horse first into a rough trot, then into a fast gallop.

Hold on, girls, she thought as she kicked Sparky's sides, gripped the saddle horn and prayed she wouldn't fall off. *We're coming.*

Zach was frustrated. They had ridden for about an hour, and he was no closer to finding his sisters than before. Bear's tracks indicated that he had wandered aimlessly around the prairie, but he had still kept basically an eastward journey, meaning he'd come from the west. The horse definitely had been on his way home to dinner. But where were the twins and Charity?

He also had an annoying feeling that they weren't alone. True, they were on Thompson land. And true, Charlie Mack was probably fast on their trail with a posse, but there was something—or someone—more. It was almost as if they were being watched. He looked around and again scanned the horizon. *Probably J.T. from the grave,* he thought wryly.

Bailey still rode behind on the black. In her own quiet way, she offered Zach strength and encouragement. He was foolish to think she would have stayed behind and worried herself frantic while they were out searching. She loved his sisters like they were her own.

He wondered briefly if he could somehow convince her to

stay. What could he offer her that she didn't already have a hundred years into the future? She was going to be a judge, no small accomplishment for a woman. He wanted her to stay, but he didn't have anything to offer her other than himself and three troublesome sisters. Could she give up everything the future entailed just to be with him? Would he, if the roles were reversed? Zach didn't know. The one thing of which he was certain was that Bailey belonged with him, no matter what year.

He slowed Bear from a slow lope down to a trot. A watering hole came into view. A stand of cottonwoods offered the few head of cattle a bit of shade. A windmill, identical to the ones on the Double Bar G, creaked and groaned as it turned in the gentle breeze. The ground surrounding the area was rocky and muddy. Another uneasy sense of foreboding washed over him. He glanced back at Bailey, who looked tired and frightened.

Rand obviously sensed something was wrong, too. He guided his horse in front of Zach's to lead the small group. As they drew closer to the water hole, he held up a hand in warning. Something was wrong. They slowed the horses to a careful walk.

Almost as if he had an internal alarm, Zach heard the threatening sound of a gun hammer cocked into place.

"That'll be far enough," a deep voice threatened.

Zach recognized Sloan's deep, slow drawl even before he turned around. "I'm looking for my sisters, Sloan. Where are they?"

Sloan lowered his rifle as Zach, Hoop, and Rand turned their horses back toward him. The man standing shook his head. "I'm out looking for Joe Junior myself. Sorry about this, I heard someone following me. I thought I'd lay low and see just who it was. I'm not a popular fellow with anyone right now," he added unnecessarily.

Zach narrowed his eyes. Sloan had talked a good tale the

other night. He said he was going to stop J.T. no matter what it took. Did he know in advance the ranch was willed to him? Had he killed his own pa? He stared at Sloan, refusing to be the first to break the silent challenge between them. Sloan stared back equally as hard, and the two men glared at each other, momentarily forgetting the other people present.

Sloan whistled, without lowering his gaze. Through the small copse of cottonwoods, his horse obediently moved toward his master. Another horse followed closely behind, his reins tied to the saddle horn of the first horse.

Reliant.

"Want to explain what you're doing with my horse?"

"I found him wandering," Sloan replied evenly. "The brown you're riding was with him, but I couldn't catch it, and I didn't have time to chase it. I figured it was unusual for your horse to be running loose on J.T.'s land, so I caught him. I planned to bring him back to you after I found the boy." Sloan finally dropped his gaze to search for his tobacco pouch. He reached for the fixings and started to roll a smoke.

"Not J.T.'s land anymore, is it?" Rand said coldly, his hand resting on his hip.

"Ain't that the sad truth?" Sloan looked up, then glanced between Rand and Zach. "He was a bad man living, and he's even meaner from the grave. Joe Junior hightailed it out of the house before I could tell him I have no interest in becoming a rancher."

"Hope was probably riding my horse," Zach offered quietly as he studied Sloan carefully. "The other two were on the brown. I believe that Hope and Joe Junior have been secretly meeting for the past few weeks. They may be together."

"The tracks are headed to an old line shack about five miles from here. That's where I was headed when I stopped to see who was behind me." Sloan quickly walked to his horse. "We'd better hurry."

"Do you know more than you're telling, mister?" Rand obviously didn't trust Sloan, didn't much like him either, from all appearances. The lawman's hand still rested on his pistol. Sloan returned Rand's steady gaze without a word.

"We don't have time for games, Thompson," Rand warned. "Those girls could be in danger."

Sloan shrugged as he put a foot in the stirrup to mount his horse. "I believe Joe Junior killed J.T.," he replied solemnly. "There's some mighty strong evidence that says I'm right, too."

"Such as?" Rand pressed.

"Those things need to come from the boy, not from me."

"Toss me your gun, Sloan," Rand demanded. "As far as I'm concerned, you could have murdered J.T. and want it to look as if Joe Junior is the guilty one. How do I know you're telling the truth?"

Sloan released a long, frustrated sigh. The man had probably been in this position many times before, Zach realized with some clarity.

"You don't, Sheriff. You only have my word that I didn't murder J.T. Truth be told, I wanted to, I thought about it, but I didn't do it."

Bailey rode up beside Zach and touched his hand. They both stared at Sloan for a long, slow moment. Zach realized that this was a man who was used to no one believing what he said. Should they?

Rand moved his horse next to Sloan's and reached for the man's gun and rifle.

"No, Rand," Zach interrupted firmly. "Let him be. I believe him."

Rand snorted. He looked as if he was going to argue. The sheriff stared back and forth between the two, indecision on his face. He suddenly nodded and backed off.

Zach dismounted and led Bear over to Reliant, then tied the makeshift reins to his saddle. He then took Reliant's reins from Sloan, who stared off into the distance, his mind obviously working on what may lay ahead. Zach lifted a booted foot into the stirrup and tossed his weight into the saddle.

God help them all if he was wrong.

Chapter 21

IT WASN'T GOING to work.

There was no way to approach the cabin without being seen. Since there was nothing but rolling hills, grass, and prairie in every direction, there was no way to take Joe Junior unawares.

The afternoon sun was low in the sky as they cautiously stared at the weathered gray shack. Bailey wished she could stand and pace. She always thought better when she was moving, especially when it came to solving an unsolvable problem.

Zach, Rand, Hoop, Sloan, and she were on their knees on the crest of a hill, hidden by the tall prairie grass. They were still a good distance from the cabin; they couldn't risk moving closer. Joe Junior could easy spot them. The horses were hobbled behind them, down the slope so they couldn't be seen either.

The old cabin and its outhouse were worn and decrepit.

There was no barn, but a single horse stood tethered outside. A few scrawny trees stood near the building but not much else dotted the prairie. Bailey could see a light in the window and a thin stream of smoke billowing from the chimney.

"There's Hope," she whispered. The twin sat near the window, her head bent as if she were crying. Two other figures appeared behind her. "Faith and Charity, too. He's got them, all right."

Bailey froze. Joe Junior suddenly appeared at another window, a rifle in one hand. He seemed to be staring straight at them. Bailey held her breath, afraid to speak, fearful to move. After a long minute, Joe Junior moved back in the cabin, out of sight.

"How do we get close without being seen?" Zach asked Sloan, his gaze never leaving the scene before him.

"I've only been up here once. As I recall, there's a window in the back so you can see from all directions," Sloan answered, his voice low and serious.

"He's right, Zach," Hoop added, plucking a piece of grass and sticking one end in his mouth while he spoke. "I've ridden up here a few times myself. Even stayed overnight a couple of nights. It's built so you see for miles."

The four men were silent as they considered their options. Bailey resisted the urge to think it hopeless. Zach would figure out something. He had to—those were his sisters down there. Since Joe Junior was holding the rifle, it was pretty likely they were being held against their will, too. She studied the four men beside her. Each bore a serious expression as he studied the layout below.

"I'll go," Sloan said quietly. "If I can get him talking about the ranch, I may get close enough to disarm him. You three can ride up then."

Bailey fought her irritation that Sloan excluded her in the rescue plans. As far as these four were concerned, she was simply extra baggage to be protected. She started to object.

Zach glanced at Bailey, then covered her hand with his own and squeezed in encouragement. He turned to Sloan and shook his head. "He's already threatened to kill you. He'd sooner do it out here where there'd be fewer witnesses. He could say that you kidnapped the girls, and he killed you trying to rescue them. And, if you were dead, he'd say you killed J.T. He'd get away with murder just like his pa did."

Rand opened his mouth to speak, but Zach quickly cut him off. "If he sees the sheriff approach, he's certain to think you're there to bring him in. He may shoot first and ask questions later."

"You may be right, Zach, but that doesn't matter," Rand argued. "Last I checked, I was still the lawman in these parts. If he's kidnapped your sisters, then it's up to me to lock him up. Besides, it would be the same for you. Once he sees you out of jail, he will probably assume we know he's the murderer." He stared pointedly at Sloan. "Even though I'm not convinced this whole thing isn't staged."

"I'll go," Hoop interrupted as he moved from his position by Bailey and resettled himself between Sloan and Rand. Bailey admired the easy way Hoop dealt with the two. Like it or not, they were all in this together.

"With you in jail, it'd be right that I'm the one looking for those young 'uns." Hoop spit out the long piece of grass and pulled his pistol to check the bullets. The sound of the spinning chamber was the only thing Bailey heard. They were all wrong.

"No, Hoop," she said quietly. All four men stared at her in astonishment. She looked directly at Zach. "My reasoning is the same as Hoop's, but Joe Junior would be less wary of a woman. I have the best chance of getting inside. Once I'm in, I'll get him away from the window and you guys can storm the place."

"No." Zach's refusal was adamant. Hoop, Rand, and

Sloan clearly agreed with Zach. They turned their attention back to Hoop.

"Yes," she insisted stubbornly. "Joe Junior will think I'm harmless if I ride up on Sparky. He'll believe that I would be out looking for them, and he'll assume he can handle another female." She placed a hand on Zach's sleeve before he could refuse once more. "I promise not to do anything risky or foolish. I'll just ride up, get inside, and get him away from the windows. It'll work, I know it will."

"She's got a point," Rand admitted reluctantly.

Hoop slowly nodded, and Bailey warmed at the new respect she saw in the foreman's eyes. Sloan was quiet as he contemplated her plan.

"I don't much like a female doing a man's job," he finally said, "but your woman is smarter than most, Zach. She's sure got more guts than you could hang on a fence."

Bailey turned back to Zach, whose face was dark and unreadable. "Let me do it, Zach. They're my sisters, too."

Still kneeling, he pulled her away from the others and down the gentle slope behind them. When they were close enough to the horses, Zach rose and gently pulled Bailey up beside him, holding her hands in his own. "This is against my better judgment, Bailey."

"Trust me, Zach," she whispered. "I've made my living discerning how people react to situations, what strategy is needed to prove guilt or get a confession. Joe Junior will think I'm harmless. I'm sure of it." They considered each other carefully. Bailey hoped Zach couldn't see the trepidation in her eyes. She was scared to ride down there. Joe Junior was probably a killer and a desperate one. But this was something that had to be done, and she was the best person for the job.

Zach placed an arm around her and drew her close. His hat shielded her face from the afternoon sun, creating a shadowy illusion that they were all alone on this vast prairie.

Bailey lowered her lids as Zach's lips neared her own. The heady anticipation of his kiss was almost more than she could bear. When their lips finally met, he was tender and sweet. As if she were the most precious thing he'd ever held. She could almost believe this man truly cared for her. Perhaps, after all they'd been through—

Bailey pushed the thought from her mind. Faith, Hope, and Charity were the most important thing right now, she'd best not forget that either.

In an instant Zach's soft embrace turned forceful. He pulled her even closer as his tongue demanded access to her own. She responded with equal abandon because she understood his silent communication. He was trying to somehow give her the strength she would need to ride down to face Joe Junior. He was giving her part of himself.

He drew himself away. Her lips, hot and fiery only a moment ago, instantly turned cold. He studied her face carefully. "Don't take any chances, Bailey. Just get him away from the window, and let us do the rest."

A slight cough came from behind. Zach slowly dropped his hands to his sides and turned toward the sound. Bailey could see Sloan standing near another one of the horses. When he saw he had their attention, he headed toward them.

"You may need this." He held out a small black-handled derringer. "It probably won't kill him, but it can stop him for a minute or two. Use it if you need it."

Bailey stared at the small pistol lying on Sloan's palm. Slowly, she reached to take it from him. "Thank you, Sloan." He smiled slightly, then nodded at Zach and walked back toward the others.

"Do you know how to shoot?" Zach asked as he guided her over to Sparky, whose head was bent as he munched on the rich green grass.

Bailey checked the gun and placed the weapon in the pocket of her skirt. "I took lessons a couple of years ago."

"The same time you learned how to trip a man?" he asked with a reluctant smile. Bailey grinned. It was less than a week ago that they stood at the windmill and she'd brought him to his knees with that simple move. She felt as if she'd been here forever. Truth be known, she felt as if she belonged.

"Around that time." She nodded. "In my century, crime is so bad that people must learn how to protect themselves."

"Looks like your training is going to come in handy here. Some things never change, do they?" Zach lifted her up into the saddle. She looked down into his brown eyes, rubbed a hand across his cheek. Zach placed his own hand over hers then gently squeezed. "Be careful, love."

Bailey managed a small smile, then gathered up the reins and kicked Sparky with her heels. The horse grunted and grudgingly moved off. She called back, "I'll signal when it's safe to approach."

It took less than ten minutes to cover the distance to the cabin. As they had assumed, Joe Junior saw her approach. He opened the door, spoke to the three behind him, then stepped outside the worn building, closing the door with a firm snap. His rifle was casually wedged in the crook of his arm, but Bailey wasn't fooled. If Joe Junior had killed J.T., he wouldn't be afraid to kill her, too. Especially if he was desperate.

Bailey closed her eyes as Sparky made the last few strides. She was terrified. Never in her wildest dreams had she imagined that she'd be doing something like this. She thought being a judge was the most challenging thing that could ever happen to her. Boy, was she wrong.

"That'll be far enough, lady." Joe Junior's words were slurred, and Bailey knew he'd been drinking.

"I'm looking for Faith, Hope, and Charity. They're missing," she said, hoping her voice didn't quaver. She rested her hands on the saddle horn to stop their trembling. "I came from town and their horses were gone. I can't find them anywhere. Have you seen them?"

"No." Joe Junior stared at her defiantly. When it appeared he wasn't going to say another word, Bailey looked toward the house. He'd obviously told the girls to stay out of sight. What was she supposed to do now?

"All right. Sorry to bother you. Before I head back, may I water my horse?" It sounded innocent enough, and she might be able to get him talking. Perhaps buy some time.

"No," he said sharply. "There's a watering hole about three miles back. You git on out of here."

"OK . . . well, then . . . I guess I'll be going." Bailey pulled the reins and started to turn Sparky around. She stopped suddenly. "Joe Junior, I'm truly sorry about your father. I know what it's like to be an orphan." The young man didn't respond. He continued to stare with hate-filled eyes. Bailey sighed. She wasn't giving up; she had to get in that cabin.

"Bailey! Don't go!" Charity threw open the door and rushed outside right up to the black horse, disregarding the fact that Joe Junior held a gun. Immediately, Bailey put herself between Joe and the girl. Faith and Hope rushed out of the door behind her, their faces draining of color as they saw Joe Junior point his rifle at Bailey and their sister.

"You've come," Charity continued excitedly. "I told Faith and Hope you would! Where's Zach?" Charity looked expectantly for her brother, then turned her questioning eyes to Bailey when she saw he wasn't there.

"Yes, Bailey," Joe Junior mocked. "Where's Zach?"

She stared at their inebriated captor. This was the chance she needed. "He's still in jail, Charity," she replied softly and pulled the girl to her. "I came looking for you guys by myself. Hoop went in the other direction."

"He killed his pa, Bailey. He said so," Faith said from the door. "Now he's too yellow to take his own medicine."

"I told you to shut your mouth, girl, or you'll be joining him. Your pa, too. They both deserve to rot in hell." Joe's face reddened in anger as he moved his rifle back and forth between Bailey and Faith.

"Let us go, Joe," Bailey urged without dropping Joe Junior's gaze. "The girls have nothing to do with whatever's going on."

"I beg to differ, ma'am," he slurred. "Little Miss Hope is in this thing just as deep as I am. Ask her yourself."

Bailey glanced at Hope. "Is that true?"

The ashen-faced twin didn't reply. She covered her face with her hands, burst into tears, and hurried back into the cabin. Faith followed. Charity grabbed Bailey's hand and started tugging. Bailey looked at Joe Junior and indicated the door. "May I?"

He shrugged, then bowed in a grand drunken gesture and followed them inside. The interior of the cabin was dark despite the glow of a single oil lamp. It was also in total disarray. Joe Junior had apparently brought a few supplies, and they lay strewn across a table. There was a small cook fire in the kitchen area. She saw two unopened bottles of whiskey over by a small stack of firewood, another empty bottle on the floor underneath a rickety wooden chair. Joe picked up a half-empty bottle and lifted it to his mouth.

A daring plan quickly formed in Bailey's mind. Instead of allowing herself to become a willing victim of whatever Joe Junior planned, she had to fight back. Joe was drunk, but he clearly hadn't reached a decision about what to do with Faith, Hope, and Charity. Either that, or he was getting so drunk he'd be able to kill them, too. She needed to take charge, and to do that she'd need every bit of confidence she could muster. Bailey took a deep breath.

"Joe, dear, you sit down right here," she spoke quickly and in the most authoritative, motherly voice she could manage. "The first thing we need to do is make a pot of coffee and cook supper for you four. I'll bet none of you have eaten since breakfast." She walked right up to Joe Junior and led him to a chair near the stove, away from the window. He started to object, but Bailey bustled away and picked up a cloth from the table. She moved the meager supplies—flour, coffee, dried beef, and bullets—then wiped off the dusty table. Without so much as a glance, she took the rag to a window and snapped it to shake out the dust as if that were the most normal thing in the world.

"Get away from that window!" Joe started to rise from his chair, but Bailey smoothly walked away from the window toward the stove as if nothing were amiss. She prayed Zach had seen her signal.

"Joe, did you bring coffee?" At his nod, Bailey picked up the blue metal coffeepot. "Good, we need to get you sober. Faith, you start the coffee, and I'll start supper. After we've had a good meal, we can figure out what to do." She looked pointedly at Joe Junior. "Together."

Whether he had consumed too much whiskey, or was simply overwhelmed by what he had done, Bailey didn't know. He still clutched his loaded rifle, ready to shoot if need be, but he had allowed her to take charge of dinner, at least. Bailey watched as he closed his eyes. He was a good-looking kid. It was no wonder Hope was smitten with him, but Bailey didn't believe for a minute that she had anything to do with J.T.'s murder.

She stood by the stove and set about finding a pot to prepare dinner. Quietly, Bailey motioned to Faith to casually circle around behind him when she could. Before Faith could move, Joe opened his eyes and glanced around the room. He visibly relaxed when everything seemed normal.

Joe turned his head and met her gaze. His eyes hardened. "Hope knew what I planned to do with the knife. She killed him just as much as I did."

"When?" Bailey asked.

"The night the banker and the sheriff were at the Double Bar G. Pa had us ride over there just to cause trouble. I circled back later and met Hope by the front porch. She told me where Zach kept the knife."

"I didn't know what you were going to do with it!" Hope cried as tears welled in her eyes. She walked closer to Joe. "You said you wanted to get rid of the knife since it stood between Zach and your pa. You said once it was gone they couldn't be mad at each other anymore. You said we could be together then, Joe. And then you lied. I caught you outside Zach's office. You'd already gone through the window and stolen the knife yourself." She covered her face with her hands and let loose another wail. "You told me that you loved me!"

"You're nothing but a schoolgirl," he ridiculed. "I never loved you."

Bailey watched as Hope grew calm. She sniffed and tried to gather her dignity. "Then you never should have lied to me, Joe Junior. I thought you were different from your father, but you're not. You're just as mean and nasty as he was."

Immediately, Joe jumped to his feet and grabbed his rifle. "Why, you—"

In an instant, Faith came up behind her captor. She lifted the coffeepot full of water and threw it on Joe. Before he could recover, she jumped full force onto his back and wrapped one arm around his head, effectively covering his eyes and pulling his head back to keep him off balance. The other arm quickly reached for the rifle, and the two struggled for control.

Charity rushed in next. She grabbed both of Joe Junior's legs so he couldn't move.

Bailey reached into her pocket for the derringer and pointed it at the frenzy, but there was no way she could shoot. The instant she'd get a clear shot, the fighting group

would spin. Bailey had to start all over trying to aim at Joe.
Then Hope jumped into the fray and tried to wrestle the rifle
from Joe's grasp. She got a good hold on the butt of the rifle,
then twisted and turned, trying to get Joe to release it. The
young man held on tightly, though. Bailey saw he wasn't
about to give up, and even with three wildcats on his back,
Joe Junior was holding his own.

Then a shot went off.

Chapter 22

E<small>VERYTHING SEEMED TO</small> happen in slow motion.

The front door slammed open. Zach and Sloan burst inside, their guns aimed directly at the flailing mass of Joe Junior, Hope, Charity, and Faith. At two of the windows, Hoop and Rand appeared, breaking the glass panes, then pointing guns at the tussle.

The tangled heap collapsed to the floor.

"Hope! Charity! Faith!" She and Zach rushed to the suddenly still pile of fighters. One by one they pulled the girls from the mess. Faith and Charity were dazed but unharmed. Bailey looked at Zach and saw the fear in his eyes. He'd seen it, too. Hope had just gotten a firm hold on the wooden butt of the rifle and swung it around, away from Joe.

Had she taken the bullet? Was she hurt? Or . . . dead?

Bailey closed her eyes and sent a quick prayer heavenward. She drew a deep breath and held it inside. Zach gently lifted Hope from Joe's body and checked for a gunshot wound. Relief crossed his face when he found nothing but a few minor scratches.

Hope opened her crying eyes and smiled weakly at her brother. "I knew you'd come."

A pool of red seeped across the floor, mixing with the water Faith had dumped on Joe Junior. Bailey stared down in horror. That meant . . .

Joe Junior lay awkwardly, his face to the floor. Zach cautiously turned him until they saw where the blood originated. The bullet had hit him square in the chest.

Bailey quickly knelt beside Joe. She knew it was useless even as she searched for his pulse. She shook her head at Zach, then looked beyond his shoulder to the man by the door. Sloan's eyes were focused on his younger brother, his face expressionless.

"I had a clear shot," he said as he put his pistol away. Without another word, Sloan turned and slowly walked away.

The sun had set and darkness had already fallen by the time Joe Junior's body was carefully wrapped in a blanket and placed over Bear's back. The crickets chirped low and lazily tonight. To Zach, it was almost as if the whole prairie knew a dead man was present. The night crawlers and other animals seemed to be paying some type of respect.

Zach grunted as he tied the last knot to hold the body in place. *Respect.* It was difficult to feel any type of admiration for a murderer, much less a dead one. Even so, it was a shame. Joe Junior had had a whole life ahead of him. Now it was over.

Rand and Zach had spent more than an hour talking to his sisters, trying to determine what had happened. Joe had left a kerchief on the windmill yesterday, and Hope had met him there after the funeral while Bailey was still in town. He insisted she go with him since she was the only other one who knew about the knife.

It was Faith who actually figured out who the murderer was. When her twin was missing, Faith knew that Joe had her. Bailey had called it a mental connection between twins. Zach didn't know about that, but whatever it was that alerted Faith was to be thanked. Although she and Charity put themselves in danger, their appearance might well have thwarted Joe Junior's plan and bought much needed time before the young man killed their sister.

Zach walked away from the horse toward Rand, who was staring out into the darkness of the prairie. The moon wasn't yet high, so the sheriff held an oil lamp in one hand.

"Can you see him?"

"Out toward the north." Rand nodded his head in the general vicinity. Zach stared but saw nothing. Finally, the red glow of a cigarette tip gave away Sloan's location. Rand lifted the lamp to light the way. The two men started out toward him, neither speaking. If Sloan heard them approach, he didn't acknowledge it.

Rand spoke first, his voice low and full of regret. "I owe you an apology, Thompson."

Sloan looked over at the sheriff, his face worn and tired. He shrugged and stared back out into the darkness again.

"Hope told us about Joe's plan," Zach added. "By killing J.T. and letting me hang, he thought he'd marry Hope, take the Double Bar G, and own the largest ranch in all of Wyoming. Big plans for just a kid. When J.T. left the ranch to you, Joe's plan went awry. He got desperate."

"That's about the way I had it figured," Sloan replied. He took one last draw on what remained of his cigarette, then dropped it and ground it into the dirt with his boot.

Zach struggled for something to say. Sloan had been a suspect in the murder just like he had been. Unlike him, though, Sloan had not been treated with much kindness or given the benefit of the doubt. "I knew the boy all of his life, and I guess I still didn't know him. I'd have never thought he'd kill his own pa."

The silence continued to grow between the three men, becoming more and more tense. Finally, Sloan turned toward both of them. "I hadn't been around but for a few days when I saw a side of him I didn't like. He cornered me in the barn and wanted me to kill J.T. He said he knew I had plenty of experience and I could get away with it. He said we'd split the ranch once J.T. was dead. I refused, of course, and the boy got pretty sore, threatening to do me in along with J.T." Sloan took a long breath. "I suspect J.T. overheard the conversation. That's why he changed his will. I think he knew Joe Junior was planning to kill him, so he taunted him by threatening to leave the ranch to me."

"Why do you suppose J.T. didn't take care of the situation beforehand? Send Joe Junior away or something?" Rand asked, kneeling down on one haunch.

"That I don't know," Sloan replied. "He and I weren't on the best of terms. He didn't take me into his confidence. I imagine he never thought Joe Junior would go through with it."

"And he did leave you his prized possession, his ranch. Why?" Rand persisted.

Sloan calmly and directly met the sheriff's gaze. "That's anybody's guess, Sheriff. If I had to speculate, I'd say he might have been making his amends to my mother. He took her innocence, refused to marry her, then left without a word when he found out she was in a family way. My mother was not only ruined, but the entire family scandalized. I was a constant reminder of her heartache. Something that's about driven her near mad."

Zach's eyes remained on Sloan as he told his story. Shame washed over him. He was ready to judge Sloan without understanding him. Just like he'd done with Bailey and her story of being from the future. He had been so smug that he knew everything, yet he didn't know anything. Not about this man before him, and not about Bailey, his own wife. The woman had married him—given up part of herself—to protect his sisters.

Sloan met Zach's gaze. "I'm sorry you were in jail so long. Even though I suspected, it took me a while to figure out how Joe Junior could have gotten your knife. When I spotted your sister with him by the windmill this afternoon after the funeral, I put it all together. What I didn't know was how deeply the girl was involved." He looked back at Rand. "I wanted to find out before I told you, Sheriff. I wanted to keep her out of trouble if I could."

Rand nodded but remained silent. Zach saw a new respect form in his friend's eyes. "What will you do now, Sloan?" the lawman asked.

Sloan pulled out his tobacco pack and carefully rolled another cigarette before he answered. He removed his hat and took a match from the band. "I've always been a wanderer, but I'm thinking maybe it's time to settle down. I'm going to bring my ma and sister up from Texas. Not so sure I'm cut out to be a rancher, but she deserves some stability after what J.T. did to her." Sloan again looked at Zach. "Those hybrids of yours are interesting. Maybe I'll give it a shot."

"Either way, I'm proud to be your neighbor, Sloan." Zach offered his hand and the two men shook.

"Over this way," a voice cried, "I see a light."

"Perfect." Rand stood and arched an eyebrow. "Charlie Mack and his posse."

They expected a dozen or so men, but only one made his way closer. His gun was drawn when he came into view. Zach wondered if the sedate old man would actually shoot.

The banker quickly glanced around, undecided about what to do.

"It's over, Charlie," Rand said calmly. "We've found the killer." Confused, the banker looked from Zach to Sloan. "No," Rand added. "Zach didn't murder J.T., nor did Thompson. It was Joe Junior. The boy kidnapped Gooden's sisters and meant to do them harm. Zach busted out of jail to rescue them."

Charlie Mack had the decency to look chagrined. "When I saw you planning to break out, I thought sure that made you guilty, Zach. I didn't want to believe it, but why else would you try to escape?" He grinned sheepishly. "I should have known, though. I couldn't get up a posse in town because no one believed you would have killed J.T. anyway. The liveryman told us your sisters were missing, and the few men I had managed to convince immediately changed their minds. They said you'd be back, you just had to find those sisters and keep them out of trouble."

"You did what you thought was right, Charlie. I respect that," Zach replied. Besides, Zach thought, the man still controlled his loan. There was no need to be anything less than gracious.

"Least I can do is extend your loan for as long as you need," the banker went on. "Truth be known, I like the hybrid idea. If it proves as successful as you believe, Wyoming's cattle market will make us all rich men."

Zach grinned. "Charlie Mack, meet Sloan Thompson. He is the new owner of the Thompson ranch. Perhaps you and he need to talk."

It was almost midnight by the time the weary Goodens reached their ranch house. They had split up from Rand, Sloan, and Charlie Mack after they crossed the river. The three men had taken Joe Junior's body on to town while Zach and Hoop brought Bailey and his sisters home.

Zach dismounted from Reliant and lifted Bailey down
from behind him. She had fallen asleep on the slow ride
home, her warm cheek resting on his back. He felt oddly
protective of this woman who clearly could protect herself.
He held her by the waist and slowly brushed his body full
length against hers as he lowered her to the ground. When
her toes finally touched the soil, Bailey smiled sleepily at
him, then wrapped her arms around his neck and brought
his face forward to her own. Without hesitation, she kissed
Zach as if she were dreaming, a slow, exotic kiss that sent
tremors skirting across his body.

The noise around them broke their magical trance. Hoop
had dismounted and then helped Hope off his horse. She
had ridden behind the foreman on the ride home. Zach
knew Hoop was like a second father to his sisters, and
Hope was clutching him as if she'd never let go.

Zach reluctantly released Bailey and walked over to help
Faith and Charity off of Sparky. Hoop carried a weary
Hope into the house and gently placed her in one of the
leather chairs. Bailey and Faith followed closely behind.
Zach cradled little Charity in his arms.

"I'll see to the horses," Hoop said, tipping his hat toward
Bailey and moving toward the door.

"Give them all an extra scoop tonight," Zach said. "I'd
say they earned their oats and then some, wouldn't you?"
Hoop grinned and continued on outside without breaking
his stride.

Jin Lee bustled into the room. The small, dark-headed
man burst into his native language and started to scold the
girls for worrying him so, but Zach held up a hand for silence. Jin Lee could deal with them later. Right now they
needed a warm dinner and a hot bath.

When Jin Lee stopped his harangue long enough to
study the tired girls with their smudged faces and dirty

clothes, his brows drew together and he wrung his hands. "Are they hurt, Mr. Zach?"

Zach shook his head. "No, thank God. If you'll heat some bathwater for them, I'll fill you in on the details." The Oriental man turned back toward the kitchen. Zach bent down and picked up a sleepy Charity in his arms. He saw Bailey rise from the sofa and encourage his other two sisters to follow them up the stairs to their room.

Once inside, he deposited Charity on her bed, then crossed the room toward Bailey. "Are you up to helping them get ready for bed?" he asked.

"Sure, I want to talk to them anyway."

"You'll come downstairs when you're finished?" He hoped so. They had their own talking to do, too.

Bailey watched as the door closed behind Zach. Of course she'd stay with Faith, Hope, and Charity for a while, certainly until they drifted off to sleep. Her three angels had been through hell the past twelve hours. They needed someone to mother them.

She wasn't really sure how a mother acted, but every single night she'd pretended that her own mother was there brushing her hair and tucking her into bed. That's what mothers did, they were there for you when the going got tough, and afterwards when the tough got sleepy.

A light knock at the door brought Jin Lee with two buckets of hot water, followed by Zach with two more. Bailey dragged the copper tub from the corner, and the men poured water for the girls' baths. Then they went back downstairs for more. When they returned again, Bailey smiled her thanks and hurried them out of the room. She then turned to help Charity out of her clothes and into the bath. Bailey quickly washed the young girl's hair and scrubbed the grit and grime from her delicate skin.

Faith was next. She bathed herself while Bailey dressed

Charity in her nightgown and tucked her into bed. In less than five minutes, sweet Charity was fast asleep, with her Indian doll tight under one arm.

Faith and Hope followed the lead of their littlest sister. Neither wanted to go back downstairs for something to eat. They were too tired. Bailey waited while the twins climbed into bed together before she turned down the oil lamp and enveloped the room in darkness.

The moon had finally risen high in the sky. Its light illuminated the room, casting a protective glow over all three girls. Bailey moved to the window and stared up at the bright stars, pondering the afternoon as Faith joined Charity's deep slumber.

Sleep would not come to Hope, however. She tossed in her bed and sighed loudly. Bailey stepped closer and touched her forehead. "Are you all right?" she asked, sitting down on the edge of the bed. Faith and Charity continued to sleep undisturbed.

Hope's eyes widened, and she nodded. "Can't sleep. I guess I'm too worked up about what happened today. I really thought Joe Junior loved me, Bailey. I thought I loved him, too." Hope buried her face in her arms and started to cry. Bailey softly stroked Hope's hair.

"I understand better than you may think," Bailey encouraged softly. "I was a teenager once, too, you know. There was this boy in the seventh grade named Emil. He and his family were from Spain and had just moved to Memphis because of his father's job. I took one look at his olive skin, dark hair, and beautiful deep brown eyes, and I was hooked. For the next two years, I swooned over him so badly, the other kids teased me unmercifully."

Hope sat up in bed, trying to wipe away her tears. "What happened?"

"By the tenth grade, my ugly red hair had grown long and shiny, and my body began filling out just like yours is doing. Boys were beginning to pay attention to me. I had just about lived down my embarrassing obsession with Emil when he saw me in study hall one day."

"Did he go crazy for you then?"

"Not really. He was way too cool, if you know what I mean. But he did ask me to go to a football game. Of course I said yes. I was shocked and flattered that he finally noticed me." Bailey smiled sweetly and sighed as if it had happened yesterday, not twenty years ago. "I was the happiest girl in the world that day."

"Your dream came true, then."

Bailey gently pushed an errant strand of hair away from Hope's swollen eyelids. "It did for a while. A couple days later, I overheard a group of kids laughing in the hallway. Seems that Emil asked me to the game because of a dare. I'd never been on a date before, and his buddies challenged him to ask that 'ugly redheaded orphan.' They called it a 'sympathy date.' I thought I'd die of embarrassment."

"What happened?"

"An angel took pity on me because I transferred to another foster home within the week. For the first time in my life, I was glad to be moved. This time it was across town, and I ended up at another high school. I never went to the game, and I never saw Emil again until—" Bailey looked at Hope, who was waiting anxiously, her tears almost forgotten. "Until he appeared in court one day as a witness for the defense in a case I was prosecuting. He remembered me all right, and he pursued me for months, telling me how foolish he'd been in high school."

"Well, did you let him court you?"

"No. I found out he had a wife and two toddlers at home." Bailey shook her head and grinned. "Besides, he had gotten a beer belly and was very rough around the edges. I was much better off without him when all was said and done. I sure didn't know that when I was in school, though, just like you didn't know about Joe Junior. He had some bad problems, Hope, and even the love of a good woman like you wasn't enough to help him overcome them."

"But I loved him, Bailey," she implored.

Bailey drew the covers up and kissed Hope on the cheek. "I know, sweetheart, I know."

Chapter 23

DOWNSTAIRS, ZACH WATCHED as Hoop slathered butter and preserves on one of Jin Lee's hot biscuits. It was his third, and it didn't seem like he planned on stopping anytime soon. Zach grinned. Hell, he'd had four himself. Nothing got in the way of a cowboy and his stomach.

Zach leaned back in his wooden chair and stretched his booted legs. He was tired but happy. They'd rescued his sisters and cleared his name all in one day. "Thanks, Hoop," he said.

The older man took his attention off the biscuit long enough to look up at Zach. "For what? Rescuing our girls? Seems to me you oughta be thanking Miss Bailey. She's the one who tightened up her belt and took on a man's job. She almost had that crew neatly in hand before we ever showed up."

Hoop sat back in his chair and finished off his biscuit, savoring every bite. He reached into his shirt pocket and pulled out a folded piece of paper. Zach recognized it immediately.

"I stopped by the bunkhouse to get this. I guess you won't be needing it now."

Zach nodded and took the crumpled note he had given to Hoop just before the Reverend Martin pronounced Bailey as Mrs. Zachariah Gooden. Zach dropped it to the table without opening it. There was no need. He knew exactly what it said.

"I want her to stay, Hoop." Zach wasted no words with his friend. "I just don't know how to go about it."

Hoop stared at him thoughtfully. "I could tell the day we first went to town that she had you cinched right down to the last hole. You didn't have a chance, buddy, not with her silks and satins swishing around you like a high wind through tall grass."

Hoop drained the last gulp of coffee from his cup and stood to stretch his legs. "Ain't nothing wrong with that either. A man's gotta settle down sometime."

"I don't have much to offer other than three troublesome sisters."

"That's a hesitation to be sure," Hoop agreed. He placed a fatherly hand on Zach's shoulder. "But you're not looking at the whole picture, son. That woman's done given you her heart. You can see it in her eyes. Now, what you do with it is up to you. You ain't going to find another one smarter, braver, or better looking."

Jin Lee appeared in the doorway to clear away the dishes. Hoop patted the small man on the back. "Thanks for the grub, Jin Lee. I was hungrier than a woodpecker with a headache." Jin Lee grinned and bowed slightly, obviously pleased with Hoop's words.

Hoop picked up his hat from an empty chair and covered his wiry hair with one smooth action. He moved toward the door and reached for the handle. Zach stood and followed his foreman toward the darkness outside.

"Looks like chance is waiting on you, fella." Hoop nodded toward the swing on the far end of the front porch without breaking stride as he headed for the bunkhouse.

Zach turned and saw Bailey alone, gently rocking back and forth in the slatted wood porch swing. She hadn't yet noticed him standing in the moonlight. He drew in a breath. She'd obviously gotten a bath, too. A pink dressing gown, the one she wore her first morning here, was wrapped around her nightgown, loosely knotted at the waist. Just below her thigh, the robe had opened slightly, giving him a glorious view of one bare leg, from just above the knee all the way down to her toes. Her legs were slightly parted as she pushed the swing back and forth. Her feet were covered with delicate slippers. It was her face, though, that stopped his heart. Her features were soft and relaxed, gentle and inviting. For a second he thought she might have seen him there in the darkness and beckoned to him. He could only imagine what she wore next to her skin. He really didn't care; he wanted to rip the robe from her body and replace it with fiery kisses.

Zach cleared his throat and slowly moved toward her. She met his gaze steadily, giving him a lazy, seductive smile. He wondered if his appearance had the same effect on her. The sleepy kiss she'd given him proved that she wanted him with the same abandon.

"I thought you'd be in bed," he spoke quietly, not wanting to break the force that drew them so compellingly to each other.

"Couldn't sleep," she replied, looking away uncertainly. Had he imagined what they just shared? "I'm always like this after a big trial," she added. "I get so worked up during the day's events, it's hard for me to unwind. What about you?"

"Just finished the steak, eggs, and biscuits Jin Lee made. You weren't hungry?"

"No, I decided on a soak in the tub instead. Jin Lee brought up some fresh hot water for me."

Zach inwardly groaned. It wasn't hard to imagine her in the copper tub, soaking in rose-scented water, once again using his straight edge to shave her glorious legs. He swallowed, and deliberately strolled to the porch railing to look out into the darkness. The sky was brilliant with millions of tiny white stars dotting the horizon. Bailey stood and joined him, slipping her soft hand in his.

"It's beautiful, isn't it?" he asked, pointing heavenward. They were both quiet a moment as they considered the stars. When he could stand it no longer, Zach drew his wife closer. The heat of her skin through the thin fabric of the dressing gown wreaked havoc with his self-control. He wanted her, but was it right to ask her to give up so much for a dusty ranch with three hellions and their brother?

Bailey glanced up at him with a sly smile. "Would you believe I have a star named after me?" At his disbelieving expression, she nodded. "It's too deep in space to see it without a telescope, though. All you have to do is donate a bit of money to a research organization, and it's named in your honor."

"Do men travel to the stars in your time?"

"Men *and* women," she replied.

A twinge of disappointment took hold in Zach's heart. He'd read parts of the almanac, the future was full of excitement and challenge, two things Bailey needed to be the person she was. Why would she want to stay with him when the future had so much to offer? He had wanted to make her his wife in every sense of the word tonight. Now he hesitated.

"The girls are holding up surprisingly well." Bailey spoke softly as if she sensed his withdrawal. She left his side and returned to her seat on the swing, then met his eyes with her own. "They've been through a lot, Zach, and they need your patience and understanding. In their short lives, they've faced the death of their mother, the murder of their father, the murder of J.T., their brother in jail, their own kidnapping, then Joe Junior being gunned down in front of them. Not an easy load for kids to bear."

Zach saw a tiny glimmer of *perhaps*. Maybe it wasn't fair, but she loved the girls. Maybe she'd stay for them.

"You're right," he agreed solemnly. "I'm not sure how to handle all this." He stared at her as she gently pushed the wooden swing back and forth with her toe. The swing was meant only for two. Zach knew if he moved to sit in the space next to her, he'd never be able to keep his hands from pulling her to him.

Hell, he didn't want to keep his hands away from her. He wanted to run them through her moonlight-kissed hair. He wanted to feel her body next to his. He wanted . . . he wanted her the way a man wants a woman. Zach hesitated again. No real man would hide behind the excuse of his sisters. If Bailey stayed, he wanted it to be because she loved him as much as he loved her. That meant honesty.

He spoke softly. "You've learned that I'm not a trusting soul, Bailey. I've been responsible for so much for so long that it's not easy for me to rely on another person. Today, you proved to me what I was missing. You faced death to save my sisters . . . to save me." He could resist no longer. She looked so irresistible, so inviting there in the moonlight, he had to at least touch her.

Zach moved to sit beside her on the swing, his hard warm hand reaching for hers, closing around her long fingers. He stopped the back and forth motion, and considered her carefully. "Ever since you've been here, something about you has called to me, called straight to my soul. You and I have somehow connected deep within ourselves. Or perhaps our souls have always been connected, I don't know. Almost overnight you've become a part of my life as if you were meant to be with me all along despite the years that separate us. And my sisters," he added, stroking the tender skin of her forearm, "no other woman has been able to handle them. But you, you're their friend, sister, and mother all combined into one."

He hesitated, wondering if he was making any sense at all. "There's more to it than just that, Bailey. It's difficult for me to put into words."

She smiled shyly and lifted a hand to touch his cheek. "You're doing a pretty good job."

Her touch lit a fire that could not be hidden. Even in the dim glow of the moon, he recognized the same fire radiating from her. Very gently he pulled his beautiful wife to him, his head bent, his mouth lightly caressing her bottom lip.

"I know, Zach," she finally admitted. "I've felt it, too."

No matter what happened, he realized, even if she left for Medicine Mountain tomorrow, he wanted to remember this moment, remember the taste of her, so warm and feminine. She had soaked in rose-scented water, and her nearness caused his senses to whirl as her fragrance combined with the night air to create an exotic perfume meant only for him.

The swing seemed to start in its own slow rocking motion. His mouth moved to possess her lips more fully. Bailey settled deeper into his embrace, returning his kiss with equal abandon.

When Zach lifted his head inches to gaze into her eyes, Bailey looked suddenly shy and vulnerable. Zach reached for her hand and brought it to his lips, opening her palm and kissing it tenderly.

Bailey slowly lifted her arms and entwined her hands around his neck, pulling him with her as she leaned back against the swing. The night air was crisp through her borrowed nightgown, but she felt giddy and hot. The contact of skin against skin only intensified the ache growing deep inside her. Zach's mouth began a slow demanding exploration of her neck and shoulders. One hand loosened the belt of her robe, then reached for the tiny white buttons across the bodice and slowly began to undo them. Bailey sighed. Zachariah Gooden made her forget everything. Forget about home. Forget about being a judge. Take what Zach was offering.

As the swing continued its perpetual motion, he completed the last few buttons, leaving the bodice of the soft gown open. As much as she wanted him to, he didn't touch her there. Inside, he lightly brushed his palm across the lace of her nightgown, and the movement created a tiny puff of cool air. Her quick intake of breath brought a gentle smile to his lips as he nuzzled the tender spot just underneath her ear.

Finally, when she could stand it no more, Zach began a delightfully lazy massage of her breast that sent an urgent throb across every inch of her being. His mouth played a sensuous game with the delicate curve of her jawbone while his hands continued to communicate his desire. Her nipple was taut and anxious for him as he traced a lean finger along the delicate lace of her gown. Bailey knew she should stop before they went too far, but she didn't want to. She just plain didn't want to.

She wanted Zach and he wanted her. They belonged to each other for this moment in time. What tomorrow held, she didn't know. He stood and swept her into his arms as Rhett had Scarlet. Her heart beat a wildly erotic rhythm as Zach leaned forward to kiss her still-tingling lips again. He pushed through the front door, wasting no time by taking the stairs two at a time. They passed the girls' bedroom and hers, going further down the hall into his. Zach gently deposited her on the comfortable mattress of his bed.

A low-burning oil lamp on a nightstand in the corner cast a faint glow in the room. Bailey stared at Zach with a thirst that refused to be quenched. She'd had relationships before, but not one had made her feel like Zach did. Like she was perfect. Her rugged cowboy stared down at her; want, need, desire in his eyes. She'd never forget this moment. Never.

Zach could only stare at Bailey lying seductively on his bed. The urge to hold this vision in his arms, to whisper sweet words in her ear, and yes, to love her. All that mattered at that very moment was to convince her of his true feelings. He wanted to show her and pray that she, too, felt the strength of the bond between them.

He knelt down beside the bed and reached for Bailey's hands and drew her into a sitting position in front of him. Bailey's mouth opened slightly to run a tongue over her dry lips. She tenderly traced the line of his cheekbone and jaw with the soft skin of her palm, feeling the prickly stubble on his chin. Her fingers fluttered down to his neck and rested on the steady beat of his pulse. Zach reached up to place his hands on each side of her face and brought her face to his until they were only inches apart. The anticipation of what was destined grew unbearable.

Still kneeling beside the bed, Zach brought her hand to his mouth, then leaned forward inch by inch, his eyes intent on her lips. A sensuous smile parted his mouth when he felt the heat of her breath on his cheek. A small moan escaped her throat. When his lips finally sought hers, he knew she was powerless to do more than offer her own.

Pure rapture spiraled when they kissed. His tongue traced the soft fullness of her lips while his hands wound through her disheveled hair. Bailey opened her mouth a bit wider, allowing their tongues to meet and entwine. Zach's head came up slightly to place tiny kisses on her face and neck, as a gentle hand skimmed over her body to her waist, then further down. He touched her thigh before lifting his wandering fingers to gently massage her breast through her open gown.

She shivered with pleasure when his teeth lightly scraped her throat and bare shoulders. Zach opened the gown wider and let his tongue follow the path of his fingers around the delicate lace of the gown. Bailey caressed the curls at the back of his neck. She murmured his name with a pleasant sigh.

The thought that he should stop before this went too far tormented Zach. She might disappear tomorrow, that was true. But tonight she was here in his bed, and she belonged to him. He knew that her body longed for his touch as much as he longed for hers. Still, it had to be her choice.

"Bailey," he groaned, pulling away slightly. "We have to stop now, or—"

Bailey looked bewildered. "Do you not want me?"

He could see the hurt in her eyes. "God, yes. It's just that tomorrow—" Zach hesitated, irritated that he sounded so nervous. "You're going home."

This time it was Bailey who withdrew. "You want me to go, then?" she asked softly, disappointment lacing her words. She couldn't help the tears that formed at the corners of her eyes. She had hoped that maybe after all they'd been through, after he called her "love" and "sweetheart," that he might have changed his mind.

"Want you to?" Zach asked. "That's what you thought?" He suddenly threw back his head with a joyful laugh. "I assumed it was what you wanted, Bailey. I've wanted you since I rescued you from the ravine."

Joyful relief lifted Bailey's heart as Zach swooped her up and swung her around in his arms. They tumbled back to the bed, laughing, kissing, loving.

Zach kissed her again, this time hard and demanding. The growing ache spread to her core like a fire out of control. She pressed trembling arms around his back to bring him close enough to quench the burning. Hurriedly, he pulled the cotton gown over her head then tossed it to the floor. A sensuous jolt of cool breeze from the window only heightened the intensity.

He resisted a few agonizing seconds before running a hot tongue along her newly bared flesh. His dancing tongue pushed her closer and closer to the edge of abandon. Zach's grin turned serious as his eyes raked boldly over her lithe form.

"Bailey, you're beautiful." His mouth caressed her already sensitive nipples as his hand moved magically over her smooth breasts, gently kneading one, then the other. The tips of his fingers brushed over the rosy circles, making them draw even tighter. Searing a path down her abdomen, his hand stroked her skin, then slipped to explore the intimate warmth of her femininity, the touch soft as a feather.

Her long lashes dropped against her cheek, answering his quest for surrender. Time ceased as they used it to explore, to arouse, to give each other pleasure. Never before had Bailey felt such contentment, such satisfaction. Never before had she felt so loved.

Inhaling Zach's masculine scent, Bailey reached to unbutton the white fabric of his shirt, impatient to rub the bare skin of his shoulders and back. His nipples were hard and taut as her own, and she savored each with her lips, wanting to share the same joy he gave to her. She craved every part of him, to touch, taste, and love all of him. A guttural moan escaped his throat as her lips cast their sultry spell. Racing passion roared in her ears when his mouth slid up to hers.

He rose from the bed to discard his trousers, his eyes caressing her body's every detail. As he slowly returned to her arms, Bailey reached with seeking fingers to find his hot rigid length. A quick intake of breath, followed by a contented sigh was all she needed to hear. She took what she wanted, as did he.

Meeting her gaze, Zach groaned in pleasure to feel her warm fingers encircle his form and begin an uninhibited massage. He lifted his head again to crush his mouth against hers, kissing ardently, matching her rhythm with his power-ful tongue. His body trembled, and his breathing grew ragged.

The heat of Zach's body seared and enveloped her as he caressed her ear with low whispers. Bailey thought she heard the words "love" and "forever," but wasn't certain. Zach's hands continued to magically stroke fire against the intense fever of her intimate flesh. They were driven by a commanding need, one which made them abandon all sensi-bilities. When he positioned himself above her, she moved to let him slip inside her body as he had slipped inside her heart.

Time simply stopped at that moment.

Zach again touched his lips to his wife's, using his tongue to mimic the eternal dance of desire. He pushed deeper and began to move in a passionate rhythm. The hard muscles of his chest crushed her breasts when his hands slid underneath to lift her into his thrusts. She clung to him with trembling limbs, his heartbeat entwined with her own.

A sense of urgency drove them. Slowly, at first, then building until her body began to vibrate with burning sweet-ness. Bailey wrapped her arms around Zach's neck, entwin-ing her fingers in his hair. Fire and passion glowed within as she acquiesced to uncontrollable joy.

They cried out together when release finally came. Who knew, she thought. Who knew that loving this man was everything, and more, than she'd ever expected.

The two stayed unmoving for several long minutes. With-out breaking their bond, Zach turned on his side and cradled her head on his shoulder, his free arm wrapped possessively around her hips.

"Will you stay, Bailey? Be my wife in every sense of the word?" He caressed her ear with a whisper.

"Thought you'd never ask." She grinned, lifting a finger to gently stroke the warm skin of his arm. They kissed, this time sweetly and tenderly, and Bailey drifted off to a wonderfully restful sleep.

Chapter 24

BAILEY WOKE BEFORE first light. The room was dark and noiseless, the only evidence of the coming morning was the crisp air of a new day that filtered through the open window. Despite the chill, Bailey wasn't cold. Zach's heavy thigh was thrown across her, and the warmth of his body seeped into hers. He lay on his side facing her, his arm wrapped protectively over her chest, his hand cupping her neck. For one of the few times in her life, Bailey felt truly safe and secure.

Zach wanted her to stay as much as she craved the same. He hadn't quite said that he loved her, but he made it abundantly clear that he wanted her and needed her. She smiled sleepily, remembering the hours he spent repeatedly showing her just how much.

Yes, he made it perfectly clear.

At last, she would have what she'd always wanted, her own family and a place where she belonged. For the past few days, she had tried to push away a thought that had nagged her, but now it refused to be ignored. Despite the way she felt about Zach and his sisters, did she really belong here? Was she meant to be part of this time?

Bailey carefully moved her arm so her fingers could caress the warm skin on Zach's bare arm. He stirred slightly but didn't wake. There were so many things to consider. Would her permanent presence here alter the future? If so, would it be for good or bad? How could she know? Would she really be happy without modern conveniences like plumbing and automobiles? She'd worked hard to rise above the blows life had dealt her. She'd had a successful career as an attorney, and now she faced the responsibilities that went with a judicial appointment. She'd craved that black robe and gavel for as long as she could remember. Was she willing to forgo that success? Would she be able to give it up for a man she'd known only a week?

A man who literally lived in the past?

Finally, the real question. Even if Bailey wanted to return, was there truly any way possible? Dark Fawn, or whatever force it was that sent her here, had decided the Faith, Hope, and Charity she needed were asleep in the other room. Even if she journeyed to Medicine Mountain, would she be allowed to return to her own time? Allowed to go home?

Was that what she wanted?

Would she start to make a life for herself here, then suddenly be sent back to the twentieth century no matter what she chose?

Bailey turned her head so she could see Zach more clearly. The oil lamp had burned itself out while they slept. She had only a dim shine from the disappearing moon to make out his strong features. His breathing was deep and even as if he rested with not a care in the world. His lips were upturned just slightly, silently telling her how happy he was. Their night together had been nothing short of magical.

He'd opened his heart and loved her, then let her love him right back.

Bailey sighed. The truth was that if she never made it back to her own time, she wouldn't mind. She always believed that somewhere there was one special person who was meant for her. That man was Zach Gooden. It didn't matter that he lived one hundred and twenty-one years before her time.

She moved her fingers until they caressed his cheek. The morning growth of stubble on his jawbone and chin gently pricked at her fingers. She continued to watch her sleeping husband. "I love you, Zach," she whispered. "No matter what happens, I love you."

He opened his eyes to a lazy slit. He said not a word when he pulled her back into his arms, but Bailey knew what he silently demanded. Time belonged only to them this night, and neither wanted to waste it.

Zach started to sit up and press her back against the bed but Bailey tenderly pushed him against the pillows. The question on his face was instantly replaced with delight when she moved to stretch her body flat against his sinewy chest and abdomen. Both of his hands sought the back of her neck. One lifted her hair away from her skin, the other pressured her into meeting his lips with her own.

There was no mistaking his intentions, just as there was no mistaking what she wanted. She wanted to love this man who made her ache with want, need, and desire. If that meant staying in this time, she'd do it. Nothing in the future was worth this. Nothing.

If Zach noticed the new fervor in her kisses, he didn't seem surprised. This time, it was Bailey who controlled the taking, and she mastered it with a slow, relaxed urgency that defied time.

*   *   *

Zach Gooden was doing a pretty poor job of proving he rose every day at the crack of dawn. Bailey had already risen from the bed and grinned at the sight before her. Zach lay sprawled across the bed in all his naked glory, sound asleep. The light quilt that had once covered them was twisted and contorted, doing nothing to ward off the cool morning air. The sun had not yet peeked across the prairie, but the sky had traded its blackness for a grayish hue.

She'd always been an early riser, no matter how late she'd gotten to bed the night before. This morning was no exception. Bailey picked up her nightgown and pink robe from the floor, then stretched long and slow. Her muscles ached pleasantly. Last night was indeed a late one, and tiring, too. Sore muscles she could handle. Right now she was starving. A cup of coffee and one of Jin Lee's biscuits sounded heavenly.

She glanced longingly at her husband in the bed. Almost on cue, Zach stirred, his arm reaching for her. He woke more fully when he couldn't find her, and sat up, scanning the room. Bailey took a step forward and back into his arms.

"Come back to bed," he gently urged. "It's not even light yet."

"No, but it will be soon. I'm surprised my rumbling stomach didn't wake you. I'm hungry."

He grinned and patted her behind. "You didn't eat last night, did you? Bring me back some coffee and I'll make it worth your while."

"What woman in her right mind could resist such an offer? Hold that thought, I'll be right back."

Zach dropped back to the pillows, and Bailey heard a soft snore before she closed the door behind her. She headed down the hallway toward the stairs, resisting the urge to peek in on Faith, Hope, and Charity. The longer they slept, the longer she'd have Zach all to herself.

Downstairs, the house was as quiet as the legal library at

the courthouse. Either it was too early for Jin Lee to begin breakfast, or everyone was so tired from last night, they hadn't yet risen. Bailey strolled over to the window, pulled back the curtains, and peeked outside. Even the ranch hands had not yet stirred.

She caught sight of the picture of Zach's family portraits on the wall and walked toward them. She was part of this family now, and she planned to have another portrait made immediately. This time, it would be she who posed in the center, and her entire family, Hoop and Jin Lee included, would gather closely around for the shot.

It would be the first of many, Bailey promised herself. The first of many.

Into the kitchen she headed, turning up the wick on a low-burning oil lamp. Out of habit, she reached for the knob to turn on the stove and frowned when she realized why she couldn't find it. There wasn't any. This was no electric range like she had at home. This was a cast-iron model that ran on wood instead of electricity. No question about it, she would have a lot to learn about this time, starting with how to light the stove. She reached for a tin of matches sitting on a nearby shelf, and added a few pieces of kindling and wood to the fire chamber as she had seen Jin Lee do. After a few tries, the fire managed to catch hold and burn.

The coffee was next. Bailey picked up the blue metal coffeepot and blankly stared at it. Once again, the enormity of differences overwhelmed her. She had absolutely no idea how to make coffee without her bright white machine at home. Not even a clue as to where to start.

Near the stove was a plate of the cook's biscuits left over from the night before. She reached for one, disappointed to find it hard and cold. Who was she kidding to think she actually had something to offer Zach and his sisters? She couldn't make coffee, and a batch of hot biscuits was completely out of the question. She was going to have to learn everything all over again.

Never would she have guessed how her life would have unfolded. It seemed odd that modern science rebuffed the possibility of time travel. Then again, even if anyone ever returned from an experience such as this, who would believe them? She certainly wouldn't. Yet Zach accepted her story, reluctantly at first, but he believed her. And now he wanted her to stay. Bailey couldn't help her contented smile. She now had her family, and she was happy. Truly happy.

She shifted in the chair, stretching her weary muscles. She would regret losing her car. Horseback didn't offer the luxury of bucket seats. Her stomach growled, and she looked back at the cold biscuits. As much as she wanted to be a part of Zach's world, would it really work? Could she give up everything she had ever known, not to mention every convenience she had taken for granted, to live in this time? She glanced around the kitchen, noting the lack of any modern appliances, and caught sight of a folded piece of paper almost hidden by a container of salt. Bailey reached for it, then picked it up and unfolded it. The handwriting was long and flowing, written in ink. It was signed *Zachariah Gooden*.

Curiously, Bailey reached for the oil lamp and pulled it near, illuminating the writing. She felt the color drain from her face as she skimmed the words. Bitter disappointment flooded her as she read the note more closely. Her heart skipped a beat as betrayal replaced last night's joy. The note was a handwritten last will and testament, dated two days ago, written while Zach was still in jail.

The will specifically appointed Bailey as guardian of his sisters in the event of his death. The ranch would be divided equally between Hoop, Faith, Hope, and Charity. Control of the Double Bar G would remain with Hoop, his foreman and family friend. In the event that his wife appeared to be using his three sisters, or the ranch, for her own gain, Hoop had full authority to intercede and assume guardianship.

Using his three sisters for her own gain? Bailey didn't know whether to be shocked or outraged or intensely sad. Clearly, Zach didn't see her as she thought he had. While the suggestion of marriage had been hers, the whole point was to protect his sisters, to prevent anyone from taking advantage of them, from hurting them. She thought she was the one to do that, and despite his words, Zach thought the opposite. Why had he married her then? Why had he let her delay the trip back to Medicine Mountain when he didn't trust her?

The ramifications went even further, she realized. If Zach had hanged, his sisters would always wonder why Zach hadn't trusted her enough to watch over them. He would have destroyed any foundation she might have built for them. She'd sacrificed to help Zach Gooden, to offer his sisters security. And he took what she offered without giving anything back in return.

He had used her. Plain and simple.

It was all so clear now. Last night in the depths of their passion, he had said he wanted her and needed her. Yet not once had he said that he loved her. He needed a nanny. He needed a baby-sitter. He needed someone in his bed. He didn't need a wife or helpmate. He needed someone for his sisters, just like he had from the beginning.

Even as her legal training recognized the logic behind his action, her heart didn't. She wanted to belong to this family, but it appeared that she would always be on the outside looking in, never truly belonging. Fate had again dealt her a painful blow. Some people were meant to be loners, and Bailey was one of them.

Bailey crumpled the paper in her fist and dug deep within herself to find a new resolve. To harden her shell so no one else could hurt her so. The decision had already been made

by Zach himself. She had planned to stay for the love of
Zach and his family. Since she had neither, there was no reason to delay. No reason to sacrifice her accomplishments in
the future for a lifetime of patronizing. If it *was* Dark Fawn
who sent her here, she'd have a few choice words for her.
Bailey Cooper was going home.

She dropped the note like a scorching coal, then rushed
back up the stairs and into her own room where she quickly
changed from the nightgown and robe into her regular
clothes. Bailey scanned the room for her other belongings
before she remembered there were none. Nothing from this
time belonged to her. Nothing.

The door creaked as she left. For a long moment she
stared toward Zach's room, almost wishing she'd never
found the note, never learned of his true wishes. She sighed.
This strange twist of fate just wasn't meant to be.

She inched over to the room shared by Faith, Hope, and
Charity. As usual, it was the children who'd lose the most.
She'd come to love them like sisters. Bailey peeked inside,
then walked closer to the beds.

"Bailey?" Charity roused slightly.

"Shhhh, honey. It's not morning yet, you go back to
sleep."

The littlest of her angels sighed and snuggled back under
the covers, a contented smile on her face. Bailey kissed her
on the forehead, then wiped away her tear before it dropped
on Charity's cheek. This was for the best, Bailey reminded
herself sadly as she retreated into the hallway and down the
stairs. It was for the best.

She formulated her plan on the way to the barn. She
needed to get to Medicine Mountain quickly, and that meant
she needed a guide. Tag. She didn't want to take anything
that didn't belong to her, but she needed a horse. She'd borrow Sparky and insist that Tag return the animal to Zach.
Bailey located the saddle, and with some struggle, finally

managed to lift it onto Sparky's back. Fortunately, she'd listened when Hope showed her how to saddle a horse the morning they headed to the river. It had only been a week, but it felt like a lifetime.

It wasn't difficult to find the road into town. Sparky seemed to know the way without her guidance. He seemed quite willing to take her there, too, she noted wryly. When Tag and Mildred appeared off in the distance, heading toward her, the coincidence was too much to bear. She was meant to go, and it was time.

Tag approached slowly, limping slightly, holding Mildred's lead rope. The grungy white donkey looked extremely irritated. There was one good thing about leaving. At least Bailey would never have to see or smell a donkey again.

Tag spoke first. "I heard Zach was off the hook. Figured I'd get to the house in time for breakfast, then take ya on to the mountain."

"No, there's been a change of plans. I need to leave now."

"What's yer hurry? Runnin' from something?"

"My hurry is none of your business. You said you'd take me and I'm ready."

"Hold yer high horses, woman. We ain't talked money. A good guide to a dangerous place don't come cheap." Tag rubbed a dirty hand across his scraggly chin, staring at Bailey expectantly.

"We've been through this before. You already have my backpack, and you refused to return it. That means you have my compass, my map, my aspirin, and my phone, which you traded for Mildred's stupid halter. You've taken everything I own. What more do you want?"

"Whoa there, Nellie. Mildred don't take kindly to folks insulting her."

Bailey immediately jumped down from the horse and stormed over to the dumpy little man, meeting his stare nose to nose. "I've had it with you and your stinky donkey. You pretend to be an innocent old miner, but you're nothing but a common thief, taking advantage of people down on their luck. Keep my backpack, I don't care. It may take me longer, but I can find the Medicine Wheel on my own."

Bailey glared at Tag until Mildred stepped forward, her ears flat back. Bailey stepped back toward Sparky and put a foot in the stirrup, her eyes never losing sight of the donkey's rear feet. Mildred pushed Tag with her nose until the miner leaned over and put his ear close to her mouth. Bailey watched as Tag vehemently shook his head, then shrugged and appeared to listen. Surely it was her imagination that the donkey's lips were moving, that the animal was *talking* to him.

When the ugly ass dropped her head and walked toward a patch of fragrant green grass, Tag glanced her way without meeting Bailey's eyes. "Don't know if I'm of the same mind, but Mildred says I need to take you. She says you and she are like kin, stubborn females who know how to get what they want."

Bailey wasn't sure if she'd been complimented or insulted, but Tag had agreed. "Thank you, Tag," she said softly. "And thank you, too, Mildred."

The donkey lifted her head toward Bailey, nodded, then went back to munching the grass.

Chapter 25

ZACH AWAKENED TO sunlight streaming in his face. He stretched long and smiled at the memory of last night. Life was good. He was no longer a suspected criminal, his sisters out of danger, and he'd found the woman of his dreams.

They had been perfect together. He'd held Bailey in his arms and caught a glimpse of heaven. Not only was his wife courageous and smart, she was unbelievably passionate and wild. He'd visited a few soiled doves when he could manage to get away from his sisters, but nothing had prepared him for what he experienced with Bailey. Even just thinking about her made him ache with desire.

A sun-warmed breeze filtered through the window and danced across his naked skin. It carried the fresh morning aroma he'd come to love on this vast prairie, sweet green grass mixed with fragrant wildflowers. After their lovemaking, Zach had wrapped their bodies with a light quilt. He pulled it closer now, wishing Bailey was beside him underneath the blanket. He longed for her alluring, responsive body, a body meant for loving.

The physical satisfaction was one thing, he realized, but he almost couldn't believe what he'd felt during their union. He had thought he only wanted her to stay because of his sisters, their mutual attraction just an added benefit. Until last night, he refused to acknowledge that he was mesmerized by this woman. Plain and simple, he loved her with every inch of his heart, soul, and being. He regretted that he hadn't told her that last night, but it was all so new to him. Those would be his first words the minute she walked through that doorway.

He shifted, then rolled over in bed so he'd face her when she entered. Zach couldn't remember the last time he'd slept so late. Usually he was up before the sun had inched its way into the day. He didn't know how long it had been since Bailey went down for coffee. He had drifted off into euphoric slumber once she promised to quickly return. Chances were, he realized, his sisters had already gotten up, and she couldn't get away right now. Zach sighed and wondered how he'd ever manage to get Bailey alone when everyone in the house needed her.

Hot coffee sure sounded good. He tossed back the quilt and rose, casually heading toward his wardrobe for fresh clothes. He had so many plans, he thought, so many things to share with Bailey. Now that he had allowed someone into his shell, he wanted her there always.

Once dressed, Zach opened the white painted door and started through the hallway toward the stairs. The door to his sisters' room was still shut. They usually left it open once they were up and about. He shrugged and whistled a cheerful tune. The morning was glorious, and Bailey was his. His forever.

Zach entered the kitchen where Jin Lee was cooking

breakfast. The aroma of smoked ham and fried potatoes was welcoming. He'd worked up quite an appetite last night. Jin Lee turned from the stove and grinned.

"Morning, Mr. Zach."

Zach glanced around the empty kitchen. "Where is Bailey?"

Jin Lee shook his head and turned back to the stove. "Haven't seen her or the little misses this morning."

Zach quelled a flair of sudden worry. She was probably out on the porch. "She said she was coming down to make—"

It was then he saw the crumpled paper on the floor. Dread washed over him, draining the color from his face as he bent to pick it up. He had lied to her, and his note to Hoop was proof. Knowing the importance Bailey placed on trust and respect, he knew without question that she'd be very hurt if she had read his handwritten will.

Surely she hadn't seen his note to Hoop, he prayed silently. Surely not.

Zach clenched the paper in his hand and groaned. He had meant to drop it in the stove's fire last night, so it would never come between them. He'd forgotten all about it once he saw her on the swing last night. And then . . . and then he'd carried her upstairs.

Zach hurried over to the rack by the front door, grabbed his hat, and hurried to the barn. Bailey had insisted that Medicine Mountain held the key to her travel, so that's where she'd be headed. Within minutes, Reliant was saddled, bridled, and as anxious to run as his owner. Zach spurred his mount away from the barn. There was no time to lose. Bailey was gone, and it was all his fault. She'd put aside her own needs, delayed her chance to find a way home, because he had needed a lawyer and because she had wanted to protect the interests of his sisters. Less than a minute after he agreed with her logical reasons, Zach had gone right be-

hind her back and made her sacrifice useless. He doubted
he'd ever win her forgiveness, much less convince her of his
love, but he had to try.

He had to.

It was slow going.

Bailey couldn't believe that Tag adamantly refused to ride
Mildred, even though they could cover the distance faster. It
had taken them two hours to get to the river with Tag on
foot. She could only imagine the dreadful trip to the distant
mountain. She glanced back over her shoulder as she'd done
repeatedly for the last hour. Zach surely would be out of bed
by now. He'd probably come after her, she knew that. He'd
seek her out not because he loved her, for that word had not
been spoken between them. He'd found the perfect companion for his sisters, and her name was Bailey Cooper. On second thought, his lack of trust proved that he hadn't found the
perfect companion, he'd found one that was just suitable.
And since there were so few applicants for the job, he was
doing everything it took to keep her.

"Well?" Tag's voice brought her back to the matter at
hand. "You crossin' or you ain't?" Her guide stood close to
the river's edge waiting for her decision. The water level had
continued to decrease, but the currents remained fast and
treacherous.

Bailey swallowed to cover her fear and fought to control
the lump that rose in her throat. Each time she had battled
the river, she'd been on a horse with someone else in control. Now it was up to her. She zipped her jacket and adjusted the reins so Tag couldn't see her trembling hands,
then mustered up her courage, lifted her chin, and looked
him squarely in the eye. "Crossing."

Tag shrugged as if it didn't matter either way. He led Mildred to a level spot, then tossed his thick body over her back
with an agility that surprised Bailey. He'd ride if it was im-

portant to him, like getting soaking wet. The donkey brayed in protest as Tag guided her down to the water. Mildred balked when her front hoof and leg stepped into the cold water.

"This was yer idea, you dad-burned female. Don't change yer mind now," Tag snapped at the hesitant donkey. Quite reluctantly, Mildred took another step, then another, and another. Bailey watched as the current pushed against the two and Mildred struggled to cross with the heavy man on her back. Her compassion rose for the little mount. At least a grown horse had more strength and weight because of its size.

After several long minutes, Mildred and Tag managed to reach the other side and scramble up the riverbank. Bailey stole another worried glance behind her. She didn't think that Zach would be the type to let her go without a fight, and she didn't think she had the strength to resist those deep brown eyes. It was the look in those same eyes that had convinced her she could stay, that she could be part of this time. Now that she realized it was all a lie, she wanted to be gone. She wanted never to see him again.

Bailey tried to push Zach from her mind and concentrate on the river. Sparky, normally laid-back and easygoing, acted tense and nervous. He danced around as if he didn't want to cross. It took some doing and a few impatient kicks to his sides, but the horse reluctantly stepped up to the edge and entered the water. Bailey loosened her hold on the reins like she'd seen Zach and Hoop do, giving Sparky his head. The horse tossed his nose and concentrated on the rushing water while Bailey gripped the saddle horn until her knuckles were white.

Roots and other debris that had been swept away upriver crashed into Sparky's sides, but the horse was steady and unflappable despite his earlier hesitation. Just as they approached the river's deepest part, all hell broke loose.

A light brownish-colored snake about three feet long slithered wildly toward them. The snake raised his head as it twisted and spun in its own fight with the sweeping water. Sparky couldn't help but see the terrifying serpent racing toward them out of control.

The horse reared and tossed Bailey off his back right into the frigid water. She struggled to plant her feet on the river bottom, but it was too slick and muddy. The water pushed hard against her. Bailey struggled to stand, dropping the reins.

Sparky floundered a second, then regained his footing. He forged ahead to the other side, then scurried up the slope, leaving Bailey in the turbulent water without so much as a worried look.

"Tag!" she shouted. "Help me!"

Tag had already loosened a rope from Mildred's pack. He swiftly tethered the end into a large loop and tossed her the line. Bailey grabbed feverishly for the lariat, but his swing was short by mere inches. The force of the current pushed her along, not allowing her feet to plant on the mucky bottom. Tag rushed along the bank, trying his best to get ahead of her and toss the rope once more.

Bailey gasped for one last breath as the water pulled her under. She frantically fought her way back to the surface, grabbing hold of a huge floating root turned bottom up. Her added weight caused the root to slow, giving Tag a chance to catch up. The same terrified snake who had caused the fiasco rammed against her and coiled his clammy body around her arm and shoulder, just as Bailey had done with the root.

Bailey shrieked then jerked to dislodge the slimy body, but the snake refused to let go. Above the din of the river, Bailey heard a shout. Reliant and Zach raced along the edge of the river, jumping over brush and rocks.

"Zach!" Bailey couldn't stifle another scream. The snake

contracted even tighter; his head swung around until his eyes were inches from Bailey's own. Bailey again grasped the body and yanked as hard as she could, but the snake would not come off. Each time she managed to loosen one part of its body, another section would move to encircle her.

"Hang on, Bailey!" The man and his horse plunged into the water. The current tried to prevent them from reaching her, but Reliant pushed through. When Zach saw the long, thin snake wrapped around her, his eyes grew large. He quickly turned Reliant's head so the horse would not see the snake and balk. Then he reached down to lift Bailey into his arms.

He pulled her and the slithering animal up away from the fury of the water, and across the saddle in front of him. Bailey turned her head away as Zach grabbed the snake just behind the head. He unwrapped it from Bailey, then threw it with all of his might. It twisted and squirmed in the air, then splashed back into the river. The water immediately engulfed it, sweeping it away to certain doom.

Zach cradled Bailey against his chest as Reliant carried them safely to shore. She knew she should push away from him, maintain her distance, but she craved his nearness this one last time. Even though she felt safe and warm and protected in his arms, it didn't change anything. It was time for her to go, to at least try to find her way home.

Reliant stepped out of the water and up the bank. When the horse stopped, Zach dismounted first, then lifted Bailey from the saddle and lowered her to the ground. He gripped her arms tightly, refusing to let go. "What in blazes did you think you were doing? You could have been killed."

Despite everything, Bailey had been glad to see Zach, thankful that he'd shown up when he had. The intense anger in his voice ripped through her gratitude, separating them even further. She stared up at him, uncertain if his fury stemmed from the snake, her rescue, or her disappearance, but it didn't matter. There was fury in his eyes, and she steeled herself against it. If he thought she'd cower and beg his forgiveness, he needed to think again.

Zach jerked her body forward full-length against his own. His lips pressed down on hers with punishing force. His tongue pushed against her teeth, seeking entry, demanding retribution. Bailey stiffened in his arms, fighting an internal battle not to succumb to his challenge. There was no love in his kiss, no relief that he had found her. After a torturous moment, Zach stilled. He released her and stepped back, his expression tight and unreadable.

"Tag is guiding me to Medicine Mountain, Zach. I'm going home." Bailey calmly unzipped her soaked jacket and shrugged out of it. She followed Zach's glance down the riverbank toward Tag. The man had removed his boots so they could dry. Mildred and Sparky appeared to be hobbled, the heads to the ground foraging the little grass near the river.

Zach walked toward his horse and removed a rolled blanket tied to the saddle. He offered it to her. "Last night you promised to stay."

"Last night we both promised a lot of things. That changed when I realized that you used me to get what you wanted."

"And just what was it I wanted?"

"Someone to watch over your sisters," Bailey said bluntly. "I believed I had to get to Medicine Mountain and that time was of the essence. I put my personal needs aside to help your family in a crisis. I thought I was marrying you to protect you in the event of a trial, but more important, to guard the interests of your sisters. But that wasn't so, was it? You wanted me to raise them, but only under the watchful eye of Hoop. You didn't believe me."

"You're right," he answered coldly. "I didn't. You told a foolish story abut being from the future, and expected me to believe it without question. You insisted that I marry you because *you* thought it was the best thing to do. Would you have given your sisters to a stranger?"

Bailey paused, recognizing the truth of his reasoning but knowing that it no longer mattered. "You still should have been honest with me, Zach. And you should have never let me think—"

You should never have let me think you might love me, she finished silently. It would be so easy to tell him that, but how could she now? He'd simply sweep his worn hat off his head, say the magic phrase, and expect her to pick up right where they left off. He would say it whether it was true or not; he would say it because he needed her to stay. She couldn't love him without his love in return. It would be unbearable.

"Why should I have told you?" Zach busied himself with adjusting Reliant's saddle. He couldn't believe she refused to understand. "You thought Hoop was just as likely to have killed J.T. as anyone. It wasn't until I started really thinking about what I had read in the almanac that I decided what you were saying might be true."

He saw the confused indecision on Bailey's face, and Zach realized how frail her resolve actually was. He knew that if he tried hard enough, if he logically refuted her objections, if he badgered her with all the right reasons, he could convince her to stay. He also sensed that if he did, things would never be right between them. He had little to offer other than a mortgaged ranch and mischievous sisters. He had nothing that could compare to her life in the future.

He'd also hurt her badly by his actions, even though he'd done what he thought was best. It wasn't fair to cut her again by proclaiming his love and adding another burden to her decision. She most likely wouldn't believe him anyway. She had to stay because she wanted to. There was only one thing that might make her change her mind. "My sisters need you, Bailey. More than you know."

She recoiled as if she'd been physically struck. The color immediately drained from her face. "You just don't get it, do you, Zach? Faith, Hope, and Charity don't need me, they need you. I showed them how to be ladylike because *you* needed to see them that way. You couldn't accept them as they were, so they resorted to mischief to get you to notice *who* they were.

"Now get out of my way because I'm going to Medicine Mountain to see if there is any way possible for me to get back to 1999." Bailey threw the blanket at him, then spun on her heel and headed toward Tag, leaving Zach to glare at her retreating back. In three long strides he was at her side. He grabbed her arm until she stopped and faced him.

"Then I'm going to the mountain, too," he said, fighting for her even though he knew he shouldn't. "And when we get there, I want you to look me square in the eye and tell me that I mean nothing to you."

Once again Bailey sat on Reliant close behind Zach. She was touched that Tag refused to let Zach take her to the mountain alone. He obviously knew well that it was no use arguing with the miner. Zach then stoically ordered Tag to ride Sparky to the mountain and lead the donkey, insisting they'd make better time. Bailey doubted it. At his master's command, Reliant had moved off at a slow, steady walk and gave no indication of going any faster. Irritated, Bailey crossed her arms in front of her and studied the movement of Zach's strong back and broad shoulders. She'd sooner die than hold on to him for safety. If she relaxed against him or touched him in any way, it would be disastrous.

He wanted her to stay because of his sisters. He'd never wanted any more than that right from the beginning, no matter what she had imagined last night. Zach had made it clear that he desired her, that he wanted her, but he never once mentioned that he loved her, not even during the intense bonding they shared last night. Bailey needed his trust and respect, but above all, she needed his love.

The horses continued step by step. Zach said nothing. Even Tag sensed it was no time for idle chatter, although he cast Bailey a worried frown now and again. The grizzly old miner still held Mildred's lead rope in his hand as she followed the two horses. The donkey increased her speed until she had moved up between them, and the animals walked three abreast. Tag caught Bailey's eye and winked. There was no sense in forcing Mildred to follow back behind, she was going to do exactly what she pleased anyway.

In some ways, Bailey knew she was just as stubborn and single-minded as the white donkey. She considered an issue from every angle, determined the best course of action, then pursued it relentlessly. Not today, however. Now she wished she could toss away her reservations, throw her arms about Zach's body, and never let go. But that meant giving up all she'd worked for in her old life in the shadow of a man who did not love her. If that was the case, she could just as easily stay married to her career. She was a judge, after all.

She was confident that Faith, Hope, and Charity would be fine without her around. They were smart girls, and even though they shouldn't have had to, they had proven to Zach that they could be ladylike and resourceful at the same time. She doubted they'd let him resort to his old habits once she was gone. So the best place for her was back to her normal life where the only thing that mattered would be her judicial robe and her gavel. She'd never take that responsibility lightly, either. Not after knowing Faith, Hope, and Charity, and certainly not after seeing what hate, revenge, jealousy, and greed had done to J.T. and his two sons.

Up ahead Bailey saw the ravine where Zach had first rescued her. They approached the clearing, and she leaned slightly to glance over the edge. The crest of the gap, where they were walking, was the top of a large grassy knoll, similar to all the rolling hills in the area. The land sloped gently away in other areas, except for this one spot where the ground ripped away like an ugly scar. It jutted deeply downward, opening a wound in the earth, exposing black dirt, roots, and rocks. The horrendous ravine was a lot like J.T., she thought wryly. One bad spot amidst much that could be good.

Despite the sunny afternoon, Bailey noticed a new chill in the air. The warm sun had dried her clothes but now they felt damp and heavy. Clouds now dotted the blue sky and appeared to be building for another thunderstorm.

The path became more narrow and the horses drew closer together until Bailey's booted foot bumped soundly against Mildred's hindquarters. Instantly, the grumpy donkey flattened her ears, lifted her rear foot, and kicked out toward the offender. Bailey sat on Reliant's back, well out of danger. It was the bay horse that bore Mildred's anger. A sickening *thud* sounded when her hoof landed squarely on Reliant's back leg.

The surprised horse stumbled, snorting and blowing in pain. Zach jerked the reins to guide Reliant away from the still-kicking donkey yet keep them from tumbling over the edge of the ravine.

"Whoa there, Mildred! Stop all yer complainin' this minute!" Tag tried desperately to get control of the unruly donkey, but not before she managed to twist around tightly between the two horses, her rear end pointed toward Reliant. The donkey's sharp hoof plowed hard into the horse's belly. Reliant spun away from Mildred's second attack. Since Bailey had refused to touch Zach earlier, she had nothing to steady her balance when the horse sidestepped. Now she grabbed for Zach's shirt when she started to fall, pulling them both awkwardly off balance. Bailey looked behind her, terrified to see the edge of the ravine dangerously close. Zach struggled to stay in the saddle and keep them steady, but it wasn't enough.

She hit the ground with a painful grunt. Zach landed next, almost on top of her. Somehow he had shifted in midair so that his torso missed her body. Instead, he crashed into the dirt right on the edge of the cliff. The earth immediately gave way, taking Zach with it over the side.

"Zach!"

Bailey peered over the edge. A huge, mud-covered root jutted out from the soil about ten feet below. Zach had managed to grab its jagged edge as he fell, and now clung to it with all of his strength. The air continued to thicken as a fog enveloped the entire area. The temperature had dropped just like it had that day at Medicine Mountain. Bailey heard Zach struggling to pull his body up and stand on the root, but she could barely make out his form as the mist grew more dense. The sickening sound of mud giving way was more than she could bear.

She repositioned herself until she was flat on her stomach, her arms outstretched, reaching for Zach, terrible thoughts raging through her mind. Was this how it was all supposed to end? Was this mist like what happened at Medicine Mountain? Would she be suddenly swept away, back into her own time, leaving Zach to possible doom?

Bailey could no longer see anything but her own hands reaching down toward her husband. "I'm here, Zach. Grab my arms!" She couldn't lose him, not now. The fog encircled her, making her body leaden and sluggish. An image of her standing at the Medicine Wheel with the Indian man flashed through her mind, mentally pulling her back toward her old life. Something, or someone, was calling her home.

"No! I'm not ready yet!" She couldn't let him die, just as she knew deep within that she could never live without him. How clearly she saw that reality. She belonged here with him; it was the only place she'd ever truly be happy and content. It mattered little whether he loved her or not because her love was enough for both of them.

What mattered was that she had been blind. Faith, Hope, and Charity hadn't needed to learn from her. It was she who learned from them: faith in her love for Zach and his love for her; hope for a future of happiness, something she'd given up on long ago; and charity. Zach had taken her in despite her story of being from the future. He had been kind, and he had expected nothing in return.

Dark Fawn had truly given her faith, hope, and charity, and now Bailey needed to give it back.

Zach managed to reach up with one hand and wrap it around her wrist, but she didn't have the strength to pull him up to safety.

"Tag! Where are you?" She closed her eyes to offer a quick prayer. Suddenly, the warmth of a leathery hand covered hers, then went farther down to lock on Zach's wrist. Together, they managed to slowly pull Zach up the muddy side to safety.

"Zach!" Bailey cradled his torso in her arms and wiped away the dirt from his face. His body was scratched and bleeding, probably a rib or two was broken, but he was safe.

"I thought I was a goner," Zach said, grimacing as he shifted and tried to sit up on his own. He took a deep breath and reached to touch her cheek, then pulled her to him. "Thank you," he whispered as his lips covered hers in a kiss that rekindled a flame that had never really stopped burning.

A slight cough reminded them of another's presence. Only it wasn't Tag who stood watching over them. Bailey lifted her face to meet the steady gaze of the same Indian man who had befriended her at Medicine Mountain.

"Thank you," she said. "Thank you for giving him back to me." The wizened man silently nodded, the barest hint of pleasure settled around his mouth. After a moment he spoke.

"Dark Fawn asks if you have found the faith, hope, and charity you desired during your quest for knowledge?"

"So it *was* Dark Fawn." She glanced at Zach. "She's the Spirit who sent me to you. The one you didn't think was real."

"The spirit of Dark Fawn is very real. As real as all of this." Sweeping his hand in a broad gesture, the elderly Indian answered the question in Zach's questioning eyes. He focused again on Bailey. "It is real because your heart is here. Dark Fawn believes your heart belongs here, too. Are you certain you wish to return and never find what you truly seek?"

"Bailey," Zach said quietly, his breathing still rapid from his brush with death. "This is what you wanted, your chance to go back to your own time, to become the judge you've worked so hard to be. Just promise me that you won't forget us. Promise me you won't forget how much we love you. How much I love you."

"Zach, I—"

His fingers moved to stop her words. "I promised myself that I wouldn't say that to you. I have nothing to offer compared to what your life must be like in the future; I never will. But I've loved you since the day I pulled you from the ravine. I was just too blindsided to see it sooner. You've turned my world around, Bailey, and I'll never forget you."

Bailey tenderly stroked the hair away from Zach's damp forehead, then bent and gently kissed his lips. "You don't know how you longed to hear those words," she whispered, stroking his cheek. "You've given me more than you know, Zach. I'd lost hope on love, on finding someone to care for, someone to build a life with. I'd thought it unlikely that I'd ever have my own family and a home filled with happy children. I've found that all with you. Nothing in the future is worth that."

Zach grinned, happiness spilled across his face. He pulled

her into his arms, but Bailey stopped him. "As far as being a judge, there's no reason I can't be one here, too. It may not be easy, but I know now that nothing is impossible if it's what you want."

"All I want is you," he said, then branded her with a kiss that Bailey would remember for a lifetime.

Epilogue

THE SUN HAD set with a fiery display of vibrant red, orange, and yellow. Her own personal fireworks, Bailey thought as she, Zach, and Tag approached the ranch. She could see the welcoming glow from lamps inside the windows, and knew in her heart she was home.

In the fading dusky light, her three angels, Faith, Hope, and Charity, were wild with excitement, even though they hadn't noticed Bailey and Zach returning home. Bailey could hear their delighted giggles as they climbed up into the buggy of a visitor who must have come to call.

"Zach! Bailey! We wondered where you two were today. Hoop said you must have gone to town. Now we know why!" The girls scampered out of the buggy and rushed to their sides. Zach dismounted, gave them all a hug, and reached up to help Bailey off the horse.

Instead of a fancy-dressed visitor, it was Box Bend's blacksmith who stepped forward with Hoop. Both men nodded at Bailey. If they thought it odd how she was dressed in her wrinkled jeans and damp jacket, Bailey couldn't tell.

"Searched high and low, Zach, but I couldn't find one with yellow fringe," the blacksmith said. "Had to go all the way to Casper to get this one, but it was the prettiest I could find, just like you wanted."

Bailey stared at the brand-new, shiny black carriage. It was highly polished with narrow red stripes that ran along the smooth curves of the wood. It was big enough for all of them, with deep red leather seats and a fold-down leather cover for rainy days. It was just what Faith, Hope, and Charity needed.

Zach reached for Bailey's hand, pulled her forward, and lifted her into the buggy. Plug looked proud to be hitched to the matching black harness.

Bailey fingered the soft cushioned leather of the seats. "I'm so proud of you, Zach. You couldn't have done anything nicer for the girls."

"I didn't do it for them."

He stepped up into the carriage beside her. "I did it for you. I ordered it the first day we went to town, even though I didn't know how much I wanted you to fall in love with us—all of us—forever."

Bailey grinned as her new sisters piled into the luxurious seat in back of them. "I never had a chance, did I?"

"Nope." Zach returned her smile as he picked up the reins and cued Plug into a snappy trot. "You never had a chance."